"You got a favorite?" Elias said, looking at the cat.

It couldn't possibly have heard him all the way across the street.

While traffic was light by San Francisco standards, it wasn't non-existent. Yet that damn cat stood up, back arched in pleasure like invisible fingers were petting the fur along the length of its spine. It stood on tiptoes almost, bushy tail straight up in the air, and stared at him. *Stared* right at him.

"I'll be damned," Elias said.

He shook his head, about ready to tell himself he needed to get his head examined, and that's when he heard it.

The opening strains to an almost forgotten song.

He'd learned the song when he'd been a kid. Older than that ten-year-old who'd tried not to cry when his mom had cleaned the four-inch cut on his arm. Old enough and already musical enough that his parents had sprung for piano lessons they couldn't really afford.

The song was "Moonlight Sonata."

GUARDIANS OF THE BAY

ANNIE REED

TV *Ink*
Thunder Valley

To the talented musicians who perform at the Wharf in San Francisco. I have enjoyed your music immensely every time I've visited the City by the Bay.

To the animal rescue organizations whose hard work and dedication save the lives of countless animals—feline, canine, and all the small critters who need their care.

And finally, to my own kitties, past and present, most especially Junior. Without their excellent feline supervision, this book would have been completed very much sooner.

GUARDIANS OF THE BAY

THEN

1

San Francisco.

The Protector had visited many places in her long, long life, but she had a certain fondness for the City by the Bay, as the people in this part of the world called it. She'd been to great forests where giant redwoods and pines and cedars remained mostly untouched by human hands. She'd stood at the edge of a high cliff and looked down at a canyon so deep it seemed to split reality. She'd run through wildflowers in a high mountain meadow of such beauty it made her heart ache. But there was something about San Francisco that made it special.

Three decades ago the Protector had lived here for a time. She rarely stayed in one place for long, but San Francisco had been different. Pretty by the standards people judged their cities, but many places in the world were pretty.

Diverse. The city had certainly been that. A melting pot, as the old saying went. A place for those who were different.

The Protector was certainly different. So were her kin who lived within the city, blending in as her kin had done for thousands of years. But that wasn't what made the city special. Her kin blended in throughout the world.

Three decades ago the city had been filled with music.

The Protector and her kin didn't make music the way people did. People used their voices and instruments of all types. In the hands of skilled musicians, even sticks and stones and their own bodies could be instruments.

The Protector and her kin sang with their souls. They sang in the moonlight. They sang by the water and the creatures of the deep answered them. They sang the songs of stars and the history of the world as they knew it. Their music was ethereal. Magical. Unheard by most people, felt by only a rare few.

The music. That's what made the city special.

It didn't feel special to her now.

A monster was walking the streets of San Francisco.

The Protector was here to kill it.

2

THE FIRST TIME THE PROTECTOR CAME TO SAN FRANCISCO, SHE'D wanted to spend time with her family.

She had family the world over, but that had been the first time she'd met the family who lived within this city. The year had been 1967 as people calculated the passage of time, and the world of man had been in turmoil.

The humans who'd taken over the world by sheer numbers alone had always fought, one tribe against another. All the far-flung tribes that comprised the Protector's family had grown nervous. They worried that if the humans destroyed themselves, they would take everything else in the world along with them.

The Protector had been traveling for long months, reassuring all the distinct tribes of her kin that the Maker of All Things would continue to provide for them just as the Maker had in the past. The Protector's kin did not wage war against each other as humans did. They did not assassinate their leaders. They did not debase one another based on the color of their fur or the length of their claws.

Most of all, they did not spit in the face of their creator by spoiling the world that the Maker of All Things had created.

The Protector reminded her kin of all the amazing gifts the Maker had bestowed upon them that allowed them to survive. Their strength. Their speed. Their patience when stalking their prey. Their intelligence. Their silence when silence was required.

And the greatest gift of all, a gift the Maker had bestowed on no other creature in the world: the ability to assume the shapes and thoughts of others, even humans.

Especially humans.

Camouflage. It had allowed her kin to survive—even thrive—in a world dominated by man.

Whenever the Protector wished to be invisible in the world, she always wore the shape of an unremarkable woman. She could walk unnoticed down city streets surrounded by people as ordinary as she appeared, and no one would know she was any different from them.

The Protector still preferred her natural form. If any human saw her in her natural state, they would think she was simply a beautiful black cat with sleekly glistening fur and rich golden-green eyes with flecks of brown.

If someone had looked at her closely, her eyes would have given her away. But most people never did. They saw what they expected to see and dismissed the unexpected. The Protector and the rest of her kin looked like the cats that humans had long since domesticated.

During her first trip to San Francisco, the Protector had roamed through the city in her human form, marveling at its diversity. She'd walked down streets where rich aromas of cooking had set her stomach rumbling. She'd walked through Chinatown, and she'd avoided the homeless camped on sidewalks in the Mission District. She'd marveled at the homes in Pacific Heights and admired the architecture and history in Japantown. She'd wandered through North Beach and The Castro.

But in Haight-Ashbury she found something unexpected.

Music.

Human music.

The natural world produced its own music, if you only knew how to listen for it. The twittering squabbles among birds, the songs of whales, and the mournful howls of wolves. In the summer cicadas and crickets added their own melodies, as did frogs and toads. In the winter, the crunch of crusty snow beneath her feet provided percussion, and the cold north wind whistling through tall pines and cedars contributed a mournful melody to a world holding its breath waiting for spring.

The Protector and her kin even had their own brand of music—the ethereal songs they sang to the moon and stars.

But there was something special about the music the Protector encountered on the streets of San Francisco in the summer of 1967.

The humans called that year the summer of love. Given the amount of turmoil in the human world, such a season seemed impossible. But the reality of Haight-Ashbury had been a revelation. Not that people could live in harmony—although history had demonstrated that was rare—but that they could produce the kind of music that touched the Protector's soul.

The music had been melodious, harmonies crisp and clean, the variety and creativity astounding. Mind-altering drugs had been plentiful in the city, but she'd never partaken. Simply existing in the world in such a time and place was all the drug she'd needed.

She began to spend more time with musicians and singers than she did with her own kin. She learned to play numerous stringed instruments herself. She sang songs of love and the musicians' hatred of cruelty and war. At night, when the human musicians slept, she sang half-remembered songs of her youth to the stars and the moon. She knew the stars and moon would hear, even when the fog was so thick she could barely see the night sky with her keen eyesight.

This magical time in the city hadn't lasted. Little by little the street musicians wandered away or were forced to leave. Some succumbed to the drugs they'd taken. Some succumbed to other forms of excess.

The Protector mourned their passing, but she'd lived a very long, long time. She understood that while she might remain a constant, the world around her would always change. Nothing lasted forever, except for her duties.

She started to spend more and more time in her natural form.

She slept away the days in the vast city parks, safely hidden away with her kin from the curious eyes of passersby. At night she hunted, using her prodigious skills to provide for this portion of her vast family. She helped teach the younglings the history of their people. For the few who'd just come of age, she helped them practice their newfound ability to change forms.

She'd been happy, but even then she'd sensed a strange change that had nothing to do with the turning of the seasons. She'd scented the foggy air at night and ocean-scented breezes during the day, trying to identify the change.

The music that had touched her soul was gone.

Was that what had created this new hollowness she felt—the loss of the humans' music she had so loved? Was that the source of this new sadness she felt whenever she considered shifting into her human form?

But shifting was necessary. Shifting had kept her safe all these years. Shifting allowed her to blend in. She couldn't stop now, even if it made her sad.

She had duties to attend to.

She'd let those duties slide while she'd been entranced with the music. She needed to be elsewhere.

When she left San Francisco after that magical summer of love, she hoped that she wouldn't have to return.

But in time her duties brought her back to the city by the bay. This time it wasn't the music that drew her.

This time it was a human killer.

3

IN THE YEARS SINCE THE PROTECTOR HAD LAST VISITED SAN FRANCISCO, she had found one or two other humans who made the kind of music that touched her soul. She'd tried to ignore them, knowing the pain she would feel when she had to leave their music behind, but the music had called to her even more strongly than it had during the summer of love.

She'd even allowed herself a short interval with one such soul, a troubled young man in a troubled marriage. She'd shared her singing with him, and he'd shared his music with her.

She could have taken him under her wing, as one of the humans' sayings went. Taught him to truly use his musical ability the same way she taught younglings coming of age to use their ability to shift. She'd come to believe that musical talent such as this young man possessed was another gift from the Maker of All Things. The Maker's gifts should not be wasted.

But taking a human into her confidence was a complicated affair. Others of her kind had done so over the centuries with disastrous results. Not all humans were trustworthy. A rare few were, but how to tell until it was too late to undo what had been done?

The Protector was too important to her people. Not a queen, never a queen, but just what her title implied.

She protected her people from those who would destroy them.

She simply couldn't risk it.

In the end she had left this young man behind. She had performed her duties and tried to ignore the growing hollowness inside her.

Maybe the hollowness was another gift from the Maker.

She never once thought that perhaps the hollowness was a sign that her time in this world was at long last growing short.

4

San Francisco had changed.

The further she journeyed into the heart of the city, the more people she encountered who radiated sorrow and anger from their very essence like poison. Impatient drivers blasted their car horns at each other. Pedestrians walked with their heads down, avoiding eye contact with each other. She could have shifted from one human form to the next, changed her face and her hair and even her height, and no one she passed on the street would have noticed.

Far more homeless than she'd ever seen were huddled in dark corners and litter-strewn alleys. Most of the people who passed them by seemed to actively ignore them.

The last time she had been in this city, people had called it the Summer of Love. This felt like the Autumn of Impatience. Of apathy. Of annoyance.

The worst was the music.

None of the music she heard was melodious. None of it was magical. It was loud and discordant and so jarring it hurt even her human ears. It blared from inside passing cars. It rattled the glass in storefront windows. It burst forth from the open doors of bars when people overindulged in alcohol and easy sex.

The music itself had become a drug humans used to numb themselves to the reality of their hopeless lives.

The city was too crowded. She'd seen it happen in other human cities. The crush of humanity into such a contained space bred the twin diseases of distrust and hatred. People turned on each other. They no longer cared for their neighbors. They became self-centered and selfish. Their souls became hollow.

They'd forgotten how to live in harmony with the land, and now they were paying the price.

They had birthed a monster.

And this city was the monster's killing ground.

5

The sidewalk beneath the Protector's feet was cold and hard, and the damp air chilly against her human skin.

The streets in this part of the city were dirty. Garbage clogged the gutters, trash containers overflowed with half-eaten and rotten food. Human urine and excrement fouled alleys and walkways between buildings. It made scenting the human monster that much more difficult.

She had heard of him, of course. He'd been hunting in this city for some time now, and that fact had finally made the news.

She paid attention to news reports concerning the parts of the world where her kin's tribes lived. San Francisco was no different. When she realized what the news only hinted at—that a serial killer had made the city his hunting ground—she knew she would eventually have to stop this monster herself.

The police had been searching for this monster for months but without success. He was savvy, this killer. So far he had murdered eight young women. Most of her kin who lived in this city wore their human shapes and lived human lives. They worked human jobs, made human friends, and lived in human homes. She couldn't risk that eventually this monster would kill one of her own.

Another car sped by her on the street, angry music thrumming so loudly that the low notes vibrated inside her chest.

When had music stopped being something that celebrated the joy of living and turned into this loud, hateful thing? She tried not to miss things that no longer existed. The lone curse of living such a long, long life was the inevitable loss of all the things she loved.

Her life was especially long. She was not immortal. Immortality belonged to the Maker and the Maker alone.

Would there be another Protector when her life was finally over? Or would her kin no longer require a Protector?

A new scent in the air made the hair on the back of her neck rise. If she had been in her true form, the fur along her spine would have risen as well.

The unmistakable scent of death, strong and pungent and tinged around the edges with the crimson essence of violence.

But worse than the simple scent of death, the Protector knew that the dead was one of her kin.

6

———

THE BODY OF A YOUNG FEMALE HAD BEEN THROWN INTO A DUMPSTER IN an alley behind an abandoned bar in The Mission District. The back entrance to the bar was chained and locked, the entrance in the front boarded over.

Graffiti marred the brick walls of the building, and a mural had been painted on the boarded-over entrance. The mural depicted street musicians from a bygone era when jazz ruled the musical scene. She'd seen similar colorful murals on other boarded-up storefronts in the area. Efforts to make the empty buildings look less abandoned, she supposed.

The murdered female was sprawled on top of the trash, her long limbs splayed over empty beer bottles, fast food wrappers, and dirty diapers. Her golden-green eyes were still open but clouded over with death.

The Protector closed her own eyes against this obscenity. This once vibrant female had been thrown away like so much garbage. No one, human or kin, deserved to be treated this way.

No one except the monster.

The Protector would gladly treat the monster like garbage. Not in retaliation. No. In acknowledgement of his place in the world.

15

He *was* garbage.

She forced her eyes open. She needed to honor this young female's life by witnessing the manner of her death. She deserved no less.

She'd been in her human form when she was killed. So many of the Protector's kin chose beautiful shapes for themselves, and this young female had been no exception. Her human face was flawless, her lips full, her golden-green eyes surrounded by silky lashes. She wore dark slacks and a white blouse beneath a loose navy-blue jacket embellished with embroidered flowers of lavender and the softest ivory. Her throat had been slashed nearly ear to ear. Blood had soaked her white blouse, the edges of it dried to an ugly brownish black.

She'd been wearing low-heeled blue pumps as well. She still had a shoe on her left foot, but the other shoe lay beside her in the dumpster. Her bare right foot was covered with fur.

She'd just started to revert to her true form when the monster killed her.

The female's true form had also been beautiful. The fur on her bare foot was tiger striped in glorious ginger shot through with darker brown and black streaks. Her auburn human hair had begun to transform into more of that glorious ginger fur. Her slender fingers were tipped by razor-sharp claws, and the teeth in her partially open mouth had begun to turn into needle-sharp fangs.

The Protector's kin could only retain other shapes and forms when a spark of their life force remained, what the humans called a soul. Once the last of the life force fled the body, any other shape they'd worn would disappear entirely. To the rest of the world, her kin's dead would look like just another dead cat.

Something was making this female's life force remain in this world.

Was it anger? This poor young female's claws were covered in dried blood, but the scent was different.

It was human blood.

She'd fought back.

"Good for you," the Protector murmured. "You were brave. You made your kin proud."

The Protector took one of the female's hands in hers and raised it to her nose. The monster's blood was dry, but it was still fresh enough.

She closed her eyes again, not in horror this time but in concentration. She breathed in deep so that she could take in the monster's essence along with his scent.

A feral growl rose unbidden from the Protector's throat. Death eventually came to all. Her kin weren't immortal, only blessed with long life. But death should not come like this. Not full of anger and suffering at the hands of a lesser being.

The monster's essence told the Protector things she hadn't known about him. His love of coffee. His hatred of his parents, particularly his mother. His humiliations at the hands of the human females he'd tried to copulate with. The fantasies he entertained himself with. His meticulous planning. His self-confidence that grew with every kill. The sheer power he felt when he watched the life leave the bodies of the women he killed.

Only now his self-confidence was tinged with something new. He'd encountered something beyond his understanding of the world, and he'd still been able to kill it.

The monster now felt invincible.

He believed could kill anything. That no one could stop him, not even the unnatural things that walked this world. He knew something no one else in the entire world knew. Shapeshifters existed, and he'd killed one.

He didn't need silver bullets. The monsters died just like any other human—with the slash of his knife. How exhilarating! And where one shapeshifter existed, there would be more. He didn't have to hunt mere women anymore. All the women he'd killed—and there had been so many! Many more than the police knew about—they had just been practice. What he needed to do now was be patient. Look for beautiful shapeshifters with golden-green eyes. And when he found one, he'd kill it.

He might even tell the world what he was doing. He was keeping the world safe from monsters! He was protecting....

The Protector growled again and shook her head. The human monster's essence was foul, and she wanted him out of her mind. But she couldn't get rid of him, not just yet. She needed his essence. It would make it easier for her to track him in this city teeming with people.

The sooner she started, the better.

Before she could leave, there was something she had to do. This young female's life force was still here, but it was fading fast. More of her human shape was reverting to her true form, her body shrinking in size. Fur covered the side of her head now and the backs of her hands. In death her fur had lost its luster, but it was still soft and lovely.

The Protector wrapped her fingers around the young female's hand and bent her head in prayer.

The prayer was simple, just an offering of thanks for the life the Maker of All Things had granted this female. Many human religions had similar death rituals, but the Protector's prayers came from a time before religion became an excuse for the humans to wage war against those who did not believe as they did.

The Protector had performed this ritual countless times over her long life whenever one of her kin met an untimely end, and there had been far, far too many to count.

Throughout the centuries her kin had been vilified as often as they'd been venerated by those few humans who were clever enough to notice that the Protector and her kin were not ordinary cats. Her kin had been killed for the color of their fur. They'd been killed because of the humans they chose to associate with. Killed for sport and killed for no reason at all.

The Protector finished her prayer for the untimely dead the way she always did. She asked the Maker of All Things to honor this young female with a place in the Great Meadow where she would be free from pain and worry and regret. Free to live out the remainder of her very long life as her true self before she moved on to whatever awaited the Protector's kin for the rest of eternity.

When she was done, the Protector placed the young female's cold, dead, fur-covered hand on her blood-soaked blouse. She smoothed the female's tiger-striped fur away from her human face, then placed her own forehead against the female's, a gesture of respect and affection. A gesture of kinship.

The Protector wished she could do more. It was up to the Maker of All Things to decide the rest of this young one's fate.

As for the Protector, she had a monster to hunt. She had his scent now. Even better, she had tasted his essence. She knew him almost as well as he knew himself. She knew his haunts and his habits. It was time to find him and stop him before he could kill again.

She took two steps toward the mouth of the alley when a tiny, plaintive sound brought her up short.

A cry of sorrow.

A cry of loss.

A cry of need.

The cry of a hungry baby.

The monster had killed a mother.

7

Fury rose up in the Protector.

The monster had killed this baby's mother and left the baby alone to starve.

She would tear this monster limb from limb. She would rip his throat out. Slit his tender belly and watch his steaming entrails spill out on the ground while he still lived so that he would know he was about to die.

She would paint the city's sidewalks with his blood and scream her pleasure at his death to the stars, and then she would dance the dance of the vanquisher in the moonlight.

She would—

The baby yelped.

The yelp brought the Protector back from the blood rage born of her fury. She had experienced blood rages throughout her long life. Her life as the Protector had begun with one.

She took a deep breath to bring her emotions under control. The baby, like all the Protector's kin, could sense strong emotions in others. This baby did not need to feel the Protector's rage. It would only compound the baby's fear and sorrow and make the baby fear her.

The tiny cries were coming from inside the dumpster. The Protector elongated her human-shaped legs until she was tall enough to reach inside.

At first she didn't see the baby, then some of the paper trash moved and more cries came from beneath it. The baby had been smart for one so young. It had burrowed beneath the trash.

The Protector picked up moldy food wrappers and wadded-up paper garbage. She moved slowly and carefully so she wouldn't startle the baby.

The baby was a girl child so small that she fit in the palm of the Protector's hand. She yelped again as the Protector picked her up and held her close. She whispered kind words, nonsense words, so that the baby could feel the vibrations of the Protector's voice and know that she was safe.

To humans, this girl child would look like any other very young kitten—except for her eyes. Kittens born to the cats humans kept as pets were born with blue eyes. This orphaned baby had her mother's tiger-striped fur and golden eyes. As she grew, her eyes would deepen into the golden-green color all their kind had been blessed with.

The baby watched the Protector with those wide golden eyes. She was still so frightened she was trembling.

The Protector kept murmuring to the baby until the girl child latched onto the Protector with sharp little claws. The Protector felt her true form responding. It was instinctual. The baby was hungry, but the Protector couldn't nurse her. She'd lost that ability centuries ago.

The baby's fur was filthy and matted with dirt and spoiled food from the dumpster. The Protector couldn't feed this baby, but she could clean her.

The back door of the abandoned building had been chained closed and the single window boarded over to prevent the homeless from getting inside. But the Protector was no mere human.

She shed her human form. The clothes she'd been wearing became her fur, and her sensible shoes became the rough pads at the bottom of her hind feet. The Protector never wore jewelry or carried any of the electronic gadgets of this age. Those she would have had to leave behind when she shifted into her true form, and they were too great a temptation for humans to steal. It was bad enough she had to leave behind the messenger bag she always carried when she was in her human form, but some things—identification; the money humans always carried—were beyond her ability to mimic when she shifted.

She hid her messenger bag beneath a stack of decomposing cardboard cartons and newsprint. The things inside were replaceable. This tiny baby was not.

She took the girl child in her mouth by the scruff of her neck. There was a knothole in the board covering the window. The Protector leaped up on the ledge beneath the window and kicked at the knothole until it fell from the board, then she shrank her own form down until she was nearly as small as the tiny girl child. Still holding the girl child by the scruff of the neck, she stepped daintily through the hole in the board and jumped down easily onto the floor inside the abandoned building.

The inside of the building was nearly pitch black, but her eyesight was as phenomenal as her hearing. Rodents had made a home inside the building. They scurried away, squeaking in fright. The Protector ignored them. She wasn't here to hunt their kind.

She reverted to her true size and padded around the detritus left behind by the humans who'd inhabited the building. She found a secluded corner that stank of old cigarette smoke and the faint odor of alcohol, but at least the floor was merely dusty. She settled down and began to clean the baby's fur with her tongue.

The girl child protested at first. All young children resisted being cleaned by their mothers. The Protector had seen enough in her travels that she believed this was a universal constant.

Eventually the familiar feel of a rough tongue soothed the baby. It wasn't long before she fell asleep.

The Protector curled around the baby. The hunt for the monster who killed this child's mother could wait for an hour or two. He wasn't going anywhere. The Protector had his scent and knew his essence. This small girl child needed comfort. The Protector was surprised to discover that she needed comfort too.

Comfort and sleep.

She closed her eyes and dozed in the safety of the abandoned building.

And while she slept, she dreamed.

8

THE PROTECTOR'S EARLIEST MEMORIES—IF THEY WERE TRULY memories and not mere dreams—were of a time when she'd been as young as the orphaned kitten now sleeping curled against her belly. When she'd had the glorious golden eyes of youth, her fur had been as yellow-gold as a field of wheat at sunset, and her world had not yet been polluted by man.

Only in her dreams could she relive those early, carefree, joyous days.

She'd been a wild child, willful and headstrong, so sure of herself and her place in the world. She was the largest and strongest youngling in her tribe. She chased after butterflies but never caught them. Chattered at the birds and sprinted after bees and grasshoppers. She ran for the sheer joy of feeling the wind against her whiskers. She mock-fought with the adults until they grew tired of her and corrected her with a firm but gentle paw and a bite on the scruff of her neck.

As she grew older, the adults taught her to hunt. She learned how to stalk her prey and how to kill by breaking the neck with a decisive shake of her head. Death, the adults said, should be swift and as painless as possible, and only inflicted when the tribe had a need to eat. Her kin never hunted for sport and never rejoiced in the act of killing.

Life, as the elders of her tribe instructed her, was to be revered in all its forms because all life was created by the Maker of All Things. To do otherwise would be to disrespect the Maker, and that was not allowed.

"Hunt for food," she'd been taught. "Hunt to eat. Hunt so the tribe can survive. Live in harmony with those creatures around you. Take no more from the land than what you need, and the land will take no more from you than what it needs."

At night she sang songs to the moon and stars, releasing the joy in her heart that came from living another day in this wonderful world the Maker had made. Then she slept beneath the same moon and stars, and dreamed the dreams of the innocent, her paws and whiskers twitching in sleep.

Life had been good when she'd been young.

Then the humans came.

The tribe tried to abide by the Maker's teachings when it came to these strange beings who'd invaded the land. But it soon became clear that humans didn't revere the natural world around them.

The elders watched from a distance as humans plowed under the meadows and erected stone structures where wildflowers had once grown. They erected fences around the wheatfields to keep other creatures out. The humans hunted far more than they could eat. They hung the carcasses of those they killed over the fire and wore the skins of those they killed on top of their own. They fashioned weapons from sticks and rocks and bones. The males beat their young and their females and fought with each other.

The adults in the Protector's tribe no longer allowed the younglings to play in areas where humans could see them. The tribe started to hunt at night when the humans stayed by their fires. Some adults in the tribe began to talk of how to drive the humans away. Most advocated hurting the humans, but a few began to talk of killing them.

The elders counseled caution. "They are also the Maker's creations," the elders said. "We must trust in the Maker's wisdom in sending these strange creatures into our midst. Perhaps the Maker wishes to show them how to live in harmony with the land from our example."

To their sorrow, the tribe learned how wrong they had been when the humans began to hunt them.

At first the humans only hunted the sick and the elderly of the tribe. They used sharpened sticks and chiseled stones to wound, and then they swarmed the wounded and stabbed them over and over until blood ran thick on the ground. They hung the skins of the murdered outside the humans' dwellings and danced by firelight to celebrate their victory over beings who never meant them any harm.

And still the humans' bloodlust grew.

Killing the sick and elderly members of the tribe was no longer enough. The humans began to set elaborate traps to catch the young and healthy. At night, screams and cries of rage came from the captured as the humans tortured them, and in the morning their skins were added to the obscene display outside the humans' stone dwellings.

Nothing in the tribe's experience had prepared them for such viciousness. None of the other creatures the tribe had encountered killed out of hatred. Tortured for pleasure. The tribe tried to live the way they always had, in harmony with the world around them, but too many fell victim to the humans.

Including the Protector's mother.

The remaining members of the tribe hid in fear. They prayed to the Maker of All Things to save them from the humans. Asked the Maker to rid the land of the vile creatures, for surely the Maker had not intended to create beings capable of such atrocities. Of such irrational hatred and lust for killing.

The Maker heard the tribe's prayers. Saw the evil its human creations had unleased on the natural world. The Maker did not rid the land of what it had created, for the Maker, above all else, still believed that all life was sacred and that humans could be redeemed. Instead, the Maker granted the tribe the power to protect themselves. The Maker gave them the gift of shifting.

9

On the night that the Maker bestowed the gift of shifting on the Protector's tribe, the Maker communed with the remaining elders. The Maker cautioned the elders about the use of this gift and the consequences for its misuse.

Each member of the tribe would be given the ability to shift when they came of age. This ability would be passed down, generation after generation, provided the tribe's members used the gift as the Maker intended.

Members of the tribe could use the ability to shift to enable them to survive and live among those who would otherwise seek to destroy them. No matter the form they took, the tribe would retain their natural speed and strength and agility, but they would also gain the natural and learned abilities of the forms they assumed. Humans used tools, and if any member of the tribe chose to shift into human form, they would gain the ability to use tools. They would also gain the ability to speak as humans, for shifting not only changed the user's form but also granted them insight into how their new form lived.

They were not to use their new ability to conquer other creatures the Maker had created. All life was still precious. Members of the tribe could only use shifting to kill in order to protect themselves and the rest of the tribe from those who meant the tribe harm.

The price for misuse of shifting was death, not only of the body but of the soul. Those who used shifting to kill for other than protection of self or tribe would be forbidden to join their ancestors in the Great Meadow.

The Maker granted the elders of the tribe a new title: Guardians. Guardians would be responsible for teaching the Maker's edicts to the rest of the tribe and making sure the tribe did not use the gift of shifting to rule over lesser beings. Guardians were to safeguard the tribe and protect the tribe against those who would harm it.

The Maker then created a special type of Guardian called the Protector. The Protector was the only member of the tribe who could kill for revenge. For retribution. To prevent a perceived threat against the tribe. The Protector was tasked with insuring the tribe survived even if it meant killing all the tribe's enemies.

In addition to enhanced speed and strength, intelligence and wisdom, the Maker granted the Protector an unusually long and protected life. No mere weapon could harm the Protector, and no member of the tribe—not even a Guardian—could question the manner in which she carried out her duties. The Protector was the ultimate authority over the life and death of the tribe's enemies.

And for this great privilege, the Protector would pay a horrible price.

She would not be permitted to enter the Great Meadow when she eventually died. She would never again see her kin who passed into the Great Meadow before her. She would forever be part of the tribe yet separate from it. She was not queen nor would she ever rule the tribe. Misuse of her power would mean death, the killing blow delivered by one whom she loved.

Even though she was not an elder, the Protector was given this responsibility by the Maker. She was the largest and strongest among her kin. She believed the Maker chose her because her heart was still aching from the loss of her mother, and the Maker knew she would not hesitate to kill the tribe's enemies.

It took time for the Protector and her kin to adjust to their new abilities. With practice, they could shift into human form in the blink of an eye. They learned to transform their fur into human hair and clothes, their paws into hands and feet. They learned they could change their size at will, shrinking as small as a mouse and as large as a bear. They crafted human weapons and grasped them with thumbs that had once been dew claws. They learned how to fight with human weapons.

They learned how to use human weapons to kill.

Then they waited. They watched the humans set new traps. In their shifted human forms, the tribe understood how the traps worked and learned how to avoid them.

The humans grew frustrated. They began to believe that the mere existence of the tribe was an affront to their gods.

This concept astonished the Protector. How could any creature that the Maker of All Things created believe in gods other than the Maker? How could any creature's mere existence be an affront to their gods if the humans' existence was not an affront to the Maker? The elders of the tribe discussed these concepts late at night when the younglings slept. Surely the Maker would not allow false gods to exist, but the Protector thought otherwise. If the Maker of All Things allowed creatures as vicious as humans to exist because all life was precious, perhaps the existence of other gods was also allowed because the life of all gods was precious as well.

Even gods who demanded sacrifices in their honor.

For that, the tribe learned, was what the humans planned to do. Sacrifice the youngest and most innocent of the Protector's tribe to their false gods.

The Protector could not allow that to happen. The time had come to kill. Not for food. Not for retribution or revenge. But for survival.

The Protector's paws twitched in her sleep as she dreamed about what happened next.

In the dead of night when the moon had cloaked itself behind thick clouds, the Protector and her kin struck back.

They attacked in their shifted human forms, using human

weapons against the men who planned to eradicate the tribe. They killed every adult human male they saw, sparing only mothers and their young.

The Protector led the battle. When she found the last of the men who had tortured and slaughtered her kin, he was cowering behind a stone altar stained with her mother's blood. The smell of it filled the Protector's head with a savage rage unlike any she had ever known.

She believed that rage came from the human form she'd shifted into. This rage was born of an unquenchable lust for power and a new emotion the Protector had never felt before:

Greed.

Greed felt like poison. It filled her true self with revulsion. She let her human form slip away—she could not have held onto it if she'd tried—and the human spear she held slipped from her grasp. But instead of simply reverting to the size of her own natural self, she grew and grew until she was twice as tall as this man who thought he spoke to his false gods.

The change terrified the man. He babbled words the Protector still understood, beseeching his gods to save him. He dropped his weapons and fell to his knees. New foul scents filled the air as he lost control of his body.

The Protector showed him the same mercy he had shown her kin. She slit his belly with sharp claws the size of his fist, allowing him to see his entrails spew forth from his body and know he was about to die in agony. Then she tore his limbs from his body before she snapped his neck with a final shake of her head.

When the killing was over, the Protector and her tribe took the pelts of their murdered kin with them until they were far away from the humans' dwellings. The tribe cried and howled their sorrow beneath the cloud-filled night sky, and the Protector said the first of countless prayers she would say over the centuries for the murdered dead.

When she was finished, she discovered that her lovely golden fur had changed to the black of a moonless night.

That had been so long ago that the Protector had lost count of the years.

The tribe had found new lands in which to grow and flourish. Their descendants spread from land to land, creating new tribes as they went. Each new tribe appointed its own Guardians, and the Maker of All Things granted these new Guardians the powers they needed to perform their responsibilities.

But the Maker never created another Protector. There had been no need.

Over the centuries, her kin had grown wise to the ways of humans. Those who lived in the parts of the world where humans were plentiful wore their shifted human shapes and lived human lives, reverting to their true forms only under cover of night. Others shifted into human form only under duress. They lived in the remaining wild places of the world. In cities such as San Francisco, the wildest places were parks, such as the vast park near the base of the Golden Gate bridge.

The Protector awoke when the girl child cried. The baby's belly was far too empty for one so young.

The Protector carried the girl child back through the knothole in the board that covered the broken window. Once the Protector was sure she was alone, she regained her human form and retrieved her messenger bag. She tucked the girl child inside. To anyone who might notice, the Protector would simply look like a woman carrying a kitten in her bag, only the kitten's eyes were golden instead of baby blue.

On her way out of the alley, the Protector passed the dumpster where the girl child's mother had been killed. The young female's body was no longer there.

The Protector's prayers had been answered. The Maker of All Things had taken the female to the Great Meadow where she would be surrounded by her own kind. She would no longer need to wear a false form in order to survive in a world overrun by humans.

For the first time that day, the Protector smiled.

THE PROTECTOR FOUND THE TRIBE SHE WAS LOOKING FOR IN A PARK that was surprisingly large for such a crowded city. It was close to the abandoned building where the Protector had found the murdered female and her orphaned girl child, but far enough from the Golden Gate bridge that human automobiles would not pose a constant danger.

She left the baby girl with the tribe's Guardian, a wizened old tom, and a young female who was nursing her own baby boy. They would raise the baby and teach her what she needed to know to survive in the city.

One member of the tribe, a ginger-haired youngling with long, silky fur, sat close by. She watched the Protector with golden eyes that were just beginning to turn golden-green. This youngling had not yet come of age and had no ability to shift, but her eyes were full of longing.

Like so many of her kin, this youngling couldn't wait to grow up and learn how to shift her form.

The image of the murdered mother was still uppermost in the Protector's mind. The tribes who lived in wild places, like this one, kept to themselves. Humans called these tribes *colonies* and said those who lived there were feral. Unable to live with humans. It wasn't far from the truth.

Had the young mother lived with this tribe, or had she been one of the kin who lived most of her days in her human form? She'd had a child to protect, which should have made her wary of humans, but raising a child in the city was not easy. The Protector's kin matured slower than the cats humans kept as pets, and her kin only had a single child at a time. A girl child as young as the baby the Protector had found would have required nearly all of her mother's attention. If the young female had lived alone without the support of a tribe, that would have made her vulnerable.

Had she been easy prey for the human monster? Kin who spent their lives as "ferals" rarely ventured outside the park in human form. Younglings like this eager ginger-haired beauty made easy prey until they learned how dangerous humans could be.

Still wearing her human form, the Protector crouched down in front of the youngling.

"This city is a harsh place," the Protector said. "For your sake, learn the ways of the people who live here, but always hold yourself separate. Be watchful."

The youngling tilted her head and raised a paw in the Protector's direction, the question clear.

You don't hold yourself separate. You protect us. Why can't I do that?

"I do what the Maker of All Things decreed," the Protector said. "I do what's necessary for our kin to thrive in this world. No matter how strong and fast you become, how clever you think you are, you are not me. You do not want to become me."

The words came out harsh. The youngling blinked and lowered her head, clearly rebuked.

The Protector sighed, a human reaction. She did not want to react like a human. She wanted to be her true self.

So she let her false shape go.

She shrank down to her natural form and size. She rubbed faces with the youngling, relishing the feel of that ginger fur against her own.

Oh, how she missed the sweet scent of youth and strength and vigor! These were the times when she wished she could live out the remainder of eternity in the Great Meadow, that the mantle of Protector had not fallen on her shoulders. The closest she would ever get to the Great Meadow was to spend time with her kin in wild places that remained in the world, such as this great city park. Places where she could sleep in the shade of oaks and aspens, and run at night beneath the stars and the moon.

She was weary. She was furious at the murder of the girl child's mother. She would hunt that monster down and kill him, but for now, she was so very, very weary.

She just wanted—even for just a short time—to forget about the price her old body had paid for her long, long life. She wanted to be a youngling again, like the one who clearly looked up to her. The Protector had been honored to accept the gifts the Maker had bestowed upon her all those centuries ago. But how could a youngling really understand what it would mean to give up eternity in the Great Meadow?

How could a youngling understand what it meant never to die but to witness the deaths of kin you held dear?

Younglings didn't think about death.

Younglings thought they would never die.

This ginger-furred youngling was special. She longed to be a Protector someday. Now that the Protector was in her natural form, she could feel the youngling's longing.

The Maker of All Things would decide this youngling's destiny. If the Maker decreed that this youngling would replace her, so be it. But the Protector hoped that wasn't the case. The Protector hoped that this youngling would live out her days in peace and joy, and when her life was over, she would be granted a place in the Great Meadow.

The youngling bapped the Protector's nose with a playful paw, then flopped down on her side, gazing up at the Protector with wide, mischievous eyes. How long had it been since the Protector simply played?

Too long, she decided.

She fell on the youngling, and soon the two of them were rolling around in the damp grass beneath a towering oak. Mock-growling and kicking each other with their hind legs.

The Protector's weariness fled, replaced with the joy of simply living in the moment. She had only birthed one youngling of her own, a male child who was centuries dead now. The tiny girl child she had brought to this tribe was being cared for, and for now, the Protector could pretend she was just another member of the tribe. No more, no less.

She could be happy.

She *was* happy.

It wouldn't last, but for now she was happy.

For now, that was enough.

11

The Protector could have disposed of the human monster the same night she discovered the body of the young female he'd killed and left behind in a dumpster to rot. She'd tasted his essence. It was part fury, part need, part hunger, and part hatred. It told her where he lived. Where he worked. Where he bought his food, and the places where he selected his victims. His essence was a poisonous vapor trail staining every place he went in the city.

The Protector was an alpha hunter among her own kind, but even a new adult could follow this man's fetid stench.

But she wanted the monster to suffer. To feel what it was like to be someone else's prey.

So she decided to play with him. It had been a long time since she'd played with her prey. If anyone deserved it, this monster did.

She sat two stools down from him at his favorite deli. He was an ordinary enough looking man of no particular note. Neither young nor old, handsome nor ugly. She watched him out of the corner of her eye as he ate his sandwich. She pretended to eat her soup, but she had no appetite.

He never noticed her.

She stood in line two people behind him as he ordered coffee from a little independent coffee shop. Waited one person behind him in the checkout line at a corner grocery store. Sat in the seat behind him on the bus he rode to work.

And still his eyes slid over her human shape. She'd chosen a form and face that was deliberately forgettable. To him, she simply posed no obvious threat. She wasn't even what he was looking for in a potential victim.

Until he'd killed the girl child's mother, he'd only preyed on the weakest members of his own species. Killing her—killing something that no one else knew existed—had emboldened him. He was beginning to feel invincible, even heroic. He would rid the city of these evil beings, and the city would thank him for it.

The Protector sensed all these thoughts every time she got close to him. So she decided to let him feel *her* presence.

Some humans had the ability to hear the thoughts of her kind. Few could hear those thoughts expressed as actual words. Many more sensed her kin's emotions. Touch increased all these abilities in humans who were more attuned to the world around them than their peers, like the musicians she had known decades ago.

She brushed against him when she passed him on the street and sent him feelings of inadequacy. She browsed close to him in a crowded bookstore, bumping into his shoulder when they both reached for the same book. This time she sent him an image of a lion stalking him in the fog for which the city was famous. She even growled low in her throat, the sound so soft human ears wouldn't be able to hear it.

But the monster did.

He gave her a startled look which she ignored, then he shoved his way through the crowd and bolted out of the bookstore without buying anything.

The Protector followed him at a discrete distance.

Now he walked with his shoulders hunched up around his neck. He flinched at sudden movements on the street. He winced when the brakes on the bus he took home from work squealed, and looked over his shoulder as he boarded to make sure no one was behind him.

The Protector didn't get on the same bus. She didn't have to. His essence told her all she needed to know, including where he'd be.

That night she stood in the shadows outside his apartment building. She sent him memories of how she'd killed the man who'd butchered her mother in the name of his false god. She smiled when the light in his apartment switched on and he stood at the window, looking out at the street.

Soon. She would end his life soon.

But not tonight.

She wasn't done with him yet.

12

Humans considered themselves the alpha predators of the world. Their bodies were insufficient for the task, so they created tools they could use to prove their prowess. Guns and knives and great machines of war, modern equivalents of the wooden spears and stone knives the men who'd slaughtered the Protector's mother had used to kill.

The human monster she hunted had used a knife to kill his victims.

Now he bought himself a gun.

The Protector followed him at a distance the next night when he met with a man in a garbage-strewn alley not far from the dumpster where he'd left the girl child's dead mother. She felt the excitement in his essence as he held the cold gray metal in his hands and felt its weight. As he considered whether he should kill the man who'd sold him the gun and then decided it would be too risky.

It won't make a difference, she thought at him as he left the alley.

He flinched and looked furtively around him. He might not have understood her words, but he'd felt her intent.

The gun would make no difference, not to her. She could only be killed by someone she loved, and she did not love this man.

She had been wounded before during her long, long life. The wounds were painful, some excruciatingly so. But the wounds did not slow her down, and she always healed.

The monster could use the gun to hurt her, but even if he shot her in the face, she would still be able to kill him. Slit his belly. Make him watch his life flow out onto the cold sidewalk and know he was going to die.

She shadowed him that night, letting the fog shroud her presence. The monster kept to well-lit stores, mingling in crowded places, but most other humans gave him a wide berth. He kept touching his jacket pocket where he'd shoved the gun, and even though the night was chilly, his face was covered in sweat.

She realized she had to stop playing with him. She had wound him too tight, this monster who realized he was now the hunted instead of hunter. She'd backed him into a corner. He was jumping at shadows, continuously glancing over his shoulder. In this state, he might kill an innocent with his new gun.

Allowing innocents to die simply because she wanted to play before killing him would anger the Maker.

She had never in her long life deliberately angered the Maker. She had railed against the Maker when her mother had been slaughtered. Wailed her sorrow to the night sky and begged to know why the Maker would allow such things to happen. She would not anger the Maker now.

She would do her duty. Carry out her responsibilities. Save the city from the monster who wore the disguise of a man.

Save her kin, and avenge the girl child's dead mother.

She was the Protector of all her tribes scattered across the world. And some nights, like tonight, she was also the Protector of people who had no idea she even existed.

13

The monster had lingered far too long in well-lit places filled with people. By the time he headed home, thick fog had blanketed the city, turning streetlights into softly glowing lanterns that did little to dispel the deep shadows between buildings on the street where he lived.

The night was perfect for the Protector. Fog dampened the sounds of the city, and the monster only exacerbated his loss of hearing by covering his ears with the hood of his jacket. She could have come within a few paces behind him and he never would have heard her, but she didn't have to follow him that closely. She hadn't even ridden the same bus with him. She knew where he would eventually go. He had nowhere else. He'd never had to hide before, and he didn't know how.

She watched him turn the corner onto the side street that led to his apartment. When she was sure they were alone, she sent him a thought.

Ready to die?

He whirled around, eyes wide. "Who's there?" he said.

His words sounded flat in the fog. Even the never-ending sounds of the city—traffic noise, distant sirens, and even the horns from ships on the bay—were dampened on nights such as this.

"Someone following you, little hunter?" she asked, a hint of a growl in her voice.

He stuck a hand in the pocket of his jacket where she knew he had his gun.

"You don't want to mess with me, lady," he said, his false bravado belied by the quavering in his voice.

"Oh, but I do," she said.

She raced past him. Even shifted into her human shape, she was incredibly fast. She raked her nails across his face, drawing blood, and disappeared into the fog before he could even begin to pull the gun from his pocket.

He yelped and clutched his face as he twisted around, trying to catch sight of her.

She ran at him again, this time digging into the skin of his cheek with nails that were as deadly as sharpened knives.

He screamed, the sound filled with rage as well as pain. "Who *are* you?"

"Retribution," she said.

Blood was running down his face and through the fingers of one hand. He began to pull the gun from his pocket with the other, and she ran at him again.

This time she sliced through the thick jacket sleeve and through the flesh of his arm with razor-sharp claws before she disappeared into the fog. The gun he'd managed to pull from his pocket fell to the sidewalk. He stared at it stupidly as blood dripped from his useless fingers.

It was time to end this.

She shifted, but not into her true form. Not yet.

Instead she shifted into the form of a lion, only a lion larger than any that had walked the earth since long before even the Protector's time. She grew until she was larger than the cars that choked the city streets.

This human monster had seen lions at a zoo when he'd been a

youngling. His mother had loved the big cats just as she loved all living things. But out of all the creatures he'd seen at the zoo that day, lions had terrified him the most.

The Protector had seen that memory when she'd tasted his essence. That terror was something she could use, and exactly what he deserved.

"Time to die," she said as she padded out of the fog on paws the size of manhole covers.

He screamed again at the human words coming from her lion's mouth.

He turned to flee, the gun lying forgotten on the sidewalk where he'd dropped it.

"Help me!" he yelled into the night. "Oh, God, *help me!*"

No lights came on in the buildings he sped past. No one else was on the street. In his terror, he was running away from the streets where cars occasionally drove past, fleeing toward the shadows where he thought he could hide.

There was no place he could hide that the Protector couldn't find him.

They were alone in the night, hunter and prey.

"*Help me!*" he screamed again. "She's going to *KILL ME!*"

"Yes," she said, padding behind him on her giant paws. "I am."

14

THE LAST TIME THE PROTECTOR HAD BEEN IN SAN FRANCISCO, HER purpose had been to comfort her kin. To reassure them that they were still under her protection, and that she would do whatever was necessary to ensure their survival in a world that humans seemed intent on destroying.

The year had been 1967. Even though humans continued to wage war against each other and protests against the war grew ugly and violent, the Protector had found a kind of peace in this city. She spent time with the tribes of her kin who called this city home, and she had discovered music that touched her soul.

She had not killed except to eat.

When she left the city, she had only fond memories of her visit.

Now, several decades later, the city had changed so much it was nearly unrecognizable. Its garbage-strewn streets were as ugly and violent as the human protests she had mostly avoided. When she left this time, her memories would not be fond ones.

But she would leave knowing she had done her duty. Fulfilled her responsibilities as Protector. Kept her kin safe when she removed this human monster from their midst.

He was crashing through the bushes in a park that was not nearly as large as the one where she'd taken the orphaned girl child to be raised by her kin. Streetlights cast gauzy pools of light through the fog. The lights were spaced evenly along the sidewalks surrounding the park's grassy areas, but the monster was cutting across the darkened center.

As if he believed she wouldn't be able to see him in the dark.

"Oh, little hunter," she called after him. "You can't run fast enough, and you can't hide."

She loped out of the halo of light at the base of a streetlight and into the darkness. When she caught up with him, she swatted him with one huge paw.

He felt face-first on the grass as she loped past him, disappearing in the darkness.

When he got to his hands and knees, she swatted him again.

He tried to get up twice more, and she swatted him down each time.

He was sobbing now, grasping handfuls of grass in his fists. "You can't do this to me," he said between sobs. "You're just an *animal!*"

"Am I?"

She shifted into her human form and squatted down in front of him.

"Or am I someone you think you have the right to kill?"

His face twisted into a mask of hatred. She tasted his memories of all the women who'd said no to him. The women who'd laughed in his face when he tried to kiss them. The women he thought he deserved just because he wanted them, whether or not they wanted him.

"Women are not *things*, little hunter," she said. "My kin are not *things*. We're not *animals* for your amusement. But you?" She lifted his head up with one finger beneath his chin, her sharpened fingernail digging into his flesh. "You gave up the right to be treated as anything other than meat."

He tried to lunge at her then, but he didn't stand a chance.

She sprang over him, shifting into her cat-like form, but nearly twice the size of her natural state. She sank all her claws into the flesh of his shoulders and buttocks, pressing him down into the fog-dampened grass.

She lowered her head until her mouth was level with his ear. "Do you understand now? The true nature of the world around you? A world you were too arrogant to see?"

He whimpered. "Please let me go. I promise not to do it again. I promise *never* to do it again. Just don't kill me. *Please.*"

It wasn't in the nature of hunters to stop killing. When she'd been a youngling, she'd been very good at hunting. She'd been the best of her tribe, the biggest and the strongest. That's why the Maker of All Things had chosen her to be the Protector. The Maker knew she wouldn't hesitate to kill when the need arose.

"I wish I could believe you," she said.

"You can," he said quickly. "You can absolutely believe me. I'll even... I'll leave the city. Go live by myself somewhere with no other people. You can trust me."

He was babbling now. It was time to end it.

"May the Maker of All Things judge your soul," she said.

He stiffened at her words and tried to buck her off. Before he could do more than draw in a breath to scream, she sank her teeth into the back of his neck. She snapped her powerful jaws shut and shook her head in a quick, decisive movement, snapping his spine.

The monster was dead.

She sprang off his back and let herself shrink down to her natural size. She sat on her haunches and regarded her work.

The authorities would find his body in the morning. When they searched his apartment, they would find the trophies he'd kept from each of his kills. Except for the orphaned girl child's mother. He'd been too frightened when she began to shift into her natural form to take anything from her.

No doubt the authorities would conclude that he'd been killed by a wild animal. Perhaps a dog gone feral. The mystery of his death would remain unsolved, and the police would count themselves lucky that a serial killer had been removed from their city.

She would leave in the morning, but first she had one more task to complete. She needed to rid herself of the stench of his essence so that she could become wholly herself again.

She'd just started to lick the monster's blood off her fur when a shape detached itself from the shadow of a nearby bush and padded toward her on silent paws.

15

THE HUMANS HAD A SAYING THE PROTECTOR HAD HEARD TIME AND TIME again in her long life.

Curiosity kills the cat.

She thought humans had it backwards. Curiosity *creates* the cat. Or in the case of her kin, curiosity about the world around them allowed them to create a reality in which they could survive.

She'd been curious as a youngling. She'd chased after butterflies because she wanted to know how they could fly. She'd raced after bees and grasshoppers because they could fly and hop almost as fast as she could run. She'd watched the clouds scutter across a clear blue sky and wondered if they felt as soft as they looked.

As she grew older, her curiosity was tempered with experience. She was bigger now than grasshoppers and could easily outpace them. But they could change directions easier than she could, so she watched how they moved until she could emulate them. She was the biggest and strongest youngling in the tribe, but that wasn't enough to make her the successful hunter she wanted to be. So she asked the adults to teach her, and she'd been eager to learn.

When her kin were granted the gift of shifting, the most successful among them were the ones who'd been curious about the world around them. The ones who'd watched other creatures and learned their traits and habits. It made the transition from their natural state to *other* easier to accomplish.

The Protector recognized insatiable curiosity when she saw it.

She saw it now in the ginger-furred youngling who approached her from the shadows where she'd hidden, watching the Protector kill the human monster. The youngling's eyes were bright with excitement. She rubbed her face against the Protector's, and the Protector let her.

This youngling wanted to become a Protector one day. Had the world become so large, the tribes of their kin so numerous, that more than one Protector was necessary to keep the tribes safe? Or was the Protector's time in this world drawing to a close?

The answers to those questions were up to the Maker of All Things, and the Protector would not dare to second guess the Maker's wisdom.

While the Protector finished washing the monster's blood from her fur, the youngling sat and watched her. She didn't approach the dead monster, although the Protector watched the youngling draw in his scent.

His scent was different now that his essence had faded from the world. But there was still an air of evil around him. This youngling didn't flinch from it. She wanted to learn about it, and she wanted the Protector to teach her.

When the last of the monster's blood was gone from her fur, the Protector stood and placed a gentle paw on the youngling's shoulder. Then the Protector tilted her head and crooked her tail, and a moment later she raced off into the foggy night.

The youngling followed her, as the Protector knew she would.

The youngling had been drawn to this spot for a reason. Had been compelled to watch the Protector carry out her duties. There had to be a reason for that.

Tomorrow the Protector would begin to teach this youngling what she would need to know if the Maker of All Things did indeed intend to bless her with the duties and long life of a Protector.

But tonight?

The rest of this blessed night would be spent in play. The world was full of fog and scent and wonders that could only be experienced in their true forms. Tonight they would revel in simply being alive.

If the Protector's time was indeed drawing to a close, she intended to fill as much of the rest of it as she could with joy.

NOW

16

Elias wasn't exactly a one-man band, but he came close.

Tuesday through Sunday he entertained the tourists who flocked to Fisherman's Wharf for shrimp cocktails, oysters, clam chowder in bread bowls, and cracked crab. With his keyboard setup and guitar, he could belt out any number of classics from the days when Frank Sinatra performed live in Vegas to modern pop tunes the Baby Boomers' grandkids streamed on their phones.

He had a prime place on the corner next to a pedestrian plaza in front of one of the few open-air parking lots between the Wharf and Pier 39. He made decent enough money in tips, especially on the weekends, and sometimes he even managed to sell a few of the CDs he'd produced as demos back in the days when he'd hoped to land a recording contract. At forty-seven, his chances of getting a record deal were somewhere between slim and not in this lifetime or the next.

Definitely not the life he'd imagined for himself back when he'd been a wide-eyed kid with dreams of becoming the next Billy Joel or Elton John or even Paul Simon, without Garfunkel. But thanks to frugal living, a decent amount of money still in savings from back when he had a regular, well-paid gig, and a roommate with a steady job in the Financial District, he got by.

More than that, he got by on his own terms. Playing music six days a week instead of slaving away in some old office for a boss who was never satisfied.

No sir, he'd rather busk on the Wharf any day of the week and twice on Sunday than have to wear a suit and tie and waste his days living for his next weekend off when those weekends were never long enough.

The first time he saw the cat, he was in the middle of his first set on a slow Tuesday morning.

The August day had dawned bright and sunny, a rarity for San Francisco. There weren't a lot of visitors out and about on the Wharf yet. Even during the summer season, ten-thirty in the morning on a Tuesday was usually too early for most tourists. Ten-thirty in the morning on a sunny Saturday, the Wharf would be jam packed.

Elias could always tell first-time visitors to the Bay. They shivered in the tank tops and board shorts that had seemed like a good idea in the hundred-plus-degree swelter of the central valley but were about two layers too few for the Wharf. He wore a leather jacket most summer days to keep out the damp cold rolling in off the bay. Today he knew he'd be shucking that jacket by noon, and the tourists from the valley would be dressed just fine.

That meant less business for the T-shirt shop across Jefferson Street from the corner where Elias played. His buddy Leon did a bang-up business on cold, foggy summer days. Tourists didn't mind spending a premium for official San Francisco's Fisherman's Wharf T-shirts and sweatshirts when they were freezing their asses off.

The fluffy ginger cat was hanging around one of the two open-air entrances at the front of Leon's store. It was just sitting on its haunches, sniffing the air and looking up at the seagulls hovering overhead.

The chain restaurant on the second floor of Leon's building wouldn't open to the public for another half hour, but no doubt the cat was smelling all the early-morning food prep going on. On the Wharf side of the street, all Elias could smell was fish and the musty odor of the bay.

Traffic was light so far, and the cat was unusual enough that Elias spent some time keeping an eye on the cat while he played. It didn't look like what he thought of as a typical alley cat, like the few he saw in the neighborhood around his apartment. This one looked too clean and too well fed to be a stray, although it was hard to tell under all that fluffy ginger fur.

He didn't think it was a tomcat either. It didn't have the jowly look that his mom's old tomcat had when Elias was a kid. That thing had been mean to anyone other than his mom who tried to touch it, but it had loved up his mom something crazy. Elias had given up trying to play with it after it had opened up a four-inch cut on his arm just as easy as you please with a swipe of its front paw. He still had the scar.

You'd think after that early experience—Elias had only been ten at the time—he would have had a lifelong fear of cats, but not so much. Cats were individuals, just like the people he met on the street. One mean cat didn't mean all cats were sons-of-bitches.

As for the people he saw on the street, it took all sorts there too. Some people stopped and listened to his music for a while. Others just walked on by like he was part of the scenery.

Elias could always tell a kindred spirit, though.

Those people were rare. They not only stopped to listen for a few beats but nodded along to the beat. Or maybe mouthed the words, not quite singing, not wanting to interrupt his performance, but still touched deep inside by the music. Maybe the music brought back a treasured memory or a favorite time in their life.

Music did that to some people. It had always been that way for him.

He got the feeling the fuzzy ginger cat was one of those who really vibed to the song he was playing. Funny thing to think about a cat, but maybe whoever owned it was a music lover. It sure seemed to be paying attention to him now.

Elias finished up the song he'd been riffing on. An early Billy Joel number and one of his personal favorites.

"You got a favorite?" he said, looking at the cat.

It couldn't possibly have heard him all the way across the street.

While street traffic was light by San Francisco standards, it wasn't non-existent. Yet that damn cat stood up, back arched in pleasure like invisible fingers were petting the fur along the length of its spine. It stood on tiptoes almost, bushy tail straight up in the air, and stared at him. *Stared* right at him.

"I'll be damned," Elias said.

He shook his head, about ready to tell himself he needed to get his head examined, and that's when he heard it.

The opening notes to an almost forgotten song.

He'd learned the song when he'd been a kid. Older than that ten-year-old who'd tried not to cry when his mom had cleaned the four-inch cut on his arm. Old enough and already musical enough that his parents had sprung for piano lessons they couldn't really afford.

The song was "Moonlight Sonata."

Now, that sure as hell wasn't something in his normal repertoire. Way too classical and slow for the tourist crowd, but there really wasn't much of a crowd at all yet this morning. Just a few tourists strolling by, taking their time and gawking at the sights, interspersed with a couple of high-powered types clocking out a staccato beat on the sidewalk in their high heels or polished leather Oxfords, no doubt on their way to do a Very Important something-or-other.

But Elias was game. Hell, he considered it a challenge.

He adjusted the settings on his keyboard. "Moonlight Sonata" was definitely a keyboard song, not something he wanted to tackle on guitar. When he thought he'd set the keyboard to produce a decent enough tone, he started playing.

As soon as he riffed the first few notes, the melody came back to him. Not the simplified arrangement from the songbook his piano teacher had insisted they use, but a more elaborate version that seemed to come to Elias from wherever most of his music came from. Not exactly his soul. More like a combination of soul and heart, imagination and memory.

He rocked the solemn notes of "Moonlight Sonata" right there on his usual corner at Fisherman's Wharf on what promised to be an unseasonably hot August day. He really got into the heavy feel of it, the flow that gave the simple melody heft and meaning. He even closed his eyes as he played, something he rarely did, he got that lost in the music.

When he was finished, he opened his eyes and was surprised to find a lithe young woman watching him. She was standing just off to one side of his corner, staring at him with the most striking golden-green eyes he could ever remember seeing. Her long, thick, luxurious hair was the color of a glorious sunset and hung down to her waist in a riot of thick curls.

She was wearing a full skirt that just grazed the ground. The tiered skirt was made of some gauzy material printed with splashes of autumn colors, each tier fuller than the one above it. Her loose shirt was made of the same material and billowed around her arms before being drawn back in around her wrists.

His mom used to call a skirt like that a peasant skirt. She'd seen a woman wearing one once when she'd dropped him off at college. Said it gave her flashbacks to her old hippy days. His dad, who'd been in the car with them, said she'd never been an old hippy, just a young one.

That had been one of the last times his parents had been together. Elias shook off the memory of what had come next. He didn't want to think about it, not when a beautiful woman was looking at him with those gorgeous eyes.

He smiled at her, just his friendly professional grin, nothing suggestive. When she smiled back, her nose crinkled up and he noticed that she had a smattering of freckles across the bridge and on her cheeks. Her chin had a subtle cleft, and her smile teased out dimples in her cheeks.

She looked like the damn free spirit of a high school cheerleader.

Except he got the feeling she was older than that. Put her in a business suit and give her a little subtle makeup, and she could pass for a thirty-something professional. But her eyes—those amazing golden-green eyes—seemed to hold wisdom beyond even middle-age, which made her true age hard to pin down.

Elias felt like shaking his head. He never waxed this poetic about the people who stopped to listen to his music. They simply crossed his path momentarily, some of them kind, some of them preoccupied with their own lives. Occasionally he might make up stories for himself about what their lives were like, especially when the day was slow and he was playing his music more by rote than feeling it. But he couldn't remember ever being struck so forcefully by a stranger's... what? Charisma? Charm? Beauty?

All of that, but there was something else. Something he couldn't quite put his finger on. Whatever it was, it made this young woman almost impossible to ignore. At least for him. The few other people passing by weren't paying her the least little bit of attention, yet he couldn't seem to tear his eyes away from her face.

Almost as if she knew what he was thinking, her smile got wider. She came a few steps closer, walking with an almost sinewy grace. Maybe she wanted to leave a tip or buy one of his CDs. She wasn't carrying a purse or a tote bag or even a shopping bag, but that skirt was big enough it could certainly have a pocket or two.

Instead of reaching into a hidden pocket, she tilted her head to one side, her lashes half lowered over those incredible eyes.

"Thank you for playing my song," she said.

Her voice was breathy, almost lyrical, and about as substantial as the outfit she wore. It was the way the wind might talk if it could actually speak.

Then what she said sank in.

He'd played *her* song? When had he done that?

She hadn't asked for a song. He was pretty sure he would have remembered that. No one had been around when he'd started playing "Moonlight Sonata." The name just came to him out of the blue.

If "Moonlight Sonata" really was her song, that was a hell of a coincidence. Stuff like that didn't usually happen to him.

He realized she was waiting for him to say something.

"Anytime," he said, trying to sound nonchalant. "Stop by anytime."

"You're so kind." Her eyes twinkled with good humor, and she ducked her chin. "I might do that."

Just like that, the conversation had turned flirty. Elias could practically feel her interest wafting over him. She had to be... what? A good twenty years younger than he was? But all of a sudden that didn't matter.

She caught her bottom lip between perfect teeth, staring at him with frank interest. "You're really very good, you know," she said. "I'm glad I stopped to listen."

Before he could say anything—and probably embarrass himself if he'd misread her signals—she turned around and walked away. Her gauzy skirt flowed around her ankles almost like it was caught in a late-summer breeze. Only there wasn't a breeze yet this morning. Just pleasant sunshine.

That's when he realized she was barefoot. Some women wore sandals that were so thin they were barely noticeable, almost like a thin sheet of leather glued to the bottom of their feet, but not this woman. Her feet were definitely bare. Not the smartest thing in a place where people weren't always careful with what they dropped on the sidewalk.

He was about to call after her to tell her to be careful where she walked, but then he stopped himself. She was an adult. An intriguing, achingly beautiful young woman with an old soul, but she was still an adult. A woman who walked around the city in bare feet could take care of herself. She was a free spirit, that was all. San Francisco had been home to free spirits long before he'd played the first note of "Moonlight Sonata" back when he'd been a kid just learning to play piano.

That thought made Elias remember the cat. He turned to look at the entrance to Leon's T-shirt shop, wondering if the song had made the cat as happy as it had made the young woman.

The cat was gone.

Well, that was disappointing. And ridiculous. It wasn't like the cat had asked for the song.

As he launched into the next song, a Gordon Lightfoot standard, he tried to catch another glimpse of his young music lover. She'd been walking toward the seafood stalls on the Wharf. It was a little early for a walkaway shrimp cocktail, but he knew people whose favorite breakfast was a shrimp and crab omelet. Not *his,* but it took all types.

The crowds on the Wharf were just starting to pick up, although the pedestrian traffic still wasn't as heavy as it would be at this time on the weekends. He had a prime location for people watching. From where he sat crooning a Lightfoot favorite, he should have been able to spot her easy, even if all he caught was a glimpse of her hair.

But he didn't see her either.

Just like the cat, she was gone.

17

THREE DAYS LATER, ON A FOGGY FRIDAY MORNING, A DIFFERENT CAT showed up to listen to Elias play.

The day started out more like a typical August day in the city. Fog had rolled in overnight, thick and damp and unrelenting. When Elias set up his kit a few minutes before ten, the city was still socked in even with the light breeze blowing in off the water. Elias would definitely be wearing his leather jacket most of the day.

A good number of tourists were already out and about, hands cupped around go-cups of their favorite hot beverage of choice. Later in the day the Wharf would be choked with crowds when people from the valley and beyond finally made it across the Bay Bridge or the Golden Gate seeking relief from the heat. Most of them would be as underdressed as the early birds. Leon's T-shirt shop and the clothing stores on Pier 39 would be doing a brisk business selling hoodies and sweaters and windbreakers to people freezing their asses off.

The first time Elias had come to the Wharf, he'd been one of those underdressed tourists. He'd paid a ridiculous amount of money to park for a few hours in the garage across the street from Pier 39.

He'd walked down The Embarcadero to where it split off Jefferson Street and fed into the piers where the tour boats docked.

A lot of people on the Wharf with him that day had paid to go on one of the boat tours. Elias hadn't. He'd been far more interested in all the street performers. He'd stopped to listen to quite a few of the musicians and had even chatted up a couple about how they'd managed to snag spots in such prime tourist real estate. All while trying not to freeze his ass off.

In all the years since then he'd never taken one of the boat tours. He wasn't fond of boats or the open water, which seemed silly considering where he made his living.

But when did life ever make sense?

He'd decided that morning to shake up his usual sets. He'd been thinking about "Moonlight Sonata" a lot. The song had even invaded a few of his dreams.

In his dreams the song hadn't sounded the way he'd played it Tuesday morning. No, in the illogical way of dreams, he'd heard "Moonlight Sonata" the way the stars would sing it. Light and airy and with an ethereal tinge to each note.

Not "Moonlight Sonata" played by the light of the moon, but "Moonlight Sonata" played *with* moonlight.

Which was utterly ridiculous. He couldn't play a song with moonlight. But that was how he remembered it.

Which was strange in and of itself. He never remembered his dreams. Oh, he knew he dreamed. He had quite the dream life, in fact. He always had. But those dreams were disjointed, just odd snippets of a life not really lived. It was rare if he could remember anything that happened in his dreams once he really woke up. It was almost like dream Elias couldn't exist in the same place as real-life Elias.

He supposed that was how dreams were for most people.

But his "Moonlight Sonata" dreams were different. He not only remembered those dreams, he remembered *exactly* how the song had sounded in those dreams.

That had to mean something.

Didn't it?

After having basically the same "Moonlight Sonata" dream Tuesday night and Wednesday night, he decided the dream was trying to tell him something. Like *this is how the song should be played, stupid.* So when he got back to his apartment after his Thursday gig at the Wharf, he decided to give the moonlight version of the song a shot.

All the years he'd spent making a living with music had made him pretty good at capturing the tone and feel and melodic qualities of a song, but he sure as hell wasn't an ethereal being who could weave a melody out of moonlight. He was just a damn good musical chameleon who could cover almost any song.

Except music sung by the stars in the moonlight.

He'd fiddled and futzed with the settings on his keyboard, trying different combinations of preset sounds with others that he'd programmed in himself. He'd spent hours frustrated at his inability to capture what really should have been a simple song (simple, ha!) until he finally came up with something that bore at least a slight resemblance to the tone he remembered from his dreams.

It wouldn't—couldn't—have the exact same musical quality he'd heard in his dreams. How could it? Nobody could play a song with moonlight.

The day was still early enough, and too many people were still freezing their butts off. They'd be hurrying to wherever they planned to go, so he figured it was safe enough to give his updated version of "Moonlight Sonata" a whirl. The song might not earn him any tips, but it wasn't like he'd be getting any real tips until later on anyway. Besides, how could he resist playing his brand of starlight music on the Wharf on a foggy San Francisco morning? Talk about setting a mood.

He played his entire version of "Moonlight Sonata" but when he was done, he didn't follow up with one of his usual standards. Instead, he flowed right into a semi-upbeat version of "Ode to Joy." The songs didn't seem to go together anywhere but in his mind, but he was pretty much just playing for himself anyway.

A few of the passing tourists gave him startled looks. "Ode to Joy" wasn't exactly a tourist magnet, especially not the way he played it. He added in some runs here and there to make up for the fact he was performing it solely as an instrumental. He wasn't a half-bad vocalist, but he felt this song deserved better than he could give it in the vocal department.

He didn't expect anyone to stop and listen, not to this song, but an older couple surprised him.

Elias thought of anyone who had twenty years or more years on him as older, but he never considered anyone elderly. The closer he got to that big Five O, the more the word "elderly" sounded like an insult, and he tried never to insult anyone.

The couple who'd stopped in almost the same exact spot that the woman with the amazing eyes had stood three days ago fell in that "older" age range. The woman was slim with a pretty face and short-cropped white hair. She had an elfin look about her thanks to the point of her chin and her upturned eyes. The man with her probably had a strong, square jaw before gravity started pulling jowls down beneath his chin. His gray hair must have been what Elias's mom would have called dishwater blond at one time. There were still hints of gold in what was a remarkably full head of hair.

They must have been locals since they were both dressed for a chilly morning on the Wharf. The man had on a charcoal gray woolen coat with a forest-green knitted scarf wrapped around his neck. The woman had on a bulky white coat with black patches on the pockets. The coat dwarfed her face and made her look more than a little like a walking marshmallow.

Elias gave them a welcoming grin as he ran through the closing bars of "Ode to Joy" on his keyboard. The woman smiled back, a smile that touched the faded green of her eyes. Her companion—husband? Maybe, but neither one wore wedding rings—didn't make eye contact with Elias. Instead, the old guy stared off into the distance in the general direction of Pier 39.

Of the two of them, the woman seemed to be the one who was really into music. It wasn't so much that she was swaying slightly to the rhythm of the song, it was the radiant look on her face. Almost as if she was listening to a favorite piece of music she hadn't heard in a very long time.

If they stuck around after the song was done, Elias would ask her if she had a favorite song. He figured it might be an old standard. If she didn't, he'd play something by Frank Sinatra, maybe she'd like that too.

Then he corrected himself. She wasn't *that* old. For all he knew, she might like to hear something by Bread or even Creedance Clearwater.

He needn't have worried about it. Before he got to the last notes of "Ode to Joy," the woman turned her gaze from Elias to her companion, then she gave Elias a little shrug and an apologetic smile as the two of them walked away.

Elias suppressed a sigh.

He lived for little moments like that, but that one had been so brief. No matter how much he told himself he played the music he did because it made him happy, if that's all it really was, he could spend his days toiling away in some office and play his music at night in his room. No, he played out in the open on a busy street corner next to the Wharf, barely making enough to scrape by, because he wanted to share the music he loved with other people. To feel that momentary connection when something he loved—something he *created*—touched someone else.

Those momentary connections, far more than money, that's what made life worth living. Far better than just surviving. Than living paycheck to paycheck like Jerry and hating every minute he spent at work.

Elias's roommate worked in the Financial District. Jerry made a good living by the standards of nearly anywhere else in the country. By San Francisco standards, where the cost of living much less living well was ridiculously high, Jerry's good living was barely subsistence level. If Jerry made enough to really live on, Elias was sure he wouldn't want a roommate. The man was a good fifteen years younger than Elias, high strung and perpetually stressed out. He tolerated Elias because he needed Elias's portion of the rent just to keep a roof over his head.

Elias understood that, and he didn't take it personally. He and Jerry weren't friends. They never would be friends. Life had thrown them together, that was all.

All these thoughts passed through Elias's mind as he finished up "Ode to Joy." He wasn't watching anyone in particular while he played. Instead he just stared off into the distance, vaguely aware of the cold, gray San Francisco morning and that unique Wharf smell that was part musty ocean water, part fresh fish, shrimp, crab, and cocktail sauce, and part sourdough bread from the store on the other side of the parking lot.

Jerry probably dealt with his everyday world of office cubicles and co-workers who doused themselves in aftershave or perfume the same way. After a while, a person's senses just got numb to the things they experienced every day.

Elias huffed out a breath when he realized he was staring off into the distance just like the old guy in the woolen coat and the forest-green knitted scarf. Only Elias got the feeling the old guy didn't miss a trick. Elias might be wool gathering, one of his mother's favorite sayings, but the old guy was surveying his surroundings.

Maybe he'd been a cop, or some kind of investigator. Or hell, maybe he just had a dozen or so grandkids he had to ride herd on whenever they visited. He could just be a man looking out for the kind of trouble toddlers could get into without half trying.

Two young women walked by, each of them holding to-go cups that trailed the rich scent of fresh-brewed coffee. They were dressed in lightweight clothes, and both of them had their hands wrapped around the cups to keep their fingers warm.

Elias could sure use some of the coffee he'd brought from home. But downing the coffee in the battered thermos by his feet would spell disaster.

He had the same kind of problem all solo street performers had: he needed someone to watch his stuff whenever he had to leave his spot, say to take a bathroom break. His street gig was only four hours long. In theory, he should be able to make those four hours without needing to pee. But ever since he'd waved forty-five goodbye in the rearview mirror, his bladder decided it had other ideas. Most days he needed at least one break, especially when the weather was cold and damp like it was today.

That's why he'd made a deal with Leon.

The restroom in Leon's store was supposed to be for staff only. Elias wasn't exactly staff, but whenever he could, he sent people Leon's way. Especially tourists who were clearly freezing their asses off.

"Tell Leon that Elias sent you," he'd say, "and he'll give you ten percent off."

Leon's shop was on the wrong side of Jefferson to get a lot of foot traffic. If that ten percent discount enticed tourists to cross the street for a bargain, Leon was definitely okay with that. In exchange, whenever Elias needed a bathroom break, he'd send Leon a text and either Leon or one of his employees jogged across the street to watch Elias's equipment while Elias used the bathroom in Leon's store.

To take his mind off how good coffee would be right about now, Elias went directly from "Ode to Joy" into a few of his more traditional standards—Billy Joel and Paul Simon and even an older Eagles song.

He was getting close to the end of what he thought of as his first set, rocking out to an old Police song, when he glanced across the street. If Leon's store was crowded with customers, Elias would just suck it up for a few more songs before he texted Leon for a break.

There was a cat sitting by the front of Leon's store.

Not the long-haired ginger cat from a few days ago. This cat was almost entirely white with a few splotches of darker tabby fur on its head and along its spine. Its thin tail was totally tabby, a combination of gray and black tiger-striped fur that looked out of place on a mostly white cat.

But like the ginger-furred cat from the other day, this one's attention was totally riveted on Elias.

Like it was listening to his music.

This wasn't the ethereal moonlight music he'd been playing first thing that morning. No "Moonlight Sonata." No "Ode to Joy." This was his version of the stuff people might hear on the radio or their streaming music service of choice.

Yet the cat appeared to be totally into the music. It didn't seem to twitch when a particularly loud car drove by, and it didn't move when people walked too close to it. The cat simply sat still as a statue, head and ears pointed in Elias's direction.

Normal cats didn't behave that way, did they?

Elias had never been tempted to adopt a cat of his own, not after his mother's ill-tempered tomcat, so he had no real idea what was normal for a cat. But the fact that two different cats had sat in basically the same place and appeared to be listening to him play—that had to be weird, right?

He finished the Police song and instead of the Gordon Lightfoot song he'd intended to play next, he decided to play "Moonlight Sonata" again just to see what the cat would do.

Not the ethereal version he'd played that morning, but the version he'd first played for the young woman who'd stopped to listen to his music a few days ago. The woman with the gauzy skirt who looked for all the world like a throwback to San Francisco's hippy days.

He'd only played a few opening notes when the cat's ears twitched. It lifted its nose, and although he couldn't tell from where he was sitting, Elias could have sworn the cat was sniffing the air. The tip of its tail twitched almost in time to the beat.

Like it was *dancing*. The feline version of a ballerina.

Elias would have laughed at the thought, but a sudden chill swept down his spine. The damp cold must have finally worked through his leather jacket. He really could use that coffee.

No, that wasn't it. He wasn't feeling the damp cold of a foggy San Francisco morning. This was the cold of a moonlit meadow in the middle of winter. Or the cold of starlight. Or....

Moonlight.

The word echoed through his mind, along with something else. A thought that he was pretty sure wasn't his own.

We all dance in our own ways.

Followed closely by another:

Thank you for playing this song.

Only muscle memory kept Elias from totally flubbing up the rest of the song.

No one had spoken those words out loud, he was sure of it.

What the hell?

He blinked and gave his head a sharp shake, trying to clear his mind.

When he looked back across the street, a white-haired woman stood in the exact same space where the white cat had been just a moment ago. She was the same woman who'd stopped to listen to "Ode to Joy" earlier that morning, only now she was alone. Her gray-haired companion wasn't with her.

She was standing there smiling at him. Then she clearly mouthed the words *thank you.*

A group of three teenage girls crossed in front of Leon's shop. They didn't seem to register that the woman was there, although they walked around her. Kids that age always seemed so oblivious to the world around them. It was a wonder they didn't barrel right into the older woman.

Except... was that all it was? The obliviousness of the young?

Because when the teenagers passed the spot where she'd been just a moment ago, the woman was gone.

Not even the cat remained.

18

———

Elias had been married once.

He'd been twenty-two years old, lean and hungry and cock-sure of himself. One year away from graduation, a music major with—at his mother's insistence—a business minor.

"You have to have something to fall back on," she told him at least once a month. "Music won't pay the bills."

Music certainly hadn't at the time. It barely did now, if Elias was being honest with himself, but back then? He had to make ends meet, such as they were, by bagging groceries at one of the chain stores close to the university. He gigged when he could talk some bar or restaurant into letting him play, pure acoustic sets, just him and his guitar so as not to annoy the customers with anything other than background music. Most of those gigs paid in tips and maybe a meal thrown in at some of the better restaurants.

His school was a state university, not even close to Ivy League standards—not that an Ivy League school would have accepted him with his grades. The best thing about it was the music program.

By the time he hit college, he'd fiddled around with most instruments. After his first semester, he decided that piano and guitar were the ones that stuck. He was pretty good at both.

77

Not great, though. Certainly not concert quality.

Still, he was sure that someday he'd hit great. He just had to keep at it.

Scarlett—Lettie for short—now she was something else. That woman could sing the notes right out of the sky. Make the clouds weep for sheer joy. Make songbirds go still with envy.

At least that's what Elias thought.

Strange thing was, they didn't meet in the music department. They had no classes together. She wasn't even a music major. Her field was education, with an emphasis on prekindergarten curriculum.

They met at a bachelorette party.

He'd gone to this particular bar with a few buddies. It wasn't one of the bars he usually gigged at, and he'd been trying to talk the bartender into letting him play. In those days he always took his guitar with him whenever he went out on a Friday night. Just in case.

Scarlett, she of the long red hair, freckles, and a voice like an angel, was the bride-to-be's maid of honor. The bachelorette party was one of those things that went from bar to bar, the women all riding in a rented limo with brief stops here and there. By the time the party hit the bar Elias hoped to gig at, most of the party'd had quite a few drinks.

Scarlett hadn't. She wasn't sober sister or the designated driver— the limo driver would be taking all the women home—she just didn't like herself when she had too much to drink.

Elias found all this out after their first song together.

After she'd convinced him to join the party as their entertainment.

"We can pay you," she'd said. "You don't even have to strip."

She'd come up to him at the bar and asked him if he could play a song for the bride. She'd seen him sitting with his guitar case at his feet, and figured, as she told him later, it was worth a shot.

The only problem was she wanted him to play "Every Breath You Take" by The Police.

"That's a pretty creepy song when you think about it," he'd told her. "How about something a little more chill?"

She'd been intrigued. The song choice had been the bride-to-be's, and as it turned out, Scarlett didn't much like it either. So she'd told him why not? Do your best.

He'd followed her back to the table where the bride-to-be and her four very drunk bridesmaids sat. Instead of the Police song, he'd played "Annie's Song" by John Denver. Denver had been a guitar player, and the song worked well for Elias's vocal range.

The bride-to-be had given him a huge smooch—on the cheek, not the lips—when he'd finished, and a few of the bar patrons had applauded. Whether it was the kiss or the song, Elias never knew, but the bartender slowed down pouring drinks to watch as Elias played a second song for the bachelorette party.

Two songs after that, Elias not only had a gig at the bar the following night—an audition, the bartender had called it—he had a gig for the rest of that night. His buddies had catcalled after him as he left the bar with six women, including one very wasted bride-to-be and one gorgeous and very sober maid of honor.

In the privacy of the limousine while the driver transported the whole party to the next bar, Elias had played another song. This one, Scarlett—*call me Lettie*, she'd said—specifically requested. "Always a Woman" by Billy Joel. By the time he hit the second verse, she'd started to sing along.

He'd been blown away by her voice. Sweet and heartfelt, and with a range that he could never hope to hit, not in his wildest dreams.

"Why the hell aren't you singing for a living?" he asked when the song was done.

She'd given him a coquettish look. "How do you know I'm not?"

One of the more inebriated bridesmaids had elbowed her in the ribs. "Stop teasing the man, Lettie." And to Elias, "She's a student, just like the rest of us."

"And me," Elias had said. "Just working my way through school in case I need a 'real' job."

"And I just sing in the shower—" Lettie started.

"And a limo," the bridesmaid said.

"—for fun," Lettie had finished.

The bachelorette party had moved on to two more bars, and Elias had sung for the bride-to-be at every bar. The first bar was the only venue that netted him an audition for a more permanent gig, but he didn't care. By the time the evening was over, he'd fallen head over heels for red-haired Scarlett.

That party became their first unofficial date. Six months later they'd moved in together. Two months after that, they were married.

The marriage lasted six years.

The Lettie years, as Elias came to think of them, seemed unreal to him now. He'd been so deliriously happy. Broke, yeah sure. Never enough money, at least at first, but he'd been happy. Gloriously happy. The world he and Lettie had carved out for themselves seemed like a magical place. They made music together in the privacy of their own little apartments, but she never sang in public.

Performing was his thing, she said. Getting feedback from the crowd, even if that crowd was only a couple of drunks in a bar who'd stopped to listen and maybe applaud when he was done. That wasn't her thing. She sang because she could. Because she wanted to. Because a particular song or even a piece of song moved her.

Whenever they sang together, he felt like his soul had been touched by an angel.

He shouldn't have been surprised when it ended.

But he was, and it almost killed him.

19

ALTHOUGH ELIAS KEPT LOOKING FOR THE WHITE CAT WITH THE GRAY and black tiger-striped tail, he didn't see it again.

Or the white-haired woman, for that matter. More and more tourists crowded around the Wharf, and the traffic on the street picked up. Typical Friday at one of San Francisco's busiest tourist spots on a chilly August day.

He'd finally given in to his need for coffee to warm himself up. Some street musicians wore fingerless gloves on cold days, but he'd never gotten the hang of it. Even fingerless gloves muffled the songs he played on guitar. As for keyboarding, the gloves just made his fingers feel weird.

Kind of like how Lettie had never worn any rings other than the plain wedding band the entire time they'd been married. She used to say it was because she didn't want to lose them at work since her part-time, college-student gig was making sandwiches at a fast-food place close to the campus, but he didn't think that was all of it. Some women wore jewelry, some didn't. The pretty golden-haired woman who'd stopped to listen to him play "Moonlight Sonata" the other day hadn't been wearing any jewelry, he was sure of it.

Funny how he hadn't noticed that at the time.

81

Elias finally texted Leon about eleven-thirty. When he saw Leon heading across the street, Elias finished up his current song and dug out his *Back in Ten Minutes* sign to hang on his keyboard stand.

"Jack's the only one working today," Leon said as Elias stood up and stretched his back. "Delila called out sick. Just a head's up."

Jack.

Wonderful.

If Elias had been a stray alley cat, Jack would have been the biggest, meanest, most cat-hating Doberman in the neighborhood. Jack was well over six feet tall and at least two hundred fifty pounds of solid muscle, most of it between his ears. He listened to right-wing blowhards on various streaming services and swallowed every idiotic conspiracy theory hook, line, and sinker, as Elias's dad would have said.

Leon said he only kept Jack around because he appealed to a certain type of tourist. The ones from the flyover states or certain areas of the west coast where traditional conservative politics were far too liberal for most residents. The fact that Jack's arms and upper body were covered with tattoos didn't detract from his appeal. Most days those tattoos were on full display thanks to the muscle tanks that were his standard work attire. Jack kept his skull shaved, and his politics were always front and center thanks to those tattoos and the artwork printed on his muscle shirts.

According to Leon, the man's one saving grace—besides the fact that his mere presence was usually enough to discourage shoplifters —was his ability to (briefly) put his beliefs aside when the more liberal members of the general public stopped by the store to shop. The man knew where his bread was buttered, another saying Elias had picked up from his parents. A customer's politics didn't matter as long as they bought something.

To say that Elias's general outlook on life was far more liberal than Jack's was an understatement. And since Elias wasn't a customer, was in fact a freeloader as far as Jack was concerned, well... that meant that Jack felt he didn't have to be nice.

Elias briefly considered whether he should take his bathroom break in the sourdough bread store on the other side of the parking lot. Except he'd have to buy something since the store's restrooms were *For Customers Only*. He'd made enough in tips for a loaf of bread, if not a sandwich, but that wouldn't be his first choice.

Leon sat his skinny ass down on Elias's stool. "Listen," he said, "if that asshole gives you any shit, let me know and I'll take care of it."

Right.

Leon was nearing sixty, one of those short, skinny men Elias's mom would have called wiry. If he'd ever had much in the way of muscles, there wasn't much evidence of it now. He wore his thin, salt-and-pepper hair long and tied back with a strip of leather. The mere idea of Leon "taking care" of a guy like Jack was ludicrous.

Instead of saying that, Elias just nodded his thanks. "Don't run off my customers while I'm gone," he said. "Or hock any of my stuff."

Leon huffed out a laugh. "And don't you run off any of mine, you hear?"

The T-shirt shop occupied a fairly narrow space across the street from the Wharf. Rent being what it was, especially in this neighborhood, Leon had stuffed his store to the gills with everything and anything having to do with T-shirts, sweatshirts, and general tourist-type goods, like postcards, shot glasses, and—surprisingly—dark glasses.

Clothing racks in the center of the store were jam-packed with sweatshirts and hoodies in all sizes emblazoned with stylized versions of San Francisco landmarks. Outerwear, as Leon called it, were big sellers during the summer months, especially on days when the fog never burned off and the breeze off the bay sent tourists from the valley scrambling for something warm to wear. Leon kept his prices reasonable—more reasonable than the clothing shops on Pier 39—and most cold days he did a pretty good business.

Leon also sold preprinted tees in all styles and colors, with artwork ranging from superheroes to metal bands to cute animals (puppies, kittens, and seals were big sellers, according to Leon) to the kind of stuff Elias used to see in head shops back when he'd been in college. The walls were lined with shelves stuffed full of shirts, with examples of the shirts for sale hung on the upper walls.

The one thing Leon didn't have in his shop was a T-shirt press. No custom while-you-wait shirts. Not only did he not have the room, he didn't want the liability, or so he'd told Elias once.

"You've seen Jack," Leon had said. "You think I want that guy sticking his hands underneath a shirt press? Leaning up against it and burning one of those tattoos, then suing my ass off?"

Or sticking someone else's hand underneath a shirt press, Elias had thought at the time but didn't say.

The shop's single restroom was at the very back of the store. A beaded curtain cordoned off a narrow hallway, and a sign tacked on the wall over the curtain read *Employees Only*. The hallway ended at the shop's back door, which opened onto the ground floor of a parking garage. The little room Leon used as an office was on one side of the hallway, the single restroom on the other.

Most days when Jack was working, Elias just kept his head down and made his way to the restroom like he belonged there. If Jack had customers, he might narrow his eyes at Elias, but that was it.

But when there were no customers in the store? Like this particular moment?

Not so much.

"Hey, asshole."

Jack's voice cut through Elias's thoughts, which were centered squarely on his intended destination.

"That's for employees only," Jack said. "Not for dickheads who play shit music on the street."

The human Doberman was standing behind the checkout counter. When Leon had first purchased the store, the counter had been in the back near the beaded curtain. The previous owner had told Leon shoplifting off the front racks was a problem, so he only displayed clearance items on the racks closest to the sidewalk.

Clearance items weren't the best draw, as far as Leon was concerned. So he'd moved the checkout counter up near the front of the store and put it right in the center. An employee working the register could see the front of the store, most of the back, and along both sides. Leon had also installed security cameras on the register and on the open storefront, and then he'd moved tourist heavy items, like the Golden Gate sweatshirts, up front.

An amazing thing had happened. Shoplifting losses went down, sales of Golden Gate sweatshirts went up, and Leon was a happy camper.

Elias, however, was currently not a happy camper. Jack had his arms crossed in front of his bodybuilder's chest and a scowl on his thick face.

Elias sighed. "You know the deal. How it works."

"I know how it's *supposed* to work, but you ain't sent no customers our way." Jack's piggy eyes narrowed. "Nobody's come in and asked for their discount."

That was probably true. It had been a slow morning for tips, even for a Friday. It usually was when the morning was cold and damp and foggy. Except for the older couple, nobody had really stopped to listen to Elias's music, which meant he hadn't had an opportunity to send anyone Leon's way.

"No referrals, no bathroom," Jack said.

This kind of crap was old hat. Most days Elias could just ignore it, but for some reason, today he'd finally had enough. He stopped in his tracks and glared at Jack.

"I could always just pee right here." Elias gestured at the shelves full of T-shirts next to where he'd stopped. "You rather I do that?"

Jack uncrossed his arms and leaned over the counter. "You do that, and I beat the crap out of you." He smiled. It wasn't a pleasant sight. "You'd give me the excuse, that what you want?"

Elias shook his head. He should know better. Arguing with this man wasn't going to do any good. It was like arguing with a brick wall.

"Whatever," he said.

He gave Jack as wide a berth as the store allowed. Elias's shoulders tensed up, and he had to fight to keep from looking over his shoulder as he made his way to the back of the store to make sure Jack wasn't coming after him.

He breathed a sigh of relief when he hit the hallway and the bead curtains clattered closed behind him.

Once he made it inside the restroom, he flipped the lock on the door, something he never did. He told himself he was being ridiculous. Jack was a blowhard, but he wouldn't risk getting fired. If Elias was being honest with himself, he was in more danger out on the street. Muggings happened in the city, and not just to street musicians.

Besides, all Jack had done was jaw at him. Elias could usually handle verbal abuse. Any street performer—hell, any performer period—learned early how to handle hecklers or they didn't last long. That's all Jack really was. A heckler of a different stripe. All talk, no action.

Which was probably why Elias was totally unprepared for Jack to grab him as soon as he opened the bathroom door. Jack's meaty hand closed around the front of Elias's leather jacket, and then Jack slammed him up against the wall next to Leon's office door.

"Whatever?" Jack said. "That what you said to me?"

He pressed his forearm against Elias's neck. Hard.

"How about I show you what-the-fuck-ever, you freeloading piece of shit."

20

One of the fluorescent bulbs in the overhead fixture in the hallway of the T-shirt shop had burned out, leaving the hallway dim. This part of the shop smelled like a musty combination of old dust, old paperwork, and cooking smells filtering down from the restaurant upstairs. Funny how Elias had never noticed that before.

Then again, he'd never had a muscle-bound asshole throw him up against the wall right outside the shop's bathroom either.

Elias had lived in a lot of crappy apartment buildings where that greasy food stench was overlaid with urine and rotting garbage.

Jack's breath smelled worse than that. Whether it was a combination of stale beer and an overdose of garlic or just bad dental work coming home to roost, the stench coming out of the man's mouth was enough to turn Elias's stomach.

If Elias could have pushed Jack away, he would have just to get that smell out of his face. But Jack outweighed Elias by a good fifty pounds or more. Elias wasn't a ninety-pound weakling, but he wasn't a bodybuilder either. He had about as much chance of manhandling Jack as he did of scoring a gig as the opening act in one of the showrooms down in Vegas.

Leon didn't have any security cameras in his back hallway. Elias had asked Leon about it once. Wasn't he worried someone could walk in the shop from the back and rummage through all the stock Leon kept in his office? The first few days Elias had busked on his corner spot, he'd been worried about someone coming up behind him, knocking him over the head, and robbing him blind.

Up until then, he'd always played on a sidewalk with a nice, solid building right behind him. He'd gotten used to only having to look out for the people he could see in front of him. It didn't pay to be careless in the city, and having a solid wall behind his back gave him a nice sense of security.

It took a while to get used to playing out in the open with nothing but the pedestrian plaza at his back. Eventually he realized that since he only played until the middle of the afternoon, even the most brazen robbers wouldn't attack him in broad daylight right in front of a whole bunch of witnesses. Steal his tips and run like hell? Maybe, but that's why he kept his open guitar case close to his feet.

Leon had told him the back door was one part of the store he didn't have to worry about. The door that led into the parking garage stayed locked on the outside. The push-bar on the inside would let anyone out in case of an emergency, but no one could get in from the alley unless someone opened the door from the inside. The only security cameras he needed were the ones in the front of the store.

Well, Elias could have used a security camera in the hallway right about now. With no one watching, Jack obviously felt free to do whatever he wanted.

And what he wanted to do right now was bring down a world of hurt on Elias.

"Listen, asshole," Jack said, his voice a rough growl. "How'd you like it if I broke a couple of your fingers? Think you'd be out there doing your thing for the tourists then, hoping for a buck or two tossed your way?"

Jack's meaty forearm was pressing against Elias's windpipe hard enough to hurt. He could still breathe, after a fashion, but Jack's arm must be cutting off part of the blood to Elias's brain. His vision was starting to get red around the edges, and real panic was starting to set in.

He couldn't knee Jack in the crotch. Jack was pressed in far too close for that to work. He couldn't stomp on Jack's foot either. Jack always wore heavy motorcycle boots, and Elias just had on his usual tennis shoes. Trying to stomp the heel of his tennis shoe down on Jack's foot would be about as effective as trying to swat a fly with a piece of tissue paper.

Could he jam his fingers into Jack's eyes? Maybe, but Jack was taller than he was. The last thing Elias wanted to do was give Jack a shot at grabbing one of his hands and carrying through with the threat to break a few of Elias's fingers.

Well, maybe not the *last* thing. The last thing he wanted to do was die.

Would Jack actually go that far? Kill him right here in Leon's shop? Jack was a bully. Bullies liked to throw their weight around when they thought they could get away with it. Like now. Jack could definitely get away with it now.

But Jack wouldn't kill him. What the hell would he do with the body, right? Even someone as dim-witted as Jack had to have considered that.

Oh, but Jack could definitely hurt him. Break a few fingers. That was definitely in the realm of possibility. Not to mention what leaning on Elias's windpipe was doing to his singing voice.

Elias could get away without a perfect singing voice. Half the songs he played were instrumentals, and he could work up instrumental arrangements for the rest. Tips would go down, he was pretty sure of that, but at least he'd still be working.

He wouldn't be able to work at all if Jack broke his fingers. Elias needed all of them in working order. If he had to take off time to heal, the Port Authority would license Elias's spot to another street performer, and Elias would have to go back on the waiting list.

Jack had bent his head down so he could look Elias in the eye. Hatred burned bright and hot in Jack's piggy eyes. Something must have set him off that morning before Elias even set foot in the store.

Whether it was something a customer said—something that stuck in the man's craw—or something else was going on in his life, Elias had definitely picked the wrong day to make a smartass remark.

"What, no asshole comeback?" Jack smiled but it was the smile of someone who enjoyed pulling the wings off flies or setting ants on fire with a magnifying glass. "Cat got your tongue?"

A shiver ran down Elias's spine, but he made himself look the man in the eye.

"You need to let go of me," he said.

His voice came out as little more than a tortured rasp. Oh yeah, singing was going to be fun. Elias tried to clear his throat, hoping that Jack would let up a little.

Surprise of surprises, he did. Just a little, but enough that the red around the edges of Elias's vision started to recede.

"Let me go," Elias said, "and I'll leave, okay? That's what you want, isn't it?"

No, that wasn't all Jack wanted.

Jack wanted to hurt him. The muscles beneath Jack's tattooed shoulders bunched. The man was getting ready to do whatever he'd decided to do. Even if he didn't break one of Elias's fingers, no way was Elias getting out of this in one piece.

Maybe he could reach a hand down between Jack's legs, try to grab his junk and give it a good hard twist. Anything to make the man back off just a little.

All Elias needed to do was give himself a chance to get the hell out of the store. Jack wouldn't chase him into the street, probably wouldn't even chase him through the store, not with all the security cameras.

Of course, if Elias *couldn't* reach Jack's balls and the man figured out what Elias was up to, that would almost guarantee Elias would be in a world of hurt.

A loud cry came from inside the shop.

It wasn't a human cry. Not by half. It was part yowl, part fury, and part warning. No human baby would ever have made a sound like that.

The first cry was joined by a second. More of the same, but louder.

The sounds startled Jack just as much as they did Elias. The big man flinched, and the pressure on Elias's neck let up as Jack turned his head toward the front of the store.

Elias heaved in a shuddery breath which hurt his throat, but at least now he had enough space he could turn his head too.

He blinked, pretty sure he couldn't be seeing what he was seeing.

Two cats were in the store, right on the other side of the bead curtain.

Elias was pretty sure one was the long-haired ginger kitty he'd seen on Tuesday morning sitting right outside Leon's shop. The other looked like the white-haired cat with the dark blotches on its fur that he'd seen just an hour or so ago.

The cats that had seemed like they were listening to his music.

21

Elias didn't have a lot of experience with cats outside of the meanspirited tomcat his mom had when he was a kid.

Even when he'd been married, Lettie had never come home with a stray kitten or stray dog. In fact, the entire time they'd been married, she'd never shown any interest in pets. That probably should have been a clue, but he'd been too head-over-heels in love at the time to notice.

Right about now he wished he could read a cat's body language, because the two cats in Leon's store looked like they were rip-your-throat-out furious.

They were both crouched down, their ears flat against their skulls, eyes wide, the pupils so dark they were almost black. Their tails were whipping back and forth, and as Elias watched, the ginger kitty raised one front paw, wickedly sharp claws extended. Their cries grew in volume and then descended into deep-throated growls that sounded almost like human speech.

"What the hell?" Jack said. "Fucking cats. Get the hell out of my store!"

His yell had no effect whatsoever on the cats.

Elias wasn't sure why the cats had shown up, but right about then he'd take any kind of distraction he could get. The pressure on his neck from Jack's forearm was almost gone. Not enough for Elias to get out from under Jack's looming bulk pressing him against the wall, but almost.

"Let me go," Elias said again. "If you don't want them to hurt you."

Or me.

He didn't say that part. He certainly wasn't sure that the cats wouldn't attack him too because something had sure as hell pissed them off.

Jack turned his beady eyes back on Elias. "Why? You the cat whisperer or something?"

Under other circumstances, the question might have been hilarious. It wasn't now.

"No, man," he said. "I just play music. That's it."

Except... that wasn't entirely right.

Yes, he played music. He played the kind of music he wanted to hear, and if other people enjoyed it, so much the better. But he also played music he thought *other* people would want to hear and maybe even hear again. He did have CDs for sale, right?

What if the music he played wasn't just for *people?*

That thought would have been ludicrous just last week. Not so much now.

Still, a parking lot full of seagulls jamming along to a guitar solo was something you'd only see in a cartoon—or maybe in a horror movie. Whales talked to each other in deep water and people called that whalesong. Birds twittered and called to each other. Thunder added crashing percussion to the snare drum ratta-tat-tat of a heavy rainstorm. Nature was full of music if you knew how to listen.

His music wasn't that kind of natural music. It was something he intentionally created. The best of it conveyed an emotion or called up a memory, but was it really *communication?* A way of talking to another species?

And how the hell had someone—the cats, he told his disbelieving mind—thanked him for it without speaking? He didn't believe in mental telepathy. None of that woo woo stuff. Yet he'd heard words in his head just as clear as if someone had spoken them aloud.

"I just play music," Jack said, singsonging the words. "You're a piece of shit, you know that? Just like these cats are pieces of shit. If they don't get the hell out of my store, I'm going to break their scrawny necks."

The little white cat with the tabby tail screeched at him, almost like it had understood Jack's threat and was ready to rip his throat out. Elias had no doubt that it could. Jack might be able to kill it—it was just a small cat, after all—but that cat would do a lot of damage before it died.

"Look at those claws," Elias said. "Look at them. Cats are little tigers with razors on their feet and needles for teeth."

"So?" Jack said, all the belligerence of a lifelong bully in his tone. "They's just fucking cats."

Now the ginger-furred cat stood up, tail still whipping furiously from side to side. It seemed more substantial somehow under all that fluffy fur than just a moment before.

"Think, man," Elias said, forcing himself to look into Jack's piggy eyes "They can cut the hell out of your tattoos. They're out on the street all day. Who knows what kind of shit those claws will leave behind. You want a bunch of scars messing up your artwork?"

Jack was thinking about that. Elias could see the man working through it in that thick skull of his.

Tattoos weren't cheap. Elias had thought more than once about getting a tattoo but he couldn't justify the expense. Not even during the summer months when the tourists—and his tips—were the most plentiful. Jack couldn't be making all that much money working for Leon. Unless he had another gig on the side, no way would he be able to afford coverup ink if the cats messed up his artwork.

The hanging beads separating the store from the hallway rattled.

The cats weren't crouched anymore. And they weren't the size of housecats.

The beads didn't touch the floor. The bottom beads hung a good two feet over the scuffed linoleum. The only way a normal-sized cat could make those beads rattle was if they were holding their tails upright. These cats were still whipping their tails back and forth. All these cats had done was come halfway into the hallway. The strands of beads had separated to hang on either side of the cats' backs.

The cats had grown.

That simply wasn't possible, yet it was true. They'd *grown*.

Jack wasn't looking at the cats though. He was back to glaring at Elias. He leaned toward Elias, really putting his weight behind the forearm across Elias's neck.

"You're a fucking freeloader," Jack said. "Your kind are what's wrong with this—"

Elias couldn't breathe. He couldn't even hear the rest of Jack's rant. Blood was pounding in his head, his vision was going red, and his ears were ringing. He'd been wrong. Jack wasn't just a bully. He was a psychopath. It was entirely possible that Jack would just keep leaning on Elias's neck until he'd effectively strangled him.

Elias started to struggle. Somehow he got his arms between himself and Jack, but he didn't have any real leverage. The man really was two-hundred-fifty pounds of muscle. Jack pushed as hard as he could, but he couldn't make Jack back off.

"What the fuck?" Jack said.

He abruptly let go of Elias and took two steps toward the back door.

Elias sucked in a deep breath. The resulting coughing fit just about doubled him over.

Then he almost forgot to breathe as he got a good look at the cats.

They were only a few feet away from him, and it was no trick of the light. Both cats had at least doubled in size.

The two of them stood shoulder to shoulder in the narrow hallway, effectively blocking the way back into the store. Their heads were now bigger than Jack's hands, and the teeth in their open, hissing mouths looked like the teeth on a Doberman that had scared the crap out of Elias when he'd been little. The dog had belonged to one of the neighbors. Elias had to walk past their yard every day to and from school, and that dog seemed to take his mere existence as a personal affront.

Elias used to have nightmares that one day the fence holding that dog in would simply vanish and the dog would eat him alive. Well, there was nothing between him now and two huge—and two hugely furious—cats who were clearly big enough to eat him alive if they felt like it.

"What the *fuck?*" Jack said again.

He took another few steps toward the back door.

Elias straightened up slowly, trying not to spook the cats. He was pretty sure—at least he was hoping—that if they'd wanted to attack him, they would have done so already. But he was also pretty sure that no cat could grow to twice its size in the blink of an eye, not in the real world, but here they were, so what did he know?

The ginger cat paced toward Jack, passing close enough to Elias that he could have reached out and touched its fur. Not that he was about to do any such thing. The cat was growling low in its throat, the sound echoing off the bare walls in the hallway. And it was still *growing,* as impossible as it was to believe. Its shoulders reached halfway up his thigh.

This was a cat that could slash through his jeans and open an artery in his leg without half trying.

How in the hell was this even possible?

Jack was clearly seeing the same thing. His beady eyes looked about ready to bug out of his head. His face was the color of cottage cheese, and sweat had beaded up on his forehead. Spittle had formed in the corners of his mouth.

"Fuck *you!*" he screamed at the ginger-furred nightmare of a cat.

Then he turned and bolted out the back door.

Elias half expected the cat to charge through the door after Jack. But it just stood in the hallway, watching as the door snicked shut.

Reality set in.

He was alone with two cats that were bigger than any cats he'd ever seen. At least any housecats. Lions and tigers were no doubt bigger, but he'd never been stuck in a narrow hallway with two of them. The ginger-furred cat was between him and the back door, and the white cat was still guarding the other end of the hallway.

He might be able to lock himself in the bathroom, but he wasn't all that sure the door would hold if either of these cats decided to throw their weight against it.

Then the ginger cat turned its head and looked at him.

Elias's breath caught in his poor, abused throat.

The cat's eyes were large and luminous and golden-green, which was strange enough, but there was an intelligence in those eyes he'd never seen in any animal. This cat was self-aware. Okay, sure, he'd never had any pets of his own, never had spent any time looking into a cat's eyes, but this cat was looking at him the way a person would look at him.

The way a specific person had looked at him: the golden-haired woman who'd thanked him for playing "Moonlight Sonata" before she'd disappeared into a crowd that really wasn't all that big.

Elias felt like he could get lost in those eyes.

What the hell was going on here?

"What *are* you?" he asked. Talking hurt, and his voice came out as a cracked and raspy whisper.

He didn't really expect a response. That would be crazy, right? A part of him wondered if he was going crazy, and the only thing that convinced him he wasn't was Jack. The man had been terrified.

The cat tilted its head upward. The gesture reminded Elias of the way some people looked down their noses at street performers, like they were only one step above the homeless who camped out in doorways at night.

Then he heard a word in his head as clearly as if it had been spoken, but not by anything remotely human. The word had weight behind it. Gravitas. Like it was an ancient truth.

Guardian.

The cat turned and loped out of the hallway toward the front of the store. A moment later the white-haired cat with the tabby tail followed. It took Elias a moment to realize that the white cat had shrunk back to housecat size.

His knees gave out on him, and he slumped onto the scuffed linoleum floor.

Holy crap. The cats hadn't hurt him. Hadn't touched him. They'd *saved* him. He'd been in trouble, serious trouble, and they'd saved him.

Guarded him.

He dropped his head in his hands and wondered exactly when the world had stopped making sense.

22

Elias had a hell of a time getting back into his music. It didn't help that his neck ached and his voice sounded like someone had poured liquid sandpaper down his throat. At least his fingers were intact, there was that.

He finally gave up trying to sing. It just flat out hurt too much. Pain like that was a sign that Jack really had done some damage to Elias's throat. If he wanted to have a voice at all the next day, he needed to give his voice a break.

So he switched up the rest of his sets to instrumentals. He could play some pretty impressive instrumentals on keyboard, and he was decent enough on guitar to get by. He'd never be a guitar virtuoso—some of the people he'd watched online could put him to shame easy—but he still managed to generate a decent amount of tips in his open guitar case.

The problem with playing just instrumentals that he'd played a thousand times before was that it gave him too much time to think.

And the only thing he could think about were the damn cats.

It had taken him a few minutes after the cats left the store for Elias to get to his feet. Even then he'd kept one hand on the wall in the hallway while he took a couple of experimental steps. He was still shaky inside by the time he made his way across the street and thanked Leon for watching his stuff.

If Leon had wondered why Elias took a longer than normal pee break, he hadn't said anything. Elias certainly hadn't volunteered anything about what had just happened. Not about Jack threatening him, and certainly not about being rescued by two cats the size of Rottweilers. Elias had a pretty good working relationship with Leon and he wasn't about to give the man any reason to doubt either his sanity or start wondering whether he was doing drugs.

But *damn*. Unless someone had slipped something in his coffee—and how the hell would that have happened? He kept his thermos close by and didn't leave his coffee cup out where anyone could get at it—something impossible had happened right in front of his face. He'd seen it.

Plus there was Jack.

The last person on earth Elias could imagine sharing a hallucination with was Jack. But Jack sure as hell must have seen the same thing Elias had. Jack had bolted out the back door like the devil himself was on his tail.

Jack came back though.

At first he was just lurking around the corner of the building, smoking a cigarette and trying to look nonchalant. Except he kept turning around or looking over his shoulder.

Looking for the cats, no doubt. Elias had been doing the same thing, watching the front of Leon's store just in case the cats were still there. That's how he'd caught sight of Jack.

After he'd finished the cigarette and crushed it beneath his boot, he went back in the shop through the front entrance. By this time Leon had been back for a while. A small, mean part of Elias hoped that Leon would chew Jack out for leaving the store unattended since Jack was the only employee who'd shown up for work. None of the crap that had happened would have happened if Jack had just left Elias alone.

Of course, Jack would probably make up some story about chasing down a couple of shoplifters. Elias doubted Leon would buy it, especially if he smelled cigarette smoke on Jack's breath. Leon didn't allow smoking in the store, but he always gave his employees a couple of smoke breaks whenever they needed it.

Most days Elias hated having to relinquish his spot on the Wharf when his time was up, but he didn't have a choice. The Port Authority limited the number of official spots along the Wharf and The Embarcadero where street performers could do their thing. Elias had obtained an official license to play a maximum of four hours a day on his corner. He especially hated to pack up his equipment just about the time on the weekends when tips were getting good. At least he had the lunchtime crowd, which was better than the *tired and getting ready to face an inevitable traffic jam on the drive home* late afternoon crowd.

Today though, he was ready to pack it in for the day. He'd gotten over the shaky feeling he'd had for a good hour after he'd left the store. In its place was the kind of nervous energy he hadn't felt in years. Not since his last audition for a steady gig, and that seemed like another lifetime ago.

He'd been watching to see if he could catch a glimpse of the cats ever since he'd left the store. But he hadn't seen any cats. Not just the two cats who'd apparently saved him, but *any* cats at all. There were the normal amount of seagulls hanging around the Wharf looking for handouts. The fog had finally burned off and the sea lions were barking up a storm. He'd seen the occasional service dog, and a few women who'd walked by were carrying those nervous little dogs that constantly shivered no matter the temperature.

But that was it.

No cats.

And he *needed* to find them, if only to reassure himself that they were just cats. Just ordinary cats.

That happened to like his music, because that was normal for cats. Right.

And cats that freaking *talked* to him in his mind? Yeah, don't forget that part. The part that was definitely *not* normal. For cats or for people.

Today the performer who took over Elias's spot at two was a young acoustic guitar player who arrived with just his guitar in a soft case strapped to his back. No amp, no microphone. Elias almost envied the guy as he packed up all his equipment.

"You should enjoy the day, my man," the new guitar player told him as Elias loaded the last of his stuff into the cart he used to transport his stuff to and from where his car was parked. "It's warmed up nicely. You know. For the Bay, I mean."

Elias had been thinking about burning off some of the nervous energy still thrumming through him like a low-voltage live wire by walking down to Pier 39. He had a ridiculously expensive parking permit for the lot, which meant he didn't have to worry about leaving by a certain time or getting a ticket.

"I been down by the Square, picking up a little side money," the new guy said. "People being generous today."

He meant Ghirardelli Square, not all that far from the Wharf. Lots of tourists in that area, especially on the weekends. In a tourist-oriented area like the Square and the Wharf, the weekends included Fridays.

The new guy smiled a grin that showed a couple of gold-rimmed teeth. Elias smiled back, hoping that the smile came off better than it felt. People had been generous with him too. Besides tips, he'd managed to sell one of his old CDs. Not bad for a day when he couldn't really sing.

"Generous is good," Elias said, feeling lame even as the words left his mouth.

What he really wanted to ask the guy was if he'd seen any cats around Ghirardelli Square, and if he had, were they regular size or super-sized. But of course he couldn't. So he just smiled and nodded and wheeled the cart to his car.

After he'd stowed his stuff in the trunk—thank Detroit for mid-size cars that still came with big trunks—he started strolling along The Embarcadero toward Pier 39.

The Pier was a two-level tourist mecca. From a mini-version of San Francisco's sourdough bread store to a candy store where customers filled baskets from old-fashioned barrels full of every kind of sweet stuff imaginable—and some that probably should never have been imagined in the first place—the Pier was chock full of restaurants, ice cream parlors, clothing stores, souvenir shops, coffee shops, a gourmet spice shop, and even a carousel. Tourists could stand along one side of the Pier and gawk at sea lions on their floats or go to the other side and gaze at all the sailboats in the marina.

For those who wanted a glimpse of Alcatraz on a clear day, the far end of the Pier's lower level provided a perfect spot to stand and look out over the Bay. But even on an afternoon when the fog had burned off and the day was warming up, there was nothing at the end of the Pier to block the wind blowing in off the water. By the time Elias got there, only a very few hardy souls were standing at the railing.

He'd wanted to find a spot where he could be relatively alone to think. He figured the end of the Pier was about as close as he'd get to that. He hadn't seen any cats during his walk down The Embarcadero. He could have circled around the back side of the parking garage across the street from the Pier and walked down some of the side streets, but that would have made him feel stupid. The cats had clearly made themselves scarce. He had a feeling that if these cats didn't want to be found, he could walk for miles and never spot them.

Hell, they'd made themselves huge. For all he knew, they could make themselves crazy small too.

Shit.

Maybe *he* was crazy. Thinking cats could grow and shrink like that was certainly crazy thinking.

He leaned against the railing and gazed out at the Bay. There were a few sailboats on the water, really moving thanks to a stiff breeze on the water. The view of Alcatraz was spectacular. He could even see the Golden Gate bridge to the west.

Just another ordinary San Francisco day.

Except it wasn't, not for him.

Funny how a person could get up one morning, a morning like any other morning, and have everything he thought he knew about the world shot to shit by noon.

He shivered, and it wasn't just from the cold. He'd zipped up his leather jacket when he got close to the end of the Pier. It did a decent job of keeping most of him warm, but he was beginning to regret not grabbing his gloves from the car. His hands were getting cold, and his fingers were starting to go numb.

At least Jack hadn't broken them. At least there was that.

A few feet away from him, a woman had propped a camera with a long lens on top of the railing. The camera was aimed toward the Golden Gate, and she was bent over at the waist, peering through the viewfinder.

She looked to be in her mid-thirties, trim, her dark hair tied back in a no-nonsense ponytail that jutted out the back of a San Francisco Giants baseball cap. She had on a lightweight jacket, but it looked new enough that it was probably made of some modern fabric meant to be wind resistant and waterproof. Still, her slender fingers where she gripped the camera were chapped and reddened, and the tip of her nose along with her cheeks had a rosy glow that didn't come from the sun.

How long had she been standing at the end of the Pier, trying to get a good shot? The dedication of some people amazed him.

Then he had to laugh at himself. How long had he futzed with "Moonlight Sonata" until he got the sound that he wanted just right? And all because he'd come up with the idea from somewhere to play that song.

No, not from somewhere. From a freaking *cat*. Or a woman he'd seen just once. He wasn't sure which idea was crazier.

He'd walked down to the Pier to try to get the whole mess at Leon's out of his mind. Sure, he'd been on the lookout for the cats, but mostly he was just people watching and letting himself exist as part of the crowd. He'd even bought himself an ice cream cone. He'd watched the people around the carousel for a while and stood off to the side while a group of kids had been entertained by a juggler.

But now that he was out here at the end of the Pier, alone with his thoughts, the ice cream gone, and trying not to stare at a woman taking pictures of the Golden Gate, his mind kept going back to the cats.

The size of those freaking cats.

Had they really been that huge? *Really?* Or had it been some type of optical illusion brought on by stress and the almost certain loss of his fingers if not his life.

The woman straightened up and slipped a cap over the front of the lens. The camera was attached to a long strap slung around her neck. Once the cap was in place, she let the camera hang free from the strap.

Good precaution, that strap. Elias would be willing bet that camera setup had cost her a pretty penny. If it had slipped off the edge of the railing and into the dark water of the Bay, it would be lost forever. He'd watched a bunch of people hold their cell phones out over the water, trying to get a good angle for a selfie. If he'd tried something like that, especially with his fingers numb with the cold, he would have dropped the damn thing.

Thinking about his cell phone brought him up short.

He'd had his damn cell with him at Leon's. He carried the thing everywhere, like a good modern man should. After Jack had let him go, he could have taken a picture of the cats with his cell. Of course, he'd been too freaked to even think about taking a picture.

Still, photographic evidence would have been nice. Most of the teenagers and tweenagers he saw on the Wharf practically lived on their phones. He'd bet *they* would have taken pictures, and those pictures would be online somewhere by now.

He realized he'd been staring at the woman, even though he wasn't really focused on her, for too long. He must have made her uncomfortable because she shot him a sudden look. He was about to apologize when she stopped him.

"I heard you play earlier," she said. "I snapped a couple of pictures. Hope you don't mind."

Pictures of him. He wondered if it was before or after the Jack incident. The cats incident.

Before or after he'd started to question his own sanity. No. Why would he mind that?

"Not at all," he said instead. "Hope you enjoyed the music."

His voice still had a rasp to it, but the ice cream had gone a long way toward soothing his abused throat.

"I did," she said. "It was nice to hear instrumentals for a change."

Well, that answered one question. Definitely after the Jack incident.

"I shoot a lot of bands. Publicity shots. Concert photos. That kind of thing." She fished around in the pocket of her jacket and came up with a business card. "If you'd like to see the pictures I took, just give me a call."

He took the card. Her name was Stephanie Solvang, and the number listed had a local area code. Not that that meant anything these days. Area codes stayed with the phones no matter where people moved to.

He must have had an odd look on his face, because she added, "No charge. I only charge when I'm on a job. Today's my day off."

He slipped her card in the inside pocket of his jacket. "And you're spending it taking pictures?"

She shrugged. "It's what I enjoy doing, like I imagine you play when you're not working, and not just for practice. You love what you do, I can tell. It comes through in the music. A lot of the bands I shoot, it's just a job to them. They'd rather get drunk after the show than play that second encore."

He'd had a few gigs like that, what he'd called his day-job gigs, where he'd just been playing music because that's what he'd been hired to do. But even then, he hadn't just gotten through the music because it stood in the way of a nice, mind-numbing drunk. If he'd actually finished college, graduated with that business minor and ended up in some job like his roommate's? Yeah, then he could see himself numbing the pain of a job like that by getting drunk on a semi-regular basis.

She shivered, a full-body shiver, and rubbed her hands together to warm them up.

"Damn, I should know better than to dress like this when I'm coming out on the Pier." She eyed his leather jacket. "I think I have jacket envy. This one's supposed to keep out the wind, which it does just fine, but the cold and the damp?" She shivered again. "Not so much."

"I know what you mean," he said. "I was an idiot and left my gloves in the car."

She looked at him for a moment, cocking her head to one side.

Elias knew the look. She was getting ready to leave, and she was waiting to see if he'd offer to walk with her back up the Pier. On any other day he might have taken her up on the idea, but he wouldn't be good company today.

When he didn't move away from the railing, she held out her hand. Elias took it, shaking once and letting go.

"Remember," she said as she walked away. "Call me if you want to see those photos." She grinned. "I think they're pretty good."

The wind almost stole her words away, but Elias heard enough. And her smile? Lit up her entire face. Her pretty face, with her rosy, wind-chapped nose and cheeks.

Would he call her? Maybe. And not just to see the photographs, because the offer had clearly been for something more than just looking at pictures.

It had been a long time since Elias had spent time with a woman. Even if it went nowhere, which most of his relationships had after the Lettie years, he could probably use a couple of new promo shots of himself at work. He had a website—what performer didn't?—but he hadn't updated it in a while. Putting up new photos—photos of him doing what he loved best—might be a good idea.

He stayed at the railing for a few more minutes before the wind finally drove him away. He strolled to the central area of the Pier where the lower level was open to the sky above. It was warmer there, the sun still high enough in the sky to light up the area around the carousel.

Next time, don't be an idiot, he told himself. Bring the damn gloves, even if they just stay in your pocket.

He was halfway around the carousel when it occurred to him that he'd been an idiot for a different reason.

Leon's shop had security cameras.

He'd been so focused on the cats and wondering if he was going crazy, and then getting pissed at himself for not taking a picture with his cell phone, that he'd forgotten all about the security cameras. The white-haired cat had shrunk back to housecat size when it loped out of the hallway, but the ginger cat had still been huge. At least one of the security cameras should have caught a cat that size.

Right?

Of course, if the cameras just caught two regular-size cats by the time they reached the front of the store—or worse yet, if the cats didn't show up on the cameras at all—then what?

"Well, then," Elias muttered to himself. "I guess I'll have to jump off that pier when I come to it."

23

———

THE FIRST FEW YEARS OF ELIAS'S MARRIAGE HAD BEEN HEAVEN.

Sure, they're been broke as fuck. Two college students trying to make a life together while still paying for school and trying to keep a roof over their heads, of course they were broke. But they'd been happy. New love and lots of great sex made up for a lot.

Elias played gigs at whatever bar or coffee house or frat party would pay him, if not in cash, at least in free food that he could take home and share with his new bride. When he wasn't gigging or going to class, he bagged groceries and corralled shopping carts. Lettie had her part-time job building sandwiches in a fast-food place. Her job came with one free sandwich a day. They pretty much lived on those free sandwiches, gig-pizzas and wings, and that old college student standby: instant ramen.

They lived in a house close to campus that they shared with three other students. Elias and Lettie had the largest bedroom, another couple took the second largest, and a grad student took the third. The house only had two bathrooms, which made mornings fun when the last one in the shower discovered the hot water had been all used up. But the rent was doable and the place had a big kitchen.

That big kitchen was where Lettie discovered how much she liked to cook.

She'd always planned on becoming a preschool teacher. She said little kids liked her and she'd had a lot of experience babysitting during her early teens when her parents volunteered her to all their friends with little kids. But once she started cooking for herself and Elias, stretching their miniscule food budget as far as it could go, she discovered she really liked it. Way more than working with little kids.

They had a sit down one night over bowls of ramen that Lettie had jazzed up with a few spices and some leftover veggies from the sandwich shop.

"I want to change majors," she said. "There's no reason to keep pouring money into a major I'm not going to use."

Elias had been thinking much the same thing about his own college courses.

By that time his dad was gone, the victim of a drunk driver, and his mom was still recovering from her own injuries not to mention adjusting to life as a widow. Elias understood that he was entirely on his own in the world. In fact, if he could have afforded it—and if she'd let him—he would be sending money to his mom to help her live.

Which he could afford to do—maybe—if he dropped out of school. He liked the performance aspects of his music classes, and he even enjoyed some of the music theory classes he had to take for his minor, but the rest of it? All the bullshit stuff required for that business minor he never planned to use? Waste of money that he didn't have.

Lettie said she'd been researching culinary schools and she thought she might just be able to afford some of the smaller ones.

Only they'd have to move.

"You could transfer to a different college," she said.

Or, he'd told her, he could just quit and get a more permanent job somewhere.

Which was why they'd decided to move to Las Vegas.

Elias hadn't felt right about moving away from his mom, but she assured him that he had his own life to think about.

"Besides," she'd said. "I'm not sure I want to stay in this house. It's too big for just me, and there are too many memories here." She'd given him a hug. "I might need a fresh start too. Or a fresh restart."

Her eyes had been a little watery, but she hadn't cried.

It had been that way ever since his dad's funeral, almost like his mom wouldn't let herself cry. Maybe she'd been afraid that if she started, she wouldn't stop. His parents had been married for nearly thirty years. That was a long time to be with someone and then to be suddenly alone. They used to joke about what they'd do for their fiftieth wedding anniversary. There wouldn't be a fiftieth now.

So Elias had dropped out of college and Lettie enrolled in a culinary school in Las Vegas. They packed up their meager belongings, drove to Vegas, and moved in with one of the bridesmaids from the bachelorette party where Elias had met Lettie. The bridesmaid had transferred to UNLV and said they could stay with her while they looked for their own place, but she'd made it clear it wasn't going to be a permanent situation.

While Lettie settled in with her culinary school classes, Elias spent a couple of months working at a grocery store for minimum wage while he tried to find some kind of work as a musician. Eventually, thanks to an older guy who was a regular at the store where Elias worked, he finally got an audition to be a backup piano player for one of the casino orchestras.

He'd been nervous as all get out, worse than on performance days when his only audience was his college professor and his performance score made up half of his grade. But he'd nailed the audition and started working a couple of nights a week when the regular piano player, a woman who'd been with the orchestra for years, had her nights off.

He got his big break when she quit to have a baby. His part-time backup work turned into a full-time gig. Along with a fulltime paycheck.

For the first time in their marriage, they could afford to eat more than ramen. Lettie was ridiculously busy but ridiculously happy. When she graduated, her degree got her a job at an upscale casino restaurant at slightly higher than minimum wage. They could actually start to put money away.

Elias couldn't point to a specific moment in time when they started to drift apart. They were both doing what they wanted to do, Lettie cooking creative food and Elias playing music, which should have made them happy. Sometimes he thought it was because they'd achieved their big goals too soon in life and hadn't realized they should move the goalposts so they'd have bigger and better goals to work toward.

Or it could have been that they never seemed to have time to spend with each other.

Elias's job had him working nights until two or three in the morning. The restaurant where Lettie worked opened at eleven in the morning and closed at nine at night. Lettie worked ten-hour days four days a week, although most weeks she worked five days. The pace over those ten hours was brutal, especially during the dinner hours when the restaurant served its signature dishes, which meant she was exhausted by the time she got home.

Most days Elias was still sleeping when she left for work, and she was fast asleep by the time he got home from his job. Their days off didn't coincide. They basically became strangers who lived in the same house and occasionally spent a little time together whenever they could.

They didn't have any plans to start a family. Lettie was hoping for a promotion at work. Taking time off to be a mom would mean starting over somewhere else. Elias understood that. Hadn't he stepped into someone else's job when they left to have a baby?

Besides, for two kids in their mid-twenties, life was pretty darn good. They had a decent enough apartment that didn't cost an arm and a leg, and their savings account was growing. Sure, they rarely got to spend any time together, but that would even out one day.

He hoped.

The thing was, he missed his wife. He loved her with all his heart, but there was something about Vegas. Something wild and uninhibited. The town never seemed to sleep. Oh sure, out in the suburbs it was like any other town, but their apartment wasn't in the suburbs. They both worked in casinos, and their apartment was within walking distance of their jobs. Casino life was far different than a normal nine-to-five existence.

On his nights off, Elias went exploring. Sometimes he took in lounge acts in other casinos, or he'd walk around Fremont Street, people watching or listening to the bands that gave free concerts.

If he'd been a different personality type, he might have spent some of his surplus cash getting wasted or gambling it away, but those distractions held no interest for him. Music, that was the thing that got him high.

Vegas was the first place he spent any time hanging around musicians who busked on the street. Some of them, he discovered, played regular gigs in casino showrooms like he did, and busked as a way to make extra money. It let them play the music they wanted to play— the music of their hearts, as one musician told him—instead of the music they had to play night after night after night in their regular gigs.

That struck a chord with him.

Back when he'd been in school, bagging groceries and trying to scare up the occasional gig, his goal had simply been to make a living with music. He'd reached that goal when he got a steady job playing piano in the casino showroom. But was that really the goal? Or was it playing music he *wanted* to play. Making his own decisions about what songs he played and actually singing along?

He'd had a vague feeling for a while that something in his life was missing, and it wasn't just spending time with his wife. Was playing the music he wanted to play that missing part?

Eventually he told Lettie he was thinking about doing a little busking on the side.

Her reaction hit him square in the gut, and the worst part was that he'd never even seen it coming.

She didn't want him playing on the street "like some homeless person," she said.

"The people I work with, they know we're married," she said. "What will they think if they see you out on the street begging for money?"

He didn't know what to say. She'd never seemed to care before what people thought.

Or had she, and he'd just never noticed?

Was that why she wouldn't sing in public? Because she was afraid of what people would think?

That idea had never occurred to him. The night they'd met, she'd sung along with him. But the only other people around to hear her had been her drunken friends. Every other time they'd sung together in the early days of their marriage, it had been in the privacy of their apartment, and never when any of their roommates were around.

The only thing he could think to say was that busking wasn't begging for money. Even as he said it, he hated how defensive it sounded.

Even more, he hated that she'd put him in a position where he felt like he had to defend himself.

"It's playing for an audience," he said.

"You play for an audience now."

An audience who never saw him. He was just part of the background. The ambiance. The soundtrack for the show they'd come to see. It didn't matter if he was playing the piano or another musician took over his spot for the night. There was no creativity in something like that. It was playing music on autopilot.

If he played out on the street, even if it was just him singing along while he played guitar, he could play whatever-the-hell he wanted. If people stopped to listen? Great! If they dropped some money in his guitar case? Even better.

She refused to understand, no matter how he tried to explain it.

She was happy working behind the scenes. Happy cooking

upscale meals for people who cared as much about how the food looked on their plates as the way it tasted. Maybe that should have given him a clue. In Lettie's world, appearance mattered as much as substance.

As far as Elias was concerned, substance was more important than appearance. A great musician was still a great musician, whether they played in Carnegie Hall or on a street corner in Las Vegas.

Was that really the moment their marriage started to fall apart? Their worldviews were irrevocably different. He couldn't imagine a time in his life when appearance would matter more than substance, he just couldn't. Had she always cared more about how things looked? Had that always mattered more to her than anything else?

His heart broke a little bit that day. He'd dropped the argument, but he couldn't make himself forget what he'd learned about his wife. He tried to tell himself that no one was perfect. That he'd just been too love-blind to see that side of her. It didn't help.

Busking on the street wasn't worth risking his marriage over, but he had to do something to bring back the joy in playing music. Because if working a steady job playing the same thing over and over again, night after night, killed that musical spark inside him, what would be left? He didn't want to burn out before he hit his thirties.

There was a park within walking distance from their apartment. It wasn't like the parks around his old college campus, all expansive green lawns and park benches. This park was close to the Strip and contained not a single patch of green lawn. Instead the park was paved with decorative rocks and brickwork. Raised planters housed shade trees and hardy plants that could take the desert heat. Wide concrete benches circled the raised planters.

He'd walked through the park more than a few times when he'd gone out exploring. Nobody busked in that park—the city probably didn't allow it—but on at least one occasion there'd been a guitar player sitting on one of the benches just playing a few tunes, guitar case closed and stowed on the bench beside him. Now and then Elias also saw a few artists sketching or working on pastel drawings in the shade of the trees.

On a whim, he took his guitar with him one late afternoon when he went out walking. A nearby hotel tower was blocking the sun, and a late afternoon breeze had kicked up, cooling down the park—and most importantly the concrete benches—and he'd found a somewhat comfortable spot to sit.

He took out his guitar, closed the case and put it on the bench next to him, and started to play.

Most of the other people in the park ignored him. Some of them had earbuds in, either talking on the phone or listening to something only they could hear. But a few of them seemed to pay attention to him. One older man who'd been sitting at one of the small wrought-iron tables scattered throughout the park, reading a well-used paperback book, actually put the book aside to watch Elias play.

Elias ended up playing for over an hour. When he was done, he packed up his guitar and stood up, stretching his back and trying to get some feeling back in his butt, which had gone numb thanks to hard concrete seat. The older man came up to him, thanked him for the impromptu concert, and told him he was "pretty damn good."

That compliment was better than any tip Elias had ever received back in the days when he'd been a student gigging for whatever he could earn in tips or free food. He felt a spark inside that he'd been afraid he was losing. The elation of making music just for the pure joy of it.

He started taking his guitar to the park once a week. Sometimes he only played for a half hour. Other times he played until the sun went down and the lights in the park came on. He never sang. He felt that would be too intrusive, even with the traffic noise from the Strip only a block or so away. He just played the songs he wanted to on his guitar and played them the way he wanted to.

He started to think that playing on the street this way—not busking, just playing—was a compromise he could live with. He didn't think Lettie would be embarrassed—he wasn't asking for money, after all—but then again, he never told her about his weekly trips to the park with his guitar.

A small part of him enjoyed keeping this part of his life from her. It was a petty kind of payback for what he still thought was a pretty damn unreasonable objection. What she didn't know wouldn't hurt her.

He just never thought that it would end up hurting him.

24

Elias spent most of the rest of that Friday afternoon killing time by wandering around the touristy areas near the waterfront.

He went up to Ghirardelli Square, stopping often along the way to listen to street musicians and watch a few of the visual artists. He bought an overpriced hotdog and a bottle of water from a hole-in-the-wall food joint and sat at an outside table, taking his time to finish a meal that had nothing to do with seafood while he listened to music on the satellite radio channel playing on the restaurant's sound system. He even listened for a while to the music playing on a boombox a caricature artist had brought with him to keep himself company while he waited for his next commission.

Elias had done this type of thing most of his life, even when he'd been living in Vegas. He liked all sorts and styles of music. While he preferred some of the music his parents used to listen to when he was a kid—certain Beatles songs still brought back memories of his mom's homemade chocolate chip cookies—he had no problem incorporating modern hits into his repertoire.

Research, Jerry would have called it. Jerry did market research on his days off. Elias listened to music. He supposed it was the same type of thing, only Elias would have bet his research was more fun than Jerry's.

Most days he'd only take an hour or two for this kind of thing, then he'd go back to the apartment, set up his keyboard, plug in his headphones, and fiddle around with some of the new stuff he'd heard. He'd try different arrangements, figure out which key was the best for his vocal range, and basically play the new stuff over and over again until he got it down to the point where he figured he could perform the song in public.

Practice, his old piano teacher would have called it. Feeding the inner artist was how Elias thought of it. Even if people like Jack thought all Elias did was beg for spare change, he was still an artist.

Today was different. He wouldn't be heading home anytime soon to futz around with a new song.

He wanted to take a look at the security footage in the T-shirt shop to see if any of the cameras caught a glimpse of the cats. He'd have to convince Leon to let him see the footage, and he'd have a better shot at that if he went back right before Leon closed the store for the night. On Fridays, Leon kept the shop open until nine, which mean Elias had a lot of time to kill.

He spent the afternoon and evening walking through neighborhoods he hadn't been in for so long he couldn't remember.

From Ghirardelli Square, he walked west on Bay Street nearly to Fort Mason, but there wasn't much in the way of street music that far from the Wharf, and Bay Street took him too far away from the waterfront. So he made his way back to the Square, then walked down to Beach Street, past the Maritime Museum, past the art galleries. Past cable cars loaded with tourists, past upscale restaurants and pricey hotels, and past homeless who'd started to gather their things and claim their spots for the night.

As he walked, he kept one eye out for cats. Any cats.

There had to be cats, even in this part of the city. People lived in apartments over the street-level stores and restaurants. Especially in the neighborhoods farther away from the Wharf and Pier 39, and especially in the apartments near the park surrounding Fort Mason.

But Elias didn't see so much as a single cat in an upstairs window, staring down at the outside world, much less any cats on the street or lurking in alleys.

That was odd, he had to admit.

By the time he got back to the Wharf, the sun had slid behind the night's incoming fog bank and the streetlights were all on. Since this was Friday night, traffic was still heavy. Music with a heavy bass beat thrummed from more than a few cars, counterpoint to the music spilling out the front doors of the bars he passed.

His feet were telling him he hadn't done this much walking in months. Now that the sun was down, he was beginning to regret not only leaving his gloves in his car, but not grabbing his watch cap when he locked his instruments in the trunk. He was going to need a nice hot bath when he finally made it back to his apartment.

A nice bath and maybe a pot of instant ramen gussied up with a scrambled egg and some fresh green onions.

He'd passed some nice seafood restaurants on his walk back to the Wharf, ones that advertised fresh crab and upscale seafood dishes, which made him think of Lettie. The last he'd heard, she'd been working at an upscale seafood restaurant down in San Diego, in line for a head chef position. He'd thought about calling her to wish her well, but she wouldn't want to hear from him.

The chain restaurant that occupied the second floor of the building over Leon's T-shirt shop was still doing bang-up business by the looks of things, but Leon had already closed one of the two roll-down metal doors at the front of his shop. Jack was nowhere in sight. Thank goodness for small favors.

Leon looked up in surprise when Elias walked into the store.

"Hey, man, what you doing here?" Leon asked. "I was just about to lower the last boom."

"Timed it right then," Elias said. "You mind if I take a peek at your security footage?"

Leon frowned at him. He gave off an old hippy gone to seed vibe, what with his long hair, scraggly beard, and the tie-dyed shirts he wore almost like a uniform. But beneath that free love, we're all friends here exterior, Leon was a businessman who kept a close eye on his bottom line.

"You spot someone working the Wharf?" he asked.

Pickpockets or thieves, he meant. But that's not what Elias was looking for.

Cats. He was looking for cats. Really *big* cats.

And if he told Leon that? Yeah, the man would think he was crazy.

So he decided that since Leon had given him a plausible reason to look at the tapes, he might as well stick with that.

"Something like that," Elias said.

Leon stared at him for a minute, like he was trying to figure out what was up. Then he shrugged. "Okay," he said. "Just give me a sec."

Elias hung out by the checkout counter while Leon lowered the boom on the shop's remaining door. The chains on the side of the roll-down door clattered in their own kind of rhythm. Street music that said *I don't trust you not to rob me blind.*

Which, now that Elias thought about it, was the whole basis of his friendship with Leon. It wasn't like they hung out outside of each other's work. Hell, Elias didn't even know if Leon was married. If he was gay, straight, bi, or otherwise. He was just Leon, the guy who owned the T-shirt shop and the guy Elias trusted to watch his instruments when he had to pee.

Once Leon had thrown the locks on both sides of the door, he took Elias back to his office. The little room was crammed with metal shelves that held boxes and tubs of office supplies, stacks of computer paper, boxes full of T-shirts, sweatshirts, and all the other stuff Leon sold in the store, and tubs filled with paper file folders jampacked with more paper. The effect was more than a little claustrophobic.

Leon's desk was an old wooden thing with tiny drawers on both sides and a footwell in the center. An old-fashioned desk blotter covered most of the top, and a paper planner type calendar was open off to the side.

Someone taking a quick glance at all the paper and the old

wooden desk would think Leon was strictly an old-school technophobe. Until they caught a glimpse of his computer setup.

Not one, but two desktop computers bracketed the old wooden desk. Two flatscreen monitors were mounted to the wall behind the desk.

Leon must have seen Elias's look of surprise when he took in the monitors.

"Belt and suspenders, man," he said. "This old building's hell with electrical. I've got a battery backup, but I learned my lesson when this place fried the first computer I ever had."

Both monitors were displaying screensavers, little bands of light chasing each other around the screens. Leon tapped a few commands on one of two keyboards, and the monitor on the right came to life. Four windows appeared, each of them showing a different view of the store.

Four cameras. Elias had thought Leon's store only had three, two on each side of the open storefront and one over the checkout counter aimed toward whoever was standing on the customer side of the counter. The fourth camera was actually pointed at the person working the register.

Leon must have had some trouble with employees stealing from him. That was the only reason Elias could think of that he'd have that fourth camera.

Or maybe he'd installed it to keep an eye on Jack. To make sure the man wasn't acting hostile toward the customers whenever Leon wasn't out in the store to keep tabs on him.

None of the cameras had audio capabilities. It was all video in black and white, although the picture quality was far better than the blurry security camera images Elias caught sometimes on the nightly news.

"What time frame are you looking at?" Leon asked.

Elias hadn't checked the time when he'd taken his pee break. "When I was over here earlier," he said.

Leon clicked on a few commands, and the four cameras reset to new views.

On the monitor Elias watched Leon leave the store and a couple of minutes later watched himself come in through one of the open doorways. The camera aimed at Jack captured the man jawing at Elias, caught his belligerent expression and the tense way he held himself.

Elias wasn't the only one watching Jack.

"What'd he say to you?" Leon asked.

Elias made an effort to appear calmer than he felt. He had a vivid memory of what had happened next out of camera range, but he still didn't want to involve Leon in that.

"Just usual Jack bullshit," he said. "You know Jack."

"Yeah."

That one word told Elias that Leon saw right through his attempt to act casual.

"My *employee* needs to learn to keep his damn mouth shut when I'm not around," Leon said.

Elias didn't say anything. What could he say? That Leon should cut the man some slack? That Jack might be a different man now that he'd seen the same thing Elias had? Only Jack had run while Elias stayed.

He wondered if Jack had heard a voice in his head, and if he had, what the voice had told him.

A minute later, the camera trained on the register recorded Jack walking out of frame.

"Where the hell did he go?" Leon said, more to himself than to Elias.

Elias didn't say anything to that either.

"Anybody else in the store then?" Leon asked.

Anybody?

"Not that I saw," Elias said, which was the truth.

Nothing happened on camera for the next couple of minutes. No customers came in the store. None of the people on the street stopped by the front of the store to check out the touristy stuff. The cameras trained on the front entrances just showed people walking by on the sidewalk in front of the store.

Elias's breath caught when he saw a momentary streak near the bottom of one of the cameras trained on the front entrances. Had that been the cats running into the store? The streak had been fast, almost like a glitch in the recording. Or maybe he just wanted so badly to see some physical evidence that the cats had been there, he'd imagined it.

"What the hell was that?" Leon asked.

So he'd seen it too.

Leon tapped a few keys on the keyboard. The camera feeds paused, then backed up. When he started them up again, the feeds clicked forward frame by frame.

The streak Elias had seen, what he'd told himself might only be a glitch, showed up as two blurry distortions at the bottom of two frames. Nothing was there the frame before, and in the following frame, the distortions were gone.

That had to be the cats, he knew it. But they'd only appeared in two frames, and they certainly weren't identifiable as cats.

How was that possible? Just how fast did they have to be running to show up on the camera feed like that? He couldn't even imagine.

"Can you tell what that was?" Leon asked.

He'd stopped the feeds on the first frame with the streaks, and he was leaning in so close to the computer monitor that he looked like a man trying to read the fine print on an extended warranty.

"All I see is a blur," Elias said, because that's all it was.

"Huh," Leon said. "That's fucking weird, man."

That wasn't the half of it. Elias was still waiting for the rest of it—security footage from after the cats had grown to the size of Rottweilers.

Leon started the footage going forward again, this time back to a normal pace.

Nothing else showed up on any of the security feeds until one camera caught Elias leaving the store. He had his head tilted down, so the camera didn't catch his face.

When Elias had come out of the hallway, he'd looked around the store for the cats. He'd survived them once, but he had no idea how long his luck would last. For all he knew, some other impossible thing might be hiding among all the hoodies and sweatshirts hanging from racks in the front of the store.

But he'd been alone. There hadn't even been any customers browsing near the front doors.

It was probably a good thing that the security camera hadn't caught a good look at his face. He probably looked like a man who was trying to figure out if he'd finally taken a dive off the deep end of sanity and into a world where all that crazy shit from Disney cartoons turned out to be real.

But the only thing the security camera had recorded was him leaving the store. No cats, big or small. And no glitches either.

As far as the security feed was concerned, no cats had been in the store period.

Leon turned away from the computer monitor and sat back in his desk chair. The chair looked as old as Leon. It's springs squawked in protest as Leon leaned back further to cross one ankle over his knee.

"I didn't see anybody lifting anything off the front," he said. "You?"

He was looking at Elias like he knew something was up, but he wasn't sure what.

Elias cleared his throat. "No, man. I thought I did. When I was coming back from the bathroom, I didn't see Jack up front. I thought I saw a kid grab something and take off, but I guess I was wrong."

"He wasn't doing something up front?"

Leon meant Jack, and the *something* was stocking the shelves or refolding shirts. Those things wouldn't show up on the camera feeds.

Elias shook his head. "Didn't see him."

"Huh." Leon rocked a little in his chair, producing more squawks from the tortured springs. It was probably a good thing Leon was a skinny old fart, or the chair wouldn't have held up as long as it had. "I wonder where he went."

Elias knew damn well where Jack had gone. He'd even seen Jack sneak back in the store after Leon had gone inside. Jack must have timed his entrance well if Leon hadn't seen him come in from outside.

Jack might have some explaining to do the next time he showed up to work. Like why he'd left the store unattended, and it wasn't just a sudden need to use the bathroom since the store only had one and Elias had been using it.

Elias has some explaining to do to himself. He'd come here to see if the security cameras had caught an impossibility on tape. They hadn't.

How was that possible?

How was any of this possible?

"You know," Leon said. "if you think you're seeing people ripping us off when they're not, you might need a break from relying on the kindness of your fellow man."

He folded his hands over his lap and peered up at Elias.

"It's none of my business," he said, "and I'd be the first to admit that people in general can be assholes—Jack's a prime example—but you and me, we're in the people business. We both got product to sell. You gotta give John Q. Public the benefit of the doubt, or they're gonna catch on real quick that you ain't out there singing because you love the work and you're appreciative when they stop and listen."

Leon was talking about burnout. The kind street musicians got when they felt underappreciated and definitely under-tipped. When they thought no one cared about the music. When they went too many days failing to make a connection. Or when they thought someone was stealing from their meager tips.

That wasn't exactly Elias's current problem, not that he could tell Leon that.

"Gotcha," Elias said. "Guess I might need to take a few days."

Especially if he was seeing giant cats where only housecat-sized cats existed.

Only if he took a few days, someone else would take over his spot. He'd been in that spot for so long that other performers recognized that from ten in the morning until two in the afternoon, that spot was his.

He thanked Leon for taking the time to show him the camera

feeds. "Sorry to have kept you for nothing," he said as he and Leon walked out the back.

"Hey, man, I'm glad it was for nothing," Leon said. "Better than having to count inventory to see what's missing, you know?"

Leon finished with the last of the locks on the back door and fished his cell phone out of his jacket pocket. He used one of the apps on his phone to turn on the shop's alarm system, then put the cell back in his pocket.

Would something like an alarm system present much of a problem to the cats if they really wanted to get in the shop? They'd certainly managed to get in and out without being seen on the security cameras. They might have a problem with the physical locks—no opposable thumbs. Elias had seen videos of cats opening doors, but these locks were keyed deadbolts on both sides.

Then he caught himself.

What the hell was he thinking? He must be more tired than he realized. More brain fried.

He needed to go home, maybe break into one of the bottles of beer he kept in the fridge for those rare times when he felt like having a drink. Tonight certainly qualified. A beer and bed, and then maybe things would look better—more normal—in the morning.

Leon kept a motorcycle in the garage behind the store. His parking spot was on the ground floor, so Elias walked along with him to his bike.

Elias didn't know much more about motorcycles other than they were loud and a hell of a lot more dangerous to ride than a car. Leon's was a big thing, with a windscreen up front and metal saddlebags in the back. Leon looked like a little kid as he climbed on board.

Once when Elias had mentioned he'd never ridden on a motorcycle, Leon had offered to take him on a nice *slow* ride around the city. Elias had thought about taking one of San Francisco's infamous steep streets on the back of the bike and said thanks but no thanks. He'd lived in the city for a long time and he didn't even like driving those steep hills in his car.

Leon had laughed at him, but he hadn't called Elias a pussy. To each his own, was all he'd said.

Elias waved goodnight as Leon started up the motorcycle. The bike's engine echoed off the concrete and bounced around Elias's skull like a loud industrial metal song. The song built to a crescendo when Leon gunned the engine as he pulled out of the parking spot and made his way to the exit.

Damn, but that thing was loud. Leon had mentioned once that he thought about installing a sound system on the bike, but what would be the point? Elias couldn't even hear his footsteps on the garage's concrete floor.

His own footsteps, or the heavy footfalls of the person coming up behind him.

He didn't even realize he wasn't alone until it was too late.

25

Summers in Vegas were hot. Seriously hot. Sometimes a sudden, violent thunderstorm interrupted the heat, but the storms rarely lasted for long and never really cooled things off.

The park where Elias went to play the kind of music he wanted to play had some shade, but not a heck of a lot. The city had tried, he'd give the planners that. They'd planted trees here and there. The bit of shade they provided didn't really cut it when the temperature topped a hundred-ten without a single cloud to hide the sun in the washed-out desert sky.

After the high-rise hotels cast their tall shadows over the park in the late afternoon? That's when sitting on the concrete benches became tolerable.

Late afternoons in Vegas were a kind of magic time, halfway between daylight, when the city belonged to the nine-to-fivers who wore suits and worked in office buildings, and nighttime, when Vegas became a version of the Sin City tourists flocked to hoping to experience things they couldn't tell the folks back home about.

For Elias, late afternoons in the park were a different kind of magic.

Late afternoons were when he could play the kind of music he wanted to play on his old acoustic guitar. After playing the same songs on the piano night after night in a casino showroom orchestra pit, no one could tell him that the freedom to make music the way he wanted to *wasn't* magic.

He still had the same guitar he'd hauled around to bars and restaurants trying to score a gig when he'd still been in college. The case was a little battered—sometimes he felt a little battered too—but the guitar still made sweet music.

He never played loud enough to bother anyone (he hoped) and definitely not loud enough to be heard much beyond where he sat thanks to the never-ending stream of traffic on nearby streets. He played around with different arrangements of songs he'd learned long ago or that he heard on the street somewhere. Sometimes he just played whatever melody popped into his head, chasing notes along the frets like they were playful puppies or kittens just out to have a good time.

The one thing he didn't do was sing. He wasn't performing, not really. He was just playing whatever he wanted to hear.

When he was in a poetic frame of mind, he thought of himself as part of the unique and somewhat quirky tapestry that made up life in Vegas, just as much a part of the city as the fountains at the Bellagio or the quirkiness of The Fremont Street Experience.

And if someone else in the park wanted to hum along? Or tap a finger to the beat of his song on the book they were reading? Well, they were just part of that tapestry too. It meant someone out there was enjoying what he played.

It meant that he wasn't an intrusion. Or, heaven forbid, an embarrassment.

The way Lettie had shot him down when he'd brought up busking made him wonder if part of her had always been embarrassed that he sang for tips. That was an ugly possibility he didn't want to think too closely about.

Because if Lettie—if his *wife*—had been embarrassed even back then by something that was such a part of who he was, what else about him did she find lacking?

Was she just tolerating him?

Another ugly thought.

It didn't take a genius to realize they'd been pulling apart from each other. Their lives seemed to be heading in two different directions, and that scared him. He didn't want to lose her, but he didn't want to lose himself either.

Stuff like that had a way of chasing itself round and round in his head when he spent too much time by himself, and outside of work, he had a whole heck of a lot of time to himself. Even when they were together, it still felt like he was all alone.

She would already be asleep when he got home from work. He'd climb into bed next to her. Feel her there, soft and warm beside him. She rarely woke up, but there were moments when she'd roll over and snuggle into him, and he would wrap his arms around her.

He lived for those moments.

But when he woke up the next morning, she'd always be gone. She usually left him a note, and sometimes she'd leave something in the refrigerator for him to heat up. Most of the time it was something she'd brought home from work the night before. Or it was something new she was working on that she wanted him to try.

She was always working so damn hard, trying to prove herself. He knew that. He even understood it on an intellectual level.

But those late mornings when he had the apartment to himself, eating some fancy dish alone at their little two-person kitchen table, he felt so alone and lonely that he actually missed the days when they'd been broke. When they'd shared a house with too many roommates and there'd never been enough hot water for everyone to take a shower. Their meals might not have been fancy, but at least they'd been together more often than not.

And they'd been happy.

Hadn't they?

Hadn't they?

It got to the point that he couldn't stand the empty feeling of his apartment, so he started going to the park more and more often.

In the beginning, he'd only gone once a week on one of his days off. Then he started going on both his days off. On those days he always made sure he was home when Lettie got home from work, but it was always the same routine. She'd shower, they'd spend a little time watching something on television, then she'd go to bed exhausted. If he offered to cook her dinner, she would always say she ate something at work, so after a while he simply quit offering.

After a while, he started playing at the park even on nights he worked. He simply went from the park to work and stowed his guitar with one of the security guards. He was self-aware enough to realize that playing in the park was becoming an obsession. A way to avoid facing the problems with his marriage, but he figured it was cheaper than therapy.

And a whole hell of a lot more enjoyable.

Besides, he wasn't hurting anyone.

He kept right on telling himself that.

Until he met Tess.

26

THE ATTACK FROM BEHIND WAS SO SUDDEN, SO COMPLETELY WITHOUT warning, that Elias couldn't manage to do anything to break his fall.

He landed flat on his face on the parking garage's concrete floor. Something in his nose gave way with a gush of something warm, and a bright red knot of pain burst into life on his forehead.

The heavy blatt of Leon's motorcycle was fading away into the night. Elias's ears were ringing in the sudden silence.

Leon was gone. He hadn't seen anything, or he wouldn't have left. No other cars were roaring to life in the garage. The sounds of nightlife on the Wharf were distant and muted.

Elias was alone with whoever'd hit him.

He couldn't stay on the ground. He had to get up. If he didn't, he had no chance of defending himself.

He tried to get his hands beneath himself to push himself upright. A solid kick to his ribs made him curl around the new explosion of pain instead.

He was suddenly sure he was going to die here, in this parking garage, just another victim of a vicious mugging. He didn't have much, but whoever'd attacked him wouldn't know that.

He expected to feel rough hands shove into his pockets, searching for a wallet. Or maybe his attacker would stab him first. Slide a knife in between his ribs, searching for something vital to slice so he'd end up bleeding out on the dirty concrete.

Or maybe his life would end with a sudden gunshot. A sudden flare of bright light before all that he was and ever would be disappeared forever.

Except none of that happened.

Before Elias could do more than contemplate the ways he was about to die, his attacker landed one more goal-scoring kick, this one a solid blow to his kidneys.

Pain that made his other injuries seem like a walk in the park almost made him black out.

He didn't scream, couldn't draw in a breath to scream. His entire body was rigid with pain. His hands were clenched into hard fists, every muscle so tight they might never relax again.

He tried to steel himself for the next attack. If he did black out this time, it would be game over. His mind was screaming at him to get up, get up, *get up!* But all he wanted to do was curl into himself. It would be so easy to make himself small enough so that no one would ever hurt him again.

He'd been in a few fistfights when he'd been younger, but he'd only come away from those with skinned knuckles. One time a blow to his mouth had loosened his front teeth. He'd never been beaten, really beaten, in those long-ago schoolyard brawls.

He wondered if that's how his attacker was going to kill him—by kicking him to death. Maybe stomp on his back and break a few vertebrae or bring a booted foot down on the back of his neck hard enough to snap his spine. Land a solid blow to the side of his head that would scramble his brains badly enough that even if he lived, he wouldn't be Elias anymore. He'd just be a vegetable hooked up to machines that kept him alive.

He needed to get the fuck up and defend himself. Somehow. He couldn't just lie there and take it. He'd be damned if he was going to end up just another statistic. Another mugging victim, left to die alone for no good reason.

He started cursing at himself. He wasn't sure if he was actually saying the words or just thinking them, but he wanted to make himself angry. If he got angry enough, he'd forget about the pain. Forget every except the need to get the fuck—

That's when his attacker simply walked away.

The heavy tread of his attacker's boots were clocking away on the concrete, not rushed, not running.

Just... walking away.

Elias hadn't heard the attacker come up behind him. The man had been stealthy then, but now he... what—*wanted* Elias to know that he was leaving? That he could have robbed him, could have killed him, but just wanted to beat him up instead?

What in the actual hell?

Elias held his breath, afraid to believe it was all over and he wasn't dead.

Maybe it was a trick. Maybe his attacker thought he *was* dead. If Elias just stayed still, stayed right where he was on the cold, damp, concrete floor of the parking garage, his attacker would stay gone.

He let his breath out slowly, trying to be as quiet as possible. His back was throbbing, the side of his ribcage where he'd been kicked was a dull, steady ache. His head—the back of his head—just plain hurt, but so far he didn't have a headache.

He almost laughed at that. *So far* he didn't have a headache. Borrowing trouble, his mom would have said. She'd borrowed a whole lot at the end. Cancer had kicked the shit out of her far worse than Elias's attacker had beaten him.

Eventually Elias convinced himself that his attacker wasn't coming back.

He needed to get up. If he *could* get up. If his back would let him.

The night had grown unnaturally quiet. He didn't hear anyone out on the street. No music from passing cars. No conversations or laughter from people leaving the restaurant. Even the sea lions had gone quiet for the night.

When was the city ever this quiet?

Or was it always this quiet at night, and he'd never been around to notice?

Not that it mattered. The only thing that mattered was getting himself upright and back to his car. Everything else was just details.

He got his arms beneath himself and pushed, grunting with the effort so he wouldn't cry out at the pain. Sweat broke out on his forehead, but he managed to push himself upright.

The pain in his back, by far the worst, settled into a hot, steady ache. It hurt to breathe, but that was mostly his ribs. The headache he'd worried about started beating in time to the beats of his heart, but the pain came from his battered nose, not the back of his head.

Elias felt the back of his head. He had a good lump forming there already, but his hand didn't come away wet with blood. At least there was that. He had bled on the concrete where he'd fallen, but that had come from his nose. The bleeding there had seemed to slow down. His nose was tender to the touch, but that was it. Nothing crunched when he touched the bridge of his nose, and at least he could touch it, so he took that as a good sign.

He needed to finish getting up. Someone would eventually see him and call 9-1-1. There'd be questions from the police, and what could he tell them anyway? He hadn't seen who'd attacked him. They'd write up a report and file it away, and that would be that.

The police might even call the paramedics, and Elias definitely didn't want to deal with that. Back when he'd been gainfully employed, he'd had decent health insurance. No more. He could deal with bills from an urgent care visit if that became necessary, but not the cost of an ambulance ride or treatment in an emergency room.

Not for a street mugging when he hadn't been stabbed or shot. Or robbed. The money he'd made that day was still in his pocket.

"You're one lucky bastard," he told himself.

His fingers were all in one piece. It would have been so easy for his attacker to stomp on his hands instead of kicking him in the ribs. That would have disabled him. As it was, even with his voice still on the raspy side, the tools of his trade were all basically intact. It could have been so much worse.

He forced himself to get to his feet.

The process was slow and painful. When he finally made it upright, the world swayed around him for a moment, as unsteady as the first time he'd ridden out an earthquake. His stomach rebelled against the sensation. But he didn't black out and the nausea was mercifully brief.

The first couple of steps he took sent bolts of pain down his legs, but each successive step seemed to get easier. Either he was working through the pain or he was just getting used to it.

He stopped near an overhead light at the garage's exit and fished in his jacket pocket for the napkin that was left over from his hotdog lunch. He used the napkin to dab at his nose and where the blood had run down his face. The napkin came away bloody, but there wasn't as much blood as he'd feared.

This whole attack made no sense. But when had random violence ever made sense? His attacker hadn't said a word, hadn't even grunted with the effort of kicking him. What had been the point?

Did there even have to be a point?

A lot of people were just flat out violent. Elias had been in the wrong place at the wrong time. He'd been an easy target for someone looking to take out their frustrations on a random stranger. He really was lucky his attacker hadn't been armed with a gun or a knife.

Tomorrow was Saturday. Tourists would be coming to the Wharf in droves. That would make for a good day in tips. Elias didn't want to miss the day.

He could rest tonight. Ice up his face and his ribs. Choke down some soup, maybe. He had a few cans in the cupboard he kept for when tips were on the slim side and he didn't want gussied-up boxed mac and cheese. If he needed to—and he probably would—he could perform in dark glasses. And if his voice was a bit more on the nasal side than normal, the tourists wouldn't know. They'd probably think the dark glasses and the nasal voice were just part of his act.

He could do this.

That thought played on a loop in his head as he shuffled down the street toward the parking lot and his car. The block and a half had never seemed so long before. At least he didn't have a long drive ahead of him. The joys of living in the city instead of commuting to Oakland or Berkley and having to face Bay Bridge traffic every day.

He could do this.

He just had to put one foot in front of the other.

The night had grown foggy. Heavy fog always muted the sounds of the Wharf. That's why the night had sounded unnaturally quiet. It was just the fog.

The fish vendors on the Wharf were closed for the night. Even the restaurant over Leon's shop would be closing in another hour or two. There were no nightclubs down here, nothing to draw the late-night party crowd.

He could do this.

He had a full-blown headache now. Every step jarred his back and made his head throb, but every step got him closer to his car.

He could do this.

He shuffled down the side street like a wraith in the damp misty night. The traffic lights on the corner ahead and the streetlights all looked like they'd been wrapped in thick, glowing cotton. The streetlights didn't reach far, almost like the fog was conspiring with the shadows at the edges of the street to keep anyone from looking too closely into the dark.

Elias never glanced at the shadows at the base of the building that housed Leon's shop. His world had collapsed into the pain each new step brought and the four words echoing inside his head. They'd almost taken on a lyrical quality, like the refrain of a song no one ever wanted to write.

He could do this.

He didn't see the old man huddled against the weathered brick on the outside of the building. Nearly a wraith himself, the man wasn't much more than an ancient, flesh-covered skeleton cocooned in layers of faded shirts and sweatshirts and a filthy jacket. A woolen blanket was wrapped around his shoulders like a cape.

A ginger cat was crouched in the shadows next to the man. Elias wasn't looking for cats any longer, and he never saw this one.

He never saw the tip of the cat's tail flick angrily, or its ears swivel to follow the sounds of his footsteps on the sidewalk as he made his slow way toward his car.

Never heard the low growl rumble deep in the cat's throat as it breathed in a different scent. A scent far too subtle for any human to smell. A scent the cat was only too familiar with.

The scent of recent violence.

The old man stroked the cat's tense back. "They never learn, do they," he whispered.

The cat's tail flicked again, harder this time, a whip camouflaged by fluffy ginger fur.

The old man tilted his head as if he was listening to something only he could hear. He shivered, not with the cold, but from an old lesson he'd learned the hard way.

"Do you think that's wise?" he asked.

The cat turned her head to glare at him.

He took his hand away from her back and bowed his own head. He had known the cat for a very long time. He should know better than to question her decisions, but sometimes she acted rashly. Still acted like the young thing she'd been when they first met. Before she'd revealed herself to him.

Before she'd bound his life to hers.

Before he'd realized exactly what that would mean.

"Just be careful," he said.

He didn't want to imagine what life would be like without her. Her life was driven by emotions and instincts and obligations he couldn't hope to understand. That put her in jeopardy more often than not. She never seemed overly concerned for her own safety. He was the one who worried for the both of them.

"Promise me," he said. "Tell me you'll be careful."

The cat rubbed her head against his gnarled fingers. Not a promise, just a gesture of affection.

He'd take it.

He watched her trot off into the foggy night. Not following the bloodied man who'd shuffled past them, but in the opposite direction. She was on the hunt.

The old man shivered again. He wrapped the woolen blanket tighter around himself, drew his legs up until he could rest his head on his knees, and settled in to wait.

27

ELIAS HAD BEEN PLAYING A VARIATION ON AN OLD FOLK SONG, HIS EYES closed, just letting his fingers pick and strum their way through the melody, when he heard someone humming along. That wasn't unusual. A lot of people who came to the park in Vegas where he played hummed along to whatever he was playing. Sometimes he thought they weren't even aware of it.

But this was different.

The woman humming had a lovely, almost ethereal lilt to her voice. And she wasn't humming the melody but a perfectly on-point harmony to the notes he was playing.

At first her voice reminded him of the way Lettie sang in the limo the night they'd first met. His heart skipped a beat, and his fingers flubbed the next few notes before they found their rhythm again.

Had Lettie found him somehow? Found him and decided to sing along, after a fashion?

Of course, when he opened his eyes, it wasn't Lettie.

One of the most beautiful women he'd seen in a long time was sitting on the concrete bench just a few feet away from him. Her own eyes were closed, her face lifted slightly as she hummed the harmony line to the song.

Vegas was full of beautiful women, both natural beauties and those whose attributes had been enhanced with a little surgical intervention. But so many of those women looked like they'd come off an assembly line meant to produce someone's idea of the ideal woman. As horrible as it sounded, beauty like that got old after a time.

This woman?

She wasn't a stunning beauty, the kind that stopped traffic on the street. She wasn't even a fresh-faced, girl-next-door type. No, even just sitting down with her eyes closed, she exuded the kind of presence that came with absolute self-confidence. Charisma, he supposed, the kind that only a very few people in the world possessed.

That was the first thing he noticed about her.

Not that her looks were anything to sneeze at. She had long, dark brown hair that hung past her trim waist in thick curls. Her face was unlined, and her skin had a flawless, healthy glow with only the slightest hint of makeup. Her chin came to a graceful point. Her eyebrows were naturally full, not tweezed to near invisibility, and dark brown like her hair.

But she definitely had a presence. Something that he supposed certain movie stars and politicians had. An indefinable thing that drew other people to them.

He was certainly drawn to her. More than that though, he felt like she was someone who might be important to *him*.

His fingers faltered on the strings again. She opened her eyes and looked at him.

Her eyes were a lovely golden-green, tilted up just slightly at the outside corners.

"Don't stop," she said. "It's lovely."

Her speaking voice was as rich and full as he imagined it would be. Not loud, no... not loud at all, and the words didn't come out like a command. Still, he couldn't have said no to her if he tried.

Just like he couldn't have looked away from her warm, golden-green eyes.

He kept playing, and she kept humming along. Sometimes she sang a word or two, not like someone who'd just remembered a few words, but more like she meant to sing those exact words and only those words.

When the song was over, she ducked her chin. The move made her look young, and the quick smile she gave him seemed almost shy.

"Thank you," she said. "I haven't heard that song for a very long time. It brought back...." She hesitated, then tilted her head slightly to one side. "Fond memories."

Her voice was like silk. Cultured in a way most people weren't.

The way she spoke reminded him of a professor he'd had for one of his music appreciation classes back in college. The professor had trained in Europe and played with orchestras in places he'd never heard of. She had a classical music education in the most traditional sense, and she had what he'd always thought was a cultured accent. Not British, not any nationality he could recognize. Definitely not American in any way, shape, or form. Just... different.

That's what this woman reminded him of. No surprise there. Vegas was a tourist destination for people from around the world. But she didn't look like a tourist. Not one bit.

"I should be thanking you," he said. "That's going to go down on my list of coolest things ever."

Back then he'd actually said things like that and hadn't been embarrassed about it. If Lettie had heard, she would have been. She might have even had a list of her own for all he knew: things Elias does to embarrass me.

"Oh, you have a list, do you?" the woman asked.

"I do." He tapped the side of his head with one finger. "Right up here."

She arched one eyebrow. "And where am I going to be on that list?"

He pretended to give the question serious consideration. Then he said, "Somewhere near the top."

"But not the top."

He shook his head. "Sadly, no," he said.

One corner of her mouth quirked up in a grin. "Feel like sharing what is at the top of your list?"

Actually, he did. He really did.

Before he realized he was going to do it, he said he'd be happy to share his top five coolest things ever—over a cup of coffee.

She'd given him a long, appraising look, which included where his left hand rested on the neck of his guitar.

His left hand, including the plain gold band on his ring finger.

He thought she'd say no, but she'd surprised him. She said yes.

He packed up his guitar and the two of them strolled to a nearby coffee shop that wasn't a Starbucks.

As they ordered fancy coffee drinks that bore a closer resemblance to milkshakes than coffee, he told himself this wasn't a date. It couldn't be a date. He was married. All he was doing was sharing a cup of coffee with someone who apparently enjoyed old folk songs as much as he did. They'd spend a little time together before they each went on their separate ways. It had nothing to do with Lettie.

So why was his heart beating a bit faster than it should have?

The woman introduced herself as Tess. She never gave him a last name or told him what she did for a living. She was dressed in jeans and a lightweight tee and tennis shoes, and she walked with the grace of a natural athlete. She didn't seem oblivious to the world around her, like a lot of people did, all caught up in their own little worlds. No, he got the distinct impression that she noticed everything going on around her. All the sights and smells, and most of all—the people.

They spent nearly two hours over their coffees. She leaned toward him over the little table where they sat, her attention focused entirely on him, while he was talking. He even gave her his list of the top coolest things ever, most of which he made up on the spot.

She never called him on his bullshit, even though she must have known he wasn't serious. Instead she listened to him the way no one had listened to him in a long time—like what he was saying was the only thing she was interested in hearing. And what a rush that was.

He had no idea how old she was. When he asked her why she'd liked the song so much that she'd hummed along, she told him that she used to hear songs like that when she'd lived in San Francisco for a time. It had been one of her favorite places, she'd said. Vegas wasn't, not until she'd heard him playing in the park.

"You made this city better for me," she said.

The compliment had taken him by surprise. He'd tried to joke his way out of a moment that was threatening to turn into something serious. Except even the joke turned into something he hadn't meant to admit.

"Me and my silly old songs that no one cares about," he said. "I'm nothing special, you know. You can hear better down on Fremont Street."

Where Lettie didn't want him to play.

Tess pushed her hair away from where it had fallen over her shoulder. She wasn't wearing any jewelry. No rings on her fingers, no bracelets on her wrists. She wasn't even wearing little earrings in her ears like the ones Lettie wore at work.

"You're wrong," Tess said. "There's something special about the way you connect with your music and connect your music to others who can truly hear it. That's why I stopped. Why I sat down and shared the song with you."

Her golden-green eyes had grown intense. He could get lost in those eyes without even half trying.

"There's a special kind joy in doing that," she said. "Joy in making—"

Memories.

The thought came to him so naturally he believed it was his own. That he'd just completed her sentence in his head instead of saying it out loud.

In that first heady month when he and Lettie had been newly in love, they used to complete each other's sentences, then they'd laugh about it. Saying that's how they realized they were perfect for each other because they were perfectly in sync.

How long had it been since they'd done that? Too long.

Here he was, completing a virtual stranger's thought in his head.

"The right songs," Tess was saying, "can take you back to a happier time. But you know that. That's why you play."

That was certainly part of it, not that he'd consciously realized it before. When he was playing in the park, just him and his guitar, it was like he was back in college. Back when he and Lettie had been happy.

But it was also the connection she talked about. Those little toe taps and finger taps from people who were listening to him, whether they realized it or not. The occasional atta' boy from a complete stranger. It was like he was sending out a musical message in a bottle and getting a message back in return.

What did they say? Music was the universal language?

Music had brought him and Lettie together, but they hadn't shared music in a very long time. Their connection was unraveling.

"I think I'm losing my wife," he said, surprising himself by admitting something he'd never meant to say out loud. Saying it out loud made it real.

He expected Tess to clam up. That wasn't something you said to a beautiful stranger who wasn't your wife, not over coffee. Not even after a couple of drinks in a low-rent bar somewhere.

Instead she simply nodded, a barely there dip of her chin. A hint of sadness crept into her intense gaze.

"Yes," she said. "I believe you are."

He didn't ask her how she could knew. At the time, he thought it was just because they'd spent hours together having coffee while he'd been trying—and failing—not to flirt.

Only later, after they'd said goodbye—a final goodbye, he knew without her having to tell him—that he began to think it was something more than that. That the connection Tess had talked about, the one she said they had through his music, gave her some kind of insight into *him*. Almost like she'd sensed his unhappiness, like she seemed to sense everything else in the world around her.

Tess was special. Even more than that, she was different. She'd touched his cheek when they'd said goodbye, the only time either one of them had touched the other. Her touch left his skin tingling.

"Protect yourself out there, musician," she'd said. "No matter what you believe, you are special. There aren't many like you around."

"Really?" he'd asked, feeling foolish but vulnerable at the same time.

"Really." She'd given him an enigmatic look. "And even fewer like me."

Then she'd smiled at him, a wide smile that made her look like a teenager, and walked away.

He'd watched her until she lost herself in the crowd, then he took his guitar and started walking toward home. He'd left the park earlier than usual to go have coffee. Late afternoon was giving way to evening, the neon lights on the Strip creating a false sunrise.

He would have just enough time to shower before the night's show. Then he'd go home and climb into bed next to his sleeping wife, and if he was lucky, she'd roll over and snuggle against him.

But he knew he wouldn't be thinking about his wife even while she was sleeping next to him.

He'd be thinking about the woman whose light touch on his cheek he could still feel.

28

JACK FELT ONLY MARGINALLY BETTER AFTER HE DOWNED HALF A BOTTLE of beer at his favorite Friday night watering hole. It had been a hell of a day, and he needed a beer to wash it all away.

Hell, he'd need half a dozen to wash all that weird shit away. Half a dozen and a sexy lady to make him forget what he was pretty sure he hadn't actually seen. Because shit like that didn't happen in the real world, right?

The real world was made up of stuff he could see and taste and eat and drink. Especially drink. Even Frisco had bars like this one. Places tourists didn't go to. Places where they played old-style country western music—none of that new shit—and served peanuts in the shell along with drinks that a working man could still afford.

His daddy used to call neighborhood bars like this one watering holes. When Jack was little and his daddy took him along for rides on the back of his motorcycle, they always stopped at his daddy's favorite watering hole.

The place hadn't been much to look at, but because his daddy said it was his favorite place, it had been Jack's favorite place too. The bar had a wooden floor and battled-scarred tables and music was always playing on a jukebox. Jack got to sit on a stool at the bar and

153

the bartenders gave him soda in a real glass. Sometimes they'd even put a cherry on top. They called him Sport and gave him a dish of peanuts in the shell while his daddy went into a back room to do grownup business.

The first time Jack had dropped one of the shells on the floor, he'd climbed off his stool to pick it up. The bartender had stopped him.

"You just throw them things on the floor like a real man," the bartender had said. "That's how it's done, Sport."

The bartender was a big burly man with muscular, tattoo-covered arms and shoulders and a mustache that drooped down on both sides of his mouth. He had a big laugh to go with his big shoulders, but he never laughed at Jack and he was never mean to Jack.

Jack had loved his daddy the way only a son who idolizes his father could. But Jack had loved that bartender too. He was the first one who'd called Jack a little man. That was important to a kid whose dad was *the* man. Somebody that everyone in the bar treated with respect. Some people even seemed afraid of his daddy.

When he was little, Jack hadn't understood why anyone would be afraid of his daddy. His daddy was never mean to Jack or Jack's mom, never yelled at them. Sometimes people yelled when his daddy was in the back room at his favorite watering hole, and one time there'd been a big noise like a chair had fallen over, but Jack's daddy always had a smile for him when they left on his daddy's motorcycle.

Life had been good for Jack when he'd been little.

Until the day his daddy came home and threw a bunch of clothes in a backpack. He gave Jack's mom a stack of money, kissed her hard, and told her to get a new life.

Jack had followed his daddy outside. When his daddy got on his motorcycle, Jack asked to go along.

"Not this time," his daddy had said. He'd given Jack a long look, told him to be good for his momma, then he'd driven off.

He never said goodbye.

Jack's momma had packed up a few of their things, tossed them in the trunk of the old car she drove, and ordered him to get in the back seat.

He hadn't wanted to, but she scared him. She was scared herself, so scared that she threatened to tan his hide if he didn't move and move *now*.

That's when he started to cry, and he never cried. His daddy said men didn't cry, and that bartender had called Jack a little man.

Jack had tried to stop his tears, to be good for his mom like his daddy told him to, but he was just beginning to realize that rides on the back of his daddy's motorcycle were over. No more peanuts in the shell. No more cherries in his sodas. No more being called a little man or Sport.

His momma had hugged him, said she was sorry, but they had to leave.

He'd asked her how daddy would be able to find them if they left their house behind.

"He can't," his momma had said. Then she'd said the thing that scared him even more. "He won't even try."

Jack never knew what happened to his daddy. As for his favorite bartender, the one who'd called him a little man, a few years later he'd seen the bartender's picture in one of the newspapers someone had left behind at the laundromat where he went with his momma on Saturday mornings. The newspaper said that the bartender had been killed during a robbery.

Jack had felt hollow inside, but he hadn't cried. The bartender wouldn't have respected his little man if Jack had cried over him. Men, little or otherwise, didn't cry.

When he got old enough, he got his first tattoo in honor of that bartender. He got serious about bodybuilding, and the more his muscles got muscles of their own, the more tattoos he got on his arms and shoulders. Most of the tattoos didn't mean much of anything. Skulls and roses and a grinning long-haired rocker in a top hat. But each tattoo had a cherry or a peanut embedded somewhere in the design.

Tribute. As much as Jack's daddy had instilled in his son a love of watering holes, that bartender had made a lasting impression.

Tonight's bartender wouldn't have made an impression on anybody. He was short and skinny. His mustache didn't so much droop as it looked like it had surrendered in shame. He wouldn't have called any kid a little man. He wouldn't even know how important something like that could be to a kid whose father had walked out on him.

Jack finished off his beer and signaled for a second. He took a long pull from the bottle and belched. Beer was about the only thing that tasted as good going down as it did with a good burp.

The beer and the night's business were going a long way toward restoring his faith in the world as it was supposed to work.

The knuckles on his right hand only ached a little bit. He'd been stupid to hit the fucking freeloader in the head with his fist. He should have used a bottle or a bat, but since the whole thing had been a crime of opportunity (not that Jack thought of it as a crime, but more along the lines of righteous retribution), he hadn't been prepared. But the asshole went down anyway. Smacked that cement with his face, and then he just stayed there like the pussy he was, like he was asking for it.

Jack hadn't actually hit anybody in a long time. He had to admit that it felt *good*. Felt like he claimed a bit of that aura of power his daddy used to have. Jack's daddy had been badass. Even though he'd left Jack and his mom behind, she'd never said a bad word about him. The kids at his new school? Yeah, they had, but only once or twice, and then Jack had shut that shit down.

He'd shut that freeloader down but good. All it took were a few well-placed kicks. That guy would be pissing blood for a week. He just wouldn't be pissing it in Leon's store. Guys like him never fought back.

Jack leaned back on his stool and contemplated his half-empty bottle.

Two beers a night, that's what he always held himself to unless he was walking home. Tonight he might make an exception even though he'd ridden his Harley to the bar. He always found a place to park his Harley, unlike all those idiots who kept cars in the city, and tonight he'd wanted to feel the rumble of the bike's big engine between his legs. He hadn't taken the motorcycle out for a spin in too long. Hard to give the beast its head in the city. Maybe next week he'd head up the Pacific Coast Highway. If the weather held, he could ride the bike all the way up to the Oregon coast.

Or maybe he'd take his ride south instead. Visit all them beaches down in L.A. Impress a few bikini babes with his muscles and tattoos.

He drained his bottle dreaming about all the babes he'd had in his life, and there'd been quite a few. Especially down in L.A. There were some crazy-ass bitches down there who dug bikers like him. Get a couple of them in the sack. Leon owed him a couple of days off. Hell, maybe he'd call out sick tomorrow and just take off.

If he called out sick tomorrow, he could have another beer tonight. Three would be just enough to give him a decent buzz and leave him with a clear enough head in the morning for a road trip down south.

He swiveled on his stool to signal the bartender, and that's when he saw the woman.

She was sitting by herself four stools away at the end of the bar. He couldn't tell for sure—two beers and the bar's dim lighting made it hard to tell anything for sure—but he thought he saw a sprinkling of freckles across the bridge of her nose and her cheeks. Her hair was an amazing shade of golden red with streaks of light brown, and it hung in long curls almost to her waist. She was wearing some sort of gauzy, flimsy blouse, open just enough in the front to offer a tantalizing view of the swell of her breasts, and he thought he could see freckles there too.

Where else did those freckles go?

He might just make it his mission to find out.

Who knew. Maybe she'd like a ride on his Harley. Maybe she'd like a ride on him.

He wasn't sure how he'd missed seeing her when she first came in. He was usually pretty good at spotting the pretty ones. She certainly hadn't been in the bar when he first got there, he knew that for sure.

She had a dainty glass of some kind of liqueur in front of her. Jack had seen a couple bottles of the stuff sitting on the bar back, but in a place like this he figured that was for show. Who the hell sipped liqueur when a good selection of beer was available?

He took his empty bottle down the bar to the stool next to the woman.

"Mind if I sit here?" he asked.

With some bar babes, he would just sit down. With this one, he wanted to be polite. It never hurt to be polite, his mom used to say. He had a feeling polite might win him brownie points with a woman like this.

She turned amazing golden-green eyes on him. Golden-green with tiny flecks of brown. Her eyes seemed to reflect the light from behind the bar.

"Not at all," she said.

Her voice was melodious. As Jack sat down, he confirmed that her freckles did indeed go down her cleavage as far as he could see.

The bartender must have been chatting her up. He shot Jack a glare, which Jack ignored. A skinny shit like the bartender had no chance with a classy, liqueur-drinking woman.

Jack pointed at his empty bottle, and the bartender got the message and brought him another. Jack offered to buy the woman a second glass of whatever she was drinking, but she declined.

The thing about Jack, the thing that kept him employed, was he could be charming when he wanted to be. Even after three beers and the nice little buzz they delivered, he was charming enough that he convinced the woman to come outside with him to see his Harley.

He figured that once they were outside he could find a dark corner and slip a hand down the front of her blouse, check out those lovely breasts of hers. And maybe if he was really lucky, he could find out if her hair really was that amazing color. He might even get her to straddle him while he straddled his ride. Wouldn't that be sweet? He'd actually done that a few times, felt the rumble of the Harley's engine while a biker babe rode him. He didn't think he'd ever come so hard in his life.

He was thinking about that, letting thoughts of getting lucky get him all hard while he led her out the front door of the bar, his hand wrapped around hers as she walked behind him. The night had turned chilly thanks to the fog, and all she had on was that gauzy blouse and a skirt of the same stuff that brushed her ankles. She might actually appreciate him warming her up.

That's when he felt the first prick of her nails on his skin.

"Watch out for the tats," he said. "You wouldn't want to wreck a man's ink, now would you?"

Instead of apologizing or letting up, the prick of her nails turned into needle-sharp stabs into the back of his hand.

"Hey!"

Jack tried to jerk his hand away, but her grip had turned to iron. Now he could swear he felt blood running down his hand. The same hand he'd used to knock the freeloader in the head.

He'd never been into blood play. He'd planned on getting lucky in some dark corner—the restaurant next door had a fenced-in seating area out front that was nice and dark and secluded now—but if she needed to spill some of his blood to get herself off, he was done with her. There were always more good-looking women in the world he could get lucky with.

He turned around, intending to tell her that he wasn't into this shit, but the words dried up before he could get a single one out.

Her nails weren't the only thing that had changed about her.

Her eyes had grown large in her head. They were nearly twice the size they'd been in the bar, and they'd taken on a feral glint in the fog-muted light from a nearby streetlight. She smiled at him, displaying teeth that had grown large and pointed. While he watched, her long hair seemed to shrink back into her head as fur took its place. Her clothes turned into more golden-red fur that covered her skin. Covered all those lovely freckles he'd been so intent on tasting.

He thought about screaming, but his tongue felt like it was stuck to the roof of his mouth. The beer he'd had was threatening to make a return trip. He had a sudden, visceral memory of the cats in the hallway in the shop, the ones that had grown bigger than any cats had a right to be.

What the fuck?

It was the beer. It had to be the beer. He'd never done drugs, had never wanted to mess with his brain that way, so this wasn't some weird sort of flashback. It had to be the beer.

Because shit like this just *Did Not Happen* in the real world.

"Don't stop now, lover boy," she said.

He was just aware enough to realize that her voice had taken on the same kind of feral tone as her eyes.

Jack's brain finally kicked into gear. He yelped and tried to dislodge her hand, but her fingernails—her *claws,* oh my God, *claws!* —had sunk in deep.

She yanked him toward the front of the restaurant and threw him —*threw* him!—over the wrought-iron fence as if he weighed next to nothing. He hit the ground so hard that his head bounced and his vision doubled.

She was incredibly strong. Stronger than she had any right to be.

He'd never been beaten in a fight, not like this. And not by a woman, because she *had* to be a woman, right? What else could she be?

Before he could even begin to believe there might be things in the world like whatever the hell she was, she'd bounded over the fence and pounced on him. She centered all of her weight on his chest. She didn't seem to be as big as she should have been, no longer person-sized, but still big enough that her weight compressed his chest and kept him from sucking in enough air to scream.

She swiped her claws down his arm, shredding his biker jacket and the skin beneath. Sharp pain radiated from his shoulder to his wrist. He brought his other arm up in a roundhouse blow. He couldn't get much momentum behind it, not flat on his back, but the blow he landed on the furry side of her jaw should have knocked her flat.

It didn't.

Faster than his eyes could track, she turned her head and sank her teeth into his wrist. She shook her head hard just once, and he felt bones in his wrist snap.

Now he screamed.

She let go of his wrist and bit through his throat. His scream dissolved into bubbly gurgles.

Jack stared up into the foggy night as blood pumped out of his ruined throat onto the concrete. He tried to scream again, but nothing came out. His broken wrist was useless, and he couldn't seem to make his other arm work.

His last coherent thought before the world faded was of that long ago bartender who'd called him a little man. Jack wasn't a little man anymore. He was a big man. A strong man. A man who'd learned how to take care of himself and his mom after his daddy left them all alone in the world.

In the end it hadn't mattered.

None of it had mattered at all.

Tears he wasn't aware of leaked from his eyes. By the time those tears mixed with the growing pool of blood beneath his head, Jack was dead.

The oversized cat on his chest sat back on her haunches, her tail flicking back and forth. She surveyed the dead man. His heart had stopped. His essence that she'd followed to this bar was already dissipating.

This night's hunt was done.

She hopped off his chest, careful to avoid stepping in the gory mess. She listened for the sound of running feet, if anyone was coming in response to the man's scream. All she heard was the muffled sound of music blaring from the bar's sound system.

No one was coming to help. So typical of humans.

She found a deeply shadowed spot at the back of the seating area. She sat down and began the serious business of cleaning her fur.

From the deep shadows across the street, an elderly tom padded toward her on silent paws. The ruff around his neck was thick and heavy, his head large, the eyes deep set. His paws were wide with long fur between the pads. Age had bleached his once golden fur of much of its color.

She didn't have to hear him to know he was there. She always knew when he was near. He'd been there the entire time, and he hadn't tried to stop her.

She raised her head to look at him. He flicked his tail at her, annoyance clear in the gesture.

No matter. He was merely a Guardian, like her. But she would be more someday.

Someday soon, she would be the Protector.

She went back to washing her face. She'd been messy, but her anger had gotten the better of her. She'd been angry since that morning. The old tom knew what she was like. Young and impulsive, he said. Too young and impulsive, her emotions always too close to the surface.

The old tom believed her nature made her unsuitable to be a Guardian, but the Protector had chosen her. Had trained her.

She'd been a mere youngling then. The old tom had been annoyed at the Protector's choice. He was Old Blood, and Old Blood could trace their lineage back to the very first ancestors gifted with the ability to shift. It made him rigid in his thinking. Unable to adapt to the world as it existed, not as it had once been.

Those of the Old Blood believed the New Blood like her were tainted with the stain of distant kin who could not change their shapes. They believed New Blood were impure. But New Blood were better equipped to survive in the modern world. Most spent their lives in human form in order to blend in. New Blood formed connections with humans, believing those humans could be useful if properly trained.

The old tom refused to live as a human. On the rare occasions when he wore a human shape, he shifted into the form of an old man, but he never fully integrated into the shape. He rarely spoke, even though their kin had been granted the gift of human knowledge and speech. The old tom preferred to shift into the form of a lion, like the Protector had all those years ago when she'd killed the man who'd killed one of their kin.

The people who lived in this city didn't expect to see a lion pad out of the fog on a moonless night. Humans who threatened the tribe, deliberately or through callous disregard for living things that shared this world with them, fled in terror when they saw the old tom in his lion form.

That was the duty of the Guardians. To safeguard their tribe.

Unlike Old Blood, New Blood believed the humans they formed connections with were a part of the tribe. New Blood protected those humans.

The old man who ran his fingers down her spine and shared his food with her was part of her tribe. He'd opened his heart to her even after she'd allowed him to see her true nature.

She hadn't planned to include the musician in the tribe, but his music had touched her soul. She had encouraged others in her tribe to listen to his music. To thank him if they so chose. So far, only one other had done that—the old tom's life partner. She'd reported that she'd been able to communicate her thanks to this particular human.

Very few humans were able to hear the kin's thoughts. The musician must have been touched at some point in his life. He'd impressed the old tom's partner enough that she'd helped deliver a warning to the muscle-bound man who'd threatened the musician.

That man should have heeded the warning. Should have left the musician alone.

He hadn't. He'd attacked the musician. Injured him.

Injured a member of *her* tribe.

Her duty as a Guardian had been clear. She could not allow that to happen again, so she made sure it wouldn't.

She had no regrets about what she'd done.

She never did.

29
_____

Elias woke up a half-hour before dawn the next day with a headache that threatened to split his skull in two. His back was killing him, and it took him far longer than it should have to lever himself out of bed.

He shuffled to the bathroom for some ibuprofen, and was relieved when his piss didn't turn the toilet bowl red. He wasn't so relieved when he looked at his face in the mirror.

Purple bruises had bloomed around both his eyes. More bruises surrounded the lump on his forehead. His nose was swollen and sore, and he couldn't really breathe through it. His mouth felt dry—far drier than it ever had in Vegas—even after he downed a second glass of water. He must have been breathing through his mouth the whole time he'd been sleeping.

Not that his sleep had been all that restful. The ice he'd put on his face and his back when he got to the apartment had only numbed the pain for just so long.

He lifted up the old T-shirt he wore to bed to get a good look at himself. The bruises around his eyes didn't hold a candle to the huge bruises on his ribs and his back over his kidneys. His attacker must have been wearing steel-toed boots. Those bruises were going to take

165

a long time to go away. It might be even longer before he could take a deep breath—or bend over—without pain.

At least he thought—he hoped—his ribs weren't broken. He'd been in a car accident once while he'd been living in Vegas, something only slightly more serious than a fender bender. He'd gone to the emergency room to stitch up a gash on the side of his head and to have his ribs looked at. The verdict on his ribs had been bruised but not broken, and the pain back then had been far worse.

Whoever had attacked him last night hadn't kicked him hard enough to break anything. Even his nose still looked straight, and his attacker had stayed away from Elias's hands. No broken fingers. He could still play.

Only he wouldn't be able to sing. Not unless he wanted to sound like a nasal version of himself. And even though his throat felt better, he doubted he'd be able to take a deep enough breath to hold a note properly anyway.

Today was Saturday. A Saturday in August. It was bound to be a busy day on his little corner of the Wharf. He couldn't afford to miss out on whatever tips he might make, and Saturday tips were usually the best of the week. If he fortified himself with ibuprofen, if he got the swelling in his nose to go down some more, he might be able to fake his way through an instrumental version of his four-hour gig.

He padded into the apartment's tiny kitchen on bare feet and rummaged through the freezer until he found a half-used bag of frozen corn. He'd wrapped ice in a washcloth and held it to his head last night, but now he wanted something that would shape itself to the lump on his forehead as well as over the bridge of his nose. He had a pair of old sunglasses he could wear to cover his eyes, but the glasses wouldn't fit right if he couldn't get the swelling in his nose to go down.

He tried to break up the hard-as-a-rock snowball of corn inside the plastic bag as quietly as he could. When Elias had dragged himself home the night before, Jerry was already in his bedroom with the door shut, either asleep or entertaining someone. Jerry's bedroom door was still firmly shut. Jerry had Saturdays off, and Elias didn't want to wake him.

Apparently he wasn't quiet enough. The bag of frozen corn was just starting to work its magic on his head when Jerry stumbled into the kitchen.

"What the hell are you banging out...."

Jerry trailed off as he got a good look at Elias's face.

"Holy shit!" Jerry said. "What the hell happened to you?"

Elias started to shrug then thought better of it. "Someone jumped me last night," he said. "Didn't mean to wake you."

Jerry blinked at him. He wasn't fully awake yet. Elias was usually gone by the time Jerry managed to haul himself out of bed on Saturday mornings to make his first of the day's several cups of coffee. By rights, Jerry should still be sleeping.

After another couple of blinks, Jerry asked if anyone had called the cops.

"The guy didn't take anything," Elias said.

"He beat the crap out of you," Jerry said.

This time Elias did risk a shrug, just a little one. The pain in his back and ribs wasn't quite as bad as it had been when he first woke up. Even his headache had gone from skull-splitting to a dull ache. Over-the-counter drugs for the win.

"He was gone by the time I picked myself up off the pavement. And before you ask, nobody saw anything."

Least of all him. What was that old saying they taught kids? Be aware of your surroundings? Or was that something only women got told? Be aware of your surroundings and watch out for anything suspicious. Elias thought that after years of performing on the street being careful was hardwired into his DNA. Apparently not so much.

"You should get yourself checked out," Jerry said. "Head injuries are nothing to sneeze at." He rubbed at his face with one hand. "I ever tell you what happened to a buddy of mine in college?"

Elias wasn't quite in the mood for someone else's tales of woe, but this was the most Jerry had talked to him in ages. Most of the time they just grunted at each other if they happened to pass in the hall or be in the kitchen at the same time.

"Don't think so," he said.

The package of frozen corn was turning his face into an ice cube, but hopefully it was shrinking the swelling. He would need to decide soon if he was going to try to play today or just pack it in.

"I used to play soccer," Jerry said. "Not on an official team or anything, just pickup games on weekends."

Elias had never heard of pickup soccer. Pickup basketball or maybe a grab-ass version of flag football, but soccer? Where the hell had Jerry gone to college, anyway?

"One day this guy, this bruiser of a football player, he decides soccer's a great way to expand his horizons," Jerry said. "So he gets in on the game. He's an aggressive player. Good on his feet, lots of stamina. Asshole could run up and down the field like nobody's business, so he's got everyone thinking he's really good, and maybe he is. Only he's not that great when it comes to moving the ball. He gets tangled up with my buddy when they both go after the ball, and this guy, he shoves my buddy backward."

Elias could visualize the whole thing. Big guy gets out of control and shoves little guy around. It made him happy he'd never gone out for sports. Even in high school he'd been too busy with music to pay much attention to whatever sport the jocks wearing letterman jackets were playing.

"My buddy," Jerry said, "he falls flat on his back."

Jerry demonstrated with a slap of his hand on the kitchen counter.

Jerry started fussing with his coffeemaker, a single-cup brewer that Elias thought was a waste of money. Elias made his coffee the old-fashioned way, with a coffeemaker that produced an entire pot at a time.

"The thing is," Jerry said, "there's this sprinkler head buried in the lawn where he fell. Not one of those plastic things that split when they freeze up, but one of those brass numbers. I'll give you a hint: brass versus skull, brass always comes out on top."

Elias could almost feel the impact. Hell, he had felt an impact just like that last night, only it was the front of his skull and the unforgiving object was concrete.

"Shit," he said.

"Yeah. Shit. Exactly." Jerry rubbed his face again as he watched the coffeemaker start to spit out its first cup of the day. "Anyway, my buddy decides he's a tough guy and he's not going to let a little thing like a potential concussion get him down. Only it wasn't just a concussion."

Jerry had his back to Elias, paying way more attention than necessary to the coffeemaker.

"He actually made it to class before the headache knocked him as flat as that football player did," Jerry said. "Puked all over himself and the chick sitting next to him. They took him to the hospital in an ambulance, then they cut open his skull."

Jerry turned to look at Elias. Jerry's expression was carefully impassive, but his eyes were dark and shadowed.

"I can still remember the diagnosis," Jerry said. "Subdural hematoma. A lot of people don't survive something like that."

Elias was almost afraid to ask. "Did he?"

The coffeemaker spit out the last bit of coffee with a spurting hiss. The aroma of fresh brew filled the little kitchen. Elias couldn't remember a cup of coffee ever smelling that good. Considering the state of his nose, it was a miracle he could smell anything at all.

Jerry picked up his mug and held it with both hands like he needed to warm his fingers.

"Yeah," he said. "My buddy was one of the lucky ones. He wasn't quite the same after that though. Had a hard time with his classes, and his grades went to shit. Said he couldn't remember things, sometimes he thought he saw things out of the corner of his eye that weren't there. He tried to laugh it off, said stuff like 'Brain injury, better than drugs,' shit like that." He took a sip from his mug. "He ended up dropping out."

He grimaced, then took a carton of half-and-half from the fridge.

He poured a generous portion into his mug, took another sip, and nodded to himself.

"I lost track of him after that," Jerry said, "but I never forgot what happened to him. My dad would say it's a cautionary tale, and he's not wrong." He tapped the side of his head with one finger. "Don't fuck with your brain. It's a good lesson to live by."

He put the half-and-half back in the fridge, then took his coffee back to his bedroom and shut the door.

Elias shut his eyes. The attack had been hours ago. His headache was getting better, not worse, and he definitely didn't feel like puking. That had to be a good sign, right?

He readjusted the bag of corn, shifting it to his other hand so that he could make some coffee for himself.

He was fine. Every knock on the head didn't lead to a... what had Jerry called it? A subdural something-or-other? The swelling in his nose must be going down considering how well he could smell the coffee. He hadn't eaten anything when he got home the night before. Now his stomach was starting to complain about that.

He drank his coffee—black, no half-and-half, thank you very much—as he cooked an egg for himself and toasted two slices of whole wheat bread. He ate standing up in the kitchen as the world on the other side of the window over the sink gradually lightened. No spectacular dawn, not this morning. Just a slow slide into a fog-shrouded new day.

He was pretty sure he could get his hair to cover most of the knot on his forehead. Even if his dark glasses sat funny on his nose and voice was breathy and sounded like he had a clothespin holding his nostrils shut, he could do this. It was only four hours, after all. Four hours that could make or break his month.

He was okay. He'd be okay. Knocked around a bit, sure, but he'd been lucky. He'd take the warning for what it was and be more careful about his surroundings. Be more aware of things. Be more watchful.

That was good as far as it went. Part of him wanted to arm himself to the teeth like some Rambo wannabe. He supposed that was a natural reaction. But he wasn't a fighter. He should probably take a few self-defense classes, but thinking every stranger was out to get him? That was a crappy way to live.

He definitely wasn't going to start seeing things that weren't there. He wasn't going to turn into another cautionary tale like Jerry's old college buddy.

Only later did he wonder if maybe he should have taken Jerry's advice that foggy August morning—gone to see a doctor instead of going to the Wharf to do his job like he did every Saturday.

If he had, would things have turned out differently?

The hell of it was he didn't know, and he never would.

30

Elias found an old black Trilby in the back of his closet, something he'd worn on stage when he had a three-week gig backing up a blues singer in a club down the coast in Monterey. The hat had been with him for a bunch of years now. It was a tight fit with the bump on his forehead, not to mention the sore spot on the back of his head, but at least the hat would stay firmly in place if a breeze kicked up off the bay.

He completed his hide-the-bruises look with a pair of dark glasses. The bag of frozen corn had knocked down the swelling enough that his glasses almost sat where they were supposed to on the bridge of his nose.

He could even breathe through his nose.

Sort of.

He tried singing in the car as he drove down to the Wharf. As he'd suspected, his voice had a nasal quality and he sure as hell couldn't hold any long notes thanks to his bruised ribs, but he doubted the tourists would know the difference. Leon would, but Leon didn't normally hang around to hear Elias sing. It wasn't like he had any other regulars.

So heartfelt ballads? Out of the question for today. Lightweight folk songs, he could probably manage those. And since his fingers had come out of the attack unscathed, he might even be able to manage some of the more complicated instrumentals on guitar and his keyboard. He loved playing some Stephen Stills' old numbers on guitar, not to mention "Classical Gas," and those usually drew in good tips.

It had taken him longer than usual to get ready for work, which meant he got to the Wharf later than he liked. The parking lot where he had his monthly pass was already three-quarters full, which meant he had to park farther away from his corner than he would have liked. His monthly pass didn't come with an assigned spot. Even if it had, some tourists—hell, some people period—seemed to think that the rules didn't apply to them, and they'd park in his spot whether it was assigned or not.

At least he'd found a spot to park. If he'd been any later, he might have been out of luck period.

By the time he downed a couple more ibuprofen and got out of his car, it was nearly nine forty-five. He couldn't start playing before ten, but he usually tried to set up between nine and nine-thirty. He still had to haul all his gear over to his corner. He had a collapsable cart he used to carry his keyboard and stand, his portable power supply, his amp, his stool, his microphone and mic stand, all the necessary cables, and the plastic tub with the CDs he had for sale. His guitar case had a carry strap, and he usually slung the guitar around his back. Thanks to the cart, he could haul everything to his spot in a single trip.

That wasn't going to work today.

Even if he wanted to, he couldn't sling his guitar onto his back. He wasn't even sure he could lift his amp out of the trunk and into the cart. His keyboard was a professional model, which meant it wasn't all that light either. He'd never hurt his back before, and he hadn't given any thought before now about how much harder it was going to be to just get his equipment out of the car. He'd left all the heavy stuff in his trunk when he'd taken his battered self home the night before.

He needed help, and he didn't have any. A few tourists were

already out and about on the pedestrian plaza, but asking a stranger to help haul some of his expensive equipment wouldn't be his first choice.

Elias stood by his car, trying to figure out what he should do.

He might be able to get Leon to help. Leon worked weekends, either on the register or restocking and straightening the displays. But he always had at least one employee with him, especially during the summer. He might be willing to take a few minutes to help Elias out since it wouldn't mean leaving the store unattended.

Except when Elias glanced over at the shop, the rollup doors were still closed, and the shop looked like it was locked up tight.

What was up with that? Leon always opened at nine on Saturdays because the restaurant upstairs was open for breakfast on the weekends.

Elias didn't want to go around through the garage to knock on Leon's back door. No, thank you. Elias wasn't exactly superstitious, but there was something about tempting fate a second time that he definitely wanted to avoid. He might never go anywhere near the back of that store again, much less into that parking garage.

And if he knocked on one of the rollup doors out front? Leon would probably ignore him, figuring he was just some idiot on the street who'd decided to screw around by making noise on the metal doors.

He wasn't going to text either. If Leon wasn't open yet, it meant he was running further behind than Elias was.

So no Leon.

Elias didn't have any other friends on the Wharf. He really should cultivate at least a working relationship with some of the fish vendors, but they were always busy prepping food and dealing with customers.

He supposed he could lash his guitar to the top of all the stuff in the cart, but that didn't solve the problem of how he was going to get all the heavy stuff out of his car in the first place.

He was so focused on trying to work out the logistics of getting his equipment from his car to his spot on the corner that he didn't notice when an older couple came up to the side of his car.

"You look like you could use some help," the woman said.

Elias jerked his head up, muscles tensing.

What had he just told himself about paying attention to his surroundings? He hadn't heard anyone approaching, just the normal morning background noise of a Saturday morning at the Wharf. Sea lions barking as they fought for space on their floats down by Pier 39. Seagulls crying as they circled overhead, hunting for scraps. The squeal of a delivery truck's brakes as it turned down the feeder road that ran alongside the fish vendors' kiosks.

The couple had stopped a few feet away, careful not to invade his personal space. They were no threat, but he'd gone into fight or flight mode anyway. Oh yes, he was definitely experiencing a bit of PTSD here, wasn't he. That was going to make playing today loads of fun.

Elias hardly ever wore dark glasses, and he wasn't used to the way they leached color out of an already foggy morning. It took him a moment to realize this was same the couple who'd stopped to listen to him play "Ode to Joy" the day before. The dark glasses had turned the woman's white hair a shade of silvery gray, but he recognized the same elfin point of her chin and the upturned eyes that gave her an impish look. She'd foregone the heavy coat she'd worn yesterday in favor of a bulky sweater.

Elias's heartbeat kicked up another notch when he realized this was the same woman who'd been standing in front of Leon's store.

The one who'd seemed to disappear in the blink of an eye.

But that couldn't be. She was standing here right, as solid and substantial as he was.

Her companion had the same faraway look in his eyes that he'd had before. Almost like he was scanning the surrounding area for potential trouble. Or maybe that was just Elias's PTSD talking. For all he knew, the old guy could be experiencing the initial onset of memory problems that would only grow worse the older he got.

Elias's shoulders and the back of his neck were so tight that his head was starting to pound again. He breathed in as deep as he could and told himself to relax, and hoped the couple hadn't noticed his initial reaction.

Apparently they had.

"Oh, my," the woman said. "We didn't mean to startle you." She tucked one hand in the crook of her companion's elbow. "People never seem to notice us. I suppose it's because we don't talk a lot when we're out walking. Isn't that right, Tom?"

Her companion—Tom—patted her hand where it rested on his arm, but he didn't say anything.

"Don't worry about it," Elias said. "I'm not on my game this morning, that's all."

Her gaze shifted to take in the hat and his dark glasses, then traveled down below his face. He could swear she was looking at the exact spot where his ribs were bruised, even though that spot was covered with two layers of shirts and his leather jacket.

Her lips thinned and the corners of her mouth turned down. He expected her to ask what in the world had happened to him, but all she did was huff out a breath. Then she seemed to shake off the mood as if it had never been.

"I have a feeling things will get better," she said. "But for now, I think you could use our help. Tell us what you need, dear."

Did he want their help? He didn't think either of them would take off with his stuff. He definitely didn't want either of them to hurt themselves picking up his equipment. But if he took just a partial load in the cart the first time, maybe they wouldn't mind watching his stuff while he made a second trip to the car to get the rest of his stuff.

"If you're sure," he said, "I'm going to need to make two trips to get my gear set up. If you wouldn't mind watching my stuff while I come back for the rest, I promise to be quick."

"Don't be ridiculous," the man said. "We might look old, but we're not infirm." He gestured at the back of Elias's car. "Let's see what you've got."

Elias was so surprised that he moved away from the back of his car so the man could get a look.

The older guy—Tom—peered at all the equipment, then he

grunted when he noticed the collapsable cart. He seemed to be doing some sort of calculations, then he nodded once, quick and decisive.

"One trip," he said. "What you can't get in the cart, we'll help carry."

Elias shot another look across the street at Leon's shop. The doors were still down. This couple seemed to be the only help he was about to get, and he didn't have long to decide.

Like almost every aspect of life these days, street performers on the Wharf had to follow certain rules and regulations. Elias paid an annual fee to the Port of San Francisco for his street performer's license. Licensed performers were assigned specific areas of the Wharf where they could perform. There were even rules concerning how loud their performances could get.

Elias had been doing this long enough that he always got assigned this prime corner location—call it being grandfathered in. But if he didn't start playing by ten-thirty, another performer—even an unlicensed performer—could take over his spot, and there was nothing Elias could do about it. He'd lose an entire day's income. He still had a decent amount of money in the bank that he'd saved from the days when he'd been getting a regular paycheck to cover the lost income, but that was his emergency/do not touch stash. He counted on some of that money to tide him over when storms rolled in and performing was out of the question.

He didn't consider today a real emergency. He was here. He could play. He just had to be able to set up his stuff.

He even had two people ready and willing to help him over this bump in the road. Yes, they were strangers, but they seemed perfectly nice.

What the hell was he hesitating about? Was it just part of his newly acquired PTSD?

Well, that was just stupid.

"I'd certainly appreciate it," he told them.

With their help, he managed to pack up the cart. The old man even lifted the amp and the portable power supply out of the trunk like they weighed next to nothing. Not infirm? That was an understatement. The old guy must still have a decent set of muscles lurking beneath his baggy coat.

The three of them made just one trip to Elias's corner spot. The woman carried his guitar and the bag that held all his cords and his microphone. Elias pulled the cart, even though his ribs and his back weren't happy about it. The old guy carried the folding stool Elias sat on as well as the stand for his keyboard, even though both things would have fit in the cart.

"Lightening the load," the old guy said.

The two of them stayed while Elias set up his gear. He'd come close to losing his spot. Two other musicians, guitars slung over their backs, one of them lugging an amp of his own, had been lurking nearby, scoping out the vacant corner. When they saw Elias, they strolled away in the direction of Ghirardelli Square.

"I don't know how to thank you," Elias told the couple after he'd plugged in the last of his cords and switched on the power supply.

"Play something nice," the woman said.

"Something nice?" Elias sat down on his stool. "Anything in particular?"

He was still moving slowly, deliberately taking it easy on his back not to mention his head. His headache had throbbed to life whenever he bent over. He'd have to remember to do that as little as possible.

"You'll know," the woman said. "It'll come to you."

It'll come to you?

He must have had a quizzical look on his face, because she smiled at him.

"The way these things do," she said. She paused for a moment, then added, "From time to time."

The old guy shot her a look. "Don't tease," he said. "It's unbecoming."

Funny how Elias still thought of him as the old guy even though the woman had mentioned his name. Tom didn't seem to suit him somehow. Thomas might, but not Tom.

"Do you like Sinatra?" Elias asked, then he did a quick calculation. Asking them about Sinatra might actually be insulting. They weren't *that* old. "Or maybe some early Beatles stuff?"

"The Chairman of the Board," the woman said. "I remember him. Good singer. And his buddies, the Rat Pack? They were hellions back in the day."

She smiled, and Elias saw a twinkle of amusement in her eyes. Or maybe it was just a fond memory. Music had a way of bringing back memories.

But if they were her memories, just how old was she anyway? Maybe her parents had been the ones who listened to Sinatra, Dean Martin, and Sammy Davis Jr. Elias's parents had listened to a lot of '70s soft rock, which was where he got his love of Billy Joel, Bruce Springsteen, and Stephen Stills.

"I preferred the Beach Boys," she said. "Up tempo. Easy to dance to in the moonlight on a warm summer night."

The old guy was really watching her now. He didn't look amused.

Elias knew a couple of Beach Boys songs. They were easy to play, but he wasn't sure his voice was up to singing "Surfin' Safari" just yet.

Still, he switched on his keyboard, kept the volume low like he always did when he was warming up his fingers, and ran through the first few bars.

"Something like that?" he asked her.

She stared at him, a grin on her lips and a definite glint in her eyes. "Moonlight music," she said. "Play it like that."

Moonlight music. She must have heard him play "Moonlight Sonata" the other day.

But "Surfin' Safari" as moonlight music?

A request was a request. He adjusted the controls on his keyboard to the same settings he'd used to produce what he thought of as the ethereal version of "Moonlight Sonata" then repeated the same few bars of "Surfin' Safari."

Beach Boys as played under the stars on a moonlit night. Somehow it worked.

Holy shit, it actually worked.

Elias finished running through the whacked-out version of

"Surfin' Safari," keeping it short. He would have played longer if he'd been singing, but this was definitely an instrumental only version.

The woman smiled, a radiant smile that lit up her entire face. "That was definitely something special," she said. "Thank you."

The old guy started to walk away. After a moment, the woman followed. She gave Elias another smile and a nod before she left.

The old guy? Tom? He never looked back at Elias at all.

31

BY NOON THE DAY HAD DEFINITELY WARMED UP. THE HEAVY MORNING fog had burned off, leaving the sky a gorgeous blue. Unusual for August, but Elias wasn't going to complain. Nice hot summer weather —hot by San Francisco standards anyway—brought crowds out to the Wharf.

He'd shucked his leather jacket shortly after eleven. He kept on his hat and his dark glasses which, he supposed, made him look cool. He might need to incorporate both into his everyday performances, given how much money he'd earned so far. His open guitar case had a nice stash of bills and a pile of coins, most of them quarters.

He'd even sold a couple of CDs, one to a middle-aged mom who was out for a day on the Wharf with a teenaged girl. They both stood and listened to his music for a good fifteen minutes before the mom dropped a five-dollar bill into his guitar case.

They'd actually started to walk away when the mom came back. She told him she'd just noticed he had CDs for sale, and she bought one without haggling over the price.

"We're only in town for the day," she said. "This"—she held up the CD—"will help me remember what a great day it was."

"I'm heading off to college next week," the girl said. "She gets maudlin."

The girl smiled at her mom, whose eyes had grown shiny bright with unshed tears.

Elias didn't know what to say to that. He and Lettie had never even thought about having kids.

"It doesn't take much," the mom said.

He thought the girl might give her mom a hug. If Lettie had been the kind of woman who teared up easily, he might have. But the girl just tugged at her mom's hand, said something about wanting to head back to the Pier, and off they went.

"She was giving her mom space to recover," someone else said.

Elias thought he recognized the voice. He turned to see the photographer he'd met at the end of the Pier the day before.

"Hey," he said, smiling at her while he tried to remember her name.

Stephanie? Was that it? Her business card was still in his jacket pocket, but his jacket was folded up and on the ground beneath his keyboard.

"Hey," the woman—Stephanie, he was sure her name was Stephanie—said.

She didn't have her camera slung around her neck. Today she was dressed like a tourist from the valley—scoop neck tee, jeans, tennis shoes, and a wide-brimmed hat. Her hair wasn't in a ponytail either, but hung loose around her shoulders.

She gestured toward her own face, making a circular motion with one finger.

"I like the new look," she said. "Fighting off this rare bit of San Francisco sunshine?"

He gave her a rueful grin. "Something like that."

He didn't want to tell her the real reason. She might understand, but something—ego maybe—made him want to keep that bit of information to himself. He hadn't expected to see her again, and now that he had, it seemed important that she didn't think he was someone who got beat up on a regular basis. Or even a semi-regular basis.

"I'm really not stalking you," she said. "I had an opportunity to shoot a band last night, so I stayed with a friend in the city. When the day turned out so beautiful, I had to take advantage."

"Of course you did," he said, his grin turning into something more genuine.

"And I saw you here again, and…."

She trailed off with a little shrug. And was that a bit of color rising in her cheeks? He thought it might be, but looking through his dark glasses made it difficult to tell.

He was pretty sure that she was trying to flirt with him. The first woman who'd flirted with him in a while, and here he looked like a racoon beneath his sunglasses. Timing, as someone somewhere had once said, was everything.

"So while you're here," he said, "do you have a request for this musician you're not stalking?"

He shifted on his stool to take a little tension off his aching back. He'd mostly been playing keyboards today, mainly because it hurt to turn and lift his guitar. At least the kinks in his voice seemed to have worked out the more he sang. He didn't even sound too nasally to himself when he sang, or even when he talked. Thank god for small favors.

She named a Gordon Lightfoot song that he'd played the day before. It was one of his guitar numbers, easy enough on his fingers and his voice.

He managed to pick up his guitar without a grunt or hiss of pain. He adjusted the volume for the guitar on his amp and strummed out the first chord.

She smiled at him. She kept smiling throughout the song, and when he was done, she clapped. A few other nearby people joined in.

That wasn't exactly a first, but most people—even the ones who stopped to listen—didn't applaud when he finished a song. If they liked it, they might throw a few dollars in his guitar case, but that was it.

"Thank you," she said. "I'm an old Gordon Lightfoot fan, and you did the song really well."

He nodded his thanks.

She stepped a little closer, so she could talk to him without the microphone in between them.

"Do you take a lunch break or anything?" she asked. "Maybe we could pick up a little something to eat. Stroll around for a bit. I mean, if you'd like to do something like that."

He hesitated. He was going to need help getting his equipment back to his car. Leon had already stopped by briefly to give him a bathroom break, but he'd said that was the one and only thing he could help out with today. Jack hadn't shown up for work, and Leon had to call in his daughter Jodi to cover.

"Can't leave her alone on the register for too long," he'd said. "She's not used to it."

Jodi was sixteen and was one of the lucky kids who'd never had to work a retail job. She was a graphic artist, and a fairly good one at that. Leon and his wife were giving her the time and space to work on her art instead of insisting that she get a part-time fast-food job like most of the kids she went to school with.

She only worked in the shop when Leon was in a bind. Elias guessed that he'd called his other part-time employees to cover for Jack when Jack didn't show up, but he hadn't been able to reach them. That explained why Leon was so late opening up the store.

Elias had frankly been relieved that he wouldn't have to face Jack today. Not when he looked and felt like somebody's punching bag.

"I don't take a lunch break," he told Stephanie. "But," he added before she had time to think he was brushing her off, "I only play until two. If you don't mind sticking around. Or coming back. We could grab a sandwich." He grinned. "Or an ice cream cone."

The one he'd had the day before at the Pier had been pretty good. Upscale ice cream, most likely. Way better than the bargain brand he bought at the grocery store whenever he had a yearning for fudge ripple.

"No shrimp cocktail?" she asked. The grin that lit up her face and put a twinkle in her eyes carried over to her teasing tone.

He almost shrugged but caught himself at the last moment. His back wouldn't appreciate the shrug.

And how would she feel if he kept his dark glasses on the whole time he was with her? The glasses just managed to cover the bruises around his eyes. One thing he knew about bruises was that they got worse before they got better. By the end of the day, the bruises—okay, they were black eyes, just admit it—might not fit behind the lenses of his glasses.

He supposed if things were going well after a sandwich or a couple of ice cream cones, he could fess up to what happened. He certainly didn't plan to lie about it.

"Shrimp cocktails aren't my favorite," he said. "Not after I smell fish for a few hours."

She chuckled. "I guess I can understand that."

She pulled a cell phone out of the pocket of her jeans. "Two o'clock, you said?" She tapped at the screen. "Just set myself an alarm for one-thirty so I'll have plenty of time to make it back."

She slipped the phone back in her pocket. Her jeans weren't designer, at least from what Elias remembered of the designer jeans Lettie used to wear, but they fit her slender form quite nicely.

"Guess I'll see you then," he said with a grin of his own.

"Play some good stuff while I'm gone," she said.

She gave him a little finger wave then she was off, blending in with the crowd headed toward the Pier.

Elias wanted to turn around and watch her, but she was headed in the opposite direction from the way he was sitting, and his back certainly wouldn't let him twist around like that.

Play something good, she'd said.

Well, he had his guitar on his lap and the amp was adjusted nicely. He started in on a simplified version of an old James Taylor song. It was an easy enough melody to wrap his voice around. The fact that he had a date—sort of—lent a smile to the up-tempo tune, and more than a few people slowed down to listen. Most of them dropped some money into his guitar case.

The day had started off shitty after a horrible night, but the afternoon was definitely looking up. He had a feeling Stephanie wouldn't mind helping him break down his equipment and haul it back to his car. After all, she had the kind of job that depended on the equipment she took with her.

He transitioned from the first James Taylor song to a second. Instead of people watching like he normally did, he let himself daydream a little about what the rest of the afternoon might hold.

He didn't notice the long-haired ginger cat dart across the street from the front of Leon's shop, deftly avoiding the cars stopped for the light. He didn't see the cat wind her way among the pedestrians and head toward the feeder road the delivery trucks used for the businesses at the Wharf and farther down the Bay toward the Pier.

Elias wasn't looking for cats today. Getting the crap beat out of him the night before had put the thought of cats out of his mind.

If he'd known what was going to happen, he might have paid more attention.

It had been a long time since he'd looked forward to spending time with a woman. Life could be weird, life could be bad. Then something good could happen out of the blue.

Stephanie just might be something good.

Elias couldn't wait to find out.

32

The old homeless man made his way slowly down the other side of Jefferson, heading toward Pier 39. Even though the day had turned warm, he had his woolen blanket wrapped around his bony shoulders. Beneath the blanket he was wearing his best dungarees and two of his cleanest T-shirts beneath his camo jacket. A navy watch cap covered what was left of his hair

The clothes had come from Goodwill. The well-worn boots that almost fit his feet, those he'd traded two fresh-made sandwiches from the shelter to a young vet said he wasn't going to need the boots anymore. The old man hadn't asked why.

The rest of his few worldly possessions were stuffed into the rickety shopping cart he was pushing down the street. An old sleeping bag. Another blanket. A rain poncho. A second pair of shoes. Dry socks and underwear with more fabric than holes.

The photograph of the first girl he'd ever kissed, that he carried in the inside pocket of his jacket.

He'd paid to have the photograph laminated, and then he'd wrapped it in clear plastic wrap. That kiss had been nearly sixty years ago. There'd been other kisses since then, but none had been that important.

The photograph was his most valuable thing. It was the only thing he still had from his former life. As far as the rest of the world was concerned—hell, as far as he would have been concerned twenty years ago before his life imploded—everything in the cart was trash. But the old man guarded his belongings jealously anyway. They were *his*, nobody else's. Even the shopping cart. He'd taken it so long ago that he figured he had squatter's rights.

As he passed the front of the T-shirt shop across the street from official entrance to the Wharf, he shot a glare toward the musician who was playing in spite of his injuries.

Would the musician feel the old man's jealousy?

He might. The old man's special friend had told him the musician was special as well. He was like the old man. A sensitive. Receptive to things most people never saw or heard or even dreamed existed.

He grumped to himself as he kept walking toward the Pier.

His friend, his special friend, was being careless. He couldn't control her, of course. He never could, not even when he'd thought she was just another young stray who lived in the park by his home. A mere mortal had no business even trying to control a creature like her. That had been a hard-earned lesson.

What he could do was try to protect her from herself. But he had to be careful about it. He had to be stealthy. He'd had years of practice not calling attention to himself.

In this city, he was just another member of a faceless, invisible population. People looked away from him. They didn't crowd him. They never stood next to him. He had an aura about him that had nothing to do with his clothes, his gaunt face and gap-toothed half smile, or the smell they imagined followed in his wake.

His aura was a gift from his special friend. It couldn't be seen, not even by the fortune tellers who claimed they could read such things. It only registered in the primitive part of the brain, where the fight or flight instinct was alive and well even in people long accustomed to the conveniences of modern life. People weren't exactly afraid of him. It was more like he was a non-entity, a space they filled in with their imaginations of what someone like him should look like. And smell like, for that matter.

For someone like him, the aura served as personal protection. Even dangerous people, like the muscle-bound asshole who'd battered the musician, left the old man alone.

His special friend had killed the muscle-bound asshole. She shouldn't have taken it that far. Her actions would draw the attention of the police. At least she'd had the good sense to kill him in a less than stellar neighborhood where violence wasn't unheard of.

At least she hadn't killed him near the Wharf.

But the asshole had worked at the Wharf. Sooner or later the police would come around and ask questions. They might even roust the homeless.

If they caught him unawares, if his aura wasn't strong enough, they might even force him to move on.

And what would she do then? She couldn't leave. This was her territory. From Fort Mason to well past Pier 39, and inland to Cow Hollow. Possibly beyond that, he didn't know. He'd never been that far himself, not since he'd lost the person he used to be after he accepted the reality of his special friend and her kin.

She couldn't leave her territory. She was one of its Guardians, she'd told him. She was charged with keeping her kin and all her kin's special people, like him, safe.

The old man knew what would happen if he was forced to leave her territory. He would have to leave her behind. It would be like cutting out his own heart. Would she feel the same?

He knew the answer to that too. She'd already selected someone to replace him.

The musician.

If the old man hadn't known before, he knew it now.

She was following the woman who'd flirted with the musician. Not to kill. No, the old man couldn't believe his special friend would kill the woman. Discourage her, perhaps. Hurt her. But kill her?

No, the old man's special friend wouldn't be that foolish, no matter how jealous she became of the special people who belonged to her. And she was a very, very jealous creature.

His mind skittered sideways. Even twenty years later, thinking about what she'd done hurt too much.

His special friend could be impulsive. Reckless. Determined. When he'd initially refused to believe what she was all those years ago, when he'd tried to seek help for what he believed were hallucinations or drug-induced flashbacks, she had driven away everyone in his life he'd loved. Everyone who'd tried to help him.

Even his wife.

That was a memory he wished he could forget.

All because he'd been kind enough to feed a stray cat who turned out to be so very much more than just a cat.

The musician had been touched, she said. Years ago, and he hadn't even realized it. Now that touch was coming to fruition. The old man wanted to make sure that no one else got caught up in the mess that was sure to follow.

He wheeled his cart down the busy street, head down, not making eye contact with anyone. His aura kept the people on the crowded sidewalk from bumping into him. The few who did manage to catch a glimpse of him gave him only a quick, furtive glance.

There but for the grace of God, and all that.

They didn't know that a god had already graced him, in a manner of speaking. Not any of the gods the people he shared the sidewalk with might worship, but an ancient god. The god his special friend called the Maker of All Things. He had witnessed the gift the Maker had given his special friend—the gift of shifting—and he believed. The aura that protected him had been another gift from the Maker, given to him because his special friend had interceded on his behalf.

The old man had kept the secret of his special friend's existence and those of her kin to himself for long years. He would take that secret to his grave.

A grave, he feared, that was not so distant in his future.

He was old now. His special friend had been alive far longer than any cat should and she was still considered young by the reckoning of her kin. But he was just a man. An old man. He felt the damp cold nights deep in his bones. Not even his sleeping bag and his blankets could ward off the chill. A hot cup of coffee in the morning warmed him now better than the finest Scotch ever had, but more mornings than not, coffee cramped up his stomach. Most food did.

Something was wrong with him deep inside. He should go to a free clinic, but if they put him in the hospital, he'd have to leave everything behind. He'd have to leave *her* behind. He couldn't do that.

If that meant he died sooner, so be it. He'd lived a long life. He'd been blessed by a creator he *knew* existed. That, if nothing else, was worth all the suffering he'd endured.

But while he still lived, he would do his best to protect his special friend—protect all her kin—from everyone.

Even themselves.

33

Elias started scanning the crowd for a glimpse of Stephanie a little after one-thirty.

The warm afternoon had done wonders for his back and his ribs. He was going to need a long, hot bath when he got home to keep his muscles from tensing up again, but for now the pain was manageable as long as he didn't make any sudden movements. He'd even managed to sing a few of his more enthusiastic songs, especially after he switched from his guitar back to his keyboard.

His head was another matter.

The dull headache was still a constant presence. The warmer the day got, the more his forehead hurt. He imagined that the sunshine beating down on him, a nice change to typical August weather in San Francisco, was making the bumps on his forehead and the back of his head swell beneath his hat. His hair was probably a sodden mess by now, but if he took his hat off to let his hair air out and relieve the pressure on his forehead, he might as well forget about hiding his bruises from the people who stopped to listen to his music.

Or from Stephanie.

He could just imagine what his bruises must look like by now. He hadn't been able to ice his face since he left the apartment that morn-

195

ing. His nose was slick with sweat, and he'd had to keep pushing his sunglasses back in place. He really wanted to take them off too and mop up all the sweat, but then he really would look like a poster boy for domestic abuse: *It happens to men too!*

People might slow down to look, like they'd slow down to get a look at an accident on the freeway, but facial deformities made people nervous. They wouldn't stop to listen to him play, and tips would dry up. So far the day's tips had made hauling his sorry ass down to the Wharf more than worth it. He didn't want to rock the proverbial boat.

Then there was Stephanie. She made the day worth it too.

Even if all they did was get a cup of coffee—or an ice cream cone—and wander around the Wharf, it would be worth it.

Who knew? She might even understand how he got the bruises. *If* he got up the courage to tell her. He'd have to spend a little more time with her first. Try to get a read on whether she'd be the understanding sort.

He ran through another song on his keyboard, a song originally made famous by someone in his parents' generation that had just been redone by a modern artist. He was willing to bet that most kids who heard the song on their streaming service of choice didn't know about the original version. He did the modern version, the one he'd heard yesterday when he'd been killing time eating an overpriced hotdog and doing his brand of market research.

And looking for cats. He'd almost forgotten that part. He wanted to forget about that part today.

Today was full of possibilities that *didn't* include magically growing and shrinking cats who could talk to him in his mind.

By one-fifty, Stephanie still hadn't shown up. She didn't strike him as someone who was habitually late, but then again, she had set the alarm on her phone a half hour ahead of their planned meeting. She might be one of those people who needed half a dozen alarms to make sure they got up in time in the morning.

Relax, he told himself. She'll be here.

Today's afternoon street performer was an artist who did amazing landscape paintings using masking tape, dots of paint, huge brushes like you'd use to paint a wall, and some kind of solvent.

Elias had watched him work before, fascinated by the way the man must see the world. He supposed it was similar to the way some musicians listened to an orchestra perform but really only heard the instrument the musician played. This artist must be able to break down a picture into its component parts and then figure out a way to put the components back together again.

Elias wasn't that kind of musician. When he listened to music, he could almost feel the whole thing flowing out his fingers, whether those fingers were on guitar strings or a piano keyboard. Once he got the original version down, only then did he add his own embellishments.

Playing by ear, his old piano teacher had said. It was a gift. His teacher had encouraged Elias to use that gift, but he'd also made Elias learn to sight-read sheet music. That had come in handy when he worked in the orchestra pit back in Vegas.

The street artist showed up at five minutes until two. He had all his supplies in a collapsable cart like the one Elias used for his gear. He stood off to the side listening to the last song Elias would play for the day, tapping his foot to the beat and bouncing a little, like he was gearing himself up for his performance. He wasn't wearing a hat, but he did have on a couple of layered T-shirts.

Elias finished his song right before two o'clock. Stephanie still hadn't shown up, but he needed to pack up his gear anyway. He'd have to take his time so he wouldn't overload his back, but the artist wouldn't mind. He was used to Elias packing up after his time on the corner was technically over. The artist always set up his own shop on the street side of the corner while Elias set up facing the food vendors on the Wharf.

It was a mutually beneficial arrangement. Elias got to play and hopefully collect more tips right up until two, and the artist got to set up shop closer to the sidewalk pedestrian traffic.

Technically street performers weren't supposed to block pedestrian walkways. *Interference with traffic patterns*, as the Port Authority's rules of operation for street performance called it, was against the rules. The artist's setup was so self-contained it hardly encroached at all on the sidewalk.

The artist unfolded his stool, opened the tackle box he used to store his paints and brushes, and placed a couple of pre-done canvasses on the ground next to the tackle box. The rest of the space in his wheeled cart was taken up by blank canvasses he'd paint during the afternoon.

He'd told Elias once that the pre-done canvasses drew the eyes of passersby. Actually watching him paint was what closed the deal.

"S'up?" he said with a nod at Elias's guitar case. "Looks like you had a good day."

Elias hadn't picked up the cash yet from the case. When he bent over—slowly—to pick up the cash, his sunglasses slid down his sweaty nose.

"Or maybe not such a good day," the artist said.

Crap.

Elias pushed the sunglasses back in place.

"Rough night," he said.

He stuffed the money in the pocket of his jeans. There had to be at least eighty dollars in tips, not counting the cash he'd already stuffed in his pocket for the sale of a couple of his CDs. Pretty decent haul for four hours' work. He could afford the ice cream cone or even a sandwich, and he'd still have money left over to put toward next month's rent.

"Anything I should know about?" the artist asked.

The man wasn't being intrusive. Street performers who didn't have companions to watch their backs, like Elias and this artist, looked out for each other when they could. That meant sharing information about dangerous areas around the Wharf or violent people to look out for.

"Got jumped in the garage behind the building across the street." Elias pointed at Leon's store. "I was there kind of late last night. Got distracted, wasn't paying attention to my surroundings."

That was an understatement. He'd been obsessing over the cats.

Which certainly hadn't seemed all that important today. Amazing how getting the crap beat out of you put your life in perspective. Impossibilities happened. Probably a million of them every day that he didn't know about. So acknowledge the one impossibility he'd seen and move on, unless he wanted to drive himself crazy.

Getting beat up? That made him realize how much he'd taken feeling good most days for granted. How lucky he'd been so far in his life, even with all the ups and downs. And the weird stuff.

"Hope they caught the asshole," the artist was saying. "And I thank you for the heads up about the garage. I usually walk past that thing, but I think I'll start taking a different route."

"Probably wouldn't hurt," Elias said. He certainly wouldn't be going anywhere near that garage for a while, especially not after dark.

He unplugged all the cables from his equipment, wound them up neatly, and proceeded to load his cart. He took it easy on himself. No need to hurry today. The artist was already busy putting the finishing touches on his first painting, a sailboat on the bay at sunset—a sunset without fog, of course—all set within a perfect circle on a square canvas. He'd attracted a few looky-loos, but Stephanie wasn't among them.

Elias pulled out his cell phone to check the time. Two-fifteen.

He didn't have a message. Well, of course, not. He hadn't given her his cell number.

But he did have hers. Her business card was still in the inside pocket of his jacket.

He took the card out and busied himself with putting her name and information into his phone's contact list. He didn't have a picture of her and he couldn't get a good shot of the Golden Gate bridge from here, so he settled for taking a picture of the sailboat painting the artist had just finished.

Once he got a good picture of the Golden Gate, he could use that for her instead of the sailboat painting. After all, that's how they'd met, when she'd been shooting photos of the Golden Gate.

He snorted at himself. Even after all this time, even after his marriage to Lettie had fallen apart, it seemed he was still an incurable romantic at heart. He enjoyed love songs from all eras. Those were his favorite songs to sing, not breakup or heartache songs.

Stephanie might turn out to be someone special, but even though he'd felt a connection with her, they weren't there yet. They might spend a little time together and realize they weren't right for each other. The fact that he was jumping the gun—that he knew he was jumping the gun and didn't care—drove home exactly how lonely he'd let himself become.

He had a roommate he'd spent more time talking with this morning than he had in months. He had a friendship of sorts with Leon. He had an ex-wife somewhere out in the world, and that was pretty much it.

Somehow he'd turned into one of those people who was friendly with lots of folks but had few true friends. When exactly had that happened?

And why?

Because he'd lost his heart to Lettie and decided, even if it wasn't a conscious decision, that he wasn't about to go through that again?

He'd had a few friends in Vegas. Most of them had been the other casino musicians he worked with. Sometimes they'd go catch shows in other casinos on their nights off so they could listen to the orchestras. Or they'd go to free concerts downtown at the Fremont Street Experience. On rare occasions they might go to a movie as a group.

One thing Elias had never done was go gambling. He worked too hard for his money. The idea of gambling any of it away never appealed to him.

One of his buddies, a saxophone player who was a good twenty years older than Elias, called the outings where they went to listen to other musicians "busman's holidays." Said he got it from his old man, a blue-collar assembly line worker who'd never driven a bus but took one to work six days a week.

The saxophone player had moved to Las Vegas ten years earlier to get a divorce from his wife. She'd stayed on the East Coast with the man's two young children. One night when he and Elias were walking back to where they'd parked their cars, Elias had asked him if he missed his kids.

"Oh yeah, sure," the man had said, "but they don't miss me. I'm just a paycheck they get in the mail."

Elias had given him a sideways look. "A paycheck?"

"Child support, alimony." The man had shrugged. "She kept telling me she didn't want to get married, even with the first kid on the way. After the second, when she told me she didn't love me and never really had, I finally believed her."

"So you came out here and stayed."

Elias had had his own reasons for moving to Vegas, and they'd all been about Lettie and her decision to go to culinary school. It seemed everyone he knew in Vegas had come there from somewhere else. Divorce was a pretty sad reason, but he supposed it wasn't all that unusual. From what he understood, getting a divorce in Nevada was pretty easy.

At the time, he hadn't thought much about exactly how easy it would be. Only later, after Lettie had him served with divorce papers, did he get firsthand experience.

The saxophone player had come to Vegas to get divorced. Elias's divorce was the reason he left.

At least he and Lettie never had kids. Elias wasn't just a paycheck for anybody. Lettie made more money than he did. The lawyer Elias hired to review the divorce papers had told him he had a good claim for alimony from Lettie, but Elias said no. Even though he knew it was going to kill him—she'd already broken his heart the night she moved out of their apartment—he wanted the divorce to be over and done with. He didn't want a knock-down, drag-out fight over alimony. He'd managed to save up a tidy nest egg from his regular orchestra job, and Lettie'd said she didn't want any of it.

She didn't want anything of his.

What he wanted was for her to love him the way he loved her, but that wasn't going to happen. She'd already moved on. Before the ink on the divorce decree was dry, he found out she was dating one of the facility managers at the casino where she was working in their upscale restaurant.

So with his heart in tatters, he'd moved away. He'd even given up music for a while, because music reminded him of the work he'd done while they'd been married. He brushed up his resume, took some night classes, and managed to land a job as an office dweeb.

He actually stayed at that job for two miserable years. He deliberately didn't make friends. He lived in a dirt-cheap apartment, sold his car, and took a city bus to and from work. He went back to eating cheap meals he fixed for himself. He never touched the money he'd saved up from Vegas. Most of the time he even forgot it was there.

The one thing he didn't do was sell his old guitar. He thought about it, actually had the wording of a *For Sale* ad worked out in his head, when a memory bubbled to the surface.

Playing guitar in the park in Vegas while a beautiful woman hummed along.

He hadn't thought of Tess in years.

She'd been the only woman he'd been attracted to while he'd been married. Would he have cheated on Lettie if Tess had given him half a chance? He liked to think that he wouldn't have, but he wasn't sure.

One thing he was sure about: he wasn't going to sell his guitar.

That had been the moment he started to come out of what had been a serious case of post-divorce depression. He never saw a shrink about it, but he didn't need to.

The best day of his entire tenure at his office dweeb job was the day he walked into his manager's office and handed in his resignation.

That was the last office job he'd had. He worked other odd jobs—bartending had been the best of them—while he brushed up on his musical skills. He earned enough in tips bartending to buy a decent keyboard, microphone, and amp.

When he thought he was good enough, he started going out for music gigs. He worked in backup bands at concerts. Performed as a one-man band at private parties, especially during the holiday season. He even worked for a cruise line for a time, although after a few cruises, he decided shipboard life wasn't his thing.

He'd worked other odd jobs here and there when the music gigs were few and far between. He managed to keep his head above water, no small feat. He moved from city to city, never staying more than a year or two in any one place. And while he wasn't exactly happy, he no longer suffered extended bouts of depression. Even when the money was tight.

Even when he learned that Lettie had gotten remarried.

Then one day out of the blue the saxophone player he'd been friends with in Vegas had called Elias to say he was getting married again. His new bride-to-be wanted an outdoor wedding overlooking the Golden Gate Bridge.

"Come if you're in the area," the man had told Elias. "It'll be a hoot and a half."

He'd been in a little town in southern Oregon at the time, playing guitar in a park near the town's summer season Shakespeare Festival. It wasn't a paid gig. He was just busking and living off the money he'd made at his last bartending job. Southern Oregon wasn't exactly in the neighborhood of San Francisco, and Elias's first instinct was to say no.

But there was something about the idea of setting foot in a park in San Francisco, with the Golden Gate in the background, that appealed to him. He sang songs about San Francisco. Tony Bennett's old standard was a frequent request when he played for private functions at places like the Elks Club or Rotary or any other gathering of folks nearing retirement age.

After he'd dreamed about the city for two nights in a row, he'd called his old buddy and said he'd be there.

Driving across the Golden Gate into the city had felt like coming home.

He'd lived there ever since.

34

Stephanie was not only late, she was seriously late.

By the time Elias finished packing up his equipment, the anticipation he'd felt most of the afternoon had faded. In its place, it left behind a kind of quiet disappointment that grew steadily worse.

He had to take his time breaking down his setup thanks to the steady ache in his back and ribs after he lifted his amp and the portable power supply into his cart. He even made two trips to his car since the artist agreed to watch Elias's stuff between trips. But that only took twenty minutes, then all he had to do was wait.

Elias should have been used to waiting. When you lived in the city like he did, traffic jams were just a part of life. Patience was a learned skill, and he'd gotten good at it.

He spent some time watching the artist work and trying not to scan the crowd every few seconds. The artist was fast, Elias had to give him that. Watching him create his paintings was like watching two speed chess players. He was good too. Elias was no art critic, and the styles he preferred ran toward delicate watercolors or hyper-realistic paintings that looked like photographs at first glance. Still, this guy had a knack for turning those dots of paint into a vivid, recognizable scene in just a few minutes.

Of course, as seen through Elias's dark glasses those vivid colors were muted, mere ghosts of their real colors. The muted colors seemed to match his mood, and he didn't need the reminder that he was pretty sure he was being stood up.

He contemplated buying a walkaway shrimp cocktail from one of the food stalls in the Wharf, but decided against it. He was still hoping that Stephanie would show. Shrimp cocktail followed by ice cream didn't sound appealing at all.

When his back demanded he sit down, he walked over to the pedestrian plaza in front of the parking lot. The plaza had a few concrete benches here and there, spots for weary travelers to take a load off their feet. The benches were nothing like the ones in the park in Vegas where he used to play. There were no trees in the pedestrian plaza, and no shade.

Elias had taken his jacket off a while ago. Instead of stowing it in the trunk of his car, he held onto it. If he ended up at the Pier, he'd probably need it. But right now the leather was slick with sweat from his hands, just like his forehead and the back of his neck were slick with sweat. His forehead was sore, and his headache had never totally gone away. Packing up his equipment hadn't helped.

He figured he'd give Stephanie another fifteen minutes, then he'd take himself home, take off the damn hat to give his head a break, and have a nice shower.

In the meantime, he actually found a place to sit on one of the benches in the plaza.

He could think of a million reasons why Stephanie might be late. The Wharf was crowded like it was most weekends during the summer. Not exactly wall-to-wall people, but pretty damn close. He imagined the Pier was worse. She could just be stuck somewhere.

But the later it got, the more he worried that something had happened to her. He supposed that would be his new normal now for a while. A side effect of getting the shit kicked out of him. Anytime anyone was late, he'd assume something bad had happened.

A seagull waddled over to stand in front of him, its head tilted to one side as it tried to decide if he was an easy mark. People weren't supposed to feed the gulls, but they still did, and the gulls were smart.

"Not today, my man," Elias said to the gull. "I've got your number, but I don't have anything for you to eat."

The gull squawked at him. When Elias didn't respond by tossing some food its way, the bird gave up on him and flew away.

He ended up giving Stephanie more than fifteen minutes. By the time his phone told him it was three o'clock, he decided to call her. Not to be pushy, he told himself. He was just concerned.

The call went straight to voicemail. He shouldn't have been surprised. A lot of people didn't answer calls that came from unknown numbers. He left her a voicemail to let her know the call had come from him. He stammered a bit, unsure of exactly what to say, and ended up telling her he hoped she was doing okay and did she want to reschedule?

Then he waited for a call back.

And waited.

By four o'clock it was more than clear that she wasn't coming. She hadn't even called him back. Ghosting him seemed like an odd thing to do if for no other reason than she made a living taking publicity shots. Just yesterday she'd solicited him, after a fashion, to hire her to take pictures of him performing.

He got up, gently stretched out his stiff back, and gave one more look around the Wharf. He'd thought about going to the Pier to look for her, but in this crowd they could pass each other and never know it. Now he wished he had gone to look for her. No doubt by now she was long gone.

He tried to tell himself not to be too disappointed. He'd been stood up before, and he probably would be again. He'd just thought she was different. That they'd had a kind of connection that could turn into something more.

He got in his car and left the parking lot.

Another car pulled into the spot he'd vacated, and a young couple got out, congratulating themselves for actually finding a parking spot on the Wharf this late on a Saturday afternoon. They left the parking lot holding hands, deftly avoiding a long-haired ginger cat that crossed their path.

"At least it wasn't black," the younger man said about the cat.

"No bad luck," his boyfriend said, and they both laughed.

No bad luck today.

At least, not for them.

35

THE LONG-HAIRED GINGER CAT IGNORED THE TWO MEN IN THE PARKING lot. They were no threat to her or anyone in her tribe. Most of the people on the Wharf weren't.

And the ones who were?

She took care of them. That was the duty the Maker of All Things had entrusted her with. To keep her tribe safe from whatever threatened them. To make sure her tribe not only survived but thrived. *All* members of her tribe.

Including the old man she'd adopted into her tribe when she'd been a youngling.

She'd revealed herself to him too soon, she knew that now. When she'd been a youngling, she hadn't known how fragile human minds could be.

Her kin accepted the world as it was. The ability to shift was just something all her kin were born with—Old Blood and New— although none of them were able to use that ability until they were old enough not to need constant care from their mothers. Once they became younglings, the adults in the tribe taught them how to shift. When to shift. When *not* to shift, and how to live among the humans in their world if the youngling so chose.

How was she supposed to know that humans were so very rigid in their thinking? That most of them refused to accept what their senses told them?

When she'd been a youngling, she'd lived among the part of her tribe who preferred to keep to their natural forms. She hadn't learned yet how humans perceived the world around them. She'd been too intent on learning how to become the Protector. Someday she would, she knew that. The Protector wouldn't have schooled her otherwise.

The Protector had to die in this city for the duty of Protector to pass to the ginger cat. She'd waited long years for the Protector to return, but now she was growing impatient. In recent months, she'd felt a shift inside herself. She'd grown stronger. Smarter, in both the ways of her tribe and the ways of humans. Shifting had become almost instantaneous.

Her time was almost here. She knew it in her bones. In the blood that flowed through her veins.

The old tom counseled patience. Counseled humility. Counseled caution.

She had been as patient, as cautious, as *humble* as her nature allowed. Hadn't she stayed by the old man after she'd inadvertently shattered his mind all those years ago? Helped him to regain as much of himself as he could? It had taken him so long, but still she'd stayed with him.

After he'd accepted his place in the world, she'd declared him of her tribe, a gift bestowed on relatively few humans throughout her kin's existence. She'd even implored the Maker of All Things to provide him with an aura of protection he could use whenever he chose to do so, and the Maker had answered her prayer.

The Maker couldn't help the old man now.

He was dying. She could smell it on his essence, the kind of rot that came from inside. She had smelled it on her mother, who'd been among the oldest of the New Blood in their tribe. The Maker hadn't healed her mother—the elders in the tribe said the Maker never healed the sick or brought the dead back to life—but instead had accepted her into the Great Meadow after her death.

There would be no Great Meadow for the dying old man.

The ginger cat tried to take that into account now. She should appreciate the old man while he was still with her. He'd always taken good care of her when she was in her natural form, sharing his meager food with her so that she wouldn't have to take time away from her duties to hunt. Remembering that helped to tamp down her anger now.

She had every right to be angry. The old man had done something unforgivable.

He'd interfered with her plans for the woman who'd been flirting with the musician.

For that, the ginger cat should have slashed his throat. Would have slashed his throat if his interference had turned out differently.

The woman who'd flirted with the musician was from Far Away. The ginger cat had smelled it in her essence. She couldn't risk that the woman would take the musician Far Away.

She'd smelled the scent of sexual attraction in the musician's essence while he talked to the woman from Far Away. The ginger cat knew what that meant. She'd also scented loneliness in his essence. It wouldn't take much for the musician to become entangled with the woman from Far Away, and that she couldn't allow.

The ginger cat had never begrudged the old man his occasional copulations. Some New Blood who had similar relationships even copulated with their humans while they were in their shifted human form. The ginger cat had never had, and she never would. Not even with the musician once he became fully hers.

He was already halfway there. His journey had started when she'd asked him to play music for her, and in response, he'd shared the music of his soul.

The sharing of soul music was so much more intense, so much more satisfying that mere physical copulation. The musician hadn't truly experienced that yet, but he would.

The ginger cat had shifted into her human form before the followed the woman from Far Away to the area of the waterfront the humans called Pier 39.

The humans were crowded together on the Pier, bumping and pushing against each other for position like the sea lions who jostled for spots on the floats in the Bay. The ginger cat planned to bump into the woman in just the right place and at the right moment. The woman was constantly checking her phone. Holding it out to take photographs.

If the bump occurred in an area where the railing at the edge of the Pier was weakest? Where the woman might drop her phone into the water and if the bump was hard enough, perhaps follow it herself? Surely someone would rescue the woman before she drowned.

And if they didn't? The ginger cat would have no regrets. She never did.

But the old man had caught her arm to stop her. She'd been so intent on following the woman from Far Away she hadn't sensed that the old man was using the Maker's gift of aura to follow *her*. He'd startled her enough that she'd nearly hissed at him.

"Don't," he'd told her. "It's too dangerous for you, after last night."

He never touched her unless she allowed it, and never while she was in this form. Her claws had come out, an instinctive response, and she had to make an effort to control herself.

He'd left his cart somewhere, something he never did. He was as possessive of that cart and the few things in it as she was of her tribe and her territory. He'd camouflaged himself with a bucket hat and a walking cane, not that he needed it.

"Let me," he said. "I'm old. I can get away with it."

He'd known what she'd planned. Her human form had flushed with a purely human emotion: embarrassment. In her natural form, she never experienced embarrassment. Exasperation, yes. And annoyance, but never embarrassment.

She'd yanked her arm away. "Do it well, then."

He had.

He'd tripped the woman from Far Away with his cane and managed to make it look like an accident. The wooden boards on the Pier where the woman had been walking were slick with water, and she fell hard. She dropped the phone she'd been holding. The old man, pretending to almost lose his balance as well, used his cane to knock the phone across the wet boards and into the Bay.

The woman had not followed her phone into the water. The ginger cat had been disappointed at first until the woman let out a sharp cry of pain when she tried to get up.

By this time the old man had vanished into the crowd. Even the ginger cat couldn't spot him. Thanks to his aura, none of the humans who'd seen what happened would be able to remember exactly what he'd looked like.

The ginger cat stayed behind to watch.

The woman from Far Away had injured herself in the fall. She held one arm gingerly against her body, and one of her feet was twisted at an odd angle. An employee from a nearby shop ran out to help her, but when he saw her foot, he told her to stay where she was.

The ginger cat had stayed a discrete distance behind, just another person in the crowd, continuing to watch until emergency personnel took the woman away on a stretcher.

The woman from Far Away wouldn't be meeting with the musician today. Perhaps not ever, but only time would tell. If the ginger cat needed to take more drastic measures, she would.

She'd left the Pier and found a place behind one of the buildings to shift into her natural form. She did it so quickly, in less than the blink of an eye, that even if some human had seen her, they would simply tell themselves they were imagining things. Humans believed what they wanted to believe. She'd experienced life in her human form enough by now to understand many things about humans she hadn't as a youngling.

She understood their loneliness. Their self-doubt. Their guilt over things they hadn't done, or worse—over things they had.

She felt none of these things. She was a Guardian and someday soon she would be the Protector.

She'd gone back to the Wharf and watched the musician from a sheltered spot between parked cars. She kept watching him until he finally got in his car and drove away.

He'd waited for the woman from Far Away for a long time. The ginger cat had scented his essence and tasted his disappointment. His resignation. His pain, both the pain in his body as well as in his mind when he finally accepted that the woman was not coming back.

The musician's physical pain angered the ginger cat, but she'd done what she could. The musician still lived. The muscle-bound man would never hurt the musician or anyone else again.

Had she exceeded her duty as a Guardian when she'd killed the muscle-bound man?

Old tom would argue that she had, but he was Old Blood. He corrected members of the tribe whose actions threatened the well-being of the tribe, but in her lifetime, never the humans who posed a threat.

"The Maker trusts us to use our gifts wisely," the Protector had told the ginger cat all those long years ago. "Always remember, what the Maker gives us, he can also take away."

The ginger cat had never known the Maker to take away any of her kin's ability to shift. Had never shortened any of her kin's long lives. Was what the Protector told her about the Maker true? Or had the Protector merely been trying to rein in a youngling's natural excitement at the possibilities the role of Protector would offer?

Had she exceeded her duties by killing the muscle-bound man? By allowing her human to injure the woman from Far Away?

The ginger cat growled at herself. Doubt was a human emotion and had no place in her life. She had never felt doubt before, not when she was in her natural form.

She loped away from the parking lot, deftly avoiding the two humans who exited their car. She needed to find the old man. She would need to correct his insolence, but after that, she wanted to feel his fingers run along the top of her spine. Perhaps she would even share a meal with him. He had been with her a long time, as humans counted their lifespans, and his life was drawing to a close. She would miss him when he died, but by then, the musician would have taken his place.

The musician had already seen her shift her form. Not into a human shape. No, he hadn't seen that. But he would, and soon enough. He'd already demonstrated that his mind could still function even knowing that the ginger cat was not the simple cat she appeared to be.

His mind would not shatter when she showed him her true self.

Once he became truly hers, they would sing and dance in the moonlight and make beautiful soul music together, and he would remain hers for the rest of his days.

36

A series of sharps rap on the apartment door woke Elias from a fitful nap.

He hadn't intended to fall asleep after he got home from the Wharf. He'd wanted to spend the afternoon with Stephanie, but that hadn't happened. He'd wasted a couple of hours waiting for her, and then another half hour wading through snarled traffic thanks to all the late summer weekenders heading home.

By the time he made it back to the apartment he shared with Jerry, his head was pounding. He took off his hat and threw it on his bed along with the sunglasses. He thought about taking a nice, cold shower, but his throbbing head convinced him he should try and alleviate that pain first. He grabbed the same old package of frozen corn, now hopelessly misshapen, rapped the package on the counter again to break up the mess, and held it against his forehead and the bridge of his nose.

He hissed when the cold hit his tender skin. He really should make himself something to eat but he didn't have the ambition. Instead he downed a couple of ibuprofen and stretched out on the couch in the apartment's small living room.

A few minutes later he was asleep.

It was still light outside when the pounding on his front door woke him from a disjointed dream of water and moonlight and music that wasn't quite music.

The apartment Elias shared with Jerry was on the second floor of a three-story walkup. The building had originally been another one of those houses built on San Francisco's famously steep hills that tourists thought looked so picturesque. In reality, the floors creaked, sometimes the pipes groaned when the hot water was turned on, and the walls had been repainted so often the interior doors, not to mention the windows, sometimes stuck.

Still, the owner of this particular building had tried to modernize it somewhat. The place had a security system that included cameras on the stairs, and one aimed at the building's front entrance. The door at the entrance locked automatically, and residents had to use a key to get in. Visitors had to be buzzed in.

The building only had three apartments, one on each floor. Elias hadn't heard anyone buzz their apartment, which meant either his upstairs or downstairs neighbor had let in whoever was knocking on his door.

Elias was in no mood for someone to just buzz in anybody who asked. Nothing like having the crap beat out of him to make him appreciate the little things in life, like a supposedly secure apartment.

Jerry hadn't answered the door, and apart from the knocking, the apartment was quiet. Which meant that Jerry wasn't home. They didn't check in with each other, and Elias had no idea where Jerry might have gone. For all Elias knew, Jerry had a date or maybe he'd gone out of town for the weekend.

Clearly the person at his door was a persistent sonofabitch. Elias sat up slowly, and the sodden bag of corn fell to the floor. He thought about rubbing the sleep from his eyes, then remembered that would be a horrible idea.

Napping on the couch hadn't done his back or his bruised ribs any favors. At least the pounding in his head had gone down to a dull ache.

He padded down the hallway to the front door and looked

through the peephole. Two men in suit jackets were standing in the narrow hallway on the other side of his door. Elias didn't recognize either of them.

"Yes?" he asked.

One of the men said Elias's full name loud enough to be heard through the closed door.

"Yes," he said again.

Both men held up badges to where Elias could see them through the peephole.

Cops? And not just street cops either. These two were in plain clothes, but their badges clearly identified them as members of the SFPD.

Elias studied the badges as best he could through the peephole. The badges looked legit, but how would he be able to tell if they weren't? He'd never been in trouble with the law. Every now and then he'd talked to a patrol officer, especially in Vegas, but it had been more along the lines of a *Hi, how're you doing?* conversation. No cop had ever come to see him at his home.

"Mr. Sandoval, we'd like to talk to you for a few minutes," one of the cops said. "Mind if we come in?"

What could he say to that? No? Not likely.

He unlocked the series of deadbolts on the door, then remembered how he must look. Well, there wasn't much he could do about it now.

He opened the door and stood back. The two cops came inside, giving the hallway the once over. Elias used their momentary distraction to run a hand through his hair and try to bring some of it down over his forehead.

"The living room's back that way," he said, gesturing toward the opposite end of the hall.

Both the cops were Elias's age or older. One of them turned to look at him. The cop was stoop-shouldered with long arms and large hands and clothes that hung loose on his frame. He had a large nose, heavy drooping earlobes, and thick fleshy lips. His skin was sallow, and Elias wondered if the man had been sick. Or was still sick and trying to hang onto his job long enough for his pension to kick in.

His eyes were still sharp though. He took in Elias's appearance but didn't react with surprise or concern or even suspicion. His neutral expression didn't change at all.

Would he be the good cop or the bad cop? Or was that just a fictional construct? Elias had a feeling he was about to find out.

The other cop reminded Elias of someone who'd been a lifelong gym rat. His shoulders were bulky beneath his suit, his neck thick and practically non-existent. He walked with the kind of grace only those in peak physical shape seemed to possess. Showgirls in Vegas had been in that kind of shape.

Elias thought about the story Jerry had told him that morning, the story about guy who'd been a great athlete in college until a freak accident had scrambled his brains. That guy might have looked like this cop in another twenty years or so if his luck hadn't been so incredibly bad. This cop had either survived whatever bouts of bad had come his way, or he hadn't yet had any. Which would make him incredibly lucky. Most people had at least a little bad in their lives.

Which made Elias think of Stephanie. Now that his bruised ego wasn't uppermost in his mind, he hoped nothing bad had happened to her.

Which brought him up short.

Had something bad happened to her? Was that why the cops were here? Had they listened to her phone and heard the message he'd left for her?

The cop with all the muscles stopped in front of the living room window at the back of the apartment. "Nice view," he said.

It really wasn't. The living room window overlooked the back of the building on the other side of the service alley that ran between the houses. The alley served as the access point to the building's partially below-ground garage—ground level on the downhill side, below ground on the uphill.

Although calling the space a garage was a stretch. It was really just a covered carport with no garage door.

Elias was pretty sure that from time to time some of the homeless camped out in the garage at night, but he'd never caught anyone in there. He'd never seen any leftover garbage, or worse—smelled the odor of urine. His upstairs neighbor threw out birdseed in the alley for the pigeons, but the birds never seemed to go inside the garage either.

Elias wasn't sure if he was supposed to respond to what the cop said. He decided it was best to be polite.

"It's not bad," he said. "We wouldn't be able to afford this place if we had a view of the Bay."

Bay view apartments this size went for twice the money. The amount they paid in rent was already exorbitant.

"True," the cop said, turning around. "Rents in this city price most people out of the city. I'm surprised a street performer can afford a place like this."

"Tips must be good," the other cop said. He wasn't looking out the window. He was staring at Elias.

They were fishing, but Elias wasn't sure what for. They already knew he performed at the Wharf. What else did they already know about him?

"I get by," he said. "But you're right. I couldn't afford this place on my own."

"We saw the second name downstairs," the cop with the muscles said. "What's he do, your roommate? It is a he, right?"

Now Elias looked back and forth between the two of them. He wanted to cross his arms over his chest, but he made himself keep his arms at his sides.

"He works downtown," Elias said. "In the financial district."

His forehead was alternating between aching and itching. He'd have to rummage through the freezer to see what else might be a good substitute for the bag of frozen corn. Right now, the combination of itch and hurt was making him impatient.

"Can I ask why you're here?" he said. "Why you're asking about Jerry?"

"We're just getting some background information," the sickly looking cop said. "I'm Detective Avrill. My partner's Detective Keiner. We're with the Bureau of Investigations. Strategic Investigations Unit." He gave a slight nod in Elias's direction. "Looks like you either took a tumble or somebody coldcocked you."

It had been a combination of both actually, but Elias wasn't going to say that. He didn't want to have to explain why he hadn't reported last night's attack.

"I fell," he said. "Turned out concrete's harder than my face."

"Huh," Detective Avrill said. "You fall around here?"

"In a parking garage," Elias said. "Down by the Wharf."

"Last night?" Detective Keiner asked. "After you left your friend Leon?"

Background information, my ass, Elias thought but didn't say.

"That's right," he said instead. "In the parking garage behind Leon's store."

He decided to offer up a little more information so the cops would think he wasn't holding anything back.

"I walked out with Leon after he locked up. He rides a motorcycle. That thing's noisy, and all that concrete in the garage makes it worse. I was on my way out of the garage and must have tripped over something. I don't remember seeing anything, but before I knew it, I was kissing the concrete."

"And he didn't stop to see how you were?" Keiner asked.

"He was already gone by then," Elias said. "I'm pretty sure he didn't see anything."

"But you did," Keiner said. "At least that's what you told Leon when you asked to see his store's security footage from that afternoon. You even hung around until he was ready to close just to ask him. He played all that footage for you, but you didn't see anything."

There wasn't really a question in there, so Elias didn't say anything. What the hell had these two cops been talking to Leon about anyway?

"What did you think you saw?" Avrill asked.

Elias tried to remember what he'd told Leon. Had he mentioned a shoplifter? Or just somebody suspicious hanging around the front of the store?

He started to reach for his forehead to rub the itch, then stopped himself. He was taking too long to respond to a simple question.

"Sorry," he said. "Headache."

He heaved in a breath, hoping that saying something about his headache, which was true by now, was enough to explain his hesitation.

"I just thought someone was messing around the front of the store," he said. "We keep an eye out for each other."

The two cops studied him for a moment. They might be trying to make him nervous, which was ridiculous. He was already nervous. He'd been nervous ever since he'd seen their badges at his front door. He hadn't done anything wrong, except for not reporting the attack, but that wasn't a crime.

"Yeah," Avrill said after a long moment of silence. "Bathroom breaks, discounts for referrals. Leon told us."

"How well do you know Jack?" Keiner asked.

The question came out of left field. Elias had a feeling that was on purpose.

He shrugged. The move sent a stab of pain through his back, but he didn't wince.

"He's Leon's employee," he said.

"You two get along?" Keiner asked.

Elias snorted. He couldn't help it. "He's an asshole who thinks I'm a freeloader, and he doesn't care that I know it."

"You ever have a run-in with him?" Keiner asked.

Was that how they thought he got the back eyes and the lump on his forehead? From Jack?

"Insults only," he said. "The guy outweighs me by a good fifty pounds or more."

Only that wasn't quite true. It hadn't been just insults yesterday. The memory of Jack slamming him up against the hallway outside the shop's bathroom came back in vivid detail.

That brought back the image of cats—huge cats—that shouldn't have been able to get that big, not in the space of a few seconds. A memory he'd managed to actually forget about for most of the day.

"So let me get this right," Keiner said. "You thought maybe you saw somebody messing around the front of Leon's store, and you what... hung around the Wharf all afternoon and into the night just to see if you'd been right? You didn't go tell him right after you got off work, so to speak? Didn't bother to walk across the street and tell your buddy Leon that someone might be ripping him off?"

Put that way, Elias could see how odd his behavior must look.

"Look," he said. "The shop was busy. Friday afternoons in the summer can get that way. Leon was down one employee. I didn't want to pull him away from the register to go in the back to see if the security cameras caught anything."

"Not even to tell him about a thief," Avrill said.

The two detectives were standing on opposite sides of the living room, Keiner still close to the window and Avrill by the hallway leading to the front of the apartment.

They were purposefully trying to throw off the rhythm of the conversation. Make him look back and forth between the two of them.

They weren't playing good cop/bad cop. They had a whole different game going on. Tennis as a metaphor for a police interrogation. He might not be in a little room down at their precinct, like on all those TV cop shows, but that didn't matter. He was still being interrogated.

Elias sighed. He was weary and sore, and his head was aching again from all the back and forth. Most of all, he was getting tired of being gamed.

"Jack was there all day," he said. "The guy said some really nasty things to me when I went to use the bathroom, and I just didn't want to have to deal with him again. So I hung around until I was sure he was off the clock. That's all."

"Huh," Avrill said. "You sure about that? Just insults?"

"Nothing a little more physical?" Keiner asked.

Avrill pointed at the back of his own head. "You've got a pretty good knot back there for someone who fell face first on the concrete," he said.

Elias almost winced. When he let the detectives into the apartment, Keiner had been walking ahead of him, but Avrill had brought up the rear. Elias had tried to finger-comb his hair over his forehead before he let the detectives in, but he'd forgotten about the bump on the back of his head. That bump had gone down a lot, but apparently not enough for a cop with sharp eyes.

"You sure Jack didn't give you a beating?" Keiner asked. "You're just afraid to tell us? Afraid of what he'll do if he gets really pissed off?"

Elias glanced at Avrill, but then he turned his attention back to Keiner. "I. Fell," he said, unable to stop himself from enunciating each word succinctly. If the detectives were trying to annoy him, they were doing a pretty good job. "As for Jack, you've seen that guy. He insults me. I let him. Would you really want to piss him off?"

Well, Keiner might actually be able to take Jack one-on-one. Avrill? Not so much.

So Elias turned to Avrill. "What about you? If you weren't a cop, if you were just somebody like me, would you want Jack angry at you?"

If Elias had expected a crack in Avrill's neutral expression, he didn't get it. Instead Avrill said, "Kind of a moot point now."

Elias blinked. "What?" He looked at Keiner. "First you were asking about Jerry, now you're asking about Jack. Care to tell me why?"

He expected Keiner to answer. The ball was in his court, after all. But it was Avrill who responded to Elias's question.

"Because Jack Driscoll's dead," he said.

37

JACK WAS DEAD.

Now Elias understood why two SFPD detectives were at his apartment asking him questions.

He and Jack had a contentious history. The cops wouldn't be here if Jack had just died in his sleep. No, he'd died under... what did cops call it? Suspicious circumstances?

Did the detectives suspect he had anything to do with it? That he'd gotten two black eyes and the bruise on his forehead because he'd actually been stupid enough to get into a fight with Jack? And then had—somehow—managed to kill the man?

Elias felt his legs start to go out from beneath him. He lowered himself to the couch before he fell down. There was a puddle of condensation from the bag of corn on the floor. He really should mop that up. He hoped he had a chance to mop it up. He hoped that the cops—these two detectives—wouldn't decide to take him to the precinct and book him for killing Jack.

But he hadn't done anything!

"He's dead?" he asked. "How? When?"

"So you didn't see him in the shop last night?" Detective Arvill asked instead of answering Elias's question. "Hanging around anywhere?"

"No." Elias made himself look the detective in the eyes. In his tired but somehow still sharp eyes. "The last time I saw Jack yesterday...."

He trailed off, realizing that there was no way he could tell the detectives why Jack had sculked back into the store from the front after Elias had left.

Again, he'd paused too long. There was no way the detectives wouldn't pick up on it. Not these two.

"I saw him go back in the store through the front," he said, deciding to stick to as much of the truth as he could. "After I went back to work. I saw him outside the store, hanging around the corner until after Leon went inside."

The detectives shared a look.

"You mean he wasn't in the store when you left after you used the bathroom?" Keiner asked.

"I didn't see him," Elias said. At least that was the truth.

"So he left the store while you were in the bathroom?" Avrill said. "You, someone he called a freeloader. You expect us to believe he left you alone in the store?"

Elias shrugged one shoulder, the one on the side of his back that didn't hurt as much.

"That's what happened," he said.

"And he didn't tell you he was leaving," Avrill said. "Didn't ask you hang on a minute, that he had something to do outside."

"No."

"You see anybody else with him?" Keiner asked. "While he was outside?"

"What, like he'd been meeting someone?" Elias asked.

This time Keiner shrugged, but he didn't clarify the question.

"He was smoking a cigarette," Elias said. "That's all I saw."

That was the truth too, as far as it went. Jack had left to get the fuck *away* from someone. Some*thing* that had scared the crap out of him.

"Do you really think I had something to do with this?" Elias asked. "Can you tell me that? Because if you think I...." He had to stop and clear his throat. "Are you going to read me my rights or something? Am I going to need a lawyer?"

Not that he could afford a lawyer. Not even if he dug into his savings. But if they were going to charge him with murder, he'd have no choice but to spend whatever it took to hire a good enough lawyer to convince a judge that he had nothing to do with Jack's death.

The two detectives shared another look, then Avrill shrugged.

"We're not going to charge you," Keiner said. "This is an ongoing investigation. All we can tell you is that Jack was killed last night. We're talking with everyone we know of who might have seen him yesterday. Your name came up."

Elias should have felt relieved. He wasn't being charged. They were just here fishing for information. But he still had a tight ball of dread in his belly. Jack was dead, and Elias couldn't tell these two detectives everything he knew. If he wasn't careful, they'd know he was holding something back.

"So just to get this straight," Avrill said. "You came out of the bathroom, and Jack wasn't in the store. Anybody else in the store?"

"No," Elias said.

"You sure? Nobody browsing around? Isn't that unusual on a busy Friday?"

The cats had been in the store, but Elias wasn't about to mention that. "Not that I saw."

"But you noticed Jack wasn't there," Avrill said.

"He's hard to miss," Elias said.

Or he had been.

The detectives shared another look. Neither one of them shrugged this time. Elias wondered how long they'd been partnered together. They seemed to have the kind of unspoken conversations like people who'd been married for a long time sometimes had. He'd never gotten there with Lettie. Never synced up enough with her to know exactly what she was going to say. He'd wanted to. They just never got that far.

"Okay," Keiner said. "We just have a couple more questions, then we'll be out of your hair. I'm going to describe a woman. We want to know if you've seen anyone like her hanging around the Wharf. Or in Leon's store."

Elias started to ask them if they understood just how many people he saw on the Wharf every day, especially on a busy Friday in August, but Keiner held up a hand to stop him.

"We realize this might be like asking if you've seen a particular needle in a very large haystack," Keiner said. "Just do your best."

He then went on to describe the woman with the golden-green eyes and thick, luxurious hair the color of one of those rare, fog-free San Francisco sunsets. The one who'd thanked him for playing her song after he'd played "Moonlight Sonata" on a whim.

Keiner described her right down to the clothes she'd been wearing.

Elias couldn't have hidden his reaction if he'd tried. These two detectives were sharp, and to say he wasn't at his best was an understatement.

"You think she had something to do with it?" he asked.

"Let's say she's a person of interest and leave it at that," Avrill said. "I'm guessing you've seen her."

Elias could lie, but he didn't want to. Not about this. Not if she was involved somehow with Jack's death.

"Yeah," he said. "Earlier this week, I think it was Tuesday. I saw someone like the woman you just described."

The two detectives perked up.

"You sure it was Tuesday?" Avrill asked.

Elias nodded. "I don't play on Mondays, and it was the day after my day off. In the morning."

The same morning he'd seen the ginger cat for the first time. The ginger cat that had seemed to be listening to his music.

"And you noticed her," Avrill said. "You sure?"

"There weren't a lot of people on the Wharf yet," Elias said. "She was hard to miss."

That part was certainly true.

"What was she doing?" Avrill asked.

"She thanked me for playing a song," Elias said. *Her* song, but Elias didn't mention that.

"Then what?" Avrill asked.

Elias shrugged with one shoulder again. "She left."

"Where was she headed, did you see?" That question was from Keiner.

"Toward the fish markets," Elias said.

"Did she go into Leon's store?" Keiner asked.

Had she? Elias didn't know, and he told them that. "I lost sight of her," he said. Also true.

"You ever see her anywhere near Jack?" Avrill asked.

"No."

"And you don't know her name or anything about her," Keiner said.

It wasn't really a question, but Elias answered no anyway.

The two detectives hadn't taken any notes. Elias wondered if one of them had been recording the conversation on a cell phone. Weren't cops supposed to tell you if they were recording you? Or was that just something they did during a formal interrogation, after they'd read you your rights?

Avrill reached into the pocket of his suit jacket, and Elias expected him to actually pull out a cell phone and stop the recording. Instead he pulled out a business card and held it out to Elias.

Elias took it. The card gave Avrill's full name along with two phone numbers. One was a number for the Strategic Investigations Unit. The other was a handwritten number for Avrill's cell.

"You see her again," Avrill said, "you call me. We just want to talk to her like we've been talking to you. That's all."

"Should I give her your number?" Elias asked.

"No," Avrill said. "Just call me."

Elias started to put the card in the back pocket of his jeans, but even just starting to reach around made him wince. This time he didn't try to hide it.

"You been to the doctor?" Avrill glanced at Elias's back. "You look like your face didn't take the worst of it."

"No," Elias said. "I'm fine. Just a little bruised up. Probably shouldn't have taken a nap on the couch. The older I get, the more my body barks at me when I do stupid stuff like that."

"Tell me about it," Avrill said. "Just take care of yourself. Before you know it, little problems can turn into big ones."

Was that what had happened to Avrill? He'd ignored a little health problem, and it had turned into a big one? A problem that made him lose so much weight his clothes looked like they belonged to much bigger big brother?

"I'll keep that in mind," Elias said.

It was pretty clear the detectives were done with him. Elias levered himself up off the couch and walked them to the apartment's front door.

Keiner went into the short hallway outside the apartment without another word, but Avrill turned to look at Elias once more.

"Call me," Avrill said. "If you see that woman, call me. Don't try to be cute and do any detective work yourself. That's what the city pays us for."

"You think she's dangerous?" Elias asked.

How could a woman who walked around the Wharf barefoot be dangerous?

Avrill gave him a long look, like he was trying to decide what he could and could not say.

That's when Keiner turned around. "One more thing," he said. "You or your roommate own any pets? Say like a dog? A big one?"

Elias was tempted to ask the detective if he'd seen any pets in the apartment but thought better of it. They'd ended the interview on a more congenial note, and he wanted to keep it that way.

"No pets allowed," he said. "The guy upstairs feeds the pigeons out back, but that's about it. Why?"

"No reason," Keiner said.

But Elias had the feeling Keiner didn't say anything for no reason.

Avrill told Elias once more to call him if he saw the woman, then the two detectives went down the stairs, Keiner with an easy grace, Arvill following behind, his tread far less light.

Elias still held Avrill's business card in his hand. The card felt thick and heavy, which was ridiculous. It was just a business card. The kind of thing that professionals like his roommate Jerry collected for leads and most other people just threw away.

Elias could throw this one away too, but he knew he wouldn't.

Jack was dead. He must have died badly. Elias couldn't imagine him going down easy, not someone like Jack.

Unless he'd been shot. A bullet would take down someone Jack's size just as easy as it would any other victim of gun violence.

But that hadn't been the vibe Elias had gotten from the detectives. They hadn't asked Elias if he owned any guns. Wouldn't they have asked that if Jack had been shot?

No, Keiner had asked him if he had any *pets*. Like a big dog.

Or a huge fucking *cat*?

Elias actually felt the blood leave his face at the thought. If he didn't sit down, he was going to fall down, this time for real.

The kitchen was closer than the living room. He barely managed to make it to one of the chairs at their small kitchen table.

He would have leaned over and put his head between his knees but his back still hurt too much. He settled for resting his head on his arms on the table and breathing in slow, steady breaths.

His mom used to watch an old TV cop show late at night on a cable channel Elias had never heard of. This had been after his dad had been killed by a drunk driver and his mom had trouble sleeping, as much from missing his dad as from the pain of her own injuries. He'd actually watched a couple of episodes with her when he'd gone over to visit and help her out around the house.

He couldn't remember the name of the show now—that had been a lot of years ago—but it featured a detective everyone thought was a bumbling fool but who was actually pretty damn good at his job. That detective always had just one more question on his way out the door. Most of the time that question cut to the heart of the investigation. What's more, since the audience knew who'd committed the crime from the get-go, the fun—according to Elias's mom—was watching that bumbling detective trip the bad guy up with that one last question that would solve the whole case.

Keiner had just done that to Elias.

Not that Elias was the bad guy. Elias knew he wasn't, and he was pretty sure Avrill at least also knew Elias had nothing to do with Jack's death. But Keiner had asked the question about pets—about a *big dog*—not as an afterthought, but because he wanted to trip Elias up on the off-chance Elias had something to hide.

Something that cut to the heart of their investigation.

Jack hadn't been shot.

Jack had been mauled to death by an animal. A *big* animal. One with sharp teeth and claws. That one question was as good as showing him pictures of the crime scene, wherever the hell that was.

Elias definitely had something to hide about big animals with sharp teeth. A cat big enough to kill a person if it wanted to. Elias had seen two cats who were fully capable of doing that, and those cats had been pissed the hell off at Jack.

Had they actually *killed* him?

Just because he'd pinned Elias to the wall in the hallway and threatened to break his fingers?

No, that couldn't be right.

And what did the woman have to do with anything? Did the detective think *she* owned animals capable of killing a person?

Which led to another question: Did she own the cats?

The ginger cat had been watching Elias play, had seemed to actually be listening to his music, and the next thing he knew, the woman had shown up and thanked him for playing *her* song. Did she play that song herself for the cat?

But he hadn't seen her across the street with the cat. He would have remembered that.

He didn't like the way his thoughts were headed. If this woman controlled at least one cat that could suddenly grow bigger than any cat had a right to be and then *order* that cat to hurt someone—to freaking *kill* someone—that was something Elias wanted no part of.

And what about the other cat? The one with the short white fur and dark markings? Did the woman with the golden-green eyes have something to do with that cat too? The ginger cat and the white-haired cat had threatened Jack together. Had they killed him together?

When he felt like he could sit upright without passing out, Elias leaned back in the kitchen chair. He was still holding the detective's business card.

He took out his cell phone and added the detective's information into his contacts list. When Avrill had first asked Elias to call him if he saw the woman again, Elias hadn't decided whether he would or not. He'd been somewhat attracted to her although he hadn't given her much thought since he'd met Stephanie. Now? You bet your life he'd call Avrill if he saw that woman again. Let the detectives sort it out. Like they'd said, it was their job.

When he was done with Avrill's information, he scrolled down his contacts list to Stephanie's name. He thought about calling her again just to see if she was okay. But they really didn't know each other. They'd made vague plans for the afternoon, but those plans had fallen through for some reason. He might never know what that reason was. If he was really curious, he could check out her business website then check it again in a few days to see if she'd posted anything new.

He thought about just deleting her contact information. He still had her business card in his jacket pocket. He didn't need to see her name every time he opened his contacts list.

In the end he just clicked off his phone and put it back in his pocket. Something normal in a day that had gone so sideways he felt like he'd fallen off the map.

There were cats in this world that could grow and shrink in the blink of an eye.

Jack was dead, more than likely mauled to death by a big animal.

A woman he'd met at the Wharf might own (and control?) cats capable of not only changing size but of killing a person.

Stephanie had stood him up.

He didn't want to think about any of that. He wanted a nice long shower, something to eat, and then he wanted to sleep for about a year.

He wanted to wake up tomorrow morning, look in the mirror, and not see a raccoon version of himself looking back. He wanted his back not to hurt, the day to dawn sunny and warm, and to go back to the world he thought he'd always understood. Most of all, he wanted to never see that woman or those cats again.

He thought the only three things he could really count on were the shower, food, and sleep. Anything else on his want list would be pure gravy.

38

When Elias arrived at the Wharf on Sunday morning, an old homeless man wrapped in a worn woolen blanket sat on the concrete bench in the pedestrian plaza closest to Elias's corner spot.

Elias had decided to get to the Wharf a little earlier than normal to give himself some extra time to get his equipment from the car and get set up. He'd slept well the night before, surprisingly enough considering everything that had happened. Whether from physical or mental exhaustion, he'd slept a solid nine hours. While he hadn't woken up refreshed and raring to go, an old expression of his father's, he did feel better than he had yesterday.

He didn't *look* much better. The bruises beneath his eyes had taken on more of a deep purple hue, along with the knot on his forehead. Sunglasses and hat again today, check.

At least the swelling in his nose had gone down. He could almost breath like normal, and he'd sounded like himself when he'd worked out the kinks in his voice during the drive to the Wharf. With any luck, that might last through the day.

His ribs and his back were still pretty sore. He'd never pissed blood, a good sign, and since he couldn't twist around enough to get a good look at his back, he had no idea how bad the bruises were back there. His ribs still looked like a child had fingerpainted his skin with a variety of purple and sickly greenish-yellow paints.

If he'd been the kind of kid who got in fights all the time, he might have been used to recovering from injuries like this. Now he was just too damn old to get into fights. Not that he'd started this one. Sure, he'd mouthed off to Jack, definitely not a wise move. But that had nothing to do with the beating Elias had taken. How could it? Elias wasn't exactly in the habit of hanging around the Wharf after dark. Even as stupid mean as Jack could be, he wouldn't have waited in the garage just on the off chance he'd run into Elias.

Now that Jack was dead, Elias would never know.

The thought of Jack made him glance across the street at Leon's shop. The roll-up doors were still down. Not all that unusual, given that Elias was early, and Leon didn't open until ten. Still, those closed doors gave Elias an eerie feeling.

He'd never known anyone before who'd been murdered. The detectives hadn't come right out and said murder, but it wasn't all that difficult to read between the lines.

He wondered what the detectives had told Leon. Had they given Leon any more information about how the man had died than they'd given him? Probably not, but still....

Curiosity was part of human nature. As much as Elias wanted to put all the weirdness out of his mind, he couldn't help but wonder what had happened to Jack. The man had intimidated the hell out of him, and not just because he'd thought Jack had more than a smidgen of a criminal streak. Of course, the muscles and the tattoos and all the right-wing bullshit Jack had spouted to those he'd perceived as like-minded customers—Elias had heard him a time or two—didn't help. Still, Jack had been a hardass. Elias couldn't imagine anything, even a wild animal, getting the better of him.

"Get a grip," he muttered to himself.

Too much morbid curiosity wasn't good for anyone. It especially wouldn't be good for him today. If he gave himself half a chance, he'd be thinking about what happened to Jack all damn day. The detectives had told him to stay out of it, and he planned to do just that.

Elias maneuvered his cart around a rusty old shopping cart parked next to the old homeless guy. The thing was overflowing with what looked like all the old guy's worldly possessions.

Like most city dwellers, Elias usually avoided eye contact with the homeless who camped out in the city. There weren't many around the Wharf, not during the day, and certainly not in the areas where tourists might spot them. This early on a Sunday morning, the tourists hadn't invaded yet. Most of the people Elias had seen so far were service people heading to work or runners out for a morning jog.

The day had turned out beautiful, the early morning fog already gone. Maybe that's why the old guy decided to hang out by the water. Just because someone was homeless didn't mean they couldn't appreciate the beauty of this part of the city.

Later though, if the old guy was still around, one of the cops who patrolled the streets would roust him and make him move. The city had an image it wanted to project to the tourists, and the homeless didn't fit that image.

The old guy grunted as Elias passed him.

Was that on purpose? More than a few homeless people he'd run across on the street talked to themselves. Hell, they shouted at the world in general or walked around muttering to people only they could see.

Elias turned around to find the old guy looking at him. His eyes were faded and his face was gaunt, really gaunt. Even for someone who was obviously living on the street, the old guy was exceptionally skinny, but he certainly seemed all there.

Elias gave the old guy a nod and a fleeting grin before he went back to wheeling his cart to his spot.

Then he stopped.

How many times had he come close to being homeless himself?

If he hadn't had all those steady gigs—the casino jobs in Vegas, the office jobs he'd hated—he'd be living hand-to-mouth with no nest egg to rely on when times were rough. Busking on the street didn't exactly produce a steady income. And here he was, wheeling a cart that held most of the things that were important to him in this world.

What was that old saying? There but for the grace of God....

He turned back to the old guy. "Would you like a cup of coffee?" he asked.

He'd brought his usual thermos of black coffee, and he had his water bottle too. It wouldn't be a hardship for him to offer this man some coffee. Elias had spotted a cup on the top of the old guy's shopping cart, one of the refillable jobs with a faded logo from a local coffee shop on the side. Elias didn't want to think where the man had gotten the cup or whether it was clean. He could pour some coffee from his thermos into the cup without touching it.

The old man cocked his head to one side. "Offering to break bread with me," he said.

His voice was raspy, like he didn't use it often, but it had a certain genteel quality. It made Elias wonder what the old guy's life had been like before.

He clearly wasn't one of the great unwashed, as Jack had said more than once. Sure, the man's face was little more than thin skin stretched over bones, but that skin was as clean as Elias's own. The old man's silvery beard wasn't long and unkempt, just a little too long to be fashionably scruffy. His hair was clean, at least what Elias could see of it poking out from beneath a ratty watch cap that might have been brown, might have been dark blue—it was hard to tell, just like it was hard to tell what color his blanket had originally been—but the man himself was far more put together than his circumstances implied.

"No bread, just coffee," Elias said. "Nothing fancy, just a cheap grocery store blend, but I made it fresh this morning and it's hot."

The old man inclined his head. "You are a scholar and a gentleman," he said. "I accept."

He had a walking cane in his shopping cart, but he rose from the concrete bench with more ease than Elias would have expected. Hell, Elias used to get stiff sitting on a concrete bench when he played his guitar in that long-ago Vegas park, and those benches had been more than a bit on the warm side. He knew from experience that this early in the morning the benches in the pedestrian plaza were cold and damp. Cold like that seeped into your bones. Especially if you'd been sitting on one for a while.

The old man retrieved the cup from his shopping cart, and Elias uncapped his thermos. He poured steaming coffee into the old man's cup, then half-filled the thermos's lid for himself.

The old man took a sip, then sighed as he smiled. "My compliments to your grocery store blend," he said. "And your skill brewing it."

Elias acknowledged the compliment with a nod, but he didn't say anything.

Instead he squinted out toward the Bay. The tour boats were docked at the pier, ready and waiting for this day's onslaught of tourists anxious to go out on the water. Elias's stint on the cruise line ships, relatively short as it was, had robbed him of any desire to ever voluntarily get on a boat again.

A few seagulls were out and about in the still mostly empty parking lot, looking for scraps. The sound of a boat engine revving up in one of the marinas competed with the squawking gulls and the few cars passing by on Jefferson. Early Sunday morning at the Wharf. It actually was quite pleasant. He could see why the old guy might have decided to stop here for a while.

He took a sip from the thermos lid. His mom had always packed him lunches when he was little. He'd had a Scooby Doo metal lunchbox complete with matching thermos. Of course, there wasn't coffee in his thermos back then, just milk. Sometimes on Fridays she'd mix in a dollop of chocolate syrup for a treat.

The memory made him smile.

The old guy must have noticed. "I would give you a penny for your thoughts," he said. "But as you can see...." He shrugged. "Pennies in our line of work are precious and not to be wasted on daydreams."

Elias started to lift an eyebrow at the "our" but stopped when it pulled at the tight skin around his eyes, reminding him why he was wearing sunglasses at this early hour.

"What line of work would that be?" he asked.

"We're the watchers," the old guy said.

Elias was about to protest that he was a musician, not a watcher (whatever that was), but the old guy held up a gnarled finger.

"You're a people watcher," the old man said. "I would hazard to say that you're very good at it, whether you realize it or not. You play for tips, and tips are only given by happy people. You have to make an educated guess what to play to make them happy. We can only make truly educated guesses based on our observations."

Elias blinked behind his dark glasses.

Wasn't that what he did? Tried to guess what type of music someone who stopped to listen to him—or rarer still, who stopped to talk to him—might want to hear? He'd just never thought of himself as... what... a professional people watcher?

"That's fair," he said. "So do you do the same thing? People watch?"

The old guy hesitated just long enough for Elias to notice. "After a fashion," he finally said. "I also watch other things. Watch out for other things. As best I can."

He finished off the coffee with one long swallow and put the empty cup back in his shopping cart. When he grabbed the cracked plastic handle, Elias noticed what looked like angry scratches on the back of the old guy's hand. Before Elias could suggest that he might want to put something on those scratches—Elias was pretty sure Leon had a first aid kit in his shop—the old man started to push the cart away. The wheels on the cart squealed in protest.

He was leaving, just like that.

Elias shrugged. He supposed that after living on the street, the old guy had lost some of his people skills. Not everyone said goodbye when they left.

He went back to wheeling his own cart toward his corner spot when the old man called after him.

"It would behoove you to do the same, young man," the old guy said.

Elias had no idea what that meant. "To do what?" he asked.

"To watch *out*," the old guy said. "For other things. The ones that aren't just people."

Elias's heart skipped a beat.

The old guy hadn't said to watch out for things that aren't people. He'd said to watch out for things that aren't *just* people.

"What do you mean?" Elias asked. "*What do you mean?*"

But the old guy was waving him off, hurrying away with his cart toward the feeder road that ran behind the shops on the Wharf. The old guy's shoulders were hunched forward, the cart squealing and rattling in protest.

Elias tried to shake off the chill that was running down his spine. The old guy might have sounded normal, might have even looked semi-normal, but clearly he had a screw loose somewhere in his head. People were people. Things were things. Even impossible things like cats that could grow and shrink in the space between heartbeats were still just *things,* not people.

Right?

Two joggers ran past him, huffing out breaths as they skimmed along the concrete sidewalk with jogging shoes that probably cost more than Elias made busking in a good week. Elias hadn't seen them coming—damn dark glasses—and they'd startled him more than they should have.

Some watcher he was.

He poured the rest of his coffee back into his thermos to save for later. It was time to set up his equipment and get ready for what he hoped would be a busy Sunday.

The old guy was just crazy, that was all. He'd had a lucid moment or two, then he'd slipped back into some paranoid world of his own making where normal-looking people were really monsters underneath. He'd probably read too much Lovecraft or Poe when he'd been a kid. Seen one too many horror movies before his life imploded.

Elias tried to shake off the mood by concentrating on setting up his equipment. He ran through a series of very quiet sound checks since it wasn't quite time for him to officially start playing yet. When he heard the rollup doors at the front of Leon's shop go up, he turned on his stool and waved, expecting Leon. But it was his daughter Jodi instead.

Of course, Leon would have to bring in Jodi today. Leon was down one employee—permanently.

Jodi waved back, then disappeared into the shop.

The alarm on Elias's cell phone went off, telling him it was his official start time. He decided to start off with one of the soft rock songs in his repertoire. The first of the tourists were showing up, and there was a short line of cars waiting to get into the parking lot. Less than a half hour from now all the spots would be taken and the plaza would be teeming with people.

Just another normal Sunday at the Wharf.

Another normal day of people watching and hopefully people pleasing. Nothing out of the ordinary to see. He didn't even catch a glimpse of any cats.

But the entire time he was playing, he couldn't shake a tight feeling along his spine that had nothing to do with his still-healing injuries. No, this was a feeling anyone who made a living out on the streets knew well. A feeling anyone who'd been bullied as a kid developed as a self-defense mechanism to avoid the first blow. A feeling that only the unwise ignored, even when there was no good reason for it.

The feeling of being watched.

39

The long-haired ginger cat who wasn't really a cat watched the old man talking to the musician. Watched with approval when the musician shared his coffee with the old man. Generosity was an admirable trait in a human. It only served to convince her that she'd chosen her next companion well.

The old tom thought she was foolish for choosing another human companion when the Maker was about to rid her of this one. In generations past, he told her, their kin had been slaughtered along with their human companions. Especially their female companions who'd been accused of engaging in forbidden rituals merely because they were independent and did not acquiesce to evil men who believed they ruled the world.

As a result, the old tom said, Old Blood rarely took a human companion. The old tom never had, and he never would. He barely tolerated humans even when he walked among them wearing their form.

His life partner was Old Blood too, but she was far more understanding. The old tom claimed it was because she wasn't a Guardian, and her life wasn't spent in service to the tribe. It gave her the freedom to be capricious. To indulge her whims. To tease, or even to assist the ginger cat when she felt like it.

The ginger cat knew better. Old tom's life partner reveled in the music of the stars the same way the ginger cat did. His life partner recognized elements of starsong in the music the musician played, and it drew her the same way it drew the ginger cat.

How could wanting a human companion who could create starsong be wrong?

But it was wrong for a Guardian to take *any* companion, the old tom maintained. Guardians couldn't afford to indulge their whims. They were too important to the tribe.

The argument was almost as old as the ginger cat. She had always been too impulsive, too reckless, according to the old tom.

So today, in an uncharacteristic bout of patience, she'd decided simply to watch. She'd left the old tom and his life partner sleeping in the park at the edge of their territory, safe beneath an overgrown thicket of evergreen bushes, and made her way to where her human companion usually spent his nights.

Only he hadn't been there.

She'd scented the air, searching for the unique scent of his essence. The early morning fog made it difficult, but she'd had years of practice dealing with the misty morning air of her home.

She eventually found her companion's scent and trailed it to the Wharf. He enjoyed this part of her territory more than any other, so she wasn't surprised to find him there.

She was surprised to see him sitting alone on a concrete bench, his old blanket wrapped around his shoulders and the ridiculous cart containing the rest of his worldly things by his side.

He never strayed into open areas where he could be so easily spotted. He hadn't even cloaked himself with the aura of protection the Maker had given him. That meant he wanted to be seen.

She realized why when the musician's car pulled into the nearly empty parking lot.

What was the old man up to? Did he simply want to meet his replacement? To assure himself that she'd chosen wisely?

So she kept herself hidden and watched.

The old man's interaction with the musician had been brief, barely more than a mere sharing of drink, like her kin shared food among themselves. This she approved of.

Then the old man had done something truly unforgiveable.

He'd given the musician a warning. A warning about *her*.

The fur along her spine rose in anger as her tailed whipped back and forth. It took all her self-control not to bare her teeth and hiss.

The old fool! What was he thinking?

Perhaps not everything was lost. The musician didn't understand the warning, that much was clear. When she scented his essence, it was filled with confusion and no small amount of dread. He shouted after the old man, but the old man didn't stay to explain.

Of course not. The old man's body language spoke volumes. He *knew*. He knew he'd gone too far.

Why would he try to warn the musician about her? About her kin? Had she not protected the old man all these long years? Had not her entreaties to the Maker granted him an aura he could use to protect himself?

Had she not trusted him with her most secret self?

That infuriated her the most. She'd shared the secret of shifting with the old man. A secret that if it became widely known among humans would jeopardize not only herself but the lives of all her kin.

She'd seen what humans did to the things they feared, even when their fears were unreasonable things based on the color of their skin or the people others copulated with. Violence in this city wasn't limited to teeth and claws. If the humans became aware of her kin, they would seek them out and kill them. Kill *all* of her kin. Even the Protector herself would not be able to stand against an army of humans determined to wipe all the tribes of her kin off the face of the earth.

A new thought occurred to the ginger cat.

Did her human companion regret the long years he'd spent with her? Was he trying to spare—to *spare!*—another human that same fate?

Did the old man *hate* her?

No, that couldn't be true. She would have tasted that kind of hatred in his essence, and she never had. Not hatred of her. He'd hated the other homeless who tried to steal from him. He hated the police officers who rousted him from places he thought of as his. He'd even hated the musician when he'd first became aware that she intended the musician to be his replacement.

His mind had been shattered because of her, that much was true. But after his mind had stitched itself back together, all she had ever tasted in his essence was his love for her. His trust in her. The comfort she provided when the rest of the world—the rest of the human world—had thrown him aside like so much garbage.

Even those humans he'd loved—his own life partner and his child—had turned their backs on him. The ginger cat never had.

Yet here he was, warning the musician against her and her kind. She hadn't even sensed any residual jealousy toward the musician in the old man's essence, when the old man had clearly been jealous of the musician just the day before. Today he'd been polite to the musician. He was rarely polite to anyone other than her.

What had changed?

He'd been disappointed in her when she'd killed the muscle-bound man who'd been foolish enough not to heed her warning to leave the musician alone. He had interfered with her plan to rid the world of the woman from Far Away, and she'd had to chastise him for it.

She'd been outside the musician's apartment building the evening before. Had seen the two men whose essences were full of rules and regulations and an air of authority and purpose. When they'd left the musician's apartment, they carried a hint of the musician's scent with them.

She understood they were police of some sort. She didn't need the old tom to tell her that they'd visited the musician because of the muscle-bound man's death. The old tom would tell her that she'd brought this trouble into the musician's life.

She'd thought—briefly—about guarding the musician from the

policemen the same way she'd guarded him from the muscle-bound man, but the policemen had traveled beyond the boundaries of her territory. The Protector was the only one not bound by territory, and the ginger cat wasn't the Protector. Not yet.

Her tail whipped back and forth as she stayed crouched in her hiding place near the back of a small food stall at the rear of the parking lot. The old man didn't see her as he hurried toward the road delivery trucks used to when they dropped off supplies to the restaurants on the Wharf.

After more cars arrived in the parking lot, she would be able to move to a better vantage point where the musician wouldn't be able to see her. She wanted to watch him, to taste his essence to see if she could determine whether he eventually understood what the old man had meant.

She'd have to do something about the old man. He'd interfered with her plans twice in as many days, and that she could not abide. She'd visit him tonight under the cover of darkness and fog, and then tomorrow she'd watch the musician again.

Maybe she'd come to him in her human form this time. Ask him to play for her. Bring him some of that fancy coffee drink humans seemed to prefer. Even in her human form, she couldn't abide the stuff.

The possibilities were as endless as the world around her. She only had to choose.

And when she chose, the musician would not be able to resist her.

That thought soothed her, and her tail quieted. The fur along her spine flattened, and a low rumble started in her throat. Patience was something she could learn. Today would provide an excellent opportunity to practice.

The long-haired ginger cat who wasn't a cat was so focused on watching the musician that she never sensed she herself was being watched.

The old tom had followed her to the Wharf that morning. He'd been following her for days now. Sometimes he followed her in his human form, most often accompanied by his life partner in her preferred human form. Sometimes, like now, he left his life partner sleeping in the park with the rest of their kin and followed the ginger Guardian by himself.

He could taste her essence just like he could taste the essence of the humans in this city. He knew how angry she was at her elderly human companion. For a moment he'd been afraid she would attack the old man as he wheeled his cart out of sight, but she'd stayed in her hiding spot, tail whipping around her, fur raised along her spine.

But then she'd quieted. Only the tip of her tail still twitched, and the fur along her spine settled down.

The ginger Guardian was becoming more and more reckless, and that made her a threat to the tribe. The old tom hadn't wanted to admit it, not even to himself. His life partner adored the ginger Guardian. She thought of the ginger Guardian like her own child and indulged her far too much, in the old tom's opinion.

He'd only tolerated the ginger Guardian's antics for as long as he had because of his life partner. But now?

Now he could taste in her essence what she planned for her elderly human companion. He feared that would only bring further scrutiny into the lives of the tribe who lived among the humans. Who lived *as* humans and depended on their anonymity to survive.

What she'd done to the tattooed man was barely forgivable. What she planned for her companions, old and new, was not.

He had tried to school the ginger Guardian. Tried to impart the wisdom he'd earned over long years as a Guardian himself. He'd already been a Guardian when the Protector had visited his tribe the last time. He was, in fact, one of the elders of the tribe, an Old Blood who could trace his ancestors back to the beginning. But the ginger Guardian would never listen to him. She thought she was destined to become the next Protector, and because of that, she had leeway to do things no Guardian should.

Like take human companions.

Guardians' lives should be devoted entirely to the tribe. So it had been since the time the Maker had gifted their kin with the ability to shift. Members of the tribe could take human companions and assume the risks that came with such close association with a human. Guardians were too important to the wellbeing of the tribe to take such risks.

The old tom had thought long and hard about what he should do. His duty was and always had been to guard the tribe against *all* things that could harm it. Yet kin were forbidden by the Maker from harming other kin. Kin did not war against kin. Kin did not kill kin. Even Guardians could not kill kin.

Yet he needed to do something.

As he spent that morning and into the afternoon hiding himself while he watched the ginger Guardian watch the musician, the old tom prayed to the Maker of All Things for guidance on what he should do.

By the time the musician finished playing, had packed up his instruments, and had driven away from the Wharf, the old tom had his answer.

40

Mondays were Elias's only day off. It was the one day of the week he allowed himself to sleep in, and it was glorious.

Or it usually was.

Jerry had already long gone to work by the time Elias padded out to the kitchen in his boxers and a ratty old T-shirt. The clock on the microwave read 10:23, but the floor was still chilly against his bare feet.

He should probably get dressed. There was a slim line between letting his body get the sleep it needed to get better and simply being a lazy bum. First he wanted a cup of coffee he didn't have to drink out of a thermos.

He got the coffeemaker going and put two pieces of bread in the toaster oven. The toaster oven belonged to Jerry, but Elias used it more often than Jerry did. It made decent enough toast and did a better job of heating up frozen burritos than the microwave. Elias supposed he could have scrambled himself a couple of eggs to go along with the toast, but he wasn't feeling all that domestic.

He was feeling watched.

Again.

The feeling had only diminished for a while yesterday after he

253

finished his last set. Elias hadn't realized how pervasive the feeling had gotten until it was gone.

The same street artist from Saturday had taken over Elias's spot yesterday. This time as the artist set up his paints and his canvases, he was full of chatter about Jack.

The street artist knew more about Jack's murder than Elias did. Apparently Jack had been killed next to a hole-in-the-wall dive bar over by Fort Mason. According to another street performer, a white kid who did break dancing to songs he played on a boombox, the bar had been a favorite of Jack's. The kid used to buy Jack a beer once a week in exchange for Jack not rousting him when he danced in front of the store on slow weekdays.

"They found him out front with his throat ripped out," the artist said. "By a wild animal, man. In the middle of the city. Can you believe it?"

He shook his head. Clearly the artist was having a hard time with the entire concept.

"As if we don't have enough to worry about with crazy people going around attacking us for no reason." The artist nodded at Elias's forehead. "You feeling better today?"

Elias had given him a noncommittal response, which had seemed to satisfy the artist.

Elias had been feeling relatively better for most of the day, if he didn't take into account the creeping feeling that somebody was watching him, and not in a good way. It was amazing how much better a person could feel when their nose no longer felt twice its natural size and their sunglasses actually fit.

Then when he'd driven away from the Wharf, that creepy, *I'm being watched* sensation had abruptly abated.

It felt like those mornings when the sun finally burned away the last of the day's persistent fog and the sky turned a brilliant blue. Elias suddenly felt ten times better. The last of his headache faded away. The muscles in his back and shoulders were looser than they'd been in days. Even his ribs felt better. For a moment he was nearly convinced that if he lifted up his shirt, the bruises on his ribcage would be gone.

He felt free.

Which was ridiculous, but it reminded him of the first time he'd heard Lettie's name after their divorce and all it sparked was a distant memory, not an immediate ache.

He'd felt so unexpectedly good that he decided not to go right back to his apartment like he'd initially planned. The day had turned out gorgeous, almost too warm for his leather jacket. He'd only kept it on while he was performing because it seemed to go with his hat-and-dark-glasses persona.

On a whim, he'd driven out to Presidio Park. Even though Elias had lived in the city for a good number of years now, he hadn't been to the Presidio since his saxophone playing buddy got married there.

Far out on the Pacific, a fog bank had obscured the horizon. But directly overhead the sky was a soft shade of blue with only a few wispy clouds here and there. He'd parked his car near the visitor center and walked over to the flat oval of lawn at the center of the section of the park called Tunnel Tops.

Lots of people were out eating late picnic lunches on the lawn, most of them families with kids. When the city had turned the former military base into a park, they'd made sure there were tons of things for kids to do. Playgrounds and trails and even a Lucasfilm facility with a statute of Yoda out front.

Elias just wanted to soak in the day. He'd been living in the city for a long time, but he spent most of his time either in the heavily tourist areas by the Wharf or in the neighborhood surrounding his apartment. He didn't even stray out of his neighborhood to buy groceries, shopping instead at a chain supermarket close to Ft. Mason. Sure, sometimes he caught a glimpse of the Golden Gate bridge, but he never really saw it the way a visitor to the city would.

He'd lost the wonder of the place. Well, at the Presidio, there was no way to avoid all the natural wonder around him. The park was full of wide-open expanses of lawns, low flowering plants and bushes he'd never seen before and couldn't name if he tried. There was even an entire forest of towering trees near the center of the park.

The view of the bay to the east and the enormity of the Pacific to the west from Tunnel Tops was awe inspiring. Even the Golden Gate looked spectacular, the spans glinting orange (not golden) in the afternoon sun.

There'd been a few vacant spots on benches and the Adirondak chairs surrounding the picnic area, but he felt too restless to just sit. He started walking west on one of the park's many trails, just letting his feet carry him along while he enjoyed the day.

Every now and then he caught sight of a squirrel in the underbrush. The ubiquitous seagulls circled and squawked overhead, looking for handouts and fighting over which one got first dibs. As he walked deeper into the park, the sun on his face, it was the first time that day his sunglasses and hat felt normal and natural and not an affectation to hide his injuries.

One of the trails he took led him toward the interior of the park. By the time he realized where he was headed, he was already deep in the forest. The trees towered above him, creating a canopy that dappled the sunlight and played tricks with the shadows in the thick undergrowth on both sides of the trail.

A sudden shiver ran down Elias's spine. It wasn't exactly the same feeling of being watched that he'd had most of the day. This was a feeling that he wasn't alone, which was ridiculous.

Of course he wasn't alone. The park was full of people. Not a lot of people in this section of the trail, that much was true. A middle-aged couple in matching track suits were walking a good twenty yards ahead of him. They were holding hands, and occasionally one of them would point out something to the other. A couple of teenage girls were giggling their way ahead of the couple. To Elias's ears, their laughter had the same quality as teenagers about to enter a haunted house on Halloween.

A sign off to the side of the trail warned visitors that dogs weren't allowed in this section of the park.

Why not?

Elias had seen a lot of dogs during his walk. Big dogs, little dogs. Mutts and purebreds. But he'd seen no other signs warning visitors not to bring their dogs into other sections of the park.

What was it about the forest that warranted the prohibition?

Were park officials afraid dogs would get lost in the forest? Or that their owners would get lost looking for a dog that got off its leash?

A sudden gust of wind rattled through the branches overhead, setting the leaves rustling. Elias stopped walking to listen because something had just occurred to him.

He hadn't heard any birds in this part of the park. He couldn't even hear the ocean or the never-ending sound of traffic. Except for the diminishing sound of the teenagers' nervous giggles, the wind through the trees was the only....

Something moved through the underbrush off to the side of the trail not ten feet from where he stood.

If he hadn't been standing still and really *listening*, he never would have heard it.

A squirrel? No, he thought the sound was too big for that.

There it came again. More rustling.

And was that something moving? It was hard to tell with his dark glasses on, so he slipped them off, trying to get a better look.

The shadows were deep beneath the brush. The light peeking through the leaves overhead kept moving in the wind, which made the shadows shift and move.

Another shiver ran down his spine. The feeling that he wasn't alone—that he was being *studied*—grew so intense he felt like he wanted to jump out of his skin.

He needed to get out of here. His flight or fight response was coming down hard on the side of flight.

He turned around and walked back the way he'd come so fast he was nearly running.

The feeling didn't entirely go away even after he left the forest behind. The park had lost its allure. He got back to his car, locked the doors, and drove directly to his apartment, all the while telling himself he was just imagining things.

After he'd hauled his guitar and keyboard up to his apartment, he'd booted up his laptop. It was an old thing, but it got him on the internet and even let him run a lower-end recording program. He kept telling himself that someday he would upgrade to something that him lay down multiple tracks, but so far that hadn't happened.

Something was wrong in that forest, something that made park officials prohibit dogs from that area. Something sinister?

As it turned out, it wasn't sinister. It was coyotes.

Coyotes lived in the forest at the Presidio. Park officials kept dogs out of the area during the parts of the year the coyotes were raising their pups. That was all.

Coyotes.

Was that what he'd heard? Coyotes in the underbrush? He hadn't heard any yipping or the kind of sounds he imagined coyote pups might make. Maybe that feeling of being studied was just coyotes trying to figure out if he was a threat to their pups.

Elias had no idea that coyotes lived in the city. Now he just felt silly. Thousands of people walked through the forest every year without getting attacked by a coyote, and he'd let his fears get the best of him. Just went to show what a little PTSD did to a person.

Then his breath caught in his throat.

Jack had been killed by an animal. Had his throat torn out by an animal.

Had a coyote done that?

When the detectives had asked him if he or Jerry had any pets, they'd specifically asked about a dog. A *big* one.

Elias had lived in Vegas long enough to know what coyotes looked like. He'd never gotten close to one, but he knew coyotes weren't as big as a big dog. They were probably vicious when they were protecting their young. All animals got aggressive protecting their young.

But Jack hadn't been killed in the park. He'd been killed next to a bar closed to Fort Mason.

There was a park close to Fort Mason, but it was nowhere near as big as the Presidio. Would coyotes actually range that far into the city?

Especially coyotes about to give birth to pups?

The detectives were going on the assumption someone with a big dog had sicced that dog on Jack, but Elias had seen cats that grew to the size of a big dog, and they had very, very sharp teeth. A coyote would make more sense if the world was still as normal as Elias used to think it was just a week ago.

Now? Now he knew different. Now he knew there were cats in the world who could have done the job. Hell, they'd threatened to do a number on Jack in the back hall at Leon's store. But even if Elias told the detectives what he knew, would they believe him?

Not a chance in hell.

The ding of the toaster oven's timer almost made him jump. His toast was done. He'd forgotten he'd even put bread in to toast. His coffee was done too by the smell of it.

He grabbed a plate from the cupboard and started to butter his toast when—

Come to the window.

The words sounded inside his mind as clearly as if someone had spoken them.

This time he did jump. The butter knife clattered to the counter, and he nearly dropped his toast on the floor.

He put a hand on the counter to steady himself. To reassure himself the world was still solid and substantial and *normal*.

But hearing voices in his head wasn't normal. Was something going wrong inside his head? Were auditory hallucinations a symptom of a concussion?

No, that wasn't right. He'd heard the damn cat *talk* to him in his head before he'd been attacked in the parking garage.

His heart was racing. He'd managed to spend most of an entire day *not* thinking about the cats, even after the weirdness with the old homeless man. Elias had played his songs, sang most of his regular set, and made a decent amount of tips for a Sunday.

He hadn't even thought about the cats when things got weird in the park.

So why now?

Come to the window.

The words were clearer this time. More insistent.

More of a command.

Before he realized what he was doing, he'd put his toast down and was walking toward the living room window at the back of his apartment. He wanted to stop. He didn't want to see whatever was outside his window. A part of him imagined it would be Jack standing down in the alley, his throat missing, the front of his muscle shirt bathed in blood.

The rational part of his mind tried to assure him that things like that didn't exist. But the rational part of his mind wasn't calling the shots. Either he was hearing voices that weren't there, which meant he was going crazy, or someone—some *thing*—was talking to him in his head, which meant the entire world had gone crazy.

He barked out a laugh that was more than a little unhinged.

The world had already gone crazy. He'd seen cats grow to more than twice their size in the blink of an eye, and that shit didn't happen in a sane world.

By the time he got to his living room window, his heart was beating so fast he wouldn't have been surprised if it just gave up the ghost—pardon the expression—and quit altogether. Heart attacks at his age weren't unheard of, and discounting all the miles he'd walked that last couple of days, exercise wasn't exactly a high priority in his life. Neither was eating right.

He closed his eyes. A childish rebellion—I'm here, but you can't make me look—and he really, really didn't *want* to look.

Hello.

One word. Just one word wrapped in such a gentle caress it felt like a warm blanket chasing away the chill of a foggy morning.

Except the morning wasn't foggy. The sun was shining. The buildings on the other side of the alley behind his apartment were casting deep shadows on the alley below, but Elias could still see the figure standing one story down on the sloping concrete.

Not Jack, throat ripped out, grinning up at him.

It was the woman who'd thanked him on Tuesday for playing "Moonlight Sonata."

The woman with long, thick hair the color of a sunset, and golden-green eyes.

The same woman the detectives were looking for.

Hello, Elias, she said.

Not out loud.

Only in his mind.

41
___

This was nuts.

The cats—the damn *cats*—were the ones who'd talked to him in his mind. Not this woman. It had been the cats.

Or he'd thought it had been the cats.

Was this woman behind it all? Had she been playing tricks on him all along?

Had she *hypnotized* him somehow during the brief conversation he'd had with her on the Wharf? Made him only think he was seeing the cats grow? Made him think it was the cats talking to him in his mind when it was really her?

Only that didn't make any sense either. Even hypnotized, people couldn't talk to each other in their minds.

Come down here and I'll explain it all.

Sure, she would.

He stood in front of his living room window and barked out another laugh that definitely didn't sound one-hundred percent sane. Come down there? The hell he would.

He'd put Detective Avrill's contact information into his phone. Okay, sure, he'd left his cell in his bedroom, but right now he could practically feel the need to make the call burning a hole in his brain.

263

That fight or flight response? Well, that was telling him, *screaming* at him, to go call the detective and tell him... tell him....

Tell him what?

What could he say?

That the woman Avrill was looking for was right outside the apartment? Standing plain as day in the alley staring up at him and *talking to him* in his mind?

Well, he didn't have to tell the detective everything, right? Elias could just say the woman was here and he was doing what the detective had asked him to do. Letting him know.

Only then the detective would want to know how the woman had found him.

Which was a damn good question.

Come down here and I'll tell you.

Right. Sure she would. She'd....

He nearly stopped breathing when he realized what should have been obvious.

She was *reading* his *mind!*

She had to be. He hadn't said anything out loud, but she was responding to his thoughts anyway. And if she was reading his mind, she had to know he was thinking about calling the detective.

How the hell was she reading his mind?

Elias put his hands out in a warding off gesture. This was so far beyond nuts it wasn't even in the realm of possibility. The world wasn't made like this, damn it. People didn't talk to you in your mind. People didn't *read* your thoughts as clearly as if you'd spoken them out loud. People couldn't—

People can't.

Elias blinked, and in that blink of an eye, the woman was gone. In her place a long-haired ginger cat sat in the same place staring up at him.

A regular housecat-sized ginger cat.

Elias let out a loud, inventive curse.

No, no, no, *no, no!!* This kind of shit just didn't happen. This was the stuff of movies. Of stories told by kids around a campfire to scare each other or in books shelved in the fantasy section of a bookstore.

He closed his eyes, fisted his hands and held them to the side of his head. Pressed his fists against his skull as if he could erase what he couldn't have just seen from his brain.

Look at me, Elias.

"I don't want to," he said.

Look at me!

He moaned. The command in that thought was unmistakable. This was a woman—a cat—a *being*—who was used to being obeyed. Who expected obedience.

What was worse—he felt that command pull at him. Like he didn't have a choice.

He opened his eyes and looked at the cat. From his vantage point, it looked like any other cat he'd ever seen in his life, but he knew—he *knew*—it wasn't like any other cat.

He didn't want to know this. He didn't want any of it. He didn't know why this was happening to him, but it could all just kindly fuck the hell off.

"Go away!" he shouted at the cat. He probably could have simply thought it, but he needed to shout. To yell. To *scream* if that's what it took. "Just leave me the hell alone! Go back to wherever you came from and leave me *alone!*"

The answer, when it came, was simple and final and hit him like a physical blow.

No.

42

DETECTIVE ISAIAH AVRILL STOOD NEXT TO A CORDONED-OFF AREA OF the trash-strewn strip of dirt between the back of a four-story parking garage and the tree-lined sidewalk bordering North Point Street. The trees didn't quite cover up the fact that the paint on the cinderblock wall of the garage building was faded and peeling. Things Avrill didn't want to contemplate too closely had been thrown at the wall. Some of it had stuck. Most of it had slid to the dirt and sat there, decomposing.

The area was a popular place for the homeless to camp out at night. Some of them erected tents between the trees. Others strung up tarps or blankets or whatever they could find to fashion makeshift tents. The dead man at the center of the cordoned-off area hadn't done either.

Street cops had rousted the closest street people from their shelters. They stood off to the side, peering past the cluster of official vehicles that had reported to the scene of the city's most recent—and goriest—homicide. The street cops hadn't let them dismantle their shelters yet, so none of them had left.

The patrol officers were waiting for Avrill to give the okay to let the street people retrieve their possessions. Avrill was waiting for the crime scene techs to finish processing the scene.

"Hey, man, it's fucking cold out here," one of the street people said in the general direction of a patrol officer guarding the perimeter of the crime scene. "I need my blankets."

Like a lot of street people Avrill had met during his career, this guy's age was difficult to peg. He could have been a hard-used, drug-addicted twenty or a recently displaced man in his late thirties. Thanks to the layers of grime, Avrill couldn't tell if he belonged to any easily identifiable ethnic group either.

"You got a coat on," the patrol officer shot back.

"This coat ain't worth jack shit," the guy said. "I *need* my *blankets*."

Avrill strolled over to the resident. It was still cold out, the kind of damp cold that seeped into a person's bones. Avrill had been on the scene since seven that morning. He'd had the luxury of bringing a travel mug full of hot coffee with him. The coffee was half gone now, and he'd only been here not quite a half hour. The techs and the patrol officers had been here much longer, which meant the guy asking for a blanket had been standing out in the cold for hours waiting to get back to his stuff.

"You see anything?" Avrill asked the man, gesturing to where his partner Keiner was crouched next to the dead man, going through the dead man's pockets.

Blanket Man shook his head. "I was fucking *sleeping*, man, like I told the officer. I didn't hear nothing." He paused, then added, "Didn't see nothing either," like he'd just remembered exactly what Avrill had asked.

Thin black wires snaked around each side of the guy's neck and disappeared inside the open V at the front of his coat.

Earbuds. Blanket Man had probably been listening to music. His particular shelter looked like an igloo, complete with a tiny opening, which meant he probably hadn't seen anything either.

Avrill turned to the patrol officer. "You find anything interesting inside?" he asked.

The officer nodded toward a smaller-built cop standing next to

Keiner, watching him do his job. "Ortiz did the search," he said. "With the resident's permission," he added, before Avrill had to ask.

Avrill didn't think Blanket Man had anything to do with dead man's death. The dead man had been mauled by an animal, just like Jack Driscoll. The similarity of their deaths was why Avrill and Keiner had been called out to the scene, even though the attack had occurred in a different precinct. Detectives in the Strategic Investigations Unit weren't tied to any one precinct. Sometimes that meant more traveling and more time stuck in traffic than actually working a scene. This morning, even though it was a Monday, traffic had been relatively light.

Both deaths had been clearly been the work of an animal. A very *big* animal. This attack had been especially vicious. A big animal that could do something like this would be difficult to hide in Blanket Man's small shelter, but it never hurt to be careful with procedure, just in case.

Some homeless had pets. The dogs they kept were usually small to medium in size, which made them easier to feed and care for. Avrill had even seen a few cats now and then who were clearly some street person's pet. Those pets were often their owners only true companions, and the only thing anchoring their owners to the world.

Blanket Man was visibly shivering, jittering from foot to foot. He could be cold, or he could just need a hit of whatever stash he had inside his shelter. Avrill didn't work narcotics. He didn't care whether the guy was addicted or not. Avrill had a different perspective from most cops when it came to addiction, and he tended to let things like that slide.

Keiner wouldn't let it slide. He wouldn't be nice about it either. It was one of the things about his partner Avrill didn't care for, but Keiner was a good detective. That fact made up for a lot of character flaws.

"Let me see what I can do," Avrill said to Blanket Man.

He walked over to where the other patrol officer—Ortiz—was still standing next to Keiner.

If Avrill had been standing up straight, his six-foot, one-inch frame would have towered over the much smaller Ortiz. But Avrill hadn't been able to stand up straight since a bullet punched through his belly five years ago. He'd lost a section of intestine, his spleen, and some of the mobility in his spine. He'd also gained a raging addiction to prescription painkillers.

He'd come to terms with the fact that he'd always be an addict. He rarely even downed an aspirin these days. Early mornings like today were a bitch, and he'd never be S.W.A.T.—like that had ever been a possibility even when he'd been Keiner's age—but he was still a damn good detective.

"Tell me what you found in there," Avrill said to Ortiz.

Ortiz tilted his head to look up at Avrill. "Buncha crap," he said. Then he seemed to remember this was a homicide investigation. "No blood, no weapons unless you want to count a couple of sets of plastic utensils," he said.

Avrill nodded. "Any blood on the outside?"

Ortiz shook his head. "No, and no blood trail in the dirt or on the sidewalk. Nothing that looks like someone tried to cover one up or clean it off."

Avrill nodded again. "How about you?" he asked Keiner. "Find anything interesting?"

"No ID," Keiner said, standing up as he brushed off his glove-covered hands.

Avrill was probably more gratified than he should have been when he heard Keiner's knees pop. Keiner's knees were still the original model. Until he'd been shot, Avrill's only surgery had been to replace his right knee. He didn't crouch down next to anything these days unless he had no choice.

He didn't ask Keiner if he'd gone through all of the dead man's pockets. That would have been insulting. They'd been partnered a long enough for Avrill to know that Keiner was one efficient sonofabitch. Abrasive as hell at times, but his dedication to the job made his personality a little easier to take.

Like most of the homeless who camped out on the city streets, the dead man was dressed in multiple layers. Shirts, undershirts, a hoodie, a watch cap, and a coat. The extra clothes, even soaked with the man's blood, made his skinny body look like a balloon.

"He had a couple of bucks in one pocket, some change in another," Keiner said. "It's all bagged and tagged, along with this."

Keiner reached down and grabbed a plastic evidence bag that held an old photograph. The photograph had been laminated and then wrapped in something that looked like plastic wrap from the outside of a sandwich.

"It was in an inside zippered pocket of his coat," Keiner said.

That explained the lack of blood on the photograph.

"Got an estimated time of death for me?" Avrill asked the crime scene tech who was still hovering over the body, taking photographs.

She must have been new on the job. Avrill didn't recognize her, and he knew most of the crime scene techs who worked in his Unit. Her name badge identified her as D. Winterhaven. Delores? Deborah? Delilah? From the dark circles beneath her eyes, she was probably working another double shift.

"Sometime after midnight, most likely before three," she said. "Can't be more specific, not with this crap."

She gestured with one hand to encompass the fog, the damp concrete sidewalk where the body was sprawled, and the general creeping cold that Avrill knew would burn off in another couple of hours. The weather honchoes on TV were predicting another warmer than average day for the Bay area. Crazy-making weather, one of the other detectives in the Unit called it.

"Close enough," Avrill said.

For now. He'd get a better estimate on TOD after the tech got the body back to the morgue and the M.E.'s office worked whatever magic they worked with computer databases and instruments he didn't want to think too closely about.

Funny, he'd never been squeamish around the tools of the M.E.'s trade until he'd become far too familiar with operating rooms and medical procedures and all the attendant problems of a life spent not taking nearly good enough care of himself. Keiner would know, but Keiner was still young enough he thought his body would last him forever. Or maybe he didn't and that's why he pushed himself so hard in the gym. Avrill had never asked him.

"You done with the igloo?" he asked the tech.

She frowned at him, probably wondering what the hell he meant by igloo, then realization dawned. "Yeah," she said. "Pretty much. Took a few photographs, inside"—she wrinkled her nose—"and out. Why?"

"I want to let the owner inside to get one of his blankets. You need to print anything?"

She shook her head. "Nothing in there will give me a good print."

"Good enough," Avrill said.

She went back to photographing the dead body without another word.

Avrill turned to Ortiz. "Let that guy over there"—he pointed at Blanket Man—"go inside and get a blanket. Everything else, he leaves inside for now. Make sure we have his name." Avrill remembered the wires leading down inside the man's coat. "If he's got a cell, even if it's a burner, get that number too."

Avrill hadn't found a cell in the shopping cart parked next to the dead man's body, but one more search wouldn't hurt.

It was an old, rusted cart, one that didn't have a lock on the wheels like most grocery store shopping carts did these days. The main basket was chock full of the kind of crap Avrill expected to find a homeless man carting around. A few extra sets of clothes, all neatly folded. A sleeping bag, still rolled up. Extra blankets. A rain slicker. A woven poncho. Again, all neatly folded. But no cell phone. No electronics of any kind.

Someone could have stolen the dead guy's cell, but they would have taken the entire cart. Wheeled it away to go through later. At the very least, they would have taken the sleeping bag and the blankets.

Whoever this guy had been, he was a neatnik. And clean. The stuff in the shopping cart hadn't given off the stench of someone who was too far gone to worry about cleanliness. The old guy's bearded face—what wasn't covered in blood splatter from the ragged wound in his neck—wasn't caked with dirt. He didn't have dirt under his fingernails from what Avrill could tell. The crime scene tech had already bagged the guy's hands in clear plastic for further examination when the M.E.'s office processed the body.

Avrill studied the shopping cart. The rolled-up sleeping bag bothered him. Most homeless, once they found a spot to spend the night, cocooned themselves in whatever they had that would protect them from the damp cold of a Frisco night. This guy hadn't done that. All the stuff he would use to sleep in was still in his cart.

So why wasn't the dead guy already cocooned and sleeping at midnight? The patrol officers had found his body on their regular rounds rousting homeless earlier this morning. The official parking garage for Pier 39 was only a block away, and no politician wanted a tourist's first look at the city to be a bunch of homeless camped out in close proximity to where the tourists parked their cars.

And why hadn't anyone stolen his stuff? If he'd been dead since three in the morning, that was a long time for prime stuff to go unclaimed.

Unless there was something about the way the guy died that warned other people away. Even the crazies who never seemed to sleep.

"Look at this," Keiner said.

He held up the evidence bag with the laminated photograph he'd found in the inside zippered pocket of the dead man's coat. He was shining his pocket flashlight on the back of the photograph.

It was difficult to tell through the layers of plastic, but it looked like there was a second photograph on the back of the first. It wasn't laminated but held in place against the other photo by the plastic wrap.

Avrill had on nitrile gloves just like his partner. Avrill hated the things. They reminded him too much of all the doctors and nurses who'd poked and prodded him in the hospital after they'd taken part of his damaged insides out. But the gloves were a necessity. They let him unseal the evidence bag and retrieve the photograph without contaminating any trace on the photo.

"Document this," he said to Keiner.

Keiner took out his cell. While Avrill unwound the plastic wrap from around the photographs, Keiner took pictures on his cell with one hand while he kept holding the flashlight on the photograph with the other. If Avrill had tried a stunt like that, he would have either dropped the flashlight or his cell.

The laminated photograph was of a young woman, little more than a teenage girl really. The photograph was old and faded except around the edges, which made Avrill think the photograph had been in a frame at one time.

The dead man's first love? Possibly. Or maybe a daughter or a sister. Certainly someone he'd had strong feelings about. Avrill would run an image search later to see if he could find a match. If this woman had been important to the dead guy, he might have been important enough to her that she'd remember his name. Avrill would rather not have this guy go to his grave as a John Doe.

The second photograph fell into Avrill's hand when he unwound the last bit of plastic wrap from around the laminated photo.

"It's almost like our vic wanted to keep it hidden," Keiner said.

This picture was smaller and far more recent. One edge of the photograph was ragged, like part of it had been torn off. The back of the print had a partial logo for the manufacturer of the paper the photo was printed on.

But it was the picture itself that caught Avrill's attention. It had been printed in full, vibrant color, the surface glossy. The plastic wrap had kept it from being damaged for however long the dead guy had held onto it.

The photo had clearly been taken at the Wharf. The Wharf's distinctive sign was visible in the background. From the angle, it looked like the photo had been taken from the pedestrian plaza behind the sign.

The part of the photo that had been torn away had to have been someone's selfie. Long, dark blonde hair that had been blowing in the breeze obscured part of the portion of the photo the dead guy had kept. He must not have been interested in whoever that hair belonged to. All Avrill could see of the person who'd been in the foreground was that hair and part of their scalp.

Which meant that the dead guy must have been interested in something in the background.

There was a crowd of people in the pedestrian plaza. Nothing unusual there. The place was usually crowded. Did the dead guy keep the picture because of someone in that crowd?

"Holy crap," Keiner said. "You see it, don't you?"

It took Avrill a moment, but yeah, when he did see it, his breath caught.

There she was, the woman they'd been looking for. Young with long, thick, curly hair. Golden blonde with hints of red that glistened in the sunlight. That kind of hair color didn't come out of a bottle. She was wearing a blouse made out of some sort of gauzy material in autumn hues. The lower half of her body was obscured by the blowing hair in the foreground, but Avrill would have guessed she was wearing a skirt made of the same gauzy material.

She was a perfect match for the woman who'd been seen leaving the bar with Jack Driscoll the night he died.

And this dead guy had a picture of her.

Keiner shot Avrill a look. "This can't be a coincidence. It has to be the same woman."

There were a lot of other people in the background, but the dead guy had saved this specific part of the photo. He'd kept it safe. Had kept it almost hidden. They might never know why, but Keiner was right. It was too damn weird to be a coincidence. Not when this woman had ties to both Jack Driscoll and their new vic, and they'd both been killed in such a savage way.

Maybe she owned the savage dog. Did she have her dog attack this guy and kill him because he knew her and knew what she'd done?

If the dead guy had known too much about her, Avrill didn't have wonder why he hadn't gone to the police. No matter how much certain patrol officers tried to build a rapport with the regulars on their beats, most street people viewed cops as enemies. Cops were the ones who evicted them from their houses, turned them out on the street and then rousted them from whatever spots they managed to find to catch a little sleep.

Avrill snapped a picture of the torn photograph with his own cell phone, then put everything back in the evidence bag and sealed it. The first thing they had to do was confirm this was the right woman. Avrill knew exactly who to ask.

They wouldn't even have to go far to find him. All they had to do was head over to the pedestrian plaza and wait for the musician— Elias Sandoval—to show up for his ten o'clock gig.

43

Elias didn't want to go down to the alley behind his apartment.

Nearly a week ago he'd spent most of the afternoon looking for the long-haired ginger cat who wasn't really a cat. He'd been desperate to find her, to reassure himself she really existed. That he'd seen what he thought he had.

Now?

Now he didn't want to go anywhere near her.

But most of all, he didn't want to keep having this conversation in his *head*.

He'd heard music in his head all his life. Music, lyrics, riffs and beats and rhythm. All of that was natural, just part of his interior voice. It had shocked him when he first learned that some people didn't have that interior voice thing going on inside their heads. He'd thought that must be a lonely way to live, without even your own interior voice to keep you company.

Hearing his own voice or music in his head was one thing. Having someone—some *thing*—talk to him in his mind when he definitely didn't want it was an invasion. A violation.

You hear that? he thought at the cat. You're violating me. Proud of yourself?

If a person could hear someone else's sigh in their mind, that's what he heard now.

That sigh, above all else, frightened him.

It meant she was getting impatient with him.

It also told him he was right about something else he'd thought earlier.

She didn't care what he wanted. What he felt. What he *thought*. She wanted him to come down and talk to her, and she wasn't about to take no for an answer. All his quibbling, all his ranting and raving and shouting at her, hadn't made a difference.

His mom's cat had been bad-tempered. It slept where it wanted to sleep—usually on his mom's lap, but sometimes on the chair that Elias thought of as his. If he ever tried to move that cat while it was sleeping, even if he did it gently like his mom told him to, that cat always hissed and swiped its claws at him.

His dad used to joke that the cat ruled the roost. Elias didn't think that was much of a joke now. This cat, this ginger-haired not-a-cat, was used to getting her way. She *expected* to get her way. Sure, she'd protected him in Leon's store when Jack threatened to hurt him— what had she called herself? Guardian?—but did she think that gave her the right to impose her will on him?

And what would happen if he really said no and meant it?

He didn't want to find out. Not right now. Not when his head was pounding again and the last thing he wanted to put in his knotted-up stomach was the toast and coffee he'd made for himself for his breakfast.

"I need to put some clothes on," he said out loud.

He turned away from his living room window, left his breakfast untouched on his kitchen table, and went directly to his bedroom. He slipped on an old pair of jeans, grabbed a hoodie to cover the ratty T-shirt he slept in. He thought about grabbing his sunglasses and his hat—they'd almost become part of his regular routine now—but left them behind as he went out to the hallway and slipped on the tennis shoes he'd left by the front door.

He had a bad moment when he locked the apartment door

behind himself. He had his keys, his wallet, and his cell phone, but his guitar and keyboard were still inside his apartment. He felt almost panicky leaving them behind, like he was saying goodbye to a part of himself.

Which was ridiculous. He was just going downstairs to talk to the not-a-cat. She'd promised to explain everything to him. He'd listen to what she had to say, then he'd make her understand that he wasn't interested in having her—whatever she was—in his life. Somehow, he'd make her understand.

Then he'd come back upstairs, heat up his coffee and fix himself something more substantial to eat, and spend the rest of the day watching something mindless on TV.

Anything that would help him zone out so he could forget she ever existed.

44

Avrill and Keiner took their time walking from the crime scene to the pedestrian plaza at the Wharf, but they were still almost an hour early.

The musician they wanted to talk to—Elias Sandoval—performed from ten until two, or so the guy who owned the T-shirt/souvenir shop across the street had told them. Avrill didn't mind getting there early. With any luck, they could talk to this Elias while he was setting up. Street performers were working stiffs too, and Avrill didn't want to keep the guy from earning whatever meager tips he could generate on a Monday morning when most people were already at work.

The day was promising to be another beautiful day. The fog had rolled out of the city proper, only partly shrouding the Golden Gate. Professional photographers must be having a field day shooting iconic San Francisco landscapes, but he didn't see any on his walk to the Wharf.

The sourdough bread store on the bay side of Jefferson Street was already doing a bang-up business. The aroma from the bakery inside the store combined with the rich smell of designer coffee in go-cups was making Avrill's stomach rumble. His own coffee was long gone,

281

his empty travel mug back in the car he'd driven to the crime scene. Now that his nose wasn't full of the stench of dried blood and decomposing garbage, he was actually getting hungry.

"Want anything?" Keiner asked.

What Avrill wanted was to still be in bed, or at the very least taking a long, hot shower to loosen up his back. He'd settle for a late breakfast.

"Coffee and a danish," he said.

He started to dig out his wallet, but Keiner shook him off.

"I've got it," Keiner said. He scrunched up his nose as he glanced up at two seagulls engaged in an aerial fight for dominance. "You care what kind of danish?"

"Surprise me," Avrill said.

Keiner ducked inside the store. The place looked crowded, the line long, so Avrill decided to wait outside.

The businesses on the other side of the street were still locked up tight. A middle-aged black man dressed in black slacks, a black leather jacket, and a black hat was walking toward the Pier. He was the only pedestrian on the city side of Jefferson.

A few people were sitting at the outdoor tables in front of the bread store, most of them eating some sort of pastry and drinking something hot. These weren't the tourists who'd show up later in the day. The early morning diners were dressed for the morning chill, some in down jackets, others in peacoats and heavy sweaters. Avrill even saw a couple of expensive sports team jackets.

He decided to put his time to good use. Today he'd hung his shield on a lanyard around his neck, like he did whenever he went to work a crime scene. He pulled it out from beneath his jacket so that it was easily visible. Then he approached each table, introduced himself, and showed the picture on his cell of the photograph of the woman Avrill thought of as their primary person of interest.

He didn't expect anyone to recognize her even though the quality of the original photograph was amazingly good. Keiner had said he thought the photograph had been printed on a portable printer the size of one of the old flip-phone cells.

"It's a little wireless gadget," he'd said. One of his nieces had one. "She can take a selfie with her friends and give them a print, right there on the spot."

Apparently the photograph the dead guy had wrapped in plastic was about the right size for one of those prints.

The problem was the cell's camera had been focused on the person in the foreground. The people in the background weren't quite a blur, but they weren't in sharp, clear focus either. Since the print was small to begin with, Avrill was asking people if they recognized a woman whose semi-blurry face was less than a half-inch tall.

No one who was sitting at the tables recognized her. Avrill lucked out when he showed the picture to a man who was leaning against a lamppost, smoking a cigarette and staring at his own cell phone.

"Maybe," the guy said. He peered at Avrill's phone. "Yeah, I think so. Just this last week, right?" He glanced up at Avrill. "Who is she?"

"That's what I'm hoping you can tell me," Avrill said.

The guy shrugged. "I don't know her name. I just remember that hair." He grinned. "That was some hair. And she was walking around in that outfit like the wind didn't bother her." He frowned. "And she had bare feet. Who walks around down here in bare feet?"

Nobody in their right mind. One of the city's many agencies employed people to keep the area relatively clean, but there always seemed to be bits of broken glass in the cracks in the sidewalks and the cobblestoned portion of the streets.

"So you saw her at the Wharf?" Avrill asked.

The guy shook his head. He was maybe early twenties, his dark hair medium length and curly. He had on a heavyweight hoodie zipped up almost to his neck, but Avrill thought he could see the neckline of a uniform shirt peeking out from the open V at the top of the zipper.

"At the Pier," the guy said. "I work over there." He named one of the many food kiosks that dotted the lower level of Pier 39. "That's where I saw her."

"When was this?"

The guy frowned, clearly thinking, then his frown smoothed out.

"Saturday," he said, nodding to himself. "That was it. I remember now. Yeah, Saturday afternoon. That was when the paramedics showed up. Some tourist fell down or something—I'm not sure exactly what happened, we were too busy—but we all stopped what we were doing when they carted her away on a stretcher. I mean, it's not like we see something like that every day."

He stopped to take a final drag on his cigarette. He started to drop the butt to crush it out beneath his boot, then he glanced at Avrill and seemed to think better of it. Like he thought Avrill would give him a ticket for littering.

"Anyway," the guy said, "I saw that woman in the picture in the crowd. She was just standing there watching like everyone else." The frown came back. "Only this was weird. She was smiling, you know? Not, like, hilariously smiling, but kind of like she was self-satisfied or something."

Avrill didn't let himself react, but he was starting to get a clearer picture of this woman, and he didn't like that picture at all. Someone who smiled at a stranger's misfortune? Sociopaths did that. Or someone who'd sic their attack dog on someone else, they might smile like that too.

"You were close enough to see that?" he asked.

The guy nodded. "Oh, yeah. That's how I know she was barefoot. It was like she was part of the crowd but nobody was standing all that close to her. So I got a good look, then we got busy, and I sort of forgot about her." He shrugged. "I see a lot of people during the day, you know? Until I saw that picture. That reminded me."

Avrill wondered how much of what this guy told him was true and how much was revisionist memory. Eyewitnesses were often the worst kind of witness to hang your hat on. A good lawyer could pick apart eyewitness testimony in court without even half trying.

Still, Avrill typed in the guy's name and cell phone number into a note on his phone. When the guy walked away, he made a show of dropping his cigarette butt into one of the ashtrays on the street as he headed toward the Pier.

Avrill was just making a few notes to himself on the screen next to the guy's name when Keiner came back out holding two coffees and a paper bag. Avrill saved the note, put his phone back in his pocket, and took his coffee.

"Almond croissant and a lemon danish," Keiner said, indicating the bag. "Take whatever one you want."

Avrill took the danish.

"We have another spotting of our mystery woman," he said, and relayed what the kid had told him.

Keiner raised an eyebrow. "So she's someone who hangs around this area a lot. That's good for us."

"We also have another possible witness," Avrill said. "The woman the paramedics worked on. We get those records, figure out who she is, go talk to her. Maybe find out why our mystery woman seemed so pleased about someone else's misfortune."

It was a longshot. Keiner didn't have to tell him that, but sometimes longshots paid off.

Keiner glanced at his watch. "Almost nine-thirty," he said. "Think it's about time for our musician to show up?"

Avrill nodded.

He took another bite of the danish as they started walking toward the Wharf. The pastry was flakey, the lemon filling just tart enough to have a zing. Avrill had to watch what he ate these days, but he still treated himself every now and then to a good pastry. This one was worth what might turn into a bellyache later on.

They found a spot to sit in the pedestrian plaza and settled in to wait. More people were out and about now. The fish stalls were opening up, and the guy with the T-shirt/souvenir shop across the street rolled up his doors.

At five minutes to ten a different musician stepped up to the corner where Avrill had expected Elias Sandoval to set up. This guy was tall, skinny, black kid with an acoustic guitar in a soft case strapped to his back. No stool to sit on, no microphone or amp.

"That's not Elias Sandoval," Keiner said, somewhat unnecessarily.

Avrill gestured at his eyes. "These work, you know."

Keiner grinned at him as they both stood up.

They dropped their empty coffee cups and the paper bag from the bread store in a trash can on their way to talk to the new musician.

Avrill still had his badge hanging in front of his jacket, so he took the lead. He introduced himself and Keiner.

"We were expecting Elias Sandoval today," Avrill said.

The guitar player smiled at them, showing off gold-rimmed front teeth. "Elias, he don't play on Mondays," he said. "I have this spot, ten to two. You need to see my license?"

Avrill shook his head. If the guy knew he needed a license from the Port Authority to play at the Wharf, that was good enough for him.

"Is that the only day Elias doesn't perform here?" Avrill asked.

The guitar player shrugged. "Only time I know of. He's usually here when I come by on my way to the Square. If he not here when he's supposed to be, I can stay, but that never happens. Elias, he a reliable guy."

"Does he ever play at Ghirardelli Square?" That question came from Keiner.

"Don't think so," the guitar player said. "Never seen him there. This spot, this is a good place, you know? You can make decent money here."

He flashed them another gold-tinted grin.

"Then we'll let you get to it," Avrill said.

They left the guitar player to his good spot, his open guitar case salted with a few bills and some quarters.

Keiner nodded at the T-shirt/souvenir shop across the street. "Think we need to corroborate any of that with Leon? See if he knows where Elias goes on his days off?"

"Nope," Avrill said.

Their guy got one day off to recoup from being "on" six days a week. And one day to lick his wounds. Avrill knew what it was like for a middle-aged body to recover from injuries like Elias clearly had. That shit took time and a good bit of TLC.

"I think I know exactly where he'll be," he said.

45

THE ALLEY BEHIND ELIAS'S BUILDING WAS EMPTY BY THE TIME HE GOT there. Well, not quite empty. There were a few pigeons poking at the seeds his neighbor had left out that morning, but not nearly as many pigeons as usual.

He supposed the not-a-cat must have scared them away.

And now? Had something scared *her* away?

He was about to breathe a sigh of relief when he felt her voice in his mind.

Hello again.

He whirled around.

The woman, not the cat, was sitting cross-legged on the hood of his car.

He'd parked his car in his slot in the garage. Technically it wasn't his spot. Each apartment was only allocated one of the three parking places. Since Jerry paid the majority of the rent for their apartment, it was only right that Jerry got dibs on their parking space. But their upstairs neighbor, the guy who fed the pigeons, didn't have a car. He said it was too expensive to keep one in the city. He liked to walk, there was enough public transportation that could get him wherever he needed to go, and he was fine if Elias took his parking place in the garage.

Elias hadn't grown up in a big city. He'd had his own car ever since his second year in college. He'd needed a car when he and Lettie had moved to Las Vegas. Wherever he'd lived since then, he'd always had his own car. Even here. He was just lucky his car was paid for, since he definitely needed a car to haul around all of his equipment.

His current car wasn't in the best shape. It had dings in the door panels and a pretty significant dent over the rear wheel well on the driver's side. But the paint was still the original gray, the engine didn't leak oil, and it got him where he needed to go.

It was his car, damn it, and he didn't want her sitting on it.

"Do you mind getting off my car?" he said.

She tilted her head. Her face was still beautiful, with those golden-green eyes and the freckles on her nose and her cheeks. Her hair curled around her shoulders and hung down to her waist in the same thick, luxurious curls he remembered. But he no longer found her attractive. How could he, when he knew what she was?

She slid off the hood of his car, straightening her legs with an easy grace.

"You don't," she said. "Know what I really am." She held her arms out at her sides, palms forward. "I'm just wearing this shape for your benefit. I've found it's easier to talk to humans this way."

Talk to humans while *wearing this shape?* What the hell?

Elias would have laughed at the ridiculousness of that statement if the situation wasn't so damn serious. He could feel laughter as inappropriate as gallows humor bubbling up inside him, but he couldn't let it out. He was afraid if he started, he wouldn't be able to stop.

Ever.

"So what are you?" he asked. "You're clearly not a cat." She wasn't human either. She just looked human.

She took a step toward him. He took a step backwards, and she stopped where she was, next to his car.

"Some elders say we started as cats," she said. "Before the Maker of All Things graced us with the greatest of all gifts. Others say we were never 'cats' as you know them." She shrugged, a purely human gesture. "I believe that we were always different."

She trailed one hand along the side of his car, but she didn't look away from him.

"You see, we live much, much longer than a mere cat. Our young are born with golden eyes. We can communicate without speaking out loud."

As you well know, she said in his mind.

He started, and one corner of her mouth quirked up in a self-indulgent expression he didn't like one bit.

"You'll get used to that," she said.

He definitely didn't like the sound of *that*.

"We live in tribes," she said out loud. "Some of us wear the shape of humans for most of our lives so we can live among you undetected. Others prefer our natural shapes."

He was afraid she was going to show him her natural shape—change right there in front of his face—but she kept her womanly form.

"Our kin live in all parts of the world," she said. "Some of us have been worshipped as gods. Some of us have been sacrificed to your false human gods. Some of us have been killed along with our human companions by evil men who sought power over things they could not understand."

Elias's thoughts were reeling.

According to her, there were shapeshifters living as humans right here in the city. Masquerading as humans so they'd go undetected.

Once a person accepted that as fact—if a fact like that could ever *be* accepted—the rest of what she'd said explained why they had kept themselves hidden.

Her kind had been sacrificed by humans. They'd been persecuted along with the women who'd been burned at the stake as witches. They'd probably been hunted just for existing. That's what people did throughout history—killed the things they feared. Hell, people still did that to whatever minority group was the current political or religious target du jour. Shapeshifters were the stuff of horror stories, which automatically made them things to be feared.

She stood next to his car, one hand still trailing back and forth along the side, just watching him.

Waiting for him to catch up.

Well, there was one thing she hadn't told him.

"Why me?" he asked.

Her hand kept moving back and forth. Like a cat's tail, twitching back and forth.

The corner of her mouth quirked up a little higher. She was enjoying this. Enjoying *toying* with him.

"You've been touched," she said.

"Touched?" What the hell did that mean?

"At some time in your life, you met one of my kin," she said. "You wouldn't have known it, not unless they wanted you to. But you met one of us. I felt it in your music. I tested that feeling when I asked you to play my song, and you heard my request."

Now her expression lost some of the self-indulgent look. In its place was a look of pure joy.

"You can play the music of the stars," she said. "It's what my kin sing, the music of our souls sung beneath the moon and the stars. I knew then you were a kindred spirit, even if you were only human."

Only human.

He'd practiced for days trying to replicate "Moonlight Sonata" the way he'd heard it in his mind. The way he'd dreamed of hearing it. Had he been playing this... this *creature's* music all along?

And when the hell had he been touched? He'd met so many people during his lifetime, people who'd stopped to listen to him play. Women who'd come up to him when he'd worked the cruise lines who were looking for a little shipboard romance.

"So I can play your music," he said. "That's no reason to...." He licked his lips and swallowed hard. "To do whatever the hell it is you're doing to me. You're *stalking* me. Invading my mind, and it needs to stop."

"It can't," she said. "I've already chosen you, or I would not be telling you what you need to know."

Chosen him?

"Chose me?" he said. "For what?"

Now her expression turned serious. No, more than that. Imperious.

"To be my new companion," she said.

46

Gaining access to an apartment building with a locked lobby entrance was always tricky.

The days when Avrill was a street cop trying to serve a warrant were long gone, but he still remembered all the ruses he'd used to get inside without letting the person he wanted to serve know the police were about to nab them.

Pretending to be a delivery person was high on the list. People almost always buzzed in someone with a fresh, hot pizza. So was pretending to be someone else in the building who'd locked their keys inside. That worked best in buildings with more than three apartments where everyone might not know everyone else, but they usually had an idea what their neighbors looked like.

Keiner preferred a more direct approach.

The first time they'd gone to Elias Sandoval's apartment, instead of pressing the buzzer for Sandoval's second-floor apartment, Keiner had buzzed the first and third floor apartments. They'd gotten lucky. Someone in one of those two apartments had unlocked the lobby door without even asking who they were.

Today wasn't going to be as easy.

For one thing, it was the middle of a Monday morning. It stood to

293

reason that Sandoval's roommate as well as the residents in the first and third floor apartments would be at work. Keiner's trick probably wouldn't work.

He tried it anyway, buzzing the first and third floor apartments.

No response.

"Try the musician's," Avrill said.

Keiner pushed the buzzer for the second-floor apartment. Also no response.

They could call the landlord and have him come down and open the lobby door, but that would take time Avrill didn't want to waste.

"So what's the plan?" Keiner asked.

They hadn't talked about how they were going to approach Sandoval this time around. The first time had been easy. Their back-and-forth interview technique was second nature by now, something they used to keep whoever they were talking to off balance. It was a way to shake a witness's story, if the story didn't sound legit or they felt the witness was trying to hide something.

Sandoval had caught on pretty quick, even with all the injuries he had that sure as hell didn't come from a fall. That part of his story had been bogus, but as far as Avrill could tell, whatever the musician was covering up had nothing to do with Jack Driscoll's death. The man had been genuinely shocked to hear that Driscoll was dead. That kind of shock a person couldn't fake.

Even Keiner's "one more question" technique hadn't caught Sandoval in a lie.

The musician didn't have a pet, not even a cat much less a big dog capable of doing the kind of damage that had been done to Driscoll and now the homeless man as well. Apartments with pets had a certain smell, no matter how much the people who lived there tried to cover it up. Avrill's body might not be in the best shape, but his sense of smell was just as good as it had always been.

He hadn't smelled any pet smell in Sandoval's apartment, and he hadn't seen any evidence that a pet lived there. No water bowls, no food dishes, no doggie toys or pet beds. Sandoval's clothes had no pet hair on them and neither did any of the furniture in the living room.

There wasn't even that overwhelming chemical odor of air fresheners or that crap that was supposed to kill odors in the air. Avrill hadn't needed Keiner's gotcha question to know Sandoval wasn't the owner of the dog that had killed Driscoll.

Avrill didn't suspect Sandoval in Driscoll's death. At this point, he was just someone they wanted to show the picture of the woman in the photograph the dead man had been carrying. Having two eyewitnesses verify it was the same woman was belt-and-suspenders detective work.

They could always track down the bartender first, show him the picture, and then come back to Sandoval, but they were already here. If Sandoval was just sleeping one off, Avrill was just fine with waking his ass up.

He took out his cell phone. He had Sandoval's number in his notes on this case.

"I'm gonna call him," Avrill said. "While I'm doing that, why don't you go around back and check to see if his car's here."

On the drive to Sandoval's apartment, Keiner had checked to see if the musician had a car registered in his name. Avrill thought it was a good bet considering the amount of equipment the T-shirt shop owner said he babysat when Sandoval took his bathroom breaks.

They lucked out. Sandoval had a car. Keiner had added the make, model, and license plate number to the case file notes.

Sandoval's car wasn't parked on the street. Converted houses like the one he lived in usually had limited parking available in basement garages. The musician might be one of the lucky ones who didn't have to rely on on-street parking.

The space between houses was practically non-existent. Keiner was going to have to go to the end of the block and up through the alleyway behind the buildings.

He gave Avrill a baleful look. "You don't want to admit you were wrong about the guy being home," he said.

"I don't want to admit that you're younger than me and in better shape," Avrill said. "Consider it part of your morning workout."

Keiner snorted. The call to report to the scene of the homeless guy's homicide had interrupted Keiner's morning exercise routine. The only thing the call had interrupted for Avrill was another couple of hours of sleep.

"I'll spring for lunch," Avrill said.

Keiner enjoyed a good meal. He grinned and named a restaurant they both enjoyed. Pricey, but then again what wasn't in the city.

Avrill made a shooing motion with one hand, and Keiner took off down the block, setting a brisk pace as he went downhill. He'd probably hoof it just as fast going back uphill when he reached the alley. Avrill didn't think he'd ever walked as fast, even when he had all his own original body parts.

He scrolled through the apps on his cell phone and opened the notes file for the original Driscoll case. The app conveniently highlighted Sandoval's cell number, so all Avrill had to do was touch the number and his phone placed the call.

Wonderful things, these modern cell phones.

Avrill brought the phone up to his ear and listened to his call ring Sandoval's cell.

And ring.

And ring.

47

All around Elias, the city went about its usual Monday mid-morning business.

A few pigeons picked at the seed scattered about the alley, cooing their appreciation while giving the not-a-cat woman a wide berth. Traffic passed by on the main feeder street below the mouth of the alley. Delivery trucks belched diesel with the grinding of gears, and a low-rider car thrummed a momentary blast of deafening bass beats out an open window.

Overhead, a single-engine airplane trailed an ad for a local politician running for re-election in the fall. The sky was wonderfully blue with only a few high, wispy clouds. Somewhere in the neighborhood a dog was barking, joyful, playful barks, and a young kid squealed a high, happy laugh. Someone else in the neighborhood was cooking onions and some kind of spicy meat. The barely heard ding of a bicycle bell meant some hardy soul was biking down one of the steep sidewalks in the neighborhood and wanted to give pedestrians a heads-up.

All normal, everyday stuff.

Elias wondered how the world could still be so damn normal all around him when his own world had suddenly imploded.

This not-a-cat woman, this imperious *creature*, had decided he was supposed to be her new companion. And he was just supposed to accept that, like he had no say in the matter?

He didn't even know what that meant.

He shook his head. "No," he said. "No *fucking* way."

She tilted her head to the side. "I've already protected you," she said. "That's my responsibility as Guardian. I ensure that the tribe continues to exist."

"I'm not part of your *tribe*," he said, biting the words off through stiff lips. "I'm human, remember?"

"You are," she said. "Companions are always part of the tribe." Her golden-green eyes bored into him. "I have lived most of my life with a companion. I have no intention of living without one now. I will continue to guard you. Keep you safe from"—she gestured at his forehead—"those who would harm you. In return, you will provide me with comfort and companionship."

Comfort. Companionship.

His gorge rose at the type of comfort she probably meant. He'd been with his share of women in his life, but he was sure they had all really *been* women. And it had always been by mutual choice and desire.

Not that way! NEVER that way!

The words shot through his mind with the force of a fist slamming into his skull and left his head ringing. He had to take a stumbling step to keep his balance.

His thoughts had insulted her. For a moment, he'd forgotten that she could read his mind.

"Then explain it to me," he said.

Instead of telling him, she showed him images in his mind.

Old fingers trailing along the spine of her natural shape, the long-haired ginger not-a-cat. He saw her trill with pleasure at the feeling of being loved and cared for. He saw an old man sharing his meals with her. Providing a space for her to curl up on his lap and sleep the deep sleep of one who knew her human companion would protect her from other humans while she slept.

He saw her communing with the old man the way she was communing with Elias. Heard the old man talk to her in his old man's voice while she simply conveyed her thoughts directly into his mind.

Elias blinked.

He recognized that old man's voice. His unusual way of speaking.

It was the same homeless man who'd been at the pedestrian plaza the day before. The man Elias had shared his coffee with.

The old man who'd said he and Elias were people watchers.

The old man who'd said Elias should watch out for the ones who weren't just people.

He thought about the old man. Tried to project that image in his mind.

"This is your companion?" he asked her.

She glanced away from him. "He was," she said.

Was. Elias didn't miss the past tense.

"What happened to him?" he asked. He'd just seen this man yesterday, and while he didn't look particularly well-fed, he'd seemed healthy enough.

"His life ended," she said.

Was that a hint of boredom in her voice? Or something else? Was she feigning boredom to cover some other emotion, like sorrow? She'd seemed genuinely happy in the images she'd showed him of her life with the old man. Then again, she'd chosen what images to show him. She'd had, according to her, a very long life, which meant she'd had a lot of practice communicating through images.

If she'd been human, he might have been able to read her. He was, after all, a people watcher according to the old man. But she wasn't human, something he couldn't forget.

In his pocket, his cell phone began to vibrate. He kept it on silent as a force of habit. The last thing he wanted when he was performing was to be interrupted by a call.

Well, that *had* been the last thing he'd wanted. Now the last thing he wanted was to ever see this not-a-cat woman again.

"Don't answer it," she said.

"It might be—"

Don't answer it!

He nearly reeled again. His headache had started to recede, but now it came back full force.

"Great way to protect me," he muttered, holding one hand to his aching forehead.

His cell vibrated four more times before voicemail kicked in. A few moments later his cell dinged, signaling that whoever had called had left him a voicemail.

On the downhill side of the alley, the pigeons who'd been pecking at the cracks in the concrete took to the air with a whir of wings.

The not-a-cat woman glanced in that direction, and her expression hardened into one of annoyance. Elias followed her gaze.

A man was walking up the alley toward them at a brisk pace. He was wearing a suit and tie—not something pedestrians in this neighborhood usually wore—and dress shoes. His shoulders looked bulky beneath his suit jacket.

Elias blinked. Was that Keiner, the detective who'd come to visit him Saturday afternoon with Detective Avrill?

Elias swallowed hard. What was Keiner doing here again?

Get rid of him.

He turned to ask the not-a-cat woman exactly how he was supposed to do that. He was just in time to see her shift into her natural form. One second the woman was standing next to his car, the next the long-haired ginger cat (*not* a cat) was trotting behind Elias's car, out of sight.

Elias felt the world tilt around him, like everything had just turned a quarter off true.

It was one thing to have her tell him that she was only wearing a human shape. It was another to actually see her shed that shape in the blink of an eye. She hadn't even left any clothes behind.

He was still trying to get his equilibrium back when Keiner made it to the back of Elias's apartment building. Keiner had his cell phone out.

"He's back here," Keiner said into his cell. He listened for a minute, then ended the call.

Keiner had to be in even better shape than Elias had given him credit for. The detective had basically speedwalked half a block uphill and he wasn't even winded. Or sweating. Elias would have been sucking wind if he'd tried something like that.

Thinking about normal, everyday things like being out of breath after a brisk walk was helping Elias ground himself. He tried to keep thinking nice, normal, friendly thoughts as he fought to slip into his approachable performer personality. He wasn't sure he was entirely successful, but at least he hoped he didn't look like he'd just seen a ghost.

Or a shapeshifter.

When Keiner didn't say anything, Elias decided to break the silence.

"Is there anything I can help you with?" he asked.

"We just have a couple of follow-up questions," Keiner said.

We. That meant Avrill was here too. That must have been who Keiner had called.

"You mind if we go inside?" Keiner asked. "My partner's got a bum knee. I don't want to make him walk up this hill if I don't have to."

Elias was supposed to get rid of Keiner, not invite him inside.

Residents had access to the parking garage from the first-floor hallway that ran the length of the building. The problem was that Elias's car was parked right next to the door that led inside, and the ginger not-a-cat was hiding behind Elias's car. They'd have to walk right by Elias's car to get into the house.

"Is he out front?" Elias asked, mainly to give himself a little time to think. "We can walk around. Save him the trip."

Keiner's expression didn't change, but something in his eyes made Elias think Keiner knew something else was going on.

"You guys have to walk that hill every time you want to get to your cars?" Keiner asked. His eyes flicked to the access door in the garage. "Is that only for the first-floor tenants?"

"No, we can all use it," Elias said.

Keiner shrugged. "So let's go that way. We need to let my partner in the front door anyway. No one answered their buzzers."

Elias's upstairs neighbor worked from home. He'd been the one who'd let the detectives into the building on Saturday. He'd admitted the same to Elias, but Elias had been too tired and in too much pain, not to mention still in shock at the news Jack was dead, to do more than ask the guy not to do it again. He'd said he wouldn't, but Elias knew better.

If his neighbor hadn't answered Keiner's buzzer, that must mean he was out too.

"You got your key, right?" Keiner asked.

Elias knew that was a cue to go inside with the detective.

So did the cat that wasn't a cat.

I said get RID of him!

If only Elias knew how.

48

AVRILL LEFT A VOICEMAIL MESSAGE FOR ELIAS SANDOVAL, SHORT AND to the point.

Detective Avrill. Call me.

He included his cell phone number in the message. Keiner always reminded him it wasn't necessary. Cell phones not only displayed the number of the person leaving the message but made it easy to call the same number back.

Modern technology. Sometimes Avrill felt like a Luddite in this technological world.

Which made him wonder.

How many of the shops along Jefferson down by the Wharf had security cameras? They'd asked Leon, the owner of the T-shirt/souvenir shop, if any of his store's cameras caught anything outside on the street, but he'd said no. He'd even taken them into his office and showed them the views from all four cameras.

If the woman they were looking for frequented the area, chances were she might have been caught on a store camera. The bar where Jack Driscoll had downed his last beer didn't have security cameras, not even over the register. At this point, she was a person of interest in one homicide and connected to a second. It might be worth the time

303

and effort to have one of the patrol officers canvas the stores along Jefferson—and on the Pier—to see if the woman showed up on any of their security cameras.

He was about to call the Strategic Investigations Unit to put in a request to have the officers who patrolled the area around the Wharf on foot do an initial canvas when his cell phone rang.

Keiner.

Avrill answered the call with a curt, "Yeah?"

"He's back here," Keiner said.

No wonder Sandoval hadn't answered his buzzer. He wasn't in his apartment but in whatever passed for a garage at the rear of the building.

"Keep him there," Avrill said. "Or better yet, have him let me in."

Keiner disconnected the call without saying anything else. That meant Sandoval was listening and Keiner didn't want to give anything away. Or else Keiner was pissed at having to walk all the way down for half a block and then uphill again, even though Avrill had been right to send him to go check.

Avrill had a feeling this lunch was going to cost him. Keiner might even order dessert.

Before Avrill could make the call to his Unit, a bicyclist braked to a stop in front of the building. He got off his bike, picked it up, and headed up the short flight of concrete steps to where Avrill stood waiting by the locked lobby door.

The bicyclist nodded at him. The guy was skinny, about Avrill's stoop-shouldered height, with thinning brown hair down to his shoulders. He might have even been going bald on top, but his bicycle helmet covered it up. He was dressed in the type of skintight bike shorts and bike shirt Avrill saw on most serious bike riders in the city. This guy's outfit was basic black with neon green, orange, and bright white geometric patterns on the sleeves and on the outside legs of the shorts.

Avrill held up his badge to the bike rider. "You live here?" he asked.

"Third floor," the guy said.

He gave Avrill the kind of wary look he'd come to expect from people who weren't sure why a cop was talking to them.

"Feel like letting me in?" Avrill asked. "I'm not here to see you, not unless you've seen this woman hanging around."

He brought up the woman's picture on his cell phone and enlarged it enough so it centered on the woman's face and all that long, curly hair.

The bike rider shook his head. "Nope. I haven't seen anyone like that. Not around here."

Avrill nodded, mostly to himself.

The bike rider just stood there, holding his bike, probably uncertain whether Avrill wanted to ask him anything else.

Avrill nodded toward the locked door. The bike rider produced a key from somewhere in his shorts and unlocked the door. Avrill decided to be a nice guy and held the door open while the guy maneuvered his bike inside.

"You don't park it in the garage?" Avrill asked, just for something to say.

Sometimes engaging people in casual conversation produced the kind of results he couldn't get with direct questioning. Keiner called it being a good bullshit artist.

"Things disappear back there," the bike rider said.

"Even when they're locked up?"

The bike rider shot him a look. "Even then, but you probably know that." He shrugged. "There's a lot of homeless around here. Elias—he's the guy you want to talk to, right?—he says he thinks some of them sleep in the garage since it doesn't have a gate or roll-down doors or anything."

He set his bicycle down in an alcove under the stairs leading up to the second floor. He produced a serious-looking lockset from a saddlebag beneath the bike's seat and locked the bike up, then he removed the front wheel.

"Don't trust your neighbors either," Avrill said, not making it a question.

"Better safe than sorry," the bike rider said. "I don't have a car. If I lose this puppy, I'm walking everywhere." He straightened up and frowned at Avrill. "What were we talking about?"

"The garage," Avrill said. "How your neighbor thinks the homeless camp out in your garage."

The dead guy down by Pier 39 had been homeless, but it would be quite a hike from the Pier to this neighborhood for a guy pushing a rusty old grocery cart.

"Don't get me wrong," the bike rider said. "This is a pretty good neighborhood. It's just...." He shrugged. "This city, you know? Too many people too close together, and everybody gets on everybody else's nerves. People forget to be kind to each other. Forget to be courteous. Forget they're supposed to keep their hands off other people's stuff."

Avrill wondered who'd ripped this guy off in the past, and how many times he'd been ripped off.

"I don't begrudge people who don't have a home anymore a place to sleep out of the elements," the bike rider was saying. "So long as they don't pee everywhere and don't steal stuff that doesn't belong to them. We have lockers in the garage, these big closets with padlocks on them where we can store stuff, but I won't use them. Padlocks don't stop somebody who's really determined. At least the building's secure."

It would be if the tenants didn't randomly buzz people in, but Avrill didn't say that.

The bike rider started to head upstairs, then looked back at Avrill. "You need anything else from me?" he asked.

Avrill had decided to make the call to his Unit while he waited for Keiner and Sandoval. There was a hallway beyond the alcove where the bike rider had stashed his bike. The hallway was on the uphill side of the building and led toward the back. Avrill guessed there was a door back there somewhere that opened into the garage. Keiner and Sandoval should be coming in that way.

He lifted his cell phone, gratified to see that he still had a strong signal. "Got a call to make first," he said, then added, "Thanks for the assist."

"No problem," the bike rider said.

Avrill waited until the bike rider was climbing the stairs to the third floor before he placed the call. When the Unit's dispatch officer answered, Avrill identified himself and put in his request. He gave dispatch the case number and the precinct of origin.

As part of the city-wide Bureau of Investigations, the Strategic Investigations Unit was assigned to investigate homicides wherever they occurred in the city. Avrill and Keiner would be following the Driscoll investigation and now the killing of the homeless man no matter what precincts eventually became involved. According to the Bureau's Deputy Chief, this structure was supposed to cut down on inter-precinct rivalry and make sure that the serious crimes Avrill's Unit handled were investigated by specialists in those crimes. In reality, it meant that Avrill put a lot of miles on his car chasing down leads.

Like Sandoval.

He'd just put his phone back in his pocket when something thudded against the building hard enough that he felt it through the soles of his shoes.

His first thought was earthquake. San Francisco certainly had its fair share, although earthquakes in L.A. got all the press.

That's when he heard the flat report of a gunshot.

Not an earthquake. A gunshot, and it had come from the back of the building.

Where Keiner was with Sandoval.

Avrill took off down the hallway, running as fast as his knees—the factory original and the artificial replacement—could take him.

49

THE NOT-A-CAT HAD DECIDED SHE COULDN'T CATCH HIS BREATH.

One moment he was walking with Detective Keiner toward the access door at the back of the garage, busy trying to dig his keys out of his pocket with fingers that felt cold and numb and clumsy, and the next all hell broke loose.

The not-a-cat had decided she couldn't rely on Elias to get rid of Keiner, so she was going to take matters into her own hands.

Or more precisely, into her own claws.

A blur of ginger fur, needle-sharp teeth, and razorblade claws exploded from her hiding place behind Elias's car, headed straight for Keiner.

Elias watched in horror as she grew to twice her size. Three times her size. *Four* times her size. *Five times* her size!

She was bigger now than the sabertoothed tiger Elias had seen at a museum he'd gone to with a woman he'd dated briefly after his marriage broke up. Far bigger than one of those Mini Coopers Elias sometimes saw on Jefferson Street by the Wharf. Or those expensive convertible sportscars guys going through midlife crisis bought to make themselves still feel virile even as they were going bald on top.

She was as big as a polar bear.

Keiner managed to draw his gun before she was on him.

She could have bitten his head off. Disemboweled him with her claws. Instead she swatted him with a paw the size of a serving platter and sent him flying.

Keiner crashed into the back wall of the garage next to the access door.

He slid down the wall, his head leaving a bloody trail behind him.

He was still awake and aware. Elias could see it in his eyes. But he wouldn't be for long.

Was this how she'd killed Jack? Because Elias knew—*knew*—that she'd gone after Jack exactly like this. She'd ripped his throat out, and why? Just because Jack had threatened him? Like she thought Keiner was some kind of threat?

Elias wanted to scream at her to stop, but he couldn't find his voice. He felt the scream building up inside him, but that was all. He felt paralyzed, helpless to do anything.

Was she doing that to him? Controlling him somehow? He'd never been someone who just stood by while other people got hurt.

Got dead, he corrected himself.

She was going to kill a cop. She was going to kill Keiner.

If Keiner didn't kill her first.

Keiner was raising his gun. Blood had already started to dribble out of his mouth, soaking his chin. She'd hurt him badly when she'd hit him with that huge paw. His arm was shaking, the barrel of his gun wobbling back and forth.

He didn't hesitate. He fired in the general direction of her center mass. She was big enough he must have thought he couldn't miss.

Except he did.

She shrank in the blink of an eye, and the bullet went past her. The back passenger window in Elias's car exploded in a spray of safety glass.

That seemed to break whatever hold she'd had on Elias.

"Stop!" he screamed at her. "Just stop! You've already hurt him, can't you see that? You stopped him. You don't need to—"

Keiner fired again.

This time the bullet grazed her shoulder.

She shrieked, a sound that was part pain, part surprise, and almost all anger.

She was still much bigger than a housecat. Bigger than she'd been in the hall at Leon's store. She sprang at Keiner, but instead of slashing her claws across his throat or crushing his chest by landing on him, she grabbed his gun arm and bit down.

Now Keiner was shrieking as she shook her head. He was still shrieking when his severed arm, hand still holding the gun, landed near Elias's feet.

The access door at the back of the garage flew open.

Avrill already had his gun out. He took two steps into the garage and froze, eyes wide.

"Don't!" Elias yelled. He wasn't sure who he was pleading with—the cat or Avrill. "Just don't!"

The cat turned toward him.

"He'll kill you," Elias told her. "If you hurt him, he'll kill you."

"He'll try," she said, her words perfectly understandable even spoken by her cat mouth.

All the blood drained out of Avrill's face. Elias knew how he felt. Of all the unbelievable things he'd seen that day, all the things she'd told him, hearing her speak while she was in her natural form—a much bigger version, but still her natural cat shape—was the hardest thing to accept.

"Avrill!" he said sharply to get the detective's attention. "Keiner's still alive, but he won't be for long if you don't take care of him."

Keiner was whimpering now. Blood was gushing from his severed arm, and Elias could see the ragged ends of bone. The skin on his face was nearly paper white.

Whether it was the whimper or what Elias said, something seemed to galvanize Avrill. He undid the buckle on his belt and pulled it out of the belt loops on his slacks one handed. He kept his gun trained on the cat while he looped the belt around Keiner's upper arm with one hand, but he'd need both hands to snug it tight.

"We're leaving," Elias said to Avrill, then he turned to the cat.

"We're leaving," he said again. "I have the keys to my car. We can leave. There's no need to kill anyone."

Anyone else. Elias had his doubts whether Keiner would make it.

They've seen me use my greatest gift. They will hunt me.

Elias held out his hands at his sides, palms up. "Who's going to believe them?"

Who would have believed him it he'd told anyone what he'd seen in Leon's hallway? Nobody, that's who.

"You will come with me? Willingly?" she asked out loud.

He didn't want to, but what choice did he have? He was an accessory now, if not to murder, then to assault on a police officer. Every cop in the city would be looking for him. He certainly couldn't stay here. If he managed to stay free for a little while longer, maybe he could figure a way out of this mess.

He looked at Avrill. Some of the color had come back to the detective's face. In its place was a hard, bitter anger.

"You can't run," Avrill said. "I'll find you and your...." His eyes flickered to the cat, who'd shrunk back to the size of a housecat. "Pet," Avrill finished. "No matter where you go. I'll find you."

Then his eyes widened. Elias knew why.

The cat had shifted forms again. Now she was once again the lithe young woman with golden-green eyes and long curly hair the color of a sunset. Her clothes had formed around her body, but her feet were bare, the toes tipped with razor-sharp nails. She was looking down at Avrill with disdain.

"I'm nobody's pet," she said, then she lifted her chin toward Elias. "He's *mine.*"

50

Keiner died on the operating table.

While Elias and the woman—cat—whatever—fled the scene, Avrill had used his belt as a makeshift tourniquet to staunch the flow of blood on Keiner's severed arm. By that point, Keiner had slipped into unconsciousness.

The paramedics showed up in near record time along with three patrol cars.

Avrill had waved off any questions about what had happened, instead climbing into the back of the ambulance along with Keiner. Once they got to the hospital, Keiner was rushed into surgery and Avrill was left alone in the surgical wing's waiting room with his thoughts.

He had no frame of reference for what had just happened. What he'd just seen.

How the hell was he supposed to write any of this up? He supposed he could stall the official paperwork until Keiner woke up. They'd need to get their stories straight, and to do that, Avrill would need to know what Keiner remembered. Trauma had a way of scrambling the mind. Avrill knew that firsthand. Try as he might to

313

remember the time immediately before and after he'd been shot, those hours were lost to the fog of memory.

He almost hoped it would be that way for Keiner. Nobody should have to relive an attack as savage as the one Keiner had endured.

One thing was clear. Elias Sandoval was involved in this up to his eyeballs. No, check that. Up to his bruised and battered head.

Had she done that to him? The unnamed *thing* that claimed Sandoval was her pet?

Only Keiner never woke up.

The surgeon who came to talk to Avrill said that Keiner's injuries had been too severe. His chest had been crushed. That alone would have been repairable, the surgeon said. Crushed ribs could be replaced with implants, like Avrill's artificial knee. The problem was the broken ribs had punctured Keiner's lungs in multiple places. He'd not only been bleeding from his severed arm, he'd been bleeding into his chest.

Keiner had gone into cardiac arrest on the operating table. They'd tried for as long as they could to get his heart beating again.

"Despite our best efforts," the surgeon said, "we were unsuccessful. I'm sorry for your loss, Detective."

Keiner was gone.

Avrill sat down hard on one of the molded plastic chairs in the waiting room. He rested his elbows on his knees and ran both hands through his hair.

He still had Keiner's blood on his suit. He'd have to throw the suit out. No dry cleaner in the world was going to get those stains out.

Stupid thing to think about at a time like this. Having to throw out a suit. He needed to get new suits made anyway. All of his old ones were too big. Drug withdrawal did that to a person. He'd lost almost twenty-five pounds in the first few months after he'd kicked the painkillers out of his life, and that was after the thirty he'd lost following surgery.

Stop it, he told himself. Think. Figure out what you're going to do next.

Keiner was dead. That *thing* had killed him, and Sandoval had protected it.

No one else was in the waiting room for Keiner. He didn't have any family in the city. He had one sister who lived in New Mexico. His mother was in a nursing home in Washington state, suffering from advanced Alzheimer's. His father had passed away two years ago. Avrill would have to call the sister, unless the captain planned to do the official notification himself.

Other detectives from their Unit had wanted to come sit with Avrill, but he'd sent them all away. He hadn't wanted this to turn into a death watch. Instead he'd given them a physical description of Sandoval along with enough information on his car for an APB. He knew they all wanted to do something, and chasing down Sandoval was number one on their list.

Avrill had warned them that Sandoval had a dangerous animal with him. Nobody had pressed him about what kind of animal. They'd been too shocked at Keiner's injuries and took Avrill's word that the animal had most likely killed two other people before it had attacked Keiner.

How long could Avrill keep this up? Keep pretending that what had killed Keiner was *just* a dangerous animal?

He could probably stall filling out an official report for a few days. His lieutenant would give him some leeway. There was no question that he'd take Avrill off the Driscoll case and the one they'd opened that morning for the dead homeless man. Not only did Avrill no longer have a partner, he was personally involved. If Avrill protested, the lieutenant would cite policy, and he'd be right.

Well, they could take him off. They could even make him take mandatory leave and mandatory grief counseling, but that didn't mean he was done with Sandoval.

So think, Avrill told himself. Put the pieces together, but this time focus on Sandoval.

First, the man has a run-in with Driscoll at Leon's store. Just a run-of-the-mill insult fest, according to Sandoval. Nothing he hasn't endured before. No big deal. But enough of a big deal to Driscoll that he goes outside to have a smoke and calm down, even though that leaves the store unattended.

Then that night Sandoval gets himself mugged in the parking garage behind Leon's store. That's after he cons Leon into showing him security camera footage from around the time Sandoval took his bathroom break. Instead of reporting the mugging to the police—Keiner had checked that out; there'd been no report—Sandoval makes up some bullshit story about falling down in the parking garage.

Had he seen who attacked him? Had his attacker been Jack Driscoll? Driscoll had a pretty checkered past, including an arrest following a bar fight, but the charges had been dismissed. Avrill wouldn't have put it past Driscoll to think what a great idea it would be to teach Sandoval a lesson.

But why *that* day? Sandoval's arrangement with Leon wasn't something new. What would have set Driscoll off?

If he'd been the one who'd attacked Sandoval, that had been the biggest mistake of Driscoll's life. He'd been killed later the same night.

Mauled to death by a big animal.

Sandoval has ties to a big animal. A big vicious animal. An animal he had to *convince* not to kill Keiner or attack Avrill. An animal who'd turned out to be the same woman Avrill and Keiner had been looking for all along.

Then last night a homeless man gets himself killed the same way as Driscoll.

No, that wasn't right.

The homeless man had been slaughtered. His wounds had been much more vicious. Driscoll'd had his throat torn out and his wrist broken. The homeless man's belly had been ripped open even through all the layers of clothing he was wearing. His neck had been shredded all the way to his spine, and his eyes torn from their sockets.

The M.E.'s preliminary report on the homeless man had come through while Avrill was waiting to hear the results of Keiner's surgery. The neck injury had completely severed the man's carotid artery, and he'd bled out in a matter of minutes. The other injuries—his belly wound and his eyes—had occurred post-mortem.

Those were the actions of someone who was seriously pissed off at that guy.

And this homeless man had saved a picture of the same woman. A woman who'd been spotted seeming to enjoy another woman's misfortune.

Avrill gripped his hair with his fists.

He didn't believe in coincidences. Not when they lined up like this.

Sandoval was at the center of all this. Even discounting the weirdness—and God, how Avrill wished he could discount all the weirdness he'd seen with his own two eyes—Sandoval was more than just a person of interest in both—no, check that, all *three* cases.

Avrill had never been one for horror stories. Vampires, werewolves, mummies, ghosts—those were all just stories people told each other to distract themselves from the horrors of real life. War, famine, disease, hatred and discrimination. Gang violence and school shootings. Pandemics. Politicians who cared more about power than the lives of their constituents. Billionaires who'd never be able to quench their thirst for more, more, more. There was more than enough horror in real life.

But he couldn't deny his senses. He'd relied on what he saw, he heard, even what he smelled, all his life. He'd built his career on what his senses told him. He trusted his perceptions of the world around him. If he stopped now, who would he be? *What* would he be?

Not himself. Not anymore.

He'd seen what he'd seen. He could either accept it and go from there or deny it and go quietly crazy.

And if he went crazy, what then? Would he end up living on the street like that unnamed homeless man? End up getting himself killed by something out of a horror story?

He'd be damned if he was going to go out that way.

He had a suspect. He could focus on that.

He could focus on Elias Sandoval. On tracking him down and bringing him in.

As for the *thing* Sandoval had with him?

Avrill'd had a chance to shoot her and he'd hesitated. He'd put his partner's life first, but Keiner had died anyway.

If Avrill ever saw her again, he wouldn't hesitate.

The next time, he'd shoot to kill.

51

Elias lost track of the days.

He'd never worn a watch. His cell phone told him what day it was. It told him when to get up, what the temperature would be so he'd know how to dress for work. It gave him headline news and let him play a few mindless games when he needed to wind down at night. It even gave him music on demand thanks to the streaming services he subscribed to.

All that was gone. The not-a-cat woman had thrown his cell out the window of his car as they sped away from his apartment.

"Your police can use your phone to track you," she'd said.

She'd crushed the phone with one hand before she'd thrown it away. He'd heard the glass crack. If she'd intended it as a show of strength, he'd gotten the message.

His car was gone now too, along with all his equipment still in the trunk. His old amp and microphone. The portable power supply he'd paid far too much for. His demo CDs. They'd ditched the car on a side street in a sketchy neighborhood after they'd taken out all the paperwork in the glove box that had his name or his address. They'd left the key in the ignition.

"The easier to steal," she'd said. "When the police find your car, and they will, you won't be the person driving it."

She'd let him keep an old blanket and rain slicker he'd had in the trunk, along with a flashlight from the glove box. As they'd walked away from his car, he'd been glad that his keyboard and guitar were still in his bedroom at the apartment. Not that he'd be seeing them anytime soon, but at least they were still his, not some thief's.

He'd wanted to leave the car near Presidio Park, but she'd said no. The Presidio wasn't in her territory. Fort Mason was. Cow Hollow was. The Presidio wasn't.

The first night had been horrible. He'd never camped out in his life, not even when he'd been a kid, and he hadn't known what to expect.

She'd found him a spot in an alley a few blocks away from Ghirardelli Square. All he'd been wearing when they'd fled his apartment were his old jeans, the T-shirt he always slept in, and an old hoodie. He'd put the rain slicker on over his hoodie and wrapped the blanket around himself, but it hadn't been enough to keep out the cold. He'd been hungry and thirsty, and the cold made all his injuries hurt more than they had since the night he'd dragged himself home after being attacked.

He'd shivered his way through the night. She'd stayed next to him all night in her cat form. The wound on her shoulder where the bullet grazed her had already scabbed over, and it didn't seem to hurt her anymore. At one point she'd climbed on his lap. He'd tensed up, remembering the way she'd attacked Keiner, but all she'd done was curl up and fall asleep.

Just like a cat.

The next few days—two? Three? He had no idea—passed in something of a blur. They kept to the side streets and alleys. Elias always pulled the hood on his hoodie as far forward over his face as he could. He walked with his head tilted down so that people didn't automatically see the bruises still prominent beneath his eyes. He relieved himself in public restrooms where he tried to clean himself as much as possible in dirty sinks and ate cheap convenience store food. He had less than a hundred dollars in his wallet, and that wouldn't last long. He really wanted a cup of coffee, but didn't want to spend the money. Water was a necessity, and he bought it a gallon at a time because it was cheaper that way.

Most of all, he tried to go unnoticed. That meant he couldn't go to soup kitchens or food banks. He figured the cops would circulate his picture anyplace in the city that fed or sheltered the homeless.

Most people he passed on the street ignored him. If anyone noticed him at all, it was to remark what a pretty cat he had. They had no idea just how deadly she was.

He'd asked her once if she had a name. She'd looked at him with an expression of such disdain he felt like he'd touched on some forbidden subject.

We have no need for names.

That bit of non-verbal communication was followed by images of different cats that he assumed weren't just cats. Each image was accompanied by a memory or a scent or something she called essence.

He realized that's how her people—her *kin*—recognized each other. By their essence, which was something far more than just the scents that bloodhounds followed. That's also how she'd found where he lived. By following his essence. Even in a city teeming with people, she'd been able to follow his essence.

That was fine for her kin, but he wasn't her kin. He needed a name for her, so he started to think of her as Gilda. Not because of the color of her fur or the color of her hair when she wore her human shape, but because she was keeping him in a cage. Not a cage made of gilded bars, but one made from his own guilt about what had happened to Keiner.

The detective had died. Elias had seen the detective's picture on the front page of a newspaper when he'd gone into a convenience store to buy a cheap sandwich and another gallon of water.

Elias had scanned the accompanying article. Most of it concerned Keiner's long service to the people of San Francisco. All his awards and commendations. No mention was made of the horrible way he'd died, only that he'd been killed in the line of duty.

Such a bloodless way of describing his death. Elias had tried to save Keiner's life by sacrificing his own to this being who considered him her pet, and it hadn't mattered.

He'd glared at her when he left the convenience store. She'd sat waiting patiently for him outside. He shouldn't have been surprised that she knew why he was so angry with her.

He was already dying. I tasted it in his essence. It was the only reason I didn't end him then.

That was the first time Elias thought that he should just turn himself in. Walk up to the next police officer he saw and surrender. He'd spend the rest of his life in prison, but at least he wouldn't be cold and hungry.

She'd laid her ears back against her head and hissed at him.

Then she gave him the image of the old homeless man he'd given coffee to. He'd been her last companion, and she'd shown him what she'd done to him when he'd betrayed her by trying to warn Elias about her.

Elias had almost thrown up, right there on the street, even though his stomach was empty.

Do not go back on your word. I will tolerate much while you learn your place, but not that.

And the bitch of it was that he *had* given her his word. He'd agreed to go with her willingly. He'd done it to save Avrill too. At least he'd saved that man's life.

But he'd inadvertently caused Jack's death.

That first cold night when he couldn't sleep, he'd asked her flat out if she'd killed Jack. When she admitted it, he'd asked her why.

"You'd already scared the shit out of him," he'd said.

I am a Guardian. You are part of my tribe. He injured you. I could not allow that.

That had shocked him. Had Jack had been the person who'd attacked him in the parking garage? Who'd kicked Elias in his ribs and back so hard he'd barely been able to move?

Had he considered whether Jack was the mugger before? Elias's mind was so scrambled by this point he couldn't remember.

It made a sick kind of sense. But still....

"That didn't mean he had to die!" Elias had said.

It was my duty.

That thought had a different flavor to it. He hadn't thought much about it at the time. He'd learned that thinking potentially dangerous thoughts when she was awake was just asking for trouble. She'd corrected him more than once with a swift swipe from her claws. He had new scratches on his arm now to go along with the old scar from his mom's tomcat.

But when she slept? She didn't seem to be able to hear his thoughts then.

Not that he was able to stay awake for long after they settled down for the night. She'd brought him a blanket and a coat after their second or third night on the street. She'd been in her human form then, and he hadn't asked her where she got them. All he knew was that since he was no longer freezing all night, he couldn't seem to stay awake long after the sun went down.

Shock, he figured. And hunger.

That was probably why he'd seen the lion.

He'd woken up one night from a bad dream. A dream filled with blood and teeth and claws, and women who'd been burned alive for talking to familiars, and he'd jerked awake.

The side street where they'd settled down for the night had been shrouded in thick fog that turned the streetlight at the end of the block into the soft fluff of a cotton ball. Elias had fallen asleep sitting upright with his back against the side of a building. He'd pulled his blankets closer around his shoulders, wishing he had his old hat—any old hat—to cover his head.

Gilda had been deeply asleep on his lap. Her breath was coming out in faint snores. Those snores were the most human thing about her. She would have been insulted at the thought, but she couldn't hear his thoughts now.

He'd just started to think about how he might be able to extricate himself from this hell he'd found himself in when something stirred in the fog. The shape was big and indistinct at first.

Then it had padded toward him on silent paws.

Not cat-sized paws. Something bigger.

Elias had steeled himself to get ready for one of Gilda's kin to emerge from the fog. She'd kept him away from her kin so far, whether deliberately or not, he couldn't tell. Eventually he figured one of them would show up, or she'd take him to meet with someone she trusted. Like the short-haired white kin who'd been with her in Leon's store.

He'd been ready to see an oversized cat. He hadn't been ready to see a lion.

A damn lion, complete with a magnificent ruff of fur around its neck and down its chest.

The lion sat back on its haunches and simply stared at him. The light wasn't good enough for Elias to see the color of its eyes, but he was sure they would be golden-green.

The lion stayed there for so long, simply gazing at him, that Elias eventually started to doze off. His head lolled back against the building, then he jerked himself awake, reminding himself that he wasn't alone in the alley.

But the lion was gone.

The encounter had been so odd that the next morning Elias thought it had just been part of his dream. Gilda had gazed at him for a long time with her golden-green eyes, then she'd set about washing her fur, just like any other cat.

Elias told himself that if she wasn't concerned he'd had a dream about a lion, he shouldn't be either.

He kept telling himself that until he saw the lion again, and this time he was wide awake.

<h1 style="text-align:center">52</h1>

Her new companion had given her a human name.

Gilda.

The long-haired ginger cat who wasn't a cat understood the reference. She'd tasted it in her companion's essence. She'd decided to allow it because it amused her, but also because it was a sign that her new companion was adjusting to his life as he would know it from now on.

He thought she had trapped him in a gilded cage, only the bars were made of the golden hair of her human form that had first caught his attention. An apt metaphor, as she understood the human concept.

But there was another component to her name. Her companion was suffering a strange, very human emotion over the death of the cop named Keiner. He felt responsible somehow, even though he'd stopped her from killing the human outright. That emotion also formed the bars of the cage he imagined himself in.

The ginger cat felt no such guilt. The cop named Keiner had been a threat to her tribe, and her companion was now a part of that tribe. She was a Guardian. It was her duty to protect her tribe from discovery. Keiner had discovered her existence, and therefore he had to die.

325

Her companion still thought of himself as Elias, but eventually he would forget his human name. It had taken years for her last companion to discard everything that had tied him to his old life.

Everything except the photograph he carried in his pocket.

Of course she had known about that. She also knew that he'd saved a photograph of her human form that he'd found in the trash. She'd allowed that too. Accepted it as a sign of his affection for her. But that affection had brought another emotion to the surface, one that New Blood shared with humans.

Jealousy.

New Blood often became jealous of their companions. Those who spent the majority of their lives in their human forms eventually became jealous of their human possessions and the connections they formed with other humans.

Old Blood, like the old tom, claimed not to feel that emotion. The elders counselled that jealousy would eventually destroy New Blood and lead to the discovery of their kin and the destruction of the tribe. The ginger cat believed that jealousy, when kept under control, was a necessary emotion, otherwise the Maker would not have allowed it to become part of New Blood's essence.

Her old companion hadn't controlled his jealousy. He'd tried to warn her new companion. Tried to frighten him away. That had enraged her. Still, she had gifted him with a quick death, only giving her rage full rein after he was dead.

The other policeman—Avrill, he called himself—had found the pictures the old man kept. He knew her human form. She should have killed him too when she had the chance. A lost opportunity, certainly, but there would be another. He was searching for her and her new companion. Eventually she would let him find her, and then she would do her duty as Guardian and end another threat to the existence of the tribe.

Only then, after she'd taken care of the human named Avrill, would she think about introducing her new companion to the tribe. Until then, she needed to keep him solely to herself. His mind had not been shattered like her old companion's, and he was far more strong-willed that she had anticipated. He would need more time to fully adjust.

He still dreamed of his old life.

He still dreamed of the music he used to play.

She could not allow him to make that kind of music, never again. It would tie him too closely to the human he'd been and only serve to reinforce his will. It might even turn him against her, and then she would have to kill him.

She didn't want to have to do that. What she wanted was for him to make the star music. That had been what had drawn her to him in the first place.

The gift of star music had been given to him long ago, in human terms, by one of the kin. A gift he had not known he possessed until the ginger cat had touched his mind, and he had heard her.

That long-ago touch had faded over time. Because she was a Guardian, she could still sense it in his essence, but not strongly enough to identify the kin who had touched him. Not that it mattered. The touch made him susceptible to her thoughts, and his thoughts accessible to her.

The thought she was most troubled by was his dream of the lion.

There was no reason for him to dream of the old tom. She had touched the essence of every member of her tribe, warning them to stay away while she trained her new human companion. Even the elders in the tribe had acquiesced, for even though she was New Blood, she was a Guardian, and they understood she knew what was best for the tribe.

The old tom had not responded to her warning. Instead he had kept her from sensing his essence, something only very few Old Blood could do.

Had the told tom been communicating with her new companion in his dreams?

That was forbidden. Not by the laws handed down by the Maker, but by the ancient traditions that Old Blood held sacred.

The old tom was a Guardian, but she could not allow him to flaunt the sacred laws of their kin. The laws served to protect the tribe and keep it secure from outside threats. If the old tom had violated the law, performed a forbidden act, she would have to correct him.

Not while she was a Guardian. That too was forbidden. But when she became the Protector, she would be free to correct kin as well as non-kin, even Guardians.

She felt that time was approaching soon. The Protector would be returning to the city, where she would die and the ginger cat would take her place. It was her destiny, promised to her when she was still a youngling.

When she became the Protector, after she dealt with the old tom, she would take her new companion away from this city and travel to wherever the Protector was needed by the far-flung tribes of their kin. She would no longer be bound by territory. The world would be her new territory.

She would have to adopt a new human shape, but there were so many in the world to choose from. She could choose one that suited her. She had only adopted the shape of the young, free-spirited human female because that shape had been a pleasing memory the Protector had shared with her. A pleasing memory from the time before the ginger cat had been born.

Once the ginger cat became the Protector, she could choose a human shape that was pleasing only to her. Or she might adopt many different shapes. The possibilities were endless, just like the life ahead of her.

She was more than ready for that new life to start.

53

The lieutenant in charge of Avrill's unit put him on administrative leave.

Avrill had expected it. His partner had been killed in the line of duty, which was reason enough. Avrill had compounded it by fabricating a good portion of his official report of the incident. It would have been another reason to put him on leave, although that would have involved union reps and far more meetings than a simple one-on-one with his lieutenant.

No, the reason, which his lieutenant didn't come right out and say, was that Avrill hadn't fired his weapon at the animal who had mauled his partner.

The lieutenant had given him an extra day to fill out his report. Avrill had thought long and hard about how to write up the report in a way that wouldn't have the lieutenant questioning his sanity.

In the end, he'd decided to keep the report as close to the truth as he could. He'd stated that when he exited the apartment building, Keiner was bleeding out on the floor of a three-car garage. Avrill had drawn his weapon when he heard the first gunshot, but when he arrived on the scene, he assessed that Keiner's wounds were life threatening and needed immediate attention.

329

He decided not to try to describe the indescribable and frankly unbelievable parts of what he'd seen. He simply stated in his report that Keiner's wounds appeared to have been caused by a large animal in the company of Elias Sandoval, a person of interest in the Driscoll case and the person that he and Keiner had gone to see. Sandoval and the animal were fleeing the scene in an automobile registered in Sandoval's name.

Avrill then applied a tourniquet to Keiner's severed right arm and placed an emergency call, officer down, needs assistance. He also requested an APB on Sandoval's car. When emergency personnel arrived, he accompanied Keiner and the paramedics to the hospital.

The lieutenant wasn't a stupid man. He'd earned his promotions through long, hard work. His mind was sharp as a tack. He could have taken his twenty and retired years ago, but he kept at it because it was necessary work. Avrill had known some command personnel who could give a rip about anything but their next promotion, but his lieutenant wasn't one of them. Avrill respected the man, even when he threw a printout of the report at Avrill during their meeting.

"Want to tell me the parts you left out?" the lieutenant demanded.

Like everyone in the lieutenant's Major Response Team, including Avrill, the lieutenant didn't wear a uniform. Instead he was dressed in a sharp-looking gray suit with subtle pinstripes, a white dress shirt, and a deep blue tie with a barely there print. He had to be on the near side of sixty, but he was still a fit man with a full head of salt-and-pepper hair, a trim mustache, and piercing blue eyes. Those eyes bored into Avrill.

"Sir?" Avrill said.

Those piercing eyes narrowed. "Don't bullshit me, detective."

Detective, not Isaiah. That didn't bode well.

Avrill decided not to say anything.

"According to this piece of fiction—" the lieutenant stabbed at the report with one finger "—you let a—and I'm quoting here—*large animal* leave the scene of an attack on your partner without attempting to prevent that animal from running loose and attacking innocent civilians. Two of which, I might remind you, this animal had already *killed*." The lieutenant shook his head. "You're a good cop. You've always been a good cop. You understand that 'protect and serve' means *protect the goddamn people we serve!*"

The lieutenant hadn't shouted. He didn't need to. His entire body had gone as rigid as the finger still poking at the report.

"I made a judgment call," Avrill said.

It sounded lame even to his own ears.

The lieutenant sat back in his chair. Like all of the furniture in his office, the chair was oversized, a black leather executive chair that somehow didn't make the man who sat in it look small by comparison.

"That's it?" the lieutenant asked. "That's all you've got?"

Avrill thought about keeping his mouth shut again but decided against it.

"If I can recall anything else," he said, "I'll file a supplemental report. This is what I can remember, as I'm sitting here today."

That was a bald-faced lie. Avrill hated making it, and he could tell the lieutenant hated hearing it. But the lieutenant couldn't do anything about it unless someone filed a statement that contradicted what Avrill had written, and no one would. The bicycle rider who lived on the third floor had wisely stayed inside, probably watching from an upstairs window after the gunshots stopped. By the time backup officers arrived, Sandoval and that thing he'd been protecting were already long gone.

"You're on leave," the lieutenant said. "Administrative. For now." He pushed another piece of paper across his desk toward Avrill. "Give my assistant your gun and badge along with this official notification, which I trust you'll sign. She'll make sure you have a copy."

Avrill nodded once, picked up his official notification—already filled out, he saw—and got up to leave. The lieutenant's voice stopped him before he got to the door.

"Whatever you're keeping to yourself," the lieutenant said to Avrill's back, "I hope it's worth your career. And I'm telling you—officially—to keep your nose out of this investigation. Every officer in the city is looking for your perp and his *animal*. Got that?"

Avrill didn't say anything, just went out and handed over his gun and badge and signed his form. When the assistant asked him to wait to get his copy, he told her to mail it to him.

He wasn't about to go home to sit on his ass doing nothing. He no longer had his badge and gun—not his official gun—but like every cop he knew, he had his own personal gun the department knew about and a couple the department didn't. He also had friends among the patrol officers who'd keep him up to date on the official investigation.

The first update came later that same afternoon. Avrill was out shopping at a local Goodwill when he took the call. He needed to update his wardrobe with the kind of secondhand clothes that were Goodwill's stock in trade. Where he'd be going, even suits that hung off his frame like he was a coat hanger would stand out.

"We found the car," Avrill's buddy said when he answered the call. "Some kid had taken it for a joyride. Said he found it with the keys in the ignition, like it was an open invitation or something. Glove box was cleaned out."

"What about the trunk?" Avrill asked.

Sandoval had a lot of equipment he carted to the Wharf in his car, but the techs who'd gone over his apartment with a fine-tooth comb had only found one guitar and an electronic keyboard.

"Empty. The kid tried to tell us he found it that way, but he eventually admitted he hocked the stuff."

His buddy told Avrill where the car had been found, a low-rent district where it was sure to be stolen.

Sandoval had been smart, Avrill had to give him that. Too smart for a guy who was supposed to be just a street performer. Avrill had double-checked Sandoval's record, which was squeaky clean. The only legal action he'd been involved in was a divorce in Nevada nearly twenty years ago.

"No sign of your perp, though," his buddy said. "We'll catch him. Don't you worry."

Avrill wasn't worried. Sandoval had no car. His picture and description had gone out to every form of public transportation in the city. Unless he walked across the Golden Gate bridge or decided to hoof it south, they'd find him.

If Avrill didn't find him first.

He spent half a week's salary on the kind of clothes and supplies most of the homeless in the city kept. Flannel shirts with worn cuffs and holes in the sleeves and tails. Undershirts that had seen better days and still smelled of bleach. Jeans that might have been blue in a former life. A heavy jacket with a hood, and two hoodies in dull, drab colors. He bought two woolen blankets that smelled like a combination of old cigarette smoke, strong detergent, and musty seawater. He topped his purchases off with a sleeping bag that didn't smell much better, a black rain slicker with a hood, and an olive-drab tarp.

He couldn't carry all the stuff, but he lucked out. The store had a wheeled shopping cart like he used to see the old ladies in his childhood neighborhood use to cart home their groceries from the Italian market. It wasn't a rusted grocery store cart like the dead homeless man had used, but it would do.

The clerk had given him a raised eyebrow. In his suit and cop haircut, he supposed he didn't look like a typical homeless man.

"Halloween's coming up," he said. "I'm making a display."

"Kind of in poor taste, don't you think?" the clerk said.

Avrill had given the clerk a perfunctory smile. "Don't worry. I'm donating it all when I'm done."

The clerk hadn't bought his explanation, but Avrill didn't care.

He went home, changed into his new old clothes, and packed the rest of his purchases into the cart. Then he strapped an ankle holster on his right leg and tucked one of his side pieces inside. He locked his ID and his cell phone in the wall safe in his apartment, put some bills and spare change in the front pocket of his jeans, and put some additional folding money inside the toe of his left boot. He'd already bought a burner on his way home. He activated it and tucked it in his jeans pocket along with his change.

After he locked up his apartment, he left his keys with a neighbor, explaining that he had to go on assignment. He assured the woman he'd be back within the week to claim them.

That had been nearly three days ago.

He'd spent that time on the street, living like one of the homeless. He wheeled his cart around the waterfront area, going as far as Presidio Park and then back toward the area where he'd found the dead homeless man. He slept on the street, secure in his sleeping bag which he covered with the tarp. He bought cheap food at convenience stores, stood in line at soup kitchens, and quit washing or shaving his face. He'd never worn a beard, and the stubble that had sprouted on his cheeks and chin itched like crazy.

Wherever he went, he looked for Sandoval.

He looked for the woman who'd been the huge ginger cat.

He even looked for long-haired ginger cats.

And he hadn't caught a glimpse of anyone who could have been Sandoval. He should have been easy to spot. He would still have bruising around his eyes and that lump on his forehead should be a nice puke green by now. Yes, it was a big city, but there were only so many places the homeless congregated.

There were some rough places, like Mission, where a person new to living on the streets shouldn't venture. Not if he wanted to last more than a night or two, not even if he had a creature like the cat to protect him. Yet after three days with no hits—he hadn't even seen more than a fleeting flick of a cat's tail in all that time—Avrill was ready to see if his knees would let him hike several miles, most of it uphill, to Mission.

It was probably a fool's errand. This whole undercover plan was a fool's mission, but he owed it to Keiner. Hell, he owed it to the citizens of San Francisco.

Because his lieutenant had been right. He *should* have shot the creature. Keiner had tried. He'd fired twice, but both shots had missed. Even as mortally wounded as he'd been, Keiner had tried.

Avrill hadn't.

He hadn't done what he'd sworn to do: protect and serve the people of his city. If the creature killed anyone else, it would be on him.

Could he live with that?

Strong cops, dedicated cops, had eaten their own guns after swallowing that kind of guilt.

He should have gone to the department shrink, but what could he say? That Keiner had been killed by something out of a B-grade horror movie? That he should have killed it, but he didn't have any silver bullets on him?

No, he was doing the only thing he could do. He'd keep looking for the creature and then fire the shots he hadn't before. He'd stay out here for as long as it took to find her. If he found Sandoval first, he'd make Sandoval tell him how to find her.

He wasn't going to fail.

And on that third night, as he was settling down to sleep in a fenced-off garbage alcove whose gate had been left unlocked, he saw something that made him think he was on the right track after all.

54

THE OLD TOM WATCHED THE GINGER GUARDIAN SLEEP ON HER NEW companion's lap.

She'd been foolish again, this New Blood Guardian. She'd killed a police officer. The old tom didn't mix well with humans, not even in his human shape as an irascible old man, but even he knew that the police in this city would not rest until they caught the person they believed responsible—the ginger Guardian's new companion.

The human who called himself Elias.

The old tom had trailed the two of them for days as the ginger Guardian schooled her new companion how to navigate the life she had chosen for him. She couldn't sense the old tom's essence, of course. Old Blood had abilities they did not share with New Blood.

Especially now, it was important that she not know she was being watched.

The new companion stirred in his sleep. The old tom sensed unrest when he tasted the man's essence. This human's essence was twisted with sorrow and guilt, emotions the ginger Guardian could never understand.

The old tom could. He felt sorrow at what was to come and guilt in the part he was to play in it.

337

The companion jerked awake.

The night fog hung heavy in the alley and the light was dim. The old tom faded back into the fog so the human would not see him.

Then he thought twice about hiding himself. The companion was not yet fully awake. Even if the old tom showed himself, it might be possible the human wouldn't remember.

Did he want the human to remember?

That was an intriguing question to consider.

If the human remembered, the ginger Guardian would be able to sense it in his essence. She would dismiss it, of course. She believed she was special. She believed she'd been chosen to be the next Protector. The old tom represented no threat to her.

Like all of his kin, the old tom had an innate need to play. In some New Blood, like the ginger Guardian, that need manifested in the way they manipulated the humans they interacted with while in their human form.

The old tom was not above manipulating humans. They were a lesser species, that much was certainly true, evidenced by that fact that the Maker of All Things had not gifted humans with the ability to shift. And while humans were not the prey animals the old tom most often played with, he rarely denied himself the compulsion to play with them when the opportunity arose.

Like now.

He shifted into his favorite form, that of a male lion. He did not make his shifted form unnecessarily large. He did not want to frighten the human who still called himself Elias. The old tom just wanted to show enough of himself for the human to remember.

He padded slowly through the fog on his lion form's paws, as silent as a night hawk on the hunt. He tasted the human's essence so he would know when the human saw him.

That moment was exquisite.

The human drew in a startled breath, his eyes opening wide.

The old tom nearly rolled his eyes in pleasure at the human's reaction. The ginger Guardian had not schooled him in the ways of their tribe. She had not introduced this human to any member of the tribe, had specifically warned the tribe to stay away, and he'd been shocked to find one of the kin watching him.

That's all the old tom did. He sat back on his haunches and watched the human for long moments, tasting glorious fear in the human's essence. The fear of the hunted.

How easy it would be to kill this human. The old tom could do it, end this human's life before the ginger Guardian even woke. It would end the threat this human posed to the tribe by his mere existence. The ginger Guardian had been foolish in choosing a new companion. The old tom had tried to tell her, but she wouldn't listen.

She never listened.

But killing her companion was not within the old tom's purview.

His instructions had been specific. Watch. Wait. Report. And when the time came—lead.

The time had not yet come, but it would soon enough.

The human's head eventually lolled backward. He was drifting off to sleep.

It was an odd human expression, drifting off to sleep.

The kin did no such thing. They slept or not. They conserved energy by merely existing in one place until threatened, and then they moved. They formed attachments, birthed their young and raised them in the traditions and tenets of the tribe. They played. They hunted. They lived long, long lives. And when it was time to take their place in the Great Meadow, they retreated to a secluded spot where they died, alone and unattended.

Such was the way of the world.

When this human was fully asleep, the old tom retreated into the fog, where he reverted to his natural form. He left the alley behind, journeying just far enough to make sure the ginger Guardian wouldn't be able to taste his essence but staying close enough that he could taste hers.

He crouched down, content to stay in one spot for the rest of the night, when he tasted something else.

Something new, but something familiar at the same time.

Human guilt and sorrow. Waves of it, mixed well with anger and honed with a fierce need for vengeance.

Intrigued, the old tom followed this essence. When he found the source, he was surprised.

The human was the murdered police officer's partner. The human had changed his shape to the extent that humans could. He'd donned different clothes. Failed to clean himself so that his scent was overlaid now with the decay and debris of the places where he slept. He'd allowed the hair on his face to grow, and weariness to accentuate the gauntness of his face.

There was something else. A sickness inside so subtle that the old tom doubted the human was aware of it. Would it be fatal, as the ginger Guardian's old companion would have died from his own sickness? The old tom wasn't privy to such things. Humans lived such short lives compared to Old Blood. Humans started to die from the moment they were born. Old Blood did not.

The old tom considered this human. He had seen the ginger Guardian shift. Whether he would be permitted to live with this knowledge was not the old tom's decision to make.

But in the meantime, the old tom could give this human a taste of what he was seeking. The human could not be allowed to interfere in what was to come, but this human was a Guardian of sorts for his own people. He would continue to do what he believed was right. If the old tom could have felt any kind of kinship with humans, it would be with a human such as this.

Once again the old tom shifted into his lion form. He padded out of the fog into the enclosure where the human had cocooned himself for the night.

When he was sure the human had seen him, the old tom shifted into his human form, complete with the clothes he wore as a human.

"We are territorial," he said to the human. "We do not stray beyond its borders. We protect our own, and we police our own. There is no need for you to do this."

The human stared at him with wide eyes. The human thought

about reaching for the weapon he carried on his leg—old tom could taste that in his essence—but he made no move for it.

"We police our own as well," the human said, his voice raspy and hoarse and strained. "I *have* to do this."

The old tom inclined his head in respect. He'd initially thought to play with this human as well, but now found that he couldn't. This human deserved his respect.

"You will not be allowed to interfere," the old tom said, and he allowed a hint of sadness to flavor his words. "You must understand this. If you proceed on this course, your own life may be forfeit."

"By you?" the human asked. "Are you telling me you'll kill me? Or will she?"

The old tom knew he was talking about the ginger Guardian. The disgust, the hatred in the human's essence when he thought of her was unmistakable.

"I would not be warning you if I intended to kill you," the old tom said. "I cannot speak for others of my kin."

"We have laws," the human said. "She broke them. She murdered my...." His voice broke, and he cleared his throat before continuing. "She murdered three people that we know of. The man she's with helped her. He broke the law by doing that. He needs to answer for that. They both do."

This human thought his laws were the only ones that mattered. He was so full of sorrow and guilt, anger and an unquenchable need for vengeance, that there would be no convincing him that he need not sacrifice his own life in a fruitless quest for justice.

There was no such thing as justice. There was only the rule of law as handed down by the Maker of All Things.

Justice was a human concept. While the old tom understood the concept, he did not believe in it. Humans by their actions toward each other constantly told the old tom his belief was not misplaced.

He shed his human form, shifting back to his natural shape and size. He gazed at the human, cocooned in his blankets and his sleeping bag instead of his nice, warm bed.

"Know this," the old tom said. "Our laws were given to us by the

Maker of All Things. The Maker's laws are older than your civilizations. Older than the time when the first humans came down from the trees and learned to walk upright. Our laws create harmony, not divisiveness. Our laws protect the vulnerable but never at the expense of the tribe. Can you say the same?"

With that he left the human behind.

He needed to continue watching the ginger Guardian. When the time came, he would reveal his presence to her. That time was nearly here.

When it was over, the old tom would resume his life with his tribe. He would reunite with his life partner and spend time in his natural form, as it was meant to be. Above all, he would remain vigilant.

For he was a Guardian, a sacred duty given him by the Maker.

He intended to carry out that duty until the day he left this realm and took his place in the Great Meadow, no matter who he had to watch die.

No matter who he was instructed to kill.

55

Several days after he dreamed about a lion in the fog, Elias spotted Avril in a crowd three blocks away from the parking garage at Pier 39.

Elias thought it might be the weekend, either Saturday or Sunday, given the sheer number of people jostling each other on the sidewalks near the Pier. A late August weekend was the next-to-last gasp of summer for a lot of people whose kids were going back to school. He always got good tips on end-of-summer weekends, but he supposed that part of his life was over and done with now.

He'd been trying to walk the same fine line he'd been doing for days—losing himself in a crowd while trying to remain invisible to the people in it. Gilda flat out refused to let them leave this part of the city. While the number of homeless made passing as one of them relatively easy—hell, he *was* one of them now—he still felt the invisible walls of Gilda's territory closing in on him.

He wanted to leave. He *needed* to leave. The police were hunting him, he knew it, but she was adamant. Every time the thought crossed his mind, she sent him an image of what she'd done to her last human companion.

The thing that scared him the most was knowing that eventually, if she kept that up, she'd break him. She wouldn't even let him sing songs to himself. He was beginning to lose the soundtrack that had always played in his head, and that was the worst thing of all. Every time he heard a snippet of music—from a passing car, from the open doors of a bar or restaurant—he held onto it like a drowning man clinging to a life preserver.

He'd even started digging through garbage.

The day before he'd rescued a backpack from an overflowing dumpster in a service alley behind two upscale restaurants. The backpack was empty and stained and smelled disgusting, but as far as Elias could tell, there was nothing else wrong with it except one of the shoulder straps had ripped loose. No doubt some tourist had thrown it away. At least it was an adult-sized backpack, and not a little kid's.

He'd managed to secure the shoulder strap and packed his growing stash of belongings inside. The backpack was far better than the shopping bag he'd been using.

The day was cool, the sky overcast. The weather had finally returned to typical San Francisco summer chill. Leon was probably doing a brisk business in the store. Not that Elias could ever go there again. They kept strictly to the inland side of the waterfront, haunting the side streets and back alleys, and sleeping in doorways of closed stores at night.

The afternoon was winding down, but very few people had left the waterfront to head home. In another few hours traffic on the Bay Bridge would be a nightmare. Sometimes Elias wondered what had happened to his car and all the equipment he'd had in the trunk. Then he made himself stop. He had to start accepting that all his stuff was gone. He'd never be stuck on the Bay Bridge again.

Not unless he could find a way out of this mess, which seemed less likely by the day.

Gilda had run off ahead of him, intent on finding a place where they could spend the night. She was doing that more and more often, leaving him alone but never truly leaving him *alone*, not in his mind.

She was probably testing him, like a parent giving a child more freedom, just a little bit at a time, to see how they handled it.

Elias had just turned a corner, heading in the general direction Gilda had gone, when the repair job he'd done on the backpack's strap let go. He managed to catch the backpack before it hit the ground, but just barely.

He dropped to one knee to see if he could fix the strap a second time or if he'd have to hoist the backpack over just one shoulder. The injuries to his back and ribs had mostly healed, but what with sleeping on the street, his back almost always hurt. Carrying the backpack on just one side wasn't going to do his back any good.

The crowd parted around him to give him space, and that's when he spotted the detective less than half a block away.

Except Avrill looked far different than the last time Elias had seen him.

Instead of a neat if too-big suit, he was dressed much like any other homeless man on the street. He had an old-fashioned shopping cart with him stuffed full with things Elias wished he had. A sleeping bag. Extra blankets. A tarp to cover himself when the fog turned into misty rain.

Elias ducked his head down, heart pounding. He'd seen Avrill, but had Avrill seen him?

And what was Avrill doing out here dressed like that anyway?

Was he part of an undercover operation? Would the cops mount something like that just to look for him?

Well, of course they would. He was involved in the murder of a fellow police officer. Elias would be lucky if some trigger-happy cop didn't shoot him on sight.

Except it made no sense for Avrill to be out here like this. Elias knew what Avrill looked like. Even disguised as just another homeless man, Elias would recognize him on sight. If they wanted to send officers out into the city disguised as the homeless to catch him unawares, they would have sent officers he had never met.

That, actually, was something Elias hadn't thought of before.

What if the police *had* sent more officers out here in the guise of the homeless?

Elias had never considered himself paranoid before. But that thought, the mere idea that every homeless person he saw on the street could be a cop out to arrest him, or worse? Paranoid didn't begin to cover how that made him feel.

Except....

Except now he had a choice. He could take his chances that he could keep evading the police. That eventually they'd get tired of looking for him and assume he'd managed to leave the area.

He could take a chance that if he was spotted by a cop, the cop would take him in quietly and Gilda wouldn't try to interfere.

Or he could just turn himself in to Avrill now.

Avrill was right there, Gilda wasn't. Was she sensing his thoughts now? He'd been operating on the assumption that she was always listening in on his thoughts whenever he was awake, but if she was reading his thoughts now, she would have sent him more nightmare images of her old companion covered in blood and gore. She hadn't.

Did that mean her ability to communicate directly into his mind had limits? Had she gone too far to read him?

If that was the case, he didn't have much time. She wouldn't leave him alone for long.

Elias stood up, his insides shaking as he contemplated what he was about to do. He'd called himself all sorts of coward for failing to prevent Gilda from killing Keiner. He couldn't be a coward now. He had to do this, and he had to do it before Gilda came back.

He started to leave his backpack, but force of habit now made him pick it up. No one who lived on the street ever left their stuff unattended or it would disappear. Law of the concrete jungle.

He hoisted the backpack on one shoulder. His back complained. He shifted the backpack as much as he could, trying to even out the weight so his back wouldn't seize up on him. He had to sidestep to keep his balance, and he almost bumped into a woman who'd started to walk around him.

"Sorry," he mumbled, another habit he couldn't quite shake.

Instead of making some non-committal response, like "That's all right" or "No worries," the woman said, "You don't want to do that."

Elias shook his head, not sure if he heard right. He shouldn't engage, shouldn't give the woman any reason to scream that he was assaulting her, but he couldn't help glancing up at her face.

He knew her.

His heart skipped a beat.

It had been nearly twenty years ago in a place far warmer than this San Francisco afternoon. They'd shared fancy coffee that was more milkshake than coffee and talked for hours. He had admitted to her that his marriage was in trouble, and she had told him that she knew. They'd met because she'd stopped to listen to the music he played in a park that was more concrete than green living plants.

The woman he'd nearly bumped into was Tess.

She didn't look a day older than the last time he'd seen her. How could that be? Was his memory playing tricks on him and he only thought she looked the same?

After days on the street with not enough sleep and not nearly enough to eat, it was possible he was just hallucinating.

"Tess?" he said, the word little more than a croak.

She smiled at him. It was even the same smile he remembered.

"This is going to sound trite," she said as she took his hand. His dirty, unwashed hand. "But you're going to want to come with me if you want get out of this alive."

56

Detective Isaiah Avrill, a nineteen-year veteran with the San Francisco police department, currently on indefinite administrative leave, thought he was losing his mind.

What else could an otherwise rational man believe when a cat—a shapeshifting *cat*—lectured that man about morals and a code of law that predates anything known to civilized man?

Well, Avrill knew one thing he did believe in: his duty to protect the citizens of San Francisco. That duty included protecting them from the creature that had killed Keiner. The only way he knew to find that creature was to keep looking for the one person—the one *human being*—she'd been seen with.

Elias Sandoval.

Avrill used his burner cell to make a call to the patrol officer who'd given him the heads up on Sandoval's car. He wanted to check on the department's progress in tracking Sandoval down.

"Nobody's reported seeing him board a bus, catch a cable car, ride BART, and TSA sure as hell hasn't spotted him trying to board a plane," his buddy said. "We got his picture and description circulating all over the place. Unless he hijacked a sailboat or managed to catch an Uber, he's still in the area."

All that meant was that nobody'd spotted him. By now Avrill's old unit would have torn Sandoval's life apart. They'd probably even contacted his ex-wife. And they were still coming up empty.

Avrill was about to hang up when his buddy said, "What's with this number, anyway? You lose your phone or something?"

"Or something," Avrill said. "You need me, just call this number till I tell you otherwise."

Not that the burner had a lot of minutes on it, but it would do for now.

So Sandoval was still somewhere in the city. Unless he'd convinced someone who had a boat in one of the marinas to give him a lift across the bay, but Avrill didn't think that was likely.

The talking cat who'd started out looking like a lion before changing shapes to look like an old man—and boy, was Avrill still having a hard time wrapping his mind around *that*—had said that their kind were territorial. That they didn't stray beyond the borders of their territory.

The creature had killed three people that Avrill knew of. Jack Driscoll outside a dive bar a couple blocks behind the Safeway at Fort Mason. The homeless man a block away from the parking garage for Pier 39. The third—Keiner—happened at Sandoval's apartment building on Gough Street near Green. That made for a hell of a big territory for a cat.

No, that wasn't right.

It would be a hell of a big territory for a normal cat, but he wasn't hunting a normal cat.

He was hunting a creature that could change its size. If it got big enough, it could probably cover that territory as fast or faster than someone could drive it. Except someone would see something that big and report it, right?

Or maybe not, not if they didn't want people to think they were as crazy as Avrill felt.

Still, he had a feeling that the creature wouldn't stray too far from where they'd found the homeless man's body. Sandoval's apartment building and that dive bar by Fort Mason felt like outliers. They might be part of the creature's territory, but they weren't part of her normal routine. No, she'd gone to those places for a reason.

She'd gone to the bar to kill Driscoll. That was pretty clear.

And Sandoval's apartment?

She hadn't gone there to kill anyone. Keiner had just been in the right place but at the totally wrong time. He'd gotten in her way, and she'd killed him.

The homeless man was different. He'd kept the creature's picture in his pocket, a picture somebody had accidentally snapped when they'd tried to take a selfie at the Wharf. And he'd been a denizen of the area around the Wharf. That shopping cart wouldn't have made it as far as Fort Mason, much less uphill to Sandoval's apartment. The thing would have fallen apart. Now that he'd been wheeling around the cart he'd bought at Goodwill for a few days, Avrill wouldn't even trust that rickety thing to make the trip, and his cart was in a lot better shape than the dead man's grocery store cart.

So Avrill decided to keep up his ruse, living among the homeless who congregated around the Wharf, all the while looking for Sandoval in whatever disguise he might be wearing, and looking for a long-haired ginger cat that was anything but.

As long as his body let him, that was.

Keiner'd been the one who'd been in shape. He'd tried to cajole Avrill into going to the gym, said it would actually help his one remaining factory original knee. Avrill hadn't listened. He'd just kicked his addiction to prescription pain pills right before he'd been partnered with Keiner. Avrill wasn't about to replace one addiction with another—working out obsessively like Keiner did.

Now he wished he'd gotten in at least halfway decent shape. He also wished he'd brought along a few more pairs of socks.

His feet were killing him from all the walking in secondhand boots that didn't quite fit. Nights sleeping on concrete, even inside his sleeping bag, hurt his bony ass. He didn't have to fake looking tired and haggard, and the stubble on his chin and cheeks was coming in more white than gray.

But there was something else going on that he didn't want to think about too closely.

He was having trouble catching his breath.

He'd never been a smoker, but his parents had both smoked like chimneys, as the saying went. They'd light up after every meal, with Avrill sitting between them at the table. Secondhand smoke kills used to be the saying, and that saying might just be right.

He should probably have himself checked out, but he had a healthy fear of doctors and hospitals. Even more, he feared getting hooked on pain pills again. But the damp nights were taking a toll. All the walking should be getting him in shape, but all it seemed to be doing was taking more out of him.

He'd stopped to catch his breath. Dragging his cart around pulled at his back, no matter how he tried to do it. He thought about finding a public bathroom, locking himself in a stall, and digging out some of the folded bills in the toe of his boot. He could use a halfway decent meal. Something with more protein than a turkey sandwich on white that only had a couple of thin slices of processed meat that passed as turkey.

The nicer restaurants on the Wharf wouldn't let him inside, but he could buy himself a walkaway shrimp cocktail from one of the fish vendors over by where Sandoval used to perform. Sandoval hadn't been back, not that Avrill thought he would be, but he'd checked every day anyway.

He straightened up as much as he could. He put his hands on the small of his back and stretched, turning from side to side while he watched the crowd of people walk by.

Half a block away, a man was down on one knee futzing with a backpack. He had his head bent over his work. Avrill wouldn't have noticed him at all except people were giving him a wide berth.

The man turned his head to the side, and Avrill caught his breath.

The man was Elias Sandoval.

He looked like hell. Worse off than Avrill himself. He looked like he'd lost twenty pounds in a week. The bruises beneath his eyes were mottled purple and greenish yellow. He had a week's worth of stubble on his face, and Avrill was pretty sure it wasn't just the bruising that gave his eyes a haunted look.

Avrill couldn't shout at him to freeze. He didn't have a badge or an official piece. He was too far away anyway. If Sandoval took off running, Avrill would never catch up.

What he needed to do was follow him. Figure out where Sandoval was staying the night, and once he was asleep, Avrill could call his patrol cop buddy and have him come pick the bastard up.

And the damn creature who'd killed Keiner? Avrill didn't see her, but he didn't doubt she'd be with Sandoval at some point in the night. And when Avrill saw her, he'd shoot her.

Even if the shooting got him dismissed from the force, he intended to kill that damn thing.

He went on stretching out his back, pretending he hadn't seen Sandoval but keeping an eye on him just the same.

Sandoval finished whatever he was doing with his backpack and stood up.

And just stood there for a good minute or more, not moving.

What was he up to? Had he spotted Avrill?

If he had, why wasn't he beating feet out of here?

Then Sandoval hoisted the backpack on one shoulder. The thing looked like it was stuffed to the gills. It must have been heavy because it threw Sandoval off balance. He took a stutter step to one side, almost crashing into a well-dressed woman.

The woman stopped next to Sandoval.

Incredibly, Avrill saw her smile. She said something, then she took Sandoval's hand.

This wasn't the same creature who'd killed Keiner, was it? Just in a different human form?

Avrill didn't think so. Her hair was long and curly, hanging nearly to her waist, but it was dark brown. She wasn't a stunning beauty, but she was certainly trim and athletic. She wore tan linen slacks and a bulky fisherman's knit sweater. She didn't have any kind of a jacket on over the sweater, which made Avrill think she must have had at least a T-shirt on underneath the sweater because she didn't look cold.

In fact, she looked totally in her element and totally unconcerned about any of the people around her. Her entire attention seemed to be focused on Sandoval.

After a moment, the two of them started walking away from him, heading toward Bay Street.

Avrill followed at a distance.

Once they got to Bay Street, they turned toward Mason. It wasn't as easy to follow them here since pedestrian traffic was lighter, so Avrill hung back. It was easy to keep track of the woman. People seemed to give her room on the sidewalk without actually looking at her.

One thing he had no problem noticing—she was still holding Sandoval's hand, and he was letting her.

Avrill kept looking for the cat creature or even the golden-haired woman she'd turned into, but he didn't see her. Would Sandoval just head off and leave the creature behind?

Avrill wanted Sandoval, but he wanted the creature even more. The way the creature had talked about Sandoval, it was pretty clear she thought she owned him. While Sandoval might leave the creature behind, Avrill didn't think the creature would leave him.

Until she showed herself, he decided his best bet would be to just keep tailing Sandoval and this new woman. See where the two of them went. They'd have to stop walking at some point. They'd have no choice. Because if they kept heading west, they'd eventually hit the ocean.

And when they stopped?

Well, then it would be Avrill's turn to do his duty. To serve and protect the people of the city. As to how he'd carry out that duty?

Well, that would all depend on them.

57

Her new companion was gone.

How could that be?

The ginger cat who wasn't a cat had left him alone for such a short period of time. It was how she'd trained her last human companion after his mind had knitted itself back together. The humans called it a trust building exercise. It was how the kin trained their younglings, giving them more and more freedom as they earned it.

Her new companion had become docile within the last few days. He no longer thought of escaping. When she sampled his essence, all she tasted were his current concerns—food, water, shelter for the night. He'd actually been proud of himself when he found the bag he could put all his belongings in to carry on his back.

She scented the air for his essence. Even though this portion of her territory was thick with humans today, she should be able to scent him.

She stood still near the place where she'd left him. She caught a whiff of his essence, more the memory of his essence still in the air than a trail she could follow.

A low growl built in her chest.

This wasn't right. She should be able to scent him. She was a Guardian. Her senses were better than other mere kin. She could follow the scent of human essences for miles. Hadn't she followed the muscle-bound man to the edge of her territory? Hadn't she followed her new companion to his residence?

Hadn't she scented the essence of the detective who thought he was so clever in his disguise?

She'd deliberately kept her new companion away from the areas where the detective was looking. She knew where the detective slept, and she selected sleeping spots for herself and her new companion sufficiently distant so the detective would not spot them. She'd been clever. She'd been thorough.

She should not be shut away from her new companion like this.

That thought made her pause.

Was one of the kin deliberately interfering with her ability to follow her new companion's essence?

Was that even possible?

Not for kin who were merely Old Blood or New Blood.

Was it possible for a Guardian? Like the old tom?

Now the fur along her spine rose and her tail flicked angrily back and forth.

The old tom had never responded to her request to stay away. She hadn't scented his essence anywhere near her. Was it possible he could hide himself from her? Mask his essence in a way that made him invisible to her?

That was a sobering thought. She was destined to become the Protector. She should have sufficient gifts, sufficient talents, to do whatever the old tom could, but she didn't know how to mask her own essence, much less that of her new companion.

A rush of scent washed over her, sudden and nearly over-powering.

She backed up, shaking her head and pawing at her nose.

The essence she scented wasn't her new companion's. It was the old tom's, and he was close.

She sat back on her haunches and concentrated. The old tom's essence faded in and out, overwhelming her one instant and disappearing to near nothingness the next.

He was toying with her. Not in the playful way that kin chased each other and mock-fought when the moon was high and humans had retreated to their living spaces. The old tom might be enjoying himself, but he didn't care if *she* was enjoying it as well.

She flicked her tail, annoyance radiating from her so strongly that a small child in a stroller nearby looked at her, eyes wide and startled, and began to cry.

Human children were so much more perceptive of the world around them than their parents. She tamped down her annoyance so the child would stop crying.

When she did, she felt the old tom's amusement in his essence.

Then she saw him. Only for a moment, and only in his guise as the old human man. His life partner wasn't anywhere near him. She'd been wise enough to stay away as the ginger Guardian had requested, but the old tom was right here. Practically on top of her, and she'd never sensed him until he'd wanted her to.

"Don't you want to know why?" he said softly, but she heard him just fine even over the noise of all these humans surrounding her.

She thought about shifting into her human form, but it would have been foolish. The small child had sensed her annoyance. It might be able to see her shift.

"Don't you want to know where he's gone?" the old tom asked.

It took all her willpower not to flatten her ears against her skull and yowl at him.

The old tom was talking about her new companion. He knew where her new companion was.

For a moment, she wondered if the old tom had killed her human, then she dismissed the thought as ridiculous. The old tom was Old Blood, and Old Blood lived by a strict interpretation of the rules handed down by the Maker limiting a Guardian's duties. The old tom believed only the Protector had the right to kill a human that threatened the tribe.

Her new companion posed no threat to the tribe. He was

becoming docile. Resigned to his new life. She had intended to introduce him to the tribe during the next full moon, less than a cycle away now. Had the old tom interfered with that somehow?

She knew he would sense all her questions in her essence. She didn't try to mask any of them, not that she could.

He smiled at her. The expression looked so foreign on his human face that the ginger Guardian's tail shivered, expressing her shock.

The old tom never smiled like this.

What are you hiding? she thought at him.

Instead of answering, he turned around and began walking west.

He didn't look over this shoulder to see if she was following him.

He didn't have to. She really had no choice.

58

THE LAST TIME ELIAS HAD WALKED AS FAR WEST AS FORT MASON, HE'D been killing time, waiting until it was late enough to go back to the T-shirt shop and ask Leon if he could watch the shop's security footage.

This time he was holding Tess's hand like it was a lifeline.

He had no idea why she was here or where she'd come from. He'd thought about asking, but if Gilda was still reading his thoughts somehow, he didn't want to put Tess in danger.

And she would be in danger if Gilda caught her. Gilda had clearly shown him that she was more than willing to kill anyone who interfered with her plans, and that included turning Elias into her new pet.

So he tried to keep his thoughts as innocent and innocuous as possible. It wasn't easy, not with Tess's hand, soft and strong at the same time, holding his.

He didn't even risk looking at his surroundings. He'd become used to shuffling along with his head bent down to hide his face. That's how he was walking now, dragging his feet like a toddler who'd gotten in trouble trailing after his mother. He walked when Tess walked, stopped when she stopped. He trusted her to cross busy intersections only when it was safe.

359

He kept starting at the ground, trying to keep his mind a blank.

After they crossed the last busy intersection, the crowds around them thinned out significantly. He heard new sounds now. The smack of a bat hitting a ball. Kids laughing and calling out insults at each other. A quick tap on a car horn, and the sound of car doors and trunks slamming shut.

He risked a quick look.

They hadn't walked quite as far as Fort Mason. Instead they were walking past the large public park on Bay Street.

Shit! He hadn't meant to think in such specifics. The park was large, easily four city blocks long and nearly as wide, bordered by thick shrubs and windblown trees on the side closest to the bay. Even if he tried to hide beneath one of those shrubs, Gilda could simply trail his essence and find him. But he hadn't wanted to make it any easier for her by giving her specifics.

He went back to staring at the sidewalk. Counting the cracks in the cement, looking at the weeds growing in some of those cracks. They crossed an access road into the parking lot, and a driver honked his car horn at them. Apparently they weren't walking fast enough.

Elias ignored it.

When they reached the other side of the access road and were once again on the cracked sidewalk, Tess squeezed his hand. He glanced up at her, then quickly down again.

"You haven't asked where we're going," she said.

He shrugged. The movement didn't hurt his back as much as it had just a few days ago. Maybe carrying the backpack, even on just one shoulder, was helping strengthen his back muscles and take the pressure off where Jack had kicked him.

"Or why I'm here," she said.

He didn't shrug this time.

"I figured you'd tell me if you wanted me to know," he said.

She sighed, a sound that was half exasperation and half sadness.

"I remember that song we sang," she said. "Even after all this time, I still remember that spark you had. Do you remember it?"

He didn't know if she meant the song or the spark, but it didn't matter. He remembered both like they'd happened yesterday. He didn't want to. He didn't want Gilda to sense those memories. Sharing them with her would seem like just another part of himself he was losing.

Tess squeezed his hand again.

"Your memory of me," she said. "It's not entirely accurate."

He risked another glance at her. She looked just like he remembered. The same long, dark curly hair. The same graceful point to her chin. The same flawless, unlined skin. The same confidence and charisma.

"Seems like it to me," he said.

Her pace faltered just a little, then she huffed out a small breath. "The detective's following us," she said.

Elias tensed.

Tess had told him not to do what he'd planned, and what he'd planned was to turn himself in to Avrill and be done with this never-ending life of hiding in plain sight. How Tess had known that, he had no idea. He didn't even know if she had an idea why he was hiding from the police, or how she knew that Avrill was a detective, just dressed like one of the homeless.

"Don't worry," Tess said. "He won't interfere."

"How can you possibly know that?" Elias asked. "How can you possibly know any of this?"

They'd been walking west for a long time. The sun was low on the western horizon, peeking through a break in the clouds that had blanketed the city all day. Tonight's sunset was going to be spectacular. Already the sun was tinting the world with a rich, golden glow.

The sun was painting Tess's face with that same golden glow. She smiled, her eyes twinkling like she had a secret she couldn't wait to share.

"Because we won't let him," she said.

"I can't let you—" Elias began, but the rest of what he was going to say dried up on his tongue.

The trees and bushes at the far edge of the park were casting long shadows on the expanse of grass. The kids who'd been playing ball were gone now, presumably picked up by parents who'd been waiting patiently in the cars parked in the lot. The lot was empty now, but the park wasn't.

The shadowy areas on the lawn were full of cats.

Cats of all sizes and colors, some with fur so long and fluffy they looked like clouds come down from the sky, others with short black fur with white paws and white on their chests that made them look like they were wearing tuxedoes. Several cats were mostly white with multicolored patches of fur, like they couldn't quite decide what color they were supposed to be.

A shiver ran down his spine. He couldn't even hazard a guess as to how many cats had come out from wherever they'd been, but there had to be several dozen, at least.

He saw kittens, but relatively few for the number of adult cats. A few juvenile cats—not kittens but not yet adults—chased each other across the law, but the rest of the cats simply sat on their haunches, watching him.

"Welcome to the tribe," Tess said, still smiling at him with that glint in her eyes.

Her golden-green eyes.

He looked at her in amazement. "You're... you're...." He couldn't get the rest of the words out.

She was *kin*. The woman he'd met all those years ago in Vegas was *kin!*

Not only that....

He remembered how she'd touched his cheek. How his skin had tingled where she touched him, and how he'd felt that tingle long after she was gone.

"You're the one," he said, barely breathing.

Gilda had told him he'd been touched by one of the kin at some point in his life, and that's why she'd been able to communicate with him. Why she'd chosen *him*.

"You did this to me?" he said, starting to get angry now. "When you touched my cheek? That's all it took? You exploded my life, took everything—"

She interrupted him with a gentle finger to his lips. "Far from it," she said. "It was your music. Even then, I heard the potential for starsong in the music you made, and *it* touched *me*. Very few humans are so gifted, Elias Sandoval. It's something to be cherished."

He took a step away from her. "You call this being cherished?" He gestured at his face where he knew he still had the remnants of bruises beneath his eyes. At his clothes. At his tennis shoes, which were becoming rattier with every mile he walked. "If this is what the *kin* think of as cherished—" he barked out a laugh that had no humor in it "—you can fucking keep it."

She sighed. "What the Guardian has done to you is unforgiveable. I had no idea. For that, I am sorry."

"I thought kin felt no regret," he said. That's what Gilda had told him.

"She doesn't," Tess said. "It is one of her many flaws. But I do. Many of us do, which is why they called to me."

"Why you?"

Instead of answering, she glanced over his shoulder and frowned.

Elias thought Avrill must be getting closer. Maybe he was, but that's not who stepped up next to him.

It was the old woman who'd stopped to listen to him play "Ode to Joy" what seemed like a lifetime ago.

"Because she's the Protector, dear," the old woman said, smiling at him.

The Protector? Gilda had never spoken of a Protector. She'd told him that she was a Guardian, what that meant, but he had no idea what a Protector was beyond the obvious meaning of the word. That didn't mean the word meant the same thing to the kin.

He was about to ask when the old woman turned toward Tess. "They're getting closer," she said. "Is it time?"

Tess glanced at the setting sun. "Very nearly."

"I do wish there was another way," the old woman said, and this time there was a tremble in her voice. Her eyes were shiny bright and her thin lips had drawn down in a sad bow. But no tears ran down her cheeks. Could the kin cry, even when they were in their human forms?

Tess touched the old woman's cheek, much like she'd touched Elias's all those years ago.

"As do I," she said.

The old woman nodded, then she turned toward Elias. "Time to come with me, dear. Meet the rest of your tribe."

He looked at Tess, and she nodded at him. He thought she was giving him permission to go with the old woman, but she was giving him something far more precious.

A choice.

"Will you trust us?" she asked. "You have no reason to, I understand that, but I'm still asking."

He knew what that meant. He could still turn himself in to Avrill and she'd let him.

But as much as he wanted to alleviate his guilt, to answer for the crimes he'd allowed to happen, he didn't want to put the tribe in danger. The kin here were innocent. None of them had killed Jack or Keiner or Gilda's old companion. They shouldn't have to pay for what she'd done.

He let out a shaky sigh. Heaven help him, he was going to put his faith in a bunch of shapeshifting cats.

"Yes," he said. "I'll trust you."

"Good," Tess said.

She turned away from him. She took all of two steps, then she shifted. The beautiful, charismatic woman was gone. In her place was a black cat the size of a bobcat. He watched as she loped across the wide lawn, not heading for where the rest of the kin waited, still sitting in the shadows, but toward a building at the back of the park.

Elias watched her, his mouth hanging open.

The old woman touched his arm lightly just to get his attention.

"Let's get you safe," she said. "It's almost time."

Elias adjusted the backpack on his shoulder. He didn't know what was coming. Part of him didn't want to know, but part of him was afraid he did.

The kin had called Tess—called their Protector—to come to the city because....

Was it possibly because of Gilda? Had she broken some rule of the tribe? She'd sure as hell broken human laws, but Elias had no idea what laws the tribe lived by. Clearly they had some sort of hierarchy.

What was the punishment when one of their own broke their laws?

As he followed the old woman across the lawn toward the lengthening shadows where the rest of the tribe still sat watching him, he had an idea he was about to find out.

59

THE FARTHER SANDOVAL AND THE WOMAN WALKED WEST, THE HARDER it was for Avrill to keep up.

Tailing someone in a crowd was a pain in the ass under the best of circumstances. Saturday afternoon at Fisherman's Wharf in late August definitely wasn't the best of circumstances.

The crowd on the streets surrounding Pier 39 was a nightmare of parents and kids and teenagers, most of whom were walking in clumps and walking far faster than he was. Some of them had obviously been drinking a little too much at one of the local restaurants at the Pier. The 49ers had another preseason game at home tomorrow, and some of the team's fans must have started celebrating early. There was a sports apparel shop at Pier 39. The amount of red-and-gold football jerseys, hoodies, hats and jackets and pennants made Avrill think of the days when he used to actually go to a couple of home games during the season.

That had been before he'd taken a bullet in the gut. These days he didn't even follow football except to note when the team had home games that would swell the city with out-of-town fans.

He almost lost Sandoval and the woman a few times before they left the immediate area. The farther west they walked on Bay Street, the more the character of the crowd changed. Now instead of shoppers carrying bags and gawking at their surroundings, the sidewalks were full of people heading to and from the pricey hotels on the Wharf or heading out to a local restaurant where they'd wait for an hour or more for a table. He stopped counting the number of limousines he saw after three. He doubted any of the people inside even gave him a second glance.

Most of the people on the street didn't look at him either. He was just another homeless man wheeling a cart of his belongings. Strangers didn't meet his eye. Sometimes they deliberately turned their heads away from him. Out of sight, out of mind.

A few of the homeless had already claimed doorways for the night or spots on the sidewalk next to the side of a building. Avrill glanced at each of them long enough to make sure none of them were Sandoval.

The woman was taller than Sandoval, although that might be because he was walking hunched over, shuffling his feet. That shuffle was the only thing that let Avrill have a hope of keeping up with the two of them.

He was having trouble catching his breath. It felt like the damp air of the city had invaded his lungs.

He thought about the recent pandemic. He'd taken all the booster shots available—most of the personnel in his unit had—but those vaccines weren't one-hundred percent effective.

Was he getting sick? Getting horribly sick? He hadn't had a cold in longer than he could remember, but he didn't have a cough. At least not yet.

He stopped for a moment and took a few deep breaths. That made him feel marginally better. What would make him feel better than that was nabbing Sandoval and that monster thing he was protecting.

The two of them—Sandoval and the woman—kept walking west on Bay. The farther west they went, passing buildings where the ground floor storefronts were closed for the night and only a few lights were on in the second and third-story apartments over the stores, the thinner the crowd got. Anyone out walking the streets here at this time on a Saturday night tended to be locals. None of them gave Avrill a second look, assuming no doubt that he was headed for one of the local parks to spend the night.

Was that where Sandoval and the woman were headed? Except she didn't look the type to spend the night in a park.

Another thought occurred to him.

Was she taking Sandoval *home* with her?

That would be a very, very bad idea.

Avrill didn't know much about the thing Sandoval was protecting, but Avrill had the idea she was a very jealous creature. Jealous and possessive. Sandoval had to know that by now. Would he be that callous, that desperate, that he'd put this woman's life in jeopardy just for a chance to spend a night not having to sleep on the street?

Given the last few nights, Avrill could almost—almost—understand why Sandoval might do something like that.

He didn't need to follow the two of them quite as closely now. He decided to drop back and see what happened. If he saw them go into an apartment building, he'd follow them. Knock on every door if he had to until he found her, then tell her to get the hell out while he called his patrol officer buddy to come pick Sandoval up.

And if the creature Sandoval was protecting showed up?

Avrill still had the gun strapped to his ankle. He didn't have any silver bullets—he tended to think that part of the werewolf legend was just plain bullshit—but he had enough bullets in his gun to take care of any *thing* that tried to attack him.

Especially when that creature no longer had the element of surprise.

Unlike Keiner—and probably unlike Driscoll—Avrill had already seen the creature change. He wouldn't be shocked into inaction. He wouldn't hesitate to shoot until it was too late.

He kept right on thinking that until he followed the two of them to the park on Bay right before the turnoff to Fort Mason. He was a little less than two blocks behind them now, keeping to the other side of the street thanks to the nearly deserted sidewalks. But he was still close enough to see them stop and talk.

To see an older white-haired woman walk up to them.

To watch Sandoval head across the lawn with the older woman toward the overgrown shrubs and trees on the Bay side of the park.

To see the dark-haired woman he'd been with disappear and an oversized black cat take her place.

Avrill swore to himself.

He'd been following another one of those *things* and he'd never known it. Just how many more of them were in his city that he didn't know about?

He got his answer a few moments later.

Cats emerged from the long shadows cast by the trees and shrubs thanks to the setting sun.

Dozens of cats. Maybe a hundred or more.

They were all walking toward Sandoval and the white-haired woman. It was like Sandoval was the damn Pied Piper, the way all the cats gravitated toward him.

As he watched, one of the cats shifted into the form of a young man. His long golden hair glistened in the faint sunlight. He held out a hand to Sandoval, and after a moment's hesitation, Sandoval shook it.

Another cat, this one a calico, shifted into a middle-aged woman with auburn hair. She had on slacks and a sweatshirt that had a damn 49ers logo on the front. She could have been any one of a dozen people Avrill had passed on the street back at the Pier and he never would have noticed her.

She held out her hand. Avrill expected Sandoval to shake it, but instead he slipped the backpack off his shoulder and the woman took it.

Avrill swallowed hard.

Were all these damn cats shapeshifting creatures?

Could they all do the same things the creature Sandoval was protecting had done? Grow in size? Rip someone's throat out without half trying?

The ground felt like it had shifted beneath his feet.

He'd been so sure of him, equipping himself with the things he thought he needed to survive on the street. To survive another encounter with Sandoval's creature. He'd never expected there would be more of them. He should have, after his conversation with the old man who could turn into a lion or just another cat, but he'd assumed the old man was just an aberration.

Even after the old man had said that *they* were territorial.

Avrill had never expected the old man's "they" meant this damn many.

What if there were even more of them?

He ducked into the open door of a ground floor garage, heart hammering in his chest. He hoped he was far enough back to hide him from sight. Assuming the creatures didn't have good night vision. Cats saw well at night, didn't they? Not that these creatures were cats exactly, but it was a good place to start.

He should just call his buddy now. Sandoval was here, right here. If enough officers surrounded the park, they could place him under arrest.

But what if his creature was among the cats already in the park? It was getting too dark for Avrill to make out if one of the cats had long, thick, ginger fur. If she was here, she might try to prevent Sandoval's arrest.

All the cats in the park might try to prevent that.

That was a sobering thought. S.W.A.T. might be able to handle all the creatures, even if they shifted into nightmare versions of themselves. But how the hell could he justify asking dispatch to send a S.W.A.T. team to the park to arrest just one man who didn't have a criminal record? Who wasn't armed with anything approaching a conventional weapon?

He couldn't, that was the answer. No one would take him seriously. He wasn't even supposed to be out here tracking Sandoval down. Avrill's buddy would cover for him, tell anyone who asked that he got an anonymous tip that someone had seen Sandoval in the park. But if anyone got hurt making the arrest because Avrill couldn't warn them what to expect? Avrill doubted his buddy would cover for him then.

Avrill was already living with enough guilt over Keiner's death. He didn't want more people to die, more *cops* to die because he'd made bad decisions. Then he really might think about eating his gun.

He had to deal with this himself. Keep watching Sandoval until he left the park and all the cat creatures behind. If he could get Sandoval alone, or with just one or two of the creatures, he could handle it.

Any more than that?

He didn't have enough bullets in his gun.

He'd just have to make sure that when he fired, he made each shot count.

He had to make sure he saved at least one bullet for the creature who'd killed his partner.

60

THE KIN WERE ALL WAITING IN THE PARK. NOT IN THEIR HIDING PLACES like they usually were during the day when humans were about, but in the deep shadows.

And they weren't alone.

The ginger Guardian's new companion was with them.

Humans called this time of day the "magic hour." Halfway between sunset and true dark, when the sun was below the horizon to the west but enough light still reflected off the clouds to give the world a gentle, soft-edged feel.

Humans ruined the effect of the magic hour with their street-lights and stoplights and the headlights in their cars. Some of them, like her new companion, carried flashlights to see in the dark. The ginger Guardian had never understood that. Even in her human form, her eyesight was exceptional. She had no trouble seeing her new companion standing in the deep shadows.

She had no trouble seeing two of her kin, members of *her* tribe, standing next to him wearing human forms.

The kin who lived in this park never shifted into their human forms unless absolutely necessary. Most were Old Blood who believed their true forms were the only ones necessary, even living as

373

they did in the middle of a city crowded with people. Yet they'd shifted to be with her new companion.

Her companion.

The ginger Guardian growled.

The two Old Blood who'd shifted were not Guardians. They were simply members of the tribe. By their actions, they had not only attempted to obtain dominance over *her* companion, they had endangered the tribe.

That was not allowed. She would have to correct them.

Just like she'd have to correct the old tom.

She'd followed him through the city until he came close to the park, then she'd left him behind. He'd been playing, alternating teasing and insulting her as she followed him. She'd been unable to taste the essence of any other member of her tribe, and she'd begun to wonder if he was preventing her from doing so.

When she ran ahead of him, still in her natural form, she'd been able to scent a few of the kin. Like the old tom's life partner. She was in the form of an old woman, the one she preferred.

The ginger Guardian reached out to the old tom's life partner. They had played together when the ginger Guardian had been a youngling, and she'd helped the ginger Guardian issue a warning to the muscle-bound man. But now the old tom's life partner wouldn't respond to her.

She won't.

The old tom's thought entered her mind just as clearly as if he'd spoken it out loud.

Have you forbidden it? the ginger Guardian thought back.

No. I did.

That thought came from elsewhere. From one of the kin, but not one of her tribe. The thought had a familiar flavor. It took a moment for the ginger Guardian to place it, and when she did, her heart began to sing.

The Protector!

She'd come back to the city.

The ginger Guardian had been right. She'd felt for some time that the Protector's life in this realm was coming to an end and that the ginger Guardian would be taking her place. She'd thought the change would come when the Protector's life ended naturally. When she became too old and frail to carry out her duties.

But the Protector who padded out from behind a building at the rear of the park did not look old and frail. Her essence didn't taste of imminent death. She appeared as a black cat, long and sleek and double the size of what the humans thought of as an ordinary house-cat. As if any of the kin would be content living enclosed by walls when they were in their natural state.

Humans might believe they were the only ones inhabiting this park, but at night the park belonged to her tribe. They continually disabled the streetlight meant to illuminate the rear of the park. On nights like tonight, when the fog stayed far offshore and the rising moon turned the grass silver, they danced and sang starsongs they carried in their souls.

Tonight would be a special night. Tonight was *destined* to be the night the ginger Guardian would take her rightful place as Protector, and the tribe would dance in joy beneath the stars to celebrate.

No.

The word resonated in the ginger Guardian's mind. But it was the words the Protector thought at her next which wounded the ginger Guardian to her core.

You have abused your gifts. You killed humans. You killed your own human companion when he angered you. Do you deny this?

The ginger Guardian lifted her head in defiance. *My duty is to guard the tribe. To keep the tribe safe. I did what was necessary.*

The Protector came closer. Her fur glowed in the last of the magic hour's light.

"No," the Protector said, speaking out loud now. "You are impetuous, and your actions have harmed the tribe." Her voice held a hint of sorrow. "I chose poorly, I see that now. I believed your desire to become a Protector was a gift from the Maker. I was wrong."

The ginger Guardian felt sudden anger suffuse her being.

How dare she! The Protector was old. Her time in this life was drawing to a close. She had *chosen* the ginger Guardian to be her replacement, to determine life and death not only of kin who endangered the tribe, but the humans who endangered the tribe as well.

The fur along the ginger Guardian's spine stood on end. She felt herself growing in size without conscious thought, as if her anger—her *fury*—could not be contained within her natural form.

The Protector grew in size to match her.

"The gifts the Maker gives us can be taken away," the Protector said. "You are no longer Guardian, so the Maker has decreed."

The ginger Guardian yowled her anger. "That is not for you to decide! You cannot speak for the Maker. *You* have exceeded *your* gifts!"

The Protector did not match her anger. When she spoke, her words were almost too soft to hear.

"Have you not noticed changes within yourself? You can no longer scent the essences of those close around you. Not even your new companion. Did you not wonder why?"

That was not the Maker. The Maker would not take her gifts away. He had chosen her as Guardian. He had *chosen* her as Protector! Someone had been blocking her. The old tom. Old Blood had abilities New Blood did not.

"You *lie!*" the ginger Guardian said. "*You* are harming the tribe! You are attempting to harm me. I am kin. I am part of this tribe."

She paused, considering a new idea.

The Protector was harming the tribe. It was the ginger Guardian's duty to stop that. Even if she had to fight the Protector. Even if she had to *kill* the Protector. She could do it too.

The Protector had loved her once, when the ginger Guardian had been a youngling and they'd played together. The Protector had treated the ginger Guardian as her own youngling. No member of the kin did that unless they had a bond, and the bond the Protector had formed with the ginger Guardian was made of love.

The Protector could only be killed by one she loved.

The ginger Guardian could kill the Protector. She had to if she wanted to keep the tribe safe. No other Guardian could do what the ginger Guardian could. No other Guardian was willing to take the risks, to do what had to be done when humans like the police detective discovered the kin's existence in this modern world.

The ginger Guardian knew what she had to do.

She didn't hesitate. She never hesitated.

As the magic hour drew to a close and the golden light fled the day, she grew to five times her natural size in less than a blink of an eye. Then she launched herself at the Protector, aiming for her throat.

61

The tomcat his mom used to have when Elias was a kid sometime got into scraps with neighborhood cats.

That's what his mom called them—scraps.

From Elias's point of view, the scraps had been out-and-out battles between two animals out to kill each other. The few school-yard fights he'd witnessed in elementary school were nothing compared to what the tomcat did to cats who dared to cross into his territory.

He'd watched the cats roll around in his parents' yard, clenched together in a frenzied ball of teeth and claws and ear-splitting yowls and screeches. Fur flew into the air as the cats battled it out for supremacy.

It always ended with one cat on its back, ears flat against its skull, eyes dilated until all that showed was black. Usually it was bleeding from one or both ears where teeth had bitten through thin flesh. The victor, most often his mom's tomcat, would stand over the other cat until he'd satisfied himself that his potential usurper was well and truly defeated. Then he'd stalk away—never too far—and sit down to wash his fur.

Elias's mom had warned him to never try to break up a cat fight.

379

"They won't fight long," she'd told him, "and they won't fight to the death. They'll just fight until someone gives up."

He'd trusted her on that. By that time he'd already had the scar on his arm from that cat. He wasn't keen on acquiring any new ones.

The two kin—the Protector (*Tess!*) and Elias's tormentor Gilda—had grown to incredible sizes. They attacked each other, sparring and spitting and slashing with claws as long as his arm, darting their heads at exposed necks only to end up clenched together in a ball of furious fur.

The fight was eerily silent. No yowls. No screams. No shrieks of anger or pain. But Elias didn't need any of the kin he stood among to tell him this fight was deadly serious. He didn't need anyone to tell him they wouldn't stop fighting until one of them was dead.

He couldn't see the battle clearly. There were no streetlights at the back of the park. The kin clearly didn't need light to see at night. He did, but the last thing he was about to do was take his flashlight out of his backpack and turn it on. He didn't want to call attention to the tribe.

No people were out on the street. It was almost like the park was in another world, and maybe it was. Maybe the tribe had a way of masking their existence from the humans who lived around them and came to the park to play ball, like the kids he'd seen leaving when he and Tess first got here.

He'd only heard snippets of the conversation between Tess and Gilda before Gilda launched herself at Tess.

Tess must have known the attack was coming. What did the old woman call her? The Protector? Maybe the Protector had special powers. Different powers. Stronger powers than Gilda had. Tess had parried easily, but now that the battle was going in earnest, he couldn't tell who was winning.

If Gilda won, his life as he knew it was truly over. He'd heard enough to know that Gilda thought she was supposed to be the next Protector. If a Protector had stronger powers, Elias knew he'd never be able to resist her. She'd never let him turn himself in to the police.

She'd take that as a threat to the tribe and she'd kill any cop he managed to contact.

And if Tess won? What would happen to him then?

He didn't know, and he didn't care. Tess had tried to save him. She'd brought him here to introduce him to the tribe, and she'd apologized for what Gilda had done to him. But what did that mean if she won? If Gilda was defeated?

If Gilda *died?*

Would they still consider him a member of the tribe?

If they didn't, even if they let him go, he'd still be going to jail. That much was a given. Avrill would make sure of it.

Tess had said that Avrill had been following them, but Elias hadn't seen him. He could be hiding anywhere, watching. If that was the case, Elias almost felt sorry for him. Elias had had more time to wrap his mind around the existence of the kin. Avrill had been thrown in headfirst and left to sink or swim on his own. From the way he'd looked this afternoon, knowledge of the kin had almost drowned him.

The old woman had been joined by the old man she'd been with that day on the Wharf. He was dressed the same, with the same charcoal scarf wrapped around his neck. He hadn't said anything to Elias, just nodded at him. Elias, still unsure of how to deal with the rest of the tribe, had simply nodded back.

Now the old woman placed a veined hand on his arm. "You must not run," she said. "No matter the outcome, you must not run. Tribe do not desert each other. Do you understand?"

He glanced at the other members of the tribe, cat and human forms alike. They were all sitting or standing quietly, their gazes never leaving the two kin battling to the death beneath the light of a half-moon.

"What will happen?" he asked. "When it's over?"

The kin who wore the shape of a middle-aged woman, the one who'd helped him with his backpack, turned large, luminous, golden-green eyes on him.

"No one knows," she said. "This is unprecedented in the history of the kin. We have only ever had one Protector. No one has ever challenged her."

He blinked. Tess had been their Protector for....

His mind refused to calculate how long. Gilda had told him the elders among the kin told of a time before the kin were granted the gift of shifting. A time before men came to their land. Men who hunted with spears and sharpened rocks and destroyed the meadows the kin called home.

Did that mean Tess had been alive even then?

How could she possibly win against someone so much younger? Gilda had chosen her former companion—her only companion—when she'd been a youngling. Her former companion had been old, but he hadn't been more than seventy or maybe eighty.

Elias's gut clenched around the possibility—hell, the probability—that Tess might die. Right here, right now, right in front of him.

He didn't care about himself anymore. He couldn't just let her die.

"Can't we help her?" he asked the middle-aged woman.

It was the old man who answered.

"Kin do not harm kin," he said. "It is the most important rule we live by."

So the answer was no. Elias had to just stand here and watch, and hope that when the battle was over, it wouldn't be Tess bleeding out on the silvery grass right in front of him.

He'd never felt so impotent in his life.

62

Avrill stood in his hiding place and watched two impossibly massive creatures battle it out in the park across the street from him.

He'd never seen such a surreal sight in his life, and that wasn't even counting the sheer size of the two combatants.

This fight was utterly silent.

Most street fights were nothing more than drunken brawls, and they were always noisy. Fighters taunted each other. Shouted insults at each other. Fists smacked against flesh. Shoes scraped along the pavement as the fighters circled each other. People who stood around watching added their own insults, egging the fighters on.

People like that loved to see other people beating the crap out of each other. Avrill wasn't one of them. He was sworn to protect and serve, and that occasionally meant protecting any idiots determined to beat each other to a pulp from doing just that.

He wasn't about to get in the middle of this fight.

He was sure one of the fighters was the creature Sandoval had been protecting, the *thing* that had killed Keiner. When she'd run into the park, she'd passed beneath one of the few working streetlights on the Bay Street side, and he'd spotted the long, thick ginger fur of her cat form.

She'd kept running until she reached the back of the park where the streetlights weren't working. There she'd confronted another oversized cat. Avrill hadn't gotten a good look at that one.

They'd seemed to talk—*talk!*—to each other at first. Then they'd started to get bigger, seriously bigger, until one of them had launched an attack at the other.

They'd been rolling around and fighting for nearly five minutes now without stopping, all while they kept growing in size. Yet if there hadn't been a partial moon in the otherwise clear sky, he never would have seen them. It was pretty obvious that no one in the few cars driving by on Bay Street had any idea that this impossible, surreal fight was happening right next to them in the park.

He wondered if the people who lived in the apartments on his side of the street had any idea about the cat creatures who lived right across the street from them. Probably not. Even if they'd ever seen anything weird or unnatural, they'd probably talked themselves out of believing anything like that could be real.

Most people had the luxury of doing that.

He didn't.

He'd believed that the creature Sandoval had been protecting was the only lethal creature threatening the citizens of his city. He knew better now. There was a second one, one that might be even bigger and more deadly than Sandoval's creature. Both of them posed a threat to the people he was supposed to protect.

He knew what he had to do. It might get him killed, or it might simply end with him in some psych ward somewhere getting poked and prodded and analyzed to death.

It didn't matter. His life didn't really matter anymore. He had a duty to perform, and he was the only one who could do it.

He reached down and retrieved the gun from the holster strapped to his ankle. He put it in the right-hand pocket of his jacket, in easy reach.

Two deadly creatures were battling in what looked like a fight to the death.

He knew what he had to do.
When the battle was over, he was going to have to kill the winner.

63

Elias felt like the fight went on forever.

The two kin—Tess and Gilda—never changed into their human shapes. They shifted into other things. Lions the size of a minibus. Bears so large they would make polar bears look like a child's teddy bear. Creatures he couldn't name and didn't recognize.

Everything they shifted into had fur. They never shifted into lizards or birds, and they always shifted into some type of predator.

Most eerily of all, they fought in utter silence.

The entire tribe was silent, and Elias realized they were bearing mute witness to something they never thought they'd see: a Protector fighting for her life.

He lost track of who shifted into what form. Even if they'd kept to the color of their fur, the moonlight had turned both their fur silver. He wouldn't be able to tell who won until it was all over.

And the way it looked now, the fight was almost over.

They were no longer clenched together in a blur of teeth and claws and snapping jaws. They stood circling each other, both bleeding from multiple wounds, both breathing heavily.

Elias clenched his fists. He couldn't stand to watch this.

He couldn't turn away.

Then one of them seemed unable to hold her shifted form. Instead of changing into another form in the blink of an eye, their form—that of a huge tiger—blurred, vibrating like a tuning fork.

The old woman next to him drew in a sharp breath. Elias glanced at her. Her eyes were wide, a distant streetlight glinting off their watery depths.

Was she crying?

When he turned back to the fight, it was over.

Gilda had reverted to her natural form and size. She was on her back, her eyes as round and black as a hole in the sky. Her front paws were extended toward Tess, and it was Tess now standing over her. Tess had shifted into her own natural form, a black cat, only she was still twice the size of Gilda.

Gilda said a single word.

Even in the still night, not even a car passing on the street now, Elias couldn't quite make out the word. It might have been "mercy," but he wasn't sure.

It didn't matter.

Tess struck lightning fast, Elias's eyes almost couldn't track the movement. She closed her jaws over Gilda's throat. Picked her up off the ground and shook her, a quick decisive kill move that must have snapped her neck.

Gilda's body went rigid, her front paws sticking out straight in front of her, and then she went limp.

Tess shook her again and then dropped her body on the ground.

All around him, the tribe seemed to let out a collective breath. When he glanced at the old woman beside him, actual tears were running down her face.

He knew how she felt.

Gilda had been a nightmare. She'd blown his entire life apart with no regard for his feelings. She'd *killed* three people that he knew of, and she'd felt no regret about any of it. He should hate her. He'd thought he hated her.

But as he looked at her limp body, so cat-like and small in its natural state, he felt like crying too.

64

Avrill stood rooted to his spot in the open garage, almost afraid to move.

The fight was over. It had ended so suddenly and so brutally it had taken his breath away.

The creature Sandoval had been protecting had lost. It had rolled over on its back, paws up in surrender.

But the other creature had killed it anyway. Just like a cat pretending to kill a favorite toy it had been hunting, only this hadn't been pretend and the dead creature wasn't a toy.

He should have killed the creature himself in Sandoval's garage. He wasn't sad that it was dead. It had killed Keiner and now it had suffered the same fate. Some people would call that karma. He called it justice.

That didn't solve his immediate problem. There was a second creature.

The one who'd so viciously ended the other one's life.

Avrill knew what he had to do. He couldn't let himself think too hard about it. He just had to do it.

Wasn't that what that old shoe commercial said? For the shoes that Keiner always wore to the gym?

389

Just do it?

Thinking about Keiner strengthened Avrill's resolve.

He took the gun out of his pocket. Checked the load. Reassured himself he was ready.

He tucked the shopping cart with his homeless persona's belongings further back inside the garage where he'd been hiding. No one had gone inside the apartment building while he'd been there. He'd be long gone before anyone came home now, and he certainly wouldn't be needing all the things he'd bought at Goodwill. He wasn't exactly going to donate them to charity, not in the conventional sense, but maybe someone else would find the cart. Someone who could use all that stuff.

However this ended up, Avrill wouldn't be spending another night on the street. Not this street. Not any street or alley or fenced-off garbage alcove.

He checked for traffic, but Bay Street was remarkably empty for a Saturday night. He took that as a sign.

Hoping that his knees, the original factory model and the replacement, were up to the task, Avrill took off at a dead run across the street. He didn't shout "Police, freeze!" or anything else that would identify him as a cop. Right now he wasn't a cop.

He was an avenging angel, and his weapon was a gun.

65

TESS HAD SHIFTED BACK TO HER HUMAN FORM, COMPLETE WITH LONG dark curls, linen slacks, and the too-big fisherman's knit sweater. She had blood running down both sides of her face, and Elias was sure her clothes hid even more wounds from the fight.

She knelt down on the grass next to Gilda's body. She touched the dead Guardian's paw with a manicured finger, bent her head, and murmured something he couldn't hear.

The old woman beside him sniffled. "She's asking the Maker to take pity on the soul of the dead," she said. "To accept her into the Great Meadow. It is part of a Protector's duty."

Elias didn't think Tess was doing this out of duty. Yes, she might be saying what amounted to a prayer for the dead because it was expected of her, but regret was clear in every line of her body. She hadn't wanted this.

She hadn't wanted to kill.

The kin, every last one of them, whether in human shape or their natural form, bowed their heads to join in their Protector's prayer.

Elias started to do the same when movement near the street caught his eye.

A man was running, and running hard, heading right toward where Tess knelt on the grass.

He wasn't yelling, he wasn't shouting. He was little more than a silhouette until he passed close to one of the few working streetlights at the front of the park.

Elias drew in a sharp breath.

It was Avrill. The man was Avrill, and he was holding his right arm out in front of himself.

Was that a *gun* in his hand? What the hell!

So much had happened so fast, Elias had forgotten that Avrill had even been following them. Where had he been hiding? Had he seen the fight? Clearly he had, and now he was charging at Tess.

Elias had to do something, but he was too far away to stop Avrill or even get between Avrill and Tess. So he did the only thing he could.

He shouted Tess's name.

She stood up and turned to look at him.

"It's the detective," he shouted, pointing at Avrill, who now seemed to be running with a limp even as he was gaining on Tess awfully fast. "Look out! He's got a—"

Elias never got out the rest of his sentence.

Tess turned in the direction Elias had pointed. Turned to face Avrill.

That's when the detective shot her.

66

THE FIRST SHOT HIT THE CREATURE HIGH IN THE SHOULDER.

Avrill's second shot hit her center mass.

She staggered backwards, but she didn't go down, so Avrill shot her again.

Another center mass shot.

She still didn't go down.

Avrill kept pulling the trigger. Shot after shot, all striking home.

Blood stained the front of her sweater black in the streetlight. He didn't realize he was screaming until his gun clicked on empty.

She finally went down on one knee. Her arms were hanging down at her sides, her hands clenched into fists.

He wasn't the only one screaming. Sandoval was running across the lawn, yelling a woman's name over and over. It sounded like Tess, but Avrill couldn't be sure over the ringing in his ears.

He expected the creature to fall over, but she stayed upright, one knee on the grass, the other bent and keeping her steady. Avrill didn't know how long that would last. He wanted her to just *die* already.

Someone would report the gunshots. Hell, the city had a gunshot detection system that could pinpoint the exact location of any gunshots. Patrol officers would be responding shortly, and they wouldn't be quiet about it. Active shooters, in this day and age, were an all-hands-on-deck call.

Why the hell wouldn't she go down?

Why wouldn't she *die?*

Sandoval got to the creature's side. He looked like he wanted to touch her but wasn't sure he should.

Then he glared at Avrill.

"You killed her!" Sandoval shouted. "She's not the one you were after. She didn't kill anybody! She never hurt *anyone!*"

"Yeah? She didn't do this?"

Avrill gestured toward the body of the creature she'd just killed. The one who'd killed his partner. Who'd killed Jack Driscoll. Who'd killed the old homeless man.

Except the body wasn't there.

An indentation in the grass where the body had been was as good as a chalk outline, only there was no dead cat inside.

What the hell?

The creature he'd just shot over and over again lifted her head and smiled at him. "The Maker accepted her," she said. "She's taken her place in the Great Meadow with those who've gone before."

Avrill didn't understand any of that. Dead bodies couldn't just disappear into thin air.

And cats couldn't turn into people and carry on conversations. Welcome to wonderland, Alice, San Francisco style.

Sandoval was gaping in open-mouthed shock at the creature who wouldn't die. "Tess? I don't understand. He *shot* you. You should be dead."

"He's not the one who can kill me," she said to him. Then she glanced at Avrill. "Not for a lack of trying. I should return the favor, Detective. See how you like it. I can assure you it hurts."

Avrill could have told her he knew exactly how it felt to be shot. His had been a belly wound, and that had been bad enough. He couldn't imagine taking as many shots to the chest as she had.

She got to her feet, rather unsteadily, but she was most definitely alive. And recovering rapidly from the looks of it.

Then Avrill saw claws extend from the tips of her fingers. He knew they'd be razor sharp.

"We have much to discuss, and very little time to do it," she said.

"Are you threatening me?" Avrill asked.

He certainly felt threatened, especially now that he didn't have a real weapon on him anymore. The best he could do was throw his gun at her, but it would probably just bounce off her skull and piss her off.

"I want to make sure I have your attention," she said.

Oh, she had his attention all right. She was looking more and more recovered by the moment, which made him wonder if he'd been on a fool's errand all along. Even if he'd shot the creature that had killed Keiner, would that have killed it?

Because if this creature, the one Sandoval called Tess, hadn't died from multiple shots to the chest, what were the chances that the one or two shots Avrill hadn't fired that day would have done the job?

Slim and none, that's what.

He'd been beating himself up for no reason.

"Elias has done nothing wrong," the creature called Tess said. "He was an innocent caught up in things beyond his control, and I bear some responsibility for that. I cannot allow you to restrain him. To subject him to human laws that are, in this instance, unjust."

"He protected that thing," Avrill said. "He kept me from shooting her. He went with her *willingly,* I heard him."

"I was trying to save your ass!" Now that he'd apparently recovered from yet another shock, Sandoval looked angry. Seriously, righteously angry. "She would have killed you! She wanted to. I let her blow up my entire life to keep you safe. To keep you alive."

Sandoval ran a hand through his hair.

Avrill heard the first siren, still distant but coming closer.

So could the rest of the creatures who'd been watching them. Avrill saw them all fade into the deep shadows at the rear of the park. The ones he'd thought might be people turned out to be more creatures when he saw every last one of them shift into their cat-like forms.

"I'm guessing my car's gone by now," Sandoval was saying. "Everything I used to earn my livelihood. It's all gone, right?"

Avrill nodded. "You set it up to be stolen," he said. "It sounds like it wasn't your idea."

"Finally," Sandoval said, "you got something right." He glanced at Tess. "Maybe I should let him lock me up. At least I'd get a decent night's sleep."

The cat creature's expression softened. "I can't let you do that," she said. "For better or worse, you're part of the tribe I'm sworn to protect."

She turned her gaze back to Avrill, and the steely determination in her eyes was chilling.

"I can kill you here and now," she said to him. "I should. You know we exist. You've seen us, know where this tribe lives. You're a threat. I'm the Protector. The Maker tasked me with the responsibility to keep my kin safe and hidden from human eyes such as yours. But the good news for you is that the Maker granted me sole discretion to determine how I ensure my kin's safety."

She tilted her head and considered Avrill like he was an interesting bug.

"It's up to you how I use that discretion," she said.

He'd often felt small in his life. When he'd been shot and his life had been in the hands of surgeons he'd never met. When he'd stared at the small pills in the prescription bottle and told himself he wouldn't take another one, but then he did.

When he'd ridden in the back of the ambulance with Keiner to the hospital, and then he'd been left behind in the waiting room, unable to do anything to save his partner.

He'd never felt as small as he did now with this creature watching him, waiting for his answer.

She was a holy person among her kind. She was telling him she had the power to let him go or kill him where he stood. His life depended on whether he could keep their secret.

He dropped his empty gun on the lawn next to his feet. "Who the hell would I tell about you and your 'kin'? Who would believe me?"

"And Elias?" she said.

Technically Sandoval was an accessory to the murder of a police officer. It wasn't like anyone in the department would believe Avrill if he filed a supplemental report stating what really happened. Who would believe that the large animal who'd killed Keiner had been the one controlling Sandoval, not the other way around?

But she was right. Arresting Sandoval wasn't justice. Even if she let him, which was doubtful at this point, taking Sandoval in would just be another example of locking up an innocent man because it was expedient and made for good headlines.

Avrill made a shooing gesture with one hand in Sandoval's direction. "Get the fuck out of here before I change my mind," he said. "Just don't let me see you in my city again." He shifted his gaze to Tess. "Either of you."

The creature gave him a tight smile. "Even if you do see me," she said, and then she shifted into an entirely different woman, this one with short gray hair, a dark complexion, and a tattoo of a bird of some sort on her neck, "how will you be able to tell it's me?"

Point taken.

A police cruiser turned the corner three blocks away, lights flashing but surprisingly with no siren. Avrill glanced up the street, calculating how long it would take for the officers to reach them.

He turned to tell Sandoval and the woman to get the hell out of there, but they were already gone.

Avrill sighed. He was now alone in a park with a gun. He couldn't even show the officers his badge.

He held up his hands as the patrol officers exited the cruiser, hands resting on their holstered weapons. Avrill said his name loudly, told them he was a detective with the Strategic Investigations Unit, and gave them the name of his lieutenant. They cuffed him, bagged his gun, and stuck him in the back of the cruiser while they checked his information on the cruiser's computer.

Avrill would have done the same. From their perspective, he was just another crazy homeless man trying to get out of trouble.

He didn't kid himself. He was in some serious trouble here. If it wasn't for his service record with the department, he might even find himself kicked off the force. But he did have a long and mostly clean record.

The lieutenant would confer with bureau superiors, then they'd probably decide to put him on extended administrative leave, with pay, provided he saw the bureau shrink.

Avrill was surprisingly okay with that. He needed to get himself checked out. He was breathing a bit easier now, but the image of his parents smoking over him as a child loomed large in his mind. He didn't necessarily want to subject himself to a bunch of tests, much less procedures, but it was the responsible thing to do. He'd already done more than his quota of irresponsible things for one night. Hell, for one lifetime.

As for the bureau shrink, Avrill figured he could handle that. And if the counselling reports indicated the shrink thought he was holding back? Hiding something?

They'd be right.

He'd be hiding a lot.

Some of those secrets, he'd take to his grave.

After all, who the hell was going to believe him anyway?

67

THE WEATHER IN SEATTLE REMINDED ELIAS SANDOVAL OF SAN Francisco.

He'd been busking on Pike Street for a couple of months now. He'd always heard that in Seattle it rained all the time. That wasn't exactly the case. It was the beginning of November, and so far the weather had been quite pleasant. Overcast most days, but still pleasant.

Julio, the manager of the Starbucks down the street from where Elias played, told him to just wait.

"We get snow now sometimes," Julio had said more than once. "You ever drive on hills like these?"

Elias had, but he didn't say that. In this new life he wasn't supposed to be from San Francisco. He was supposed to have moved to the Pacific Northwest from Arizona to get away from the heat.

"Just wait till you try driving on these hills in snow, man." Julio shook his head. "On ice. It's a mess, I tell you. Hills like these, nobody should ever drive on when it snows."

Julio was one of the good ones. He brought Elias coffee in the morning and usually sent out one of his baristas to give him a refill after the lunch rush was over.

Except on the weekends when the tourists invaded. Then the line at Starbucks always snaked out the door. Elias knew to bring his own coffee on the weekends.

These days he was doing what he considered "busking light." Just himself and a guitar, not even a microphone. It wasn't his old guitar, the one he'd had since he'd been in college. That guitar had gone everywhere with him and he missed it, but it was long gone now. He hoped whatever Jerry had done with it and the keyboard Elias had left in his bedroom, someone was treating them right and making good music.

The guitar he had now, he'd bought in a secondhand store. The frets fit his fingers just fine, and the sound it produced was full and rich. He didn't play any of the songs he used to play at the Wharf on the off chance one of the tourists had seen him there. The last thing he wanted was to be recognized. He'd even grown a wispy beard to go along with what he considered his new hair—longer with streaks of gray.

The gray was natural, a side effect from his time on the street, his introduction to the tribe, and most of all, witnessing that last, horrible fight. At least he still had his sanity, there was that.

And his savings.

How Tess had managed to accomplish that, he didn't know and he didn't want to know. She'd gotten him out of San Francisco, no mean feat considering the cops were still looking for him. They'd boarded one of the boats in the marina on the far side of Fort Mason. The owner, another one of the kin, had taken them north to Sausalito, where Tess rented a car.

The drive north had been a nightmare. Tess had driven the entire way, stopping only for fuel and bodily necessities. Elias kept waiting to be pulled over. For a cop to take one look at him, run his name through the system, and arrest him on the spot. He still had his wallet and his identification. He'd asked Tess if he should toss them away, but she told him it wouldn't be necessary.

He didn't understand what that meant until they stopped at a truck stop just south of Seattle. He'd accidentally started to pay for a sandwich and a bottle of water with his debit card. He'd snatched it away at the last moment, but not before the convenience store clerk had seen it.

"Rather pay in cash," he'd said lamely.

"No problem, Mr. Sanders," the clerk had said.

Sanders?

That was when Tess told him the Maker had gifted him with an aura, and that had caused the clerk's confusion.

"The Maker can't give you back what you've lost," she'd said. "This is the best gift he can give you."

As Elias understood it, the aura would prevent anyone from connecting the person he was now to the Elias Sandoval wanted for questioning by the San Francisco Police Department. For some people, that meant they'd misread his name. For others, it meant they wouldn't be able to recall his face or even realize he was there.

Not exactly the best thing for a musician who made a living wanting people to stop and listen and leave a tip on their way out the door, so to speak.

She'd taught him how to control the aura. How to strengthen it when necessary, or how to basically hit the off button—temporarily, of course.

So he'd changed his hair and grown a beard and played only current songs people might have heard on their streaming service of choice. He made enough in tips most days to cover his expenses, which he kept deliberately low.

He'd made friends, like Julio and a few other merchants and people who worked in the area, but they were only casual friends, nothing more. He figured when the weather really turned bad and he couldn't busk, he might have to take in a roommate. But that hadn't happened yet, and he was in no hurry. Right now he was just coasting, something his old workaholic roommate Jerry would never have understood.

Tess had offered to introduce him to kin that lived in the city. She said the tribe in San Francisco still considered him one of their own, which meant he was still kin, after a fashion.

"I can't stay with you," she'd told him. "I'll be needed elsewhere. If you need help...."

He was touched by the offer, but he'd said no. He didn't want to start wondering how many of the people who stopped to listen to him play were really people at all. He'd already promised himself that he would never again play anything at all like the starsong version of "Moonlight Sonata."

Tess had been true to her word. She'd only stayed with him for a short time while he got his new life sorted out. Their relationship never went beyond purely platonic, which was fine with him. She'd worn several different human shapes during the drive north, but once they'd arrived in the city, she'd reverted to the shape she'd worn when he'd first met her in Vegas.

The night she left Seattle, he'd asked her if she was immortal. She'd laughed at him, a musical sound in and of itself.

"No," she'd said. "None of us are. We just live very long lives compared to humans. I have lived longer than most."

Then he'd made a crack about how since regular bullets couldn't kill her, maybe he should keep a few silver bullets around. Just in case she decided someday that he knew too much.

He'd meant it as a joke, but her expression turned serious.

"The Maker of All Things gave great gifts to the kin," she'd said. "The gift of shifting. The gift of long life. The gift to know the minds and thoughts of the creatures whose shape we wear. But every gift comes with a cost. Sometimes the costs are dire. For me, that's meant I must always live my life alone."

He'd stared at her, dumbfounded. "Alone? That's a hell of a lonely way to live."

"Don't misunderstand," she'd said. "I have friends and companions. Not in the way *she* interpreted the word."

Elias understood "she" meant Gilda.

"But companions like you and I," she'd said. "Friends."

They'd been sitting on a bench at the top of an incline overlooking Puget Sound. The day had been warm for the beginning of

September, and he'd only needed a light jacket after the sun set in the west.

He'd still been getting used to his new surroundings. Half the time he expected to look out over the water and see the Golden Gate bridge, always surprised that it wasn't there. Tonight lights from the ferries and sailboats out on the sound reflected off the water, along with the lights on the islands across the water.

He told himself that someday he'd set foot on one of those ferries and take a ride across the water just to see one of the towns on the other side that Julio had told him about.

That's when Tess had reached out and touched his hand. His skin tingled just like it had when she'd touched him on the cheek all those years ago in Vegas.

"Do you wonder why the legends say silver is the only way to kill a shapeshifter?" she'd asked.

He'd never really thought about it, and he told her that.

"Silver is a precious metal," she'd said. "A lover might give a gift of silver as a sign of his love. While gold is more common, silver isn't unheard of. A person so loved might very well cherish such a gift even over life itself."

She'd been looking out over the water herself. Her eyes had narrowed, taking on a faraway look.

"Gold cannot be made into bullets," she'd said, and then her voice had turned cold and hard. "Silver can."

That had sent a chill down his spine that had nothing to do with the breeze coming in off the water.

She'd changed the subject then, asking him about his music and whether he was happy. He'd told her his music was good. As for happy? That was a work in progress.

He thought about that story from time to time after she'd left. During one of his breaks, or when he was alone in his small apartment, trying to read a book but not really seeing the words.

She hadn't come right out and said that the old legends were true, that silver *could* kill a shapeshifter. Eventually he decided the story had been a metaphor.

The point wasn't that bullets made of silver could kill her. It was what a gift of silver represented.

Love. Pure and simple.

Tess lived her life alone so that she would never love. A silver bullet couldn't kill her, but love could.

Back in San Francisco, on that last night, she'd said the detective wasn't *the one* who could kill her. That implied that someone could.

That implied that she'd actually allowed herself to love someone. But it had been more than that.

The tribe had been riveted by the battle between Tess and Gilda. Because they cared for Gilda and didn't want Tess to kill her? Possibly. Certainly in the case of the old woman who'd introduced him to members of the tribe.

But not everyone had cared for Gilda. The old man had seemed to actively hate her.

If the outcome of the battle had never been in doubt, would the entire tribe been that concerned?

Football fans cared passionately about the outcome of each and every game. Why? Because the outcome was uncertain. If the end result was a foregone conclusion, when one team was blowing out the other and the score was ridiculously unbalanced, even diehard fans got bored and left early to avoid the traffic.

Not a single member of the tribe had left until the battle between Gilda and Tess was over. That meant the outcome was uncertain.

The tribe had been worried Gilda would win.

Gilda could only win—could only *kill* Tess—if she'd been kin that Tess had loved at one point in her life.

Love kills. At least it did for the Protector.

When he got home that night, he'd taken his new secondhand guitar out of its soft case. He started to strum a few chords at random while he thought about living such a long life and never allowing himself to love anyone.

He'd loved Lettie, the first true love of his life. True, they'd drifted apart, but the love had never really died. But when his marriage ended, he'd cut off a part of himself. He'd been interested in a few women since then, but he'd always held them at a distance.

Stephanie Solvang, the photographer he'd met on the Pier came to mind. He might have let himself get close to love with her, but that was over. He'd looked her up online a week or so after Tess had left. She was still taking photographs of bands and singers and places around the Bay. She didn't have a blog, per se, but he eventually did see a casual photograph on her site of toes peeking out from a cast, the toenails painted bright red, with the caption "Getting better!"

He didn't know if that was her leg, and he didn't know when or how that leg ended up in a cast, but at least she was alive and well, and that's all that mattered.

He strummed a few more chords and started to hum a tune almost without being aware of it.

He was on his own, truly on his own in a way he hadn't ever been. His mother had passed away years ago, and now he couldn't even contact his ex-wife. The police in San Francisco must have contacted her about him. He couldn't take the chance she'd turn him in.

The tune he was humming started to turn into an actual melody. He chased the notes around, trying to see if they brought any words to mind.

Not words, but images.

A moonlit meadow beneath a canopy of stars so numerous they looked like someone had thrown all the glitter in the world into the heavens and it had stuck there.

Only these stars existed long before anyone had thought of inventing glitter. Long before cell phones and cameras and electric guitars and the Golden Gate bridge and ferries across the Sound.

Creatures were dancing in the moonlit meadow beneath all those glittering stars. Creatures that bore a passing resemblance to modern housecats, except for their golden-green eyes.

Intelligence lived in those eyes. Self-awareness. Care and emotion, joy and yes... love.

Was this the Great Meadow? Where the kin went after they died?

Or was he catching a glimpse of what life had been like for the kin before man came to destroy their home?

Was he playing *starsong*?

He'd vowed never to play anything remotely like his special version of "Moonlight Sonata" again, but this was different. This wasn't a reinterpretation of a classic song. This was his own song, coming from a place deep inside himself that he hadn't known existed.

Tess had said he would always be a member of the tribe, be *kin*, after a fashion. He hadn't wanted that. Had deliberately refused to accept it.

But now, maybe now he was ready to admit he wasn't the man he'd been just a few months ago. That he *was* kind of, sort of, kin.

Gilda had changed him, there was no denying that. Because of her, he'd lost everything he'd thought had been so important in his life, but really. The way he'd been living before? That was existing, just going from one day to the next. Not really living.

Not like the kin in his imagination lived.

If this starsong, as Tess called it, was a gift, something he'd been given by the Maker or God or whoever was out there in the cosmos in charge of such things, Elias wasn't about to spit in his eye. He'd been given an opportunity to discover who he really was. To make his own music, not kill time playing covers of songs made famous by someone else.

He didn't want to be famous, he never had. But play his own music?

Yeah, that sounded like a plan he could live with.

He closed his eyes and kept right on playing, and in his mind, he danced with the rest of his adopted kin beneath a canopy of glittering stars.

Be the first to know!

If you love Annie's writing, her newsletter is a great way to keep up with new releases, special promotions, and bundles where her work is featured, not to mention the occasional giveaway that's only available to her newsletter subscribers. You'll even receive a free copy of the first Abby Maxon mystery novel, *Pretty Little Horses*, when you sign up!

What are you waiting for?

Sign up at https://anniereed.wordpress.com/newsletter/ today!

ALSO BY ANNIE REED

ABBY MAXON MYSTERIES

Pretty Little Horses

Paper Bullets

MORETOWN BAY SERIES

Unbroken Familiar

Iris & Ivy

Tales from the Shadows

Not What They Seem

Spells Gone Bad

The Diz & Dee Holiday Mysteries

GRAY LADY SERIES (co-authored with Robert Jeschonek)

Gray Lady Rising

Gray Lady's Revenge

Gray Lady's Gambit

STANDALONE NOVELS

In Dreams

A Death in Cumberland

Faster

Road of No Return

A Christmas Reunion

UNEXPECTED SERIES

Unexpected Aliens

Unexpected Monsters

Unexpected Holidays

Unexpected Criminals

Unexpected Good Guys

Unexpected Futures

Unexpected Encounters

Unexpected Travels

Unexpected Hauntings

Unexpected Family

Unexpected Critters

Unexpected Cats

Unexpected Monsters

Unexpected Christmas

Unexpected Santas

COLLECTIONS

Crimes of Yesteryear

Everyday Magic

Life with Cats

Magic of the Heart

Turning the Page

Eight from the Silver State

The Patient Z Files

The Forever Soldier and Other Future Tales

WRITING AS KRIS SPARKS

Shadow Life

WRITING AS LIZ McKNIGHT

Wedding Belle Blues

ABOUT THE AUTHOR

Annie Reed has been called "one of the best writers of her generation" and for good reason. She writes in multiple genres, including urban and contemporary fantasy, mystery, suspense, science fiction, romance, and thrillers, along with the occasional story that doesn't fall into any one specific category.

She's a founding member and frequent contributor to the innovative *UNCOLLECTED ANTHOLOGY*, now starting its eleventh year of publishing themed urban and contemporary anthologies. Her short fiction appears regularly in *PULPHOUSE FICTION MAGAZINE*, *THRILL RIDE MAGAZINE*, and *MYSTERY, CRIME & MAYHEM*. She's even written official *Star Trek* fiction and admits that she's an unabashed MCU fangirl.

Annie has won awards in categories as diverse as her writing. She's been honored with appearances in five year's best mystery and crime volumes, including an amazing three years in a row in the *BEST MYSTERY STORIES OF THE YEAR* (2022, 2023, and 2024) edited by Otto Penzler. She received a Silver Honorable Mention from Writers of the Future and won a Literary Fellowship from the Nevada Arts Council. She's a multiple Derringer finalist, and one of her holiday romance stories (featuring cats, of course) was chosen to appear in study materials in Japan for students preparing for college entrance exams.

This prolific, versatile writer's longer works include the mystery novels *Pretty Little Horses*, *Paper Bullets*, and *A Death in Cumberland*, the crime novel *Road of No Return* (which also features a cat), the suspense novel *Shadow Life* written under the name Kris Sparks, and the Gray Lady space opera novels co-written with bestselling author Robert Jeschonek. Annie also writes the sweet romance Liberty Springs novels under the name Liz McKnight.

Annie currently writes and edits full time, when she's not otherwise cuddling cats. She can be found on the web at anniereed.word press.com.

A Special Request from the author:

Word of mouth is critical for any author to succeed. If you enjoyed this book, please consider leaving a review at the site where you purchased it. Even a line or two would make all the difference in the world and I would greatly appreciate it.

Thank you!